DEATH'S KNIGHT

War of the Lich, Book One

MATTHEW T. SUMMERS
JENA REY

Opal Kingdom Press

Copyright © 2021 Opal Kingdom Press

ISBN-13 978-1-952415-04-3

All rights reserved

No part of this book may be used or reproduced in any way whatsoever without written permission except in the case of brief quotations embodied in critical articles and reviews.

This book is a work of fiction. Names, characters, businesses, organizations, places, events, and incidents either are the product of the author's imagination or are used fictitiously. Any resemblance to actual persons living or dead, events, or locales is entirely coincidental.

Cover Design by RJ Creatives Graphic Design

First Edition
10 9 8 7 6 5 4 3 2 1

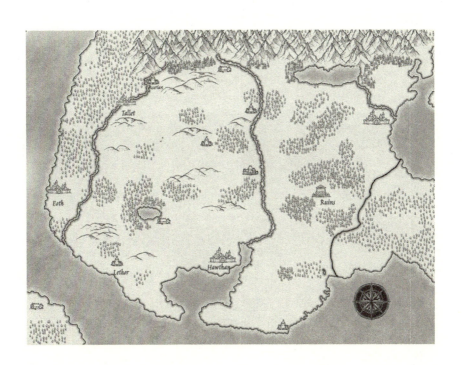

Matt: What a long, strange, fun road this has been! Just wanted to say a quick thanks to everyone that's helped me move forward - except that would take forever, so I'll just say a big "thanks!" to the whole mess! And, of course... thank YOU for reading.

Jena: As always dedicated to my sweetheart, Bryan. And to the readers: Never Give Up. Never Surrender.

CHAPTER ONE

Far in the west, the pale autumn sun dipped below the jagged edge of the mountains. Its feeble rays dragged across the land like claws, and as the light died, so too did hope. Twilight reigned, a moment of pregnant silence between light and darkness.

Then the night awoke.

True night came with a single howl, a guttural screech of hatred and defiance that no human voice gave rise to. It was quickly joined by other voices, one after another, until they echoed across the valley in snarling cacophony. To Ephema, the sound was familiar, something she had known her entire life, but familiarity didn't mean comfort. The cries of the walking dead were never comfortable.

Tonight, there was excitement to the rage, a rising tone that meant the undead were not only walking, but had found a hunt. They hunted only one thing. No one knew why the undead ignored anything that wasn't human. All anyone knew was it had to do with the necromantic magic that animated corpses and sent them wandering the world. Ephema never thought much about it. It was enough for her to know they hunted men and that, if they found her, they would hunt her too.

She cocked her head, listening as the noises drew near, frowned and scooped up her bag of roots and herbs. She strapped the bag across her shoulders to keep her hands free. The hunt was closer than she liked and common sense drove her to retreat to the proven safety of her cave.

Ephema scrambled up the narrow mountain path, jumping from side to side to keep her footing on the loose stone and dirt. The pathway was steep and treacherous by design, a barrier to the approach of the undead just as certain as the wards etched into the cave's entrance and walls. Such precautions had allowed Ephema's parents, and now her, to live outside of the heavily fortified cities in the valley below despite the danger.

By the time she slipped around the large stones that hid the cave entry from view, the skies were full of the bright points of glittering stars. In the east, the moon crested over the horizon, its light thin and silvery white. She caught her breath and lowered her bag to the cave floor. The hunting wail crescendoed and, almost against her will, Ephema returned to peer into the night. In the distance, she saw movement, humanoid shapes running and stumbling down her mountain.

If they kept going in the same direction, they were going to pass very close. She placed a hand on the small, clear sphere she wore on a silver chain around her neck. It was warm, pulsing under her fingers. She needed to take a closer look, to see who was being hunted. She carried no weapons, but maybe there was still something she could do to help. Her fingers tightened on the necklace and a tiny glimmer of light flashed deep within the globe. She murmured a soft prayer to the forgotten Goddess, Lianna, and began down the path she'd just ascended.

DARIAN STUMBLED down a trail that was little more than a goat path, desperately trying to keep his feet under him. He glanced over his shoulder and swore, putting on another burst of speed. They were still coming! The undead were not supposed to be so fast! Damn it all, nothing in his training as a Journeyman Knight of Osephetin had prepared him for undead capable of sprinting down the side of a mountain. If he survived, he was going to complain to the Training Sergeant, a thought that brought him little comfort as he half-fell, half-slid down the path.

He pulled himself through a stand of scraggly trees, breathing hard and risking another glance behind him. Only a few skeletal warriors continued to chase him, but that wasn't reassuring. A few were more than enough to kill him. His mind insisted on replaying the moment when the caravan had been attacked, how the undead had poured into the clearing, howling and clawing. When he blinked, he saw the shadows of his fallen comrades with empty eyes, in broken, blood-drenched armor. He shook the visions away with a snarl. This was not the time or place to mourn the dead, or he would join them.

Branches snagged at his leather armor, and he dropped his hand to his waist and checked the scroll case lashed to his belt pouch. The case of bone and metal held information that he prayed was worth the lives they'd paid to retrieve it. It had been the mission of the caravan, his mission alone now, to bring the scroll back to the High Temple in Hawthan. He had to outrun his pursuers and get to the next city, any city, even a way station would do. He needed a safe place with solid walls away from this infested wilderness where Knights did not cull the wandering dead.

He slid around a boulder, a gash in his calf screaming as he demanded more of his battered body. The undead broke through the brush, and he lunged over another stone. He had never heard of the undead pursuing someone so doggedly. They were predators, yes, but usually predators of opportunity. These skeletal warriors were unusually strong, and he was certain they'd been directed in their attack, though he'd not heard of such a thing before. He remembered shouted commands in a language he didn't recognize.

The deepening dark made the way increasingly treacherous, particularly for someone who was more accustomed to navigating a rocking ship than a rocky mountainside, but Darian didn't dare slow down. Each time his steps faltered the sounds of the undead drew nearer, the footfalls behind him drumming out a deadly rhythm.

He saw the edge of the tree line and broke into a desperate, hobbling run, hoping for an open path, but his hopes were swallowed when his cloak caught on a scrabbly bush. The change in momentum brought him up short by the neck, and Darian turned and yanked on the thick wool. It came free, but as it did the scent of decay assaulted his nose and a ravaged body tumbled into him.

He twisted as he fell, trying to catch himself, but the motion opened up his guard and claws raked his face, narrowly missing his eyes. Darian screamed and wrenched away, his blood hot on his cheeks. He shoved the monster back and drew his mace, his feet scrambling for purchase as the earth and stone around him gave way. He found himself caught up in a flood of moving stone and wrapped his arms around his head, praying he wouldn't crack his skull when the rock slide ceased.

Studded leather armor meant to shield his body from sword and claw did very little to protect him from the impact as he bounced down the pathway. Something in his left knee wrenched and dirt sprayed into his face. He felt himself briefly leave the ground as he went over a small precipice. When he landed, it was hard enough the wind was driven from his lungs and his vision blurred. Finally motionless, Darian lay flat on the barren ground, bleeding and broken, resigned to his death. He had failed.

Through the ringing in his ears, he heard someone approaching. His fingers flexed around the shaft of his mace, which he'd clung to through his fall. He expected a killing blow, but he wouldn't go to Osephetin's halls without trying to defend himself. Dimly, he realized nothing was happening, and the howls rang distant, moving away. Confused, he squinted through bruised eyes. The approaching figure didn't move like the undead, though in his blurred vision all he was really able to discern was the drift of pale fabric. A soft hand touched his cheek, and he bit his lip against a shriek of pain.

"It's all right." The voice was gentle, feminine. "You will be safe now. Rest." The words that followed were strange, twisting around him with the familiar power of divine incantation, though they were nothing he'd ever heard or felt before.

Lethargy filled his body and the pain retreated. Darian tried to form words, but they were lost as he tumbled into darkness.

~

Darian woke slowly, his thoughts sluggish as though he was swimming through molasses. When he finally opened one eye, he lay in semi-darkness, the only light coming from a small bowl candle sitting on a stone ledge across the room. He lay on some soft object and a thick blanket, which smelled vaguely of goat and dirt, was tucked over him. Despite the smell, the bed was warm and encouraged him to return to sleep.

The weight of the blanket made him realize he was barechested and without armor, and he pushed away his weariness and sat up. The blanket fell to his waist, but he ignored it. He searched the room and relaxed slightly as his gaze came to rest on the pile of armor neatly stacked on the floor nearby, his mace, belt pouch, and the battered scroll case lying on top.

He breathed a sigh of relief, but tensed again when a realization crossed his mind which was more disturbing than the absence of his armor.

He could move.

He could see.

Granted, he felt stiff, but he was in far less pain than many of his training sessions with the Knights had left him. How was that possible?

He frowned, trying to process the changes. He remembered being injured, bleeding and unable to walk. Darian twitched aside the blanket to look at his calf and, to his utter amazement, the deep gash was gone. Had he died? Was this how one was reborn to Osephetin's grace?

Darian flexed his fingers and took in a deep breath. No, he wasn't dead. He was breathing and this certainly wasn't the glory of the Dark Lord's Hall of the Faithful. This was… a cave. His injuries were simply gone, like magic.

Like he'd been healed.

A divine magic which hadn't existed for over a hundred years.

The conclusion was impossible, but the facts were undeniable.

"By the Dark One!" Darian's breath heaved in his chest, and he rolled out of the bed, onto his hands and knees. The Daughters of Lianna, the Eternal Mother, were the only healers in history, and they had all been driven as mad as their goddess a century ago. They killed with their power, not healed. If one of them had found him they would have killed him, not helped him. None of this made sense.

A soft hand touched Darian's shoulder and, driven by training and instinct, he grabbed it and swept the person's legs out from under them. The body landed with a muffled yelp, and Darian jumped on top of the intruder, realizing it was a woman, but not slowing his defensive attack. He pressed his arm against her throat, cutting off her breath. "Who are you? Where am I?"

She tried to answer, but couldn't. Her fingers wrapped around his forearm as she thrashed under him, managing to push his arm up enough to gasp a breath. In the dim candle light her dark eyes were wide and terrified.

He was hurting her and, despite his mission, he hesitated. She was smaller than he, and she might have saved him. Osephetin forbade hurting the innocent, and as his head grew clearer, he saw less threat and more fear in her eyes. He released the pressure against her throat just enough to let her breathe and speak, but not enough to escape.

It was enough. She drew in a breath and spat a few quick words. Pain surged up his arm where she touched him, blinding Darian with its intensity. His grip failed, and she scrambled away, throwing herself across the room and away from him.

The moment she was no longer in contact with him, his pain eased to a dull ache. Darian rubbed his head, falling back on his haunches. He assumed a defensive crouch, blinking until his vision cleared. Once he could see again, he cast about the room, surprised the woman was still present, huddled against the wall near where the candle burned.

"I…" Words failed him. What had he done? "I am sorry."

A bright light flared from a stone at her neck, and she warily pushed herself up, her bare feet pale against the stone. Though her breath was heavy, her face was set, and her lips turned in a scowl. "When the sun comes up, you will take your things and leave. Do not come back." She backed out of the room, and once she was out of sight, her steps turned from walking to running.

Darian sat alone in the flickering candle light, watching the flame burn deeper in the bowl. Unconsciously, his hand drifted to his leg, and his gaze lifted to the path where the woman had retreated.

Ephema sat in the cave entrance watching the sun rise. The light from the east wasn't very warm, simply wan and weary, especially as autumn drifted toward winter. She had not slept since encountering her violent visitor. Not that she hadn't tried, but each scratch of movement on stone had jerked her back to wakefulness, and eventually she'd given up the effort. Her throat ached as did her hip where she'd landed, and she wished, not for the first time, that her healing abilities worked on herself.

Another shift of stone caught her attention, and she turned, seeing the shadowed figure standing in her cave. She leapt to her feet, moving out of his way, but he didn't leave. In fact, he wasn't fully clothed yet, his armor left behind, leaving him in clothing which had once been sturdy, but was now battered and ripped by his trip down the mountain.

She stared at him, uncertain what he was going to do next. His strength was evident in the curve of muscle under his rich brown skin, but she'd already experienced that strength and what others might admire only increased her tension. Dirty red hair, which had looked black in darkness, fell into his eyes and brushed the collar of his shirt. She supposed he was handsome, though she had very little experience to compare him to.

Ephema's fingers closed over her necklace, taking comfort from the cool chain and the smooth stone beneath her palm. "The sun is up. You can go down the mountain now."

"Yes." His gaze was piercing, and though his movements were still stiff, they were sure as he moved closer to her. She backed away, and he stopped, holding very still as though she was a wild animal and stillness would keep her from being spooked. "I am sorry for earlier. Are you…?" He hesitated, and she read the questions in his gaze. She didn't want to know what he wanted to ask. She still wasn't sure why she'd put so much effort into saving him, besides the fact he was human and didn't deserve to die. "Are you safe here?"

The question struck Ephema as bizarre, and she couldn't contain a soft bark of laughter. "Safety. Is there truly such a thing? I live. It is enough." She knew she was being brisk with him, but she couldn't shake the vision of him leaping at her. Her fingers tightened on the chain until it dug into the back of her neck. "There…there is food and water. Take it and go. The cities will have better."

Darian shook his head. "I cannot take your food. Water would be welcome, but nothing more. You have done enough." He met her gaze, and she was certain he saw her fear as much as she tried to hide it. "I really am sorry for before. My convoy was attacked last night, and as far as I know they are all dead. My actions were rash, driven by fear and confusion. Our Lord Osephetin looks poorly on harming the innocent, and I have done you a grave disservice. Especially as I am certain now you saved my life."

Osephetin. Ephema knew that name all too well. The God of Death, the Eternal Mother's greatest love and most bitter enemy. And his…Knight? No. Her father had been a Knight, she knew this man was not. His armor was made of leather, not metal plates, and carried no bone or magic. He could not be a Knight -- at least not yet.

She repeated his words in her mind, his accent and pace of speech making her have to focus to understand him. She didn't speak much to other people. Most of the townsfolk feared her and ignored her, except when they needed something, or she wished to barter with them. "I am sorry your friends died. I did not see any others on the mountain." She hesitated before continuing. "Follow this path down, and it will lead you to a wider road and the town beyond. Do not speak of Osephetin in Aserian. His temple is closed, his disciples long gone. Those who still worship do so quietly. Many have chosen the lost god Neikan for their devotions instead. Their worship has not stopped the undead."

"What? Why? Where was the Knight in Residence?"

"He left, five years ago. No one came for a long time. When some people did, they called themselves Followers, not Knights. They were bad, and the council made them leave. No one else has come until you."

Darian frowned, but finally nodded. "This town is very far away from the High Temple. It is unfortunate, but possible, that they did not know of the need. As the people continue to spread and settle there are not enough Knights to see to everyone. I don't know about these Followers…"

"WITCH!" A voice boomed from down the hillside, bouncing around the stone and echoing into the cave, cutting Darian off.

Ephema cringed, biting down on a sigh. She recognized the voice. About twice a month, Mayor Trevin made the hike up the mountain to yell at her for some imagined slight. Last month he had blamed her for there being less water in the stream that fed the town. The month before that it had been her fault the wind had taken the shutters off of several houses during a storm.

It was annoying, but generally he yelled for a while, made the signs against the evil eye and stomped away. She was certain he didn't know exactly where her cave was, only that if he came into the general area and shouted enough, she would appear, and he could tell the townsfolk he'd done something about their troubles.

She glanced at Darian, her understanding of the man still far from complete, but instinct said the Mayor didn't need to know about him. "Stay here. I will return. He is loud, but not dangerous." She didn't wait for Darian to respond, moving quickly down the tunnel and to a narrow chimney of rock which she scurried up as easily as a mouse. The opening came out higher up the mountain and let her circle around to the path below Trevin, who was still yelling.

"Good morning, Mayor." She pitched her voice to carry, and the Mayor whipped around, startling at her sudden appearance. "Why have you come today?"

"You!" He stomped to her, his fist raised, shaking. "You sent those beasts down upon us! The guards saw them come from this direction. Do not deny it!"

Ephema tilted her head to the side, wisps of dark brown hair escaping the cloth she wore over her head. "I do not understand."

"Undead! Skeletons! With weapons even! They killed Ol' Man Harvid's goat and pounded on the gates until dawn when the guards took care of them. You are lucky our guardsmen were well prepared!"

Prepared enough to watch the undead bang on the gates until dawn, when sunrise made them easier to break apart and scatter? And what would the undead do with a goat? They ignored creatures that went on more than two legs. Everyone knew that. The questions played through Ephema's mind, but she didn't speak them aloud. It was not worth arguing with the Mayor if she did not have to.

"I have no guilt in this. I did nothing. The undead go where they will, like leaves on the wind. They are always drawn to cities. You know this. Why would last night be any different?"

Trevin leaned closer to her, and she fought not to step back. She did not trust him not to hit her if he thought it would help him. She smelled the foulness of his breath, reeking of spiced meat and mead, hot on her skin. "And do they steal cattle as well? Six head have gone missing over the last month, all of them last seen up this way. Don't think I don't know how you work with those monsters and probably bandits as well. I have been patient with your foul presence in these hills for long enough. I warn you, Witch. I will return tomorrow morning, and you'd best be gone, or we'll burn your evil out of these mountains and to the undead pits of hell with you." Spittle flew from his lips with his snarls. He slammed into her shoulder as he stomped by her, incautiously making his way down the path. If there was any justice in the world he would have stumbled, but no matter how shaky his steps were, they led him away into the leafless foliage and the valley below.

Ephema closed her eyes and rubbed her fingers across her forehead. The forest around her whispered in the winds with the creaking of branches and the shifting of stone. She hoped he would return home and sleep off the drink on his breath. Maybe by tomorrow he would forget his threats. Maybe she could return to being forgotten too and keep her home. She had no desire to leave and burning the woods was insanity; but people were known to do insane things, especially when they were afraid.

She looked up at her cave where Darian had emerged, concern etched on his dirty face, and began back up the path. "You should go. I do not know when he will return, but he will not be friendly if he thinks you were here with me."

Darian's gaze focused past her, down the mountain where the man had gone. "Would he really be foolish enough to burn the mountain?"

"He might. I do not know." She drew close enough she did not have to raise her voice. Despite her fears, between the Mayor and this man she would rather deal with the latter. "His people are unhappy. He is a bad leader, but they are afraid. He needs someone to blame for their unhappiness. He claims often I have stolen something, but I think that is only an excuse as he fattens his table."

Darian brought his gaze back to her, frowning again. "And he would risk their well-being as well as yours for that." He shook his head as though he could shake out an unpleasant thought. "You said the town was at the bottom of the mountain?"

Ephema didn't like the sound in his voice, but she gestured down the path. If he was gone, she could hide until the townspeople forgot their ire. She did not believe they would burn anything if they couldn't find her. She had been preparing winter supplies already and could stay out of the way. Perhaps in the spring she would go down again. "Not far. Once you leave the mountain there is an old road. It is not well kept, but it is easy to find. You can go to the town or around Aserian if you follow it."

"Thank you." Darian spun on his heel and walked back into the cave, his thoughts dark. There was too much amiss here, and he would be a fool not to try to help, even if it slowed his mission by a couple of hours. He had hoped to find some of his brethren today. He would feel better in the company of others of his order, but he couldn't let this woman be burned out of her home for no reason. This town was on his way back to Hawthan, he could do good and move forward at the same time.

It didn't take long to get his armor back on; it was an old habit by now and the leather fit him much better than it had over a year ago, when he'd earned it. The mace hung at his side, sliding into the thong that held it at his belt. He hoped he wouldn't use the mace forever, but despite being at the end of his eight years of training, he'd not yet become a full Knight and received his soul weapon. He would have to work with what he had, and the mace was effective against the undead of flesh or bone.

Darian picked up the scroll case, checking it over to make sure the bone and silver remained unbroken. The case hummed in his hand with divine energy, but he felt no temptation to open it, that duty was for the High Priest or the scholars. He just had to get the scroll home. Success was the best way to avenge his fallen comrades. He opened the large pouch that hung on his belt and slid the scroll case inside, grateful to have time to properly secure it this time. At least now if he got chased, he wouldn't worry about dropping it.

He smoothed the makeshift bed of rushes and rags and took one last look around the little cavern. It was difficult to believe that anyone lived in such sparse conditions, but it seemed the lady made it work for her. It was her home, and Darian felt it was important to do whatever he could to ensure her safety after he was gone.

He walked back to the cave entrance, the mace occasionally slapping against his side. The woman was crouched near where she'd been this morning, fiddling with a bundle of cloth. "You called that man Mayor, didn't you? He runs the entire town of Aserian?"

She glanced up, and he could see the bundle was filled with roots and tied to a worn water skin. She was ignoring his protests about feeding him, and it would be rude to argue. She nodded and offered the food. "Yes, he does. I think... you do not have to go there. You are strong, and there are other places beyond Aserian with walls and safety."

"I do have to go there." He knelt down to accept the bundle. "This is not necessary, but it is very appreciated."

Her fingers brushed his, and she pulled her hands back quickly. Her expression showed puzzlement as she leaned back on her haunches, and he noticed her feet were still bare. "Why do you have to go there? They will not help you."

"I don't expect them to help me, but I cannot repay your kindness by leaving you in danger. I will tell them to leave you alone." He saw the fear in her eyes, and he again regretted attacking her. He had many excuses for what he had done, but if he'd been slower to react things might have been different. "You are a kind soul, and you helped me."

He shrugged and pushed to his feet, automatically settling his mace. "Besides, there is the matter of the removal of my brothers to address and a temple to assess, so I can tell the High Priest of the needs of the people. Just because their Mayor closed the temple doesn't mean there aren't still worshipers in need here."

"But…" She blinked a few times and shook her head. "You don't… No one will find me here. If they come, they will just yell and go away. If you confront them, they will hurt you. I do not even know your name to ask for you if they do."

"They won't keep going away forever. You've been very lucky, and your cave is well hidden, but if they really searched, they'd find you eventually. The biggest reason they haven't, if I were to wager, is because they think you are capable of harming them. Even if you are, fear won't last forever. They need to know you aren't a good target." He carefully stepped around her, mindful of his footsteps in the loose dirt. It would hardly do to kick dust into her face. A smile crept onto his face, the first real one he'd had since waking. "My name is Darian, after my father. Thank you for saving my life."

He strode away down the mountain before she could protest any further. A few moments later, her quiet footsteps followed him through the dust.

CHAPTER TWO

It took nearly an hour of walking and scrambling down the mountain side before Darian spotted the town – desperately trying to be a city – that was Aserian. He found the road, such as it was, and his travel went faster, bringing him to the town by midmorning.

The town before him had, at one point, been constructed of proper stone and metalwork, but that had long been left to the elements, the walls now crawling with greenery and thick mosses. It was obvious Aserian had expanded, and the people had gone to the abundant forest around for materials to build new outbuildings and a thick, wide wooden wall to keep out the undead. At least they weren't foolish enough to try to live outside the walls, as settlers sometimes attempted. Darian had heard awful stories of the slaughter that resulted from thin fences and unprotected homes. Here, nothing was well-maintained and some areas looked to be one good sneeze away from collapse, but they had not completely abandoned common sense.

Darian kept his pace steady as he approached the town, though his mind raced as he considered everything he'd heard the Mayor say. Witch. Undead at the gates. Burn out the hills. He knew something had to be done, but how much could he, only a Journeyman Knight, accomplish? It occurred to him that – just maybe – he might have convinced his reluctant hostess to move instead of taking on the leadership of the town. That thought didn't sit well with him. She hadn't done anything wrong. He was doing the right thing. He just didn't know how he was going to accomplish it.

He adjusted his armor slightly as he walked. The journeyman armor fit better now than it had the first time he'd put it on, but it still wasn't exactly right for his frame and even the wan sunlight was making him warm. He looked forward to the day when he became a full-fledged Knight of Osephetin and his soul armor would fit like a second skin. It was what he'd always wanted, and he knew he could pass the tests if the High Priest would only let him try.

As he approached the gates to the town, his gaze followed the curve of the wall to the town's funeral yard and children's cemetery. In the back of the yard stood the massive stone of the funeral tablet. It was a horrible reminder of the extremes people had been driven to in the early days before they had learned that any flame, not just Osephetin's Eternal fires would keep the dead from rising. Darian didn't know how many years the crushing stones had been used for, and he was glad he'd never seen one that wasn't only a reminder of how bad things could be.

Near the stone stood the crematorium where bodies not given rites at a temple were burned by those appointed by the town. It wasn't in use now, as no smoke rose from the stacks. Darian stopped to look at the building and study the children's cemetery with its tiny headstones and urns. Darian didn't understand why children didn't rise after death. The High Priest often cited the purity of a child's soul as the reason, though some of the Knights privately argued that it was more about the mass of a body required for the dark magic to take hold. Either way, Darian was grateful it was the case. Fighting the undead was hard enough without fighting children.

He shook his head and turned away, continuing on. Closer to the gates, he saw that the Mayor hadn't lied about being attacked by the undead. The gates bore fresh scratches and gouges, and piles of broken, crushed bones and shreds of fabric told of the defense the town had put up. Darian knelt by one of the piles, studying the yellowed bone shards. There was no way to know if these were the same skeletons that had attacked his convoy and killed his comrades, but he hoped they were and took comfort in seeing them in pieces. If the townsfolk burned and scattered them today, they wouldn't return for some time. Maybe not at all. Undead killed with divine power stayed that way, but sometimes the towns got lucky too.

"Ho there!" A voice echoed from the gate above, and when Darian looked up, he could make out the top of a man's head, backlit by the sun. "What you doing with those bones, boy? Doncha know better than to play with cursed stuff? We beat those bastards back from the gates not two hours ago. An' Ingersol got rot from it, so they're not safe. The teams'll give them a burning and crushing later. Stop mucking with them." The warning given, he leaned his arms on the top of the wall and scratched his forehead. "Anyway. Who are you and what are you doing here? Ain't often we see folks carrying proper weapons and armory in these parts."

Darian pushed to his feet, his mind racing with the best way to respond. He couldn't just accuse the Mayor out of hand, or they'd never open the gates. He frowned a little. "I'm a bit lost, truth told." He made sure his voice was loud enough that it carried to the other soldiers he was positive were on the other side of the gate. "I'm looking for the town of Aserian. I heard the Mayor was looking for some lost cattle. But I got lost when I picked up some undead a trail or two back, and I'm all turned around. Can you point me in the right direction, please?"

A second voice joined the first. It was distant and didn't seem to be talking to Darian, but rather the man on the wall who ducked down to listen. The two went back and forth for a moment before the second voice retreated and the head popped back up at the top of the gate, much like the groundhogs Darian had chased as a child. "Mayor Trevin's been in a snit over those cattle. I'm sure he'll be right happy to hear whatever you have to say." He gestured to his right. "There's a smaller door over that way. You see it? The big gate takes too long to open if there's nothing but one body to come through. Come on over while Boris gets the Mayor."

Darian held back a smile, relieved. He'd hoped they'd go for that carrot, not that he was sure how far he could take it, but he wanted to see this Mayor for himself. He jogged over to the smaller door, which was cleverly disguised to look like part of the wall. If he hadn't known to look for it, he might have missed it all together. He knocked once. From behind the door came the sounds of latches being thrown and a bar grinding out of the way. Finally, the door swung open, allowing him access.

The interior of the town looked much like the exterior. Many of the buildings were in severe states of disrepair, patched with whatever came to hand with little eye for aesthetics over functionality. In a few spots, fresh white wash had been applied, but instead of making the buildings look better, they just made everything around them dingier.

Darian nodded at the men who'd opened the door for him and stepped aside so it could be closed again. He couldn't shake the feeling that he'd wandered voluntarily into the fox's den, but it couldn't be helped. The closest guard gave a wide smile which showed a couple of missing teeth deeper in his mouth. While the expression was welcoming, the other guards didn't seem nearly as pleased to see a stranger, much more guarded in their expressions. Their displeasure deepened as the Mayor came bustling down the street, his gait odd as he tried to hurry without appearing to run. Several other men followed him and, as curiosity spread, many of the townspeople drifted from their homes and shops to see what the rising noise was about.

Mayor Trevin came to a halt a few feet away from Darian, surveying him with a deep scowl. His eyes paused at the worn journeyman badge on the left breast of Darian's armor, but it only made him more annoyed. "Snelson! What are you doing letting this trash into town? You're supposed to question all newcomers before they are allowed entry!"

"But…I did, Mister Mayor, Sir. He said he had a message for you about those missing cows. He's a Knight too, or as close as we ever see out here. I didn't see any sign of undead nor Ephema, so I figured it was safe and you would want to talk to him yourself. I can't see where that's wrong."

"Do not mention that witch in these walls! You'll bring her evil eye down upon us!" The Mayor's scowl deepened, drawing furrows in his fat face. He glanced at the man standing at his elbow who was dressed in mismatched and poorly fitting amor. A sword hung at his hip, the weapon and its sheath well maintained despite everything else. "Sergeant, we will discuss your guardsmen's training when this is over with. Apparently, they are in much need of retraining." His narrow gaze returned to Darian, and Darian almost felt the moment the Mayor decided he was no one of any importance or use. "So you've raised my whole town with your inquiries, boy. What do you have to say for yourself?"

Darian took in a breath and held it for a moment, sending up a silent prayer for inspiration. "I must beg your forgiveness for my deception, Guardsman Snelson." He offered the apology before bringing his full attention to the Mayor. "I do not know where the cattle are, though there are a few in the meadow three trails off the main roadway."

At the words, a few men slipped from the back of the crowd, hurrying away. Darian hoped they were going after the animals he'd seen. That might help the village soften toward Ephema. He refocused on the Mayor who seemed about to launch into a tirade. "I do, however, have questions for you, Sir. Why, by the name of all that is holy, with the number of undead in these lands would you close Osephetin's temple and live without his priests? Are you mad? Without them, who gives rituals to your dead? Who keeps the fires of the Eternal Flame? Osephetin does not demand that your town worship him, but it is folly to refuse his disciples when they would aid you."

Mayor Trevin's eyes widened fractionally with guilt, but he merely snorted. "I assure all that the council handles such things. We do not need the flames of your order, nor your Knights to take care of our own. I cannot believe I came away from important meetings to be lectured by a whelp with absolutely no proof that you even ARE connected with the order. I require neither your approval nor your God. The Disciples have never done anything for us that we cannot do for ourselves. As we have proven such in their absence. You see the bones crushed before our gates. We can turn away the undead. We are the masters of our own fate!" His voice rose as he spoke, addressing not only Darian, but the crowd, who murmured in agreement. "Get this man out of my sight."

"Uh, sir?" The guardsman to the Mayor's right shifted nervously. "If…if he really is with the Knights…umm…he has a right to sanctuary at the temple."

Darian latched onto the suggestion, silently thanking Osephetin that not everyone in the town was as corrupt as the Mayor. "A claim I so make," He said quickly. He glanced over the crowd, resting his hand on the grip of his mace, but making no effort to draw it. "Think carefully, though, good people. What kind of man turns away those who would help and protect you?"

Mayor Trevin glared at the guard, who wilted before his gaze and stared at his feet, shuffling in the dirt. The Mayor snarled, the expression ugly and defiant. "He's not a Knight. He's a charlatan trying to throw his weight around. If he was really a Knight, he would have shown up last night when we were under attack, not waited until midday. He's probably in league with the mountain witch and trying to frighten us into compliance. I am your duly elected Mayor. I am the one who has taken care of you! Throw him out. If he resists…" He looked at the Sergeant. "Then you know your duty."

The guards looked at each other, a couple making half-hearted steps toward Darian before stopping. It seemed the Mayor's change in religious devotion wasn't universal. Finally, the Sergeant straightened and took a breath. His fingers flexed around the hilt of his sword before releasing it. He touched a piece of braided leather wrapped around a yellowed piece of bone, holding it against his wrist. "You heard him, Sir. Are you going to go of your own will or do you need convincing?"

The sight of the talisman was welcome to Darian who was beginning to feel very young and very outnumbered. The Mayor might be corrupt, and there was no doubt his corruption had tainted the other leaders of the town, but there were still the faithful among the people. He had to have faith. Darian shook his head, considering his options in the space of a heartbeat. "I will go of my own will. I will go to the Temple of Osephetin. I claim sanctuary in the home of my God."

The Sergeant nodded, and Darian was certain he saw relief in the man's gaze. "I'm sorry, Mayor. He has the right to sanctuary. If he is a fraud, Lord Osephetin will punish him for his claim."

Mayor Trevin gave an enraged shout and lunged forward, sweeping a sword out of one of the other guardsman's hands. "I'll not be a prisoner to false traditions! I'll rid us of him myself, and you can find your replacement!"

He slashed at Darian, not without skill, but skill which was buried beneath years of heavy living. The strike was true to its mark, but slow, and by the time it landed Darian was no longer where he'd been, ducking to one side. The sword dug into the wooden gate, pushing into the aging wood and sticking fast.

Darian tugged his mace free and spun it, slapping the wooden shaft across the Mayor's hand savagely. It wasn't enough to break bone, but Trevin yelped in pain and released the trapped sword, cradling his hand against his chest. A quick turn, and the spiked mace's edge tucked neatly under Trevin's fat chins. Darian smiled as the crowd fell to a hushed silence.

He kept his voice calm, though there was an edge to it. He hadn't invited violence, but he was certainly going to defend himself from it. "Now, maybe we can have this conversation a bit more rationally."

The Mayor's throat convulsed as he swallowed against the metal. "Bastard. I'm not afraid of you, even if you are what you claim. Get out of my town."

"Until we clear some things up, it's no longer your town. There's far too many things going on here that are wrong, and you seem to be at the center of all of it." Darian glanced at the Sergeant. "I didn't hear your name Sergeant, but I thank you for your restraint. Am I wrong in thinking that there is a town restriction against attacking someone like that? It seems like we have a lot of witnesses that I didn't strike first."

"Indeed, we do." The Sergeant bridged the gap between them, catching the Mayor by the shoulder. "He'll be put under detention for now, pending investigation. You'll be required to stay in the town until this is resolved. Given you were already going to the temple, I do not believe this will be a problem. Do I need to ask you to swear on it?"

Darian lowered the mace before it could do more harm than scraping a layer of skin from Mayor Trevin's throat. He grinned at the delight the Sergeant was taking in wrenching the Mayor's arms behind him and wondered how long the Sergeant had been waiting for an excuse for just such a moment. "No, Sir. I will be at the temple until things are set to rights there."

"Good."

Several men slipped away from the back of the crowd, though Darian couldn't see them well enough to decide if they looked guilty or bored. He put his mace away and inclined his head. "To the Eternal Rest."

The Sergeant cocked his head, pushing the Mayor in front of him. "To the Eternal Rest. Snelson will show you the way to the Temple. Try to get there without causing any more ruckus." Mayor Trevin protested each step, but his Sergeant paid no attention to the noises, bustling him along with brusque efficiency.

The crowd fell away as quickly as it had formed, though not without many long looks at Darian and the retreating form of the Mayor. Rumor and question would be rampant within only minutes. Darian decided that, more than ever, he needed back up, and he prayed the temple would help him get it. Hopefully before his very presence caused a riot.

Snelson, the gatekeeper, approached, shaking his head. "I've never seen anything like that before."

Darian rolled his shoulders, trying to get the tension that had gathered there to go away. "It wasn't exactly what I was intending, but I get the impression your Mayor has been up to no good for a long time." He paused, then added. "Don't be surprised if you see others of my Order arrive in the next day or two. I'm going to send a message. They should be full Knights and easy to recognize, but I do not know who is nearby. I'd suggest letting them in without any fuss."

"I suppose we can do that. I personally always liked the Knights. Good folk, if a little strange." He scratched his rather large nose, flicking away a piece of dirt or snot, Darian didn't look closely enough to see which and didn't want to know. "Kinda like Ephema. She's not so bad either, no matter what the Mayor says, and she doesn't bring the evil eye. She's odd, but just a slip of a thing. Harmless, you know?"

"I know. I've met her." Darian admitted as he walked along, keeping an eye out in case anyone decided to take further issue with his presence. He wasn't certain Ephema was harmless, but he didn't believe she was evil either.

Snelson sniffed, clearing his nose again. "Thought you

might have. It seemed too much coincidence that Trevin went off to confront her this morning and then you showed up. It's a good thing that she's got a friend. She's a nice girl. Polite. Helpful. Gave my daughter help with birthing pains when she had my grandson. I don't know why so many people get all upset about Ephema. She's never done anyone harm as I know." He shrugged. "But people are odd."

Darian couldn't argue that, and they fell into silence as Snelson showed him through the town. As a whole, the town seemed fairly prosperous, even given the dire times and whatever mischief their leaders were up to. Yes, it was worn down, but the small river dock bustled with industry, and people came and went selling wares and exchanging greetings.

They entered into a quieter section of town, and Snelson came to a stop, gesturing toward a sagging building a bit farther down the street. "That'd be the temple there." He chuckled. "And seems you've already got a guest."

Darian looked where Snelson was pointing and saw Ephema curled up in a small alcove between two buildings.

"I'll leave you to it. If'n you get hungry, the food is good at the Tapper and they don't water the ale, much."

Darian nodded, though he didn't look away from Ephema. "Thank you."

He didn't watch as Snelson strode away. Instead, he crossed to where Ephema sat on the ground with her arms draped around her knees. "After all the things the fat Mayor said, this is the last place I'd have expected you to come. But I'm glad to see you, Ephema."

She tilted her head as he spoke her name and a little smile turned her lips. In the light, the tattered state of her clothing and the dirt that clung to her skin was more apparent, but she seemed unbothered. He also realized she was younger than he had thought, near his own twenty-three years. "I wanted to see what you would do. I worried there would be blood."

"Thankfully, there wasn't. I'm not sure if it will remain that way. I think I only accomplished as much as I did because I surprised him. That won't last."

"Maybe. Maybe not. My Father said that men such as the Mayor surround themselves with snakes. When one is surrounded by snakes it is easy to be bitten." She shook her head slowly. "He is a mean man. He kicks his wife and children. Maybe it would be good if a snake bit him."

Darian blinked at her comparison, not entirely sure how much of her point was literal versus figurative. He shrugged. "Maybe, but he's being held tonight and that's good enough for me. I need to go to the temple. I've stirred the hornet's nest and asked for sanctuary, so that will be my only safe place in town right now." He shook his head wryly, continuing, "Not that I expect even that to remain so for very long. But hopefully the temple aviary hasn't been destroyed, and I can get some help with more authority than I have to help me untangle this mess."

Ephema nodded, pushing to her feet and rubbing the dirt from her hands on her skirt. "It was once a beautiful building. I was sad when it went dark and the Priest no longer answered the door."

"They were all beautiful once." Darian lapsed into silence as they approached the temple. The building had, as Ephema insisted, been beautiful in the past. The tall building had been built with marble and granite, the old stone still visible under dirt and disrepair. What had once gleamed white was now dirty grey with cracks that ran across the face of the stone. The wide double oak doors hung at an angle, possibly jammed from the inside.

Darian frowned as he approached. He knew many of the temples were not taken care of as well as they should have been, but this showed long years of neglect. "Tell me again what happened here? How long has the temple been abandoned?"

Ephema approached the door, running her fingers along the front panels where there had once been elegant etchings and carvings. Now they were just faded memories of the past, full of dirt and coal dust. "The Knights left five years ago. They had a mission that called them away. One priest stayed behind, an old man named Cerenus. I liked him, but I haven't seen him for many seasons either. A few moons ago others came. They said they were Followers, not Knights." She thought for a moment, counting on her fingers. "There were seven or eight of them, I think. Their armor was not good. They were all loud, drinking too much and making the Aunties uncomfortable. They tried to get into the temple, but could not get very far. They broke the doors. I was not sad when the Mayor kicked them out of town."

"Knights don't make a nuisance of themselves. I have never heard of someone from our order calling themselves Followers as a group. Most worshippers of Lord Osephetin that do not become Knights are either casual worshipers, or Disciples who are a part of the priesthood." His frown deepened as he tried to piece together what might have happened. "What happened after the Mayor kicked them out of town?"

Ephema looked over her shoulder at him, tilting her head slightly. She still seemed leery, though much less so than she had this morning. "That was when he began talking to the people about the superiority of worshipping Neikan."

"Convenient that they gave him a reason to lead the people astray. It sounds like there is a lot more to this than the

Mayor just being a bastard." Darian watched as Ephema worked around the ruined door. Her tone and mannerisms regarding the facility were those of someone familiar with the inner workings of a small temple, though Darian wondered how a girl from the mountains knew any of these things. How much more did she know that she wasn't telling him?

Everything he saw in this town bothered him, leaving Darian painfully aware of how alone he was. His hand brushed the pouch where the precious scroll case was hidden. As much as he wanted to solve the mysteries here, he was reminded that he had little time to spare. If he could get some of his brethren here, he could go to Hawthan with a clear conscience and maybe an escort. He turned his attention back to Ephema as she grunted, her shoulder wedged under the door latch as she tried to lift it. She caught her lip between her lower teeth and pushed again. "We need to go in. I feel something, but the door is stuck."

"If you'll move, I'll try." She nodded, and Darian waited for her to get clear, aware of how she kept from touching him as she moved by. He hated that she was still afraid of him. He hadn't meant to cause such harm, but what was done was done. Time to dwell on it later. He climbed into her spot and squared up so he could push with his entire body. With a grunt, he lifted up and, with a squeal of protest, the latch gave way. The door didn't swing open easily, but he gestured her over and together they pushed until there was enough space to pass.

CHAPTER THREE

The air that whooshed out of the building was musty and oppressive, and Ephema turned away, coughing. Once it cleared, she wrinkled her nose as she peered into the foyer which was lit only by the light allowed through the partially open door and a couple of slits up high where the stone was open to daylight. Darian stepped into the building first, with a confidence she didn't feel. This place held echoes of her childhood, a time when she and her parents had visited frequently, but now slipping past the crumbled stones was like stepping into a broken past.

The interior was, if anything, in worse condition than the outside. The elements had not been kind to the artwork on the walls, and the floors and ceiling were cracked and crumbling. A few long wooden beams from the ceiling hung askew, revealing holes to the outside making way for rain, wind, and bird nests. What hadn't been ruined had been stolen, pedestals that had once held small artifacts or books empty and pushed over. Ephema wanted to believe the local people would not disturb the temple, but she knew the desperation of need and want which sometimes drove people to do things they would be ashamed of in better circumstances. If the Disciples weren't here to take care of the temple, how much of a jump was it to think Osephetin had abandoned it – and them – as well?

She raised her hand, pointing toward the double doors that separated the receiving area from the chapel. "The chapel and Eternal Flame are through there." She drew closer, peering at the deep gouges on the doors where someone had tried to open them and failed. These wooden doors weren't as heavy as the outer doors, but they had held. "It is not a big temple."

Darian nodded, finishing his circuit around the room and coming to the doors. "They rarely are in outlying towns, but it's bigger than the shrines at way stations or in the outlands. This is big enough to service the population, and should have sleeping chambers, an aviary, and hopefully a working well, somewhere."

Ephema ran her fingers across a large scratch in the door before resting her hand on the latch. "The well is in the back." She remembered that much and the small cloister rooms that circled the chapel where she used to play, but she hadn't been inside since before the Knight in Residence, and her parents, had left.

She pushed the latch, expecting it to be as tightly jammed as the outer doors had been and jumped back in surprise when the doors fell back with little effort, the hinges not even squeaking. A tickling sensation ran across her skin, like a puff of warm air, somehow familiar and welcoming, as though the temple had been waiting for the right people to arrive.

She looked over her shoulder at Darian, but he didn't seem to have felt it and was still talking. As he stepped aside to avoid tripping on a smashed and discarded urn, he continued, "Depending on what kind of hurry the Disciples were in when they left, we might even be able to find you some footwear or clothing."

Ephema raised both of her eyebrows and glanced at her toes. "Is there a problem with my feet?"

Darian opened his mouth, then closed it as though he was thinking hard about what he was going to say. Finally, he shrugged and spoke. "I never said there was a problem. I just don't like seeing people without shoes when I can help them get what they need." He jerked his head in the direction of the mountain. "It can't be comfortable to walk that mountain barefoot. Some shoes will make whatever travel you have in mind easier, at least in the long run." He didn't seem to consider that her only travel was back to the cave she'd come from. He turned toward the main doors. "I'm going to try to shut the door behind us. I'd rather have some forewarning if someone tries to come in."

Ephema didn't think he was going to be able to do that, given how much effort it had taken to get the doors open as much as they had, but she didn't protest. If he wanted to try, she saw no reason to stop him, and maybe he was right to be concerned. The people were generally good people, but those who agreed with the Mayor wouldn't like anything that had happened today. There might be some who would think if Darian was gone their troubles would go with him.

As he turned away, she stepped into the chapel and began down the long aisle between the pews. The damage was not nearly as extensive in here, though the edges of the carpet were still frayed and a couple of the benches tilted in ways that would make sitting on them dangerous or impossible. Her feet brushed softly along the remains of the dark blue carpet, and she smiled to herself over the thought that she wear shoes. She hadn't needed shoes since she was a child. Her mother had seen to that, using her healing skills to turn the skin on the bottom of Ephema's feet leathery and tough. She felt the heartbeat of the world through the soles of her feet, and shoes just got in the way. But it was an interesting thought that someone might care about something so inconsequential as her feet.

Her gaze rose from the carpets to the dais, set in front of the low pit where the Eternal Flame of the temple had once burned. It didn't surprise her that the fire was out, but what else she saw did. A skeleton clad in the remains of Cerenus's robes knelt on a prayer rug spread in front of the hearth.

Ephema recognized the designs embroidered on his faded tunic and came to a complete stop. Her father had once told her that death was different for the faithful followers of Osephetin, but he didn't say in what way. Her heart pounded as she stepped backward, trying not to draw attention to herself, but not daring to look away in case the body sprang to life. "Darian…" It was the first time she'd called him by name, and what she meant to be a shout came out as a whisper. She took another step back and banged into a low pew which collapsed under the impact and sent her tumbling to the ground with a shriek.

Darian was there in a few quick steps, running into the chapel quickly enough that he made the door bang against the opposite wall. His hand was on his mace as he entered, his gaze quickly moving about the room. When nothing was an immediate threat, he visibly relaxed and knelt down beside her. "Are you all right?"

Ephema pushed part of the bench out of her way, looking between Darian and the front of the room where nothing stirred. "I...I'm fine, but there's a...a...dead man. By the flame pit. I don't feel magic from him, but he's there." Her puzzlement came out in her voice which was too shrill and too sharp. She forced herself to take a breath and to seek calm. "I don't understand why he's not attacking, or why he's not dust."

"Remember where you are." Darian offered his hand, leaning back when she ignored it and scrambled to her feet. He carefully approached the skeleton, circling it once before he knelt down beside it and reverently inspected the hooded corpse, careful not to disturb it. "He's not attacking, because he's not undead. He is a true corpse, in the ways of the old, before the dead walked the earth. He is in the natural state of repose, in the way that Lord Osephetin meant for all of us to be, in the way all things should be once they pass."

He stood, again careful not to so much as brush the corpse with his hands or clothing. "Disciples and Knights of Osephetin cannot be brought back as undead if we pass in proper servitude to the Dark One. Our Faith and His power protect us from the Lich's call, even after we have passed from this life. Such is Osephetin's reach over his faithful." He paused and shrugged before adding. "Though most of us are given rites and put to the Eternal Flame before reaching this state. It's understandable for you to be concerned."

"Oh." Ephema considered his explanation, slowly approaching the corpse again. There were things her parents had taught her, but too many places where there were gaps. Now that she knew it wouldn't attack her, she felt the quiet pull of sorrow instead of heart-pounding fear. "This would be Bishop Cerenus, wouldn't it?" At his nod of confirmation, she sighed. "I wondered why I hadn't seen him. I thought after my parents left, he might come and visit, but he never did. When I came to see him, the temple was closed, and I thought he had joined them." She knelt by the edge of the funerary pyre, looking at the long cold ashes and missing the sharp glance Darian gave her. "So, what do you do with this kind of death?"

"The same we do with all others. We give them to the fire and spread the ashes. The ashes of some of our greatest leaders are kept in the High Temple at Hawthan. Once the highest among us received burials into the earth, because they have the same purity as a child, but such burials are rarely seen, especially these days. I have seen three headstones for the first Knights of our Order, but none other."

Ephema's brow wrinkled as she considered what he told her. "My Mother said fire took souls to Liana's heaven, and returning their ashes to the world was a gift of love."

Darian's jaw tightened at the mention of the Goddess's name, but he didn't argue. Instead, he walked to the nearest hallway that led out of the chapel. "I'm going to see what else is here and try to find the aviary. Will you be all right?"

She nodded, feeling very little desire to join him in exploring. It all felt like too many reminders of what she had lost, and she was content to let him scout.

"If anything changes, call for me and I will come running." He offered a little smile with the promise and disappeared down the hallway.

Ephema touched the bruising at her neck, which still stung, and shook her head. It was hard to continue to be afraid of Darian when he offered her nothing but deference and kindness. He had hurt her. He could hurt her still, but she didn't think he would or wanted to now. He reminded her of the few Knights she'd known as a child who'd been kind to her as her Father's daughter and who had always treated her mother with respect and reverence. It was, perhaps, best to let her first impressions of Darian go and begin again.

～

THE TEMPLES of Osephetin were built around one of three designs, each taking some aspect from the High Temple in Hawthan. It took two turns down the hallway for Darian to figure out which version this temple was, and he proceeded with greater confidence. He walked past doors he knew would lead to chambers for the disciples and the Knight in Residence and kept going as the hallway curved around the building. A small door at the end opened onto what he was looking for, a narrow stairway leading to the top of the steeple tower.

He climbed the stairs carefully, though there was less damage here than he had seen in the exterior rooms. The only light came from slit windows along the wall of the staircase, but it was bright enough that he didn't turn back. The door at the stop of the stairs was partially open and, as Darian pushed it, he felt the soft touch of the wind coming in through an open window.

The aviary was only big enough to hold the fifteen or so wire bird cages that dangled from the ceiling on slowly rusting chains. Three large windows holding precious, mottled glass cast light into the room, though one window's jagged edges warranted caution. A storm had thrown a large tree branch through it creating a dangerous pile of glass and wood.

As Darian approached the cages, he peered inside the lowest-hanging ones. As expected, there were no birds, only small piles of bone and dust. Darian walked between the cages, finally choosing one of medium size. He'd only invoked the prayer for Lord Osephetin's messengers once before. Then it had been the smallest creature, only truly capable of flitting from one High Temple tower to the next, and the invocation had been achieved with the assistance of a Priest who often communed with the Dark One. Darian wasn't sure where the nearest Knights might be; so this time he needed something bigger and capable of going farther.

He crossed the room and set the cage down on a tall table meant for just this purpose. The wind through the broken window toyed with his hair and brought the scent of roasting meat into the room, making his stomach growl. He'd been eating trail rations and gatherings for over a month, and the new scent made him homesick for his sister's tavern and a meal held around a table instead of a fire pit. He took a deep breath and shoved the feelings down, knowing he couldn't afford to be distracted.

Darian opened the door to the bird cage, picking up the largest of the bones and setting it in front of him on the table. He closed his eyes, remembering the instructions he'd received only a few months ago. Lord Osephetin was the God of Death and thus the remains of all creatures fell under his rule. It was blasphemy to reanimate the dead such as the Lich did, binding the soul of man to remain when his time had ended. But when Osephetin's followers were in need, they could call upon the Dark Lord's will to fill the remains of his messengers: owls, ravens, and bats.

There was no guarantee Osephetin would grant the request, his will was not for his servants to command, and this prayer worked best for priests. But Darian had no other way to find his Brethern, and he needed help. He had to try.

Darian swallowed and whispered the summoning incantation he'd been taught. As he spoke, he tasted each word of the ritual language, like little sparks of lightning in his mouth, jumping from his tongue to his teeth until his head hummed with divine power. It got harder and harder to speak, but he remembered that happening before and pushed forward, nearly spitting each syllable until the end. With the final word of the incantation, a blue haze slipped from his lips, falling down to the counter and swirling around the skull before sinking into it.

Darian sagged against the table, his eyes barely slits as he stared at the bone.

Nothing happened.

Why wasn't it working? His need was great. He believed. He was certain he'd said the right things. What would he do if Osephetin didn't answer him?

Hesitantly, he reached out to touch the bone. It jerked away from him, blue energy jumping from it in a shower of sparks. The skull raised a few inches into the air and began to spin. From within the cage other bones and ash scuttled about and shot out of their confinement to the table. The bones clattered and sang as they bumped into each other and fused, fitting together without muscle or sinew. In an instant a skeletal raven with long skeletal bones for feathers landed on the table, cocking its head and staring at him.

Relief flooded Darian's body, and he bowed his head. "Thank you."

He touched the bone raven on the top of the head, and it leaned into his fingers as though it was an overeager cat instead of a bird made of magic. Darian smiled. Now, it just needed a mission and a message.

Darian held tight in his mind the crossed hammers and skull that were the heraldry of the Knights of Osephetin. "Find them. Bring them here." He murmured. The skeletal raven pecked his fingers and then leapt into the air. The bird skillfully passed through the broken window without damage and soared off into the daylight, vanishing quickly from sight.

All Darian could do now was wait.

Darian returned to the chapel with his arms full of fabric and books, and Ephema rose, curious to see what he'd found and grateful to once again for living company. She wasn't afraid of the skeleton now, but it was sad and the chapel felt lonely.

He looked up as she approached and smiled faintly. "I found the aviary and sent the message. We should know soon if it finds anyone."

She found it strange, but not upsetting that he included her in his 'we.' "That is good, then. What else did you discover?"

He nodded to the pile he carried. "I found some robes and other sundries, a few pairs of shoes that might be in your size, and this." He lifted a journal from the top of the pile, offering it to her. "I think it is Cerenus's journal."

Ephema took the book, running her fingers along the cracked spine. It wasn't nearly as worn as some of the other items, but it bore the oil marks of fingerprints and much usage. She opened it, squinting in the dim light to make out the words. She knew the basics of reading, but it didn't come easily to her, especially given the priest's thin, angular hand. "He didn't feel good. He says…" She held up the book, trying to find a ray of light to help her see. "I can't read it. These are not words I know, and it is too dark."

Darin nodded. "I didn't find any candles or oil lamps up there. Well, one lamp, but it was under a large rock and was very flat" He offered her the clothing and the shoes. "Here, see if these are helpful, then we can look for other supplies. It's not quite midday yet, but we might as well find out all the little secrets we can with what light we have. I have flint in my gear, and we'll need to find something to burn tonight, or it's going to be really cold in here."

She took the bundle and set everything together near the fire pit, keeping it far away from the corpse so she didn't disturb it. She didn't relish the idea of sleeping near the dead body, but maybe space could be made near the door, or one of the other rooms. "The benches are easy to break." She'd already proven that, and she knew he was right about the night being cold. It wasn't yet the white winter season, but they were on the brink of the first snows. "Can we not burn those? If the temple is restored, they will have to be replaced anyway."

Darian looked between her and the benches and ran both hands through his hair, rubbing some of the dust out. He chuckled. "Indeed, we can. You're right. When," he emphasized the word, "this temple is restored they will be replaced. There will be no need for the old ones." He turned back toward the hall he'd come from. "I'll start looking down there while you get dressed, all right?"

"Yes." She watched him go and then sorted through the piles. The robes were brown and stiff with creases where they'd been folded. She decided it was easier to add a layer rather than giving up her lighter clothing. She had wraps more appropriate to the season back at her cave, but she hadn't brought them, and she wasn't certain when she would return there. She'd come to town to see what would happen to Darian and expected to go right back, but now she wasn't sure. Something inside of her had woken, and it was restless.

Ephema didn't bother with the shoes, but wriggled into the robes, surprised at how much warmer they were. The brown fabric wasn't creative; however, it was solidly constructed. She glanced after where Darian had gone and decided to focus her efforts on the broken bench. She gathered all the pieces that she could handle easily and set them into the fire pit as far from the body of Cerenus as possible. She was considering the large end of the bench which hadn't broken when Darian returned, bringing with him a bundle of candles, a few other pieces of fabric, and a couple of fraying wristlets bearing pieces of yellowed and cracked bone.

He set his pile aside and immediately grabbed the other end of the bench, helping her to carry it forward where he disassembled it with a few quick strikes of his mace. They stacked the wood in companionable silence. Once they had a good stack of burnables, they shared a light lunch from the roots she'd sent with him before deciding which of their finds were useful, and what would be burned. Darian was insistent that none of the wristlets be burned, and Ephema didn't argue. She wasn't sure it really mattered, given the wristlets had been left behind and they had no way of figuring out what family they belonged to, but if Darian wanted to keep them that was up to him.

The remainder of the day passed swiftly, and an evening meal finished the food, neither of them feeling like going through the effort to get through the front door and visit the tavern. More food was a problem for tomorrow, and Ephema knew many of the people would deal with her no matter what the Mayor said. This was especially true because Darian had capital coin, not just the skins or herbs Ephema usually offered in trade. Coin spent no matter who you got it from. As Darian began his evening prayers and the crescent moon rose into the night sky, Ephema stretched out with a bundle of cloth beneath her head, and a fire warming her back, tumbling into an uncertain sleep.

∼

DARIAN WOKE FIRST, the sounds of distant shouting bringing him to full awareness. He reached for the mace that lay at his side, resting his hand on the wooden shaft while he listened. He decided that the commotion wasn't at the doors but beyond them. The thought brought some comfort. A glance at Ephema told him she was still asleep, but from her expression her dreams were troubled. He checked the fire and added fuel to the pit before he crouched at her side.

He brushed her shoulder carefully, but even with that light of a touch her eyes flew open. There was a moment of panic in the green depths of her eyes before realization hit, and she rose up on her elbows, scooting away. "Where…who…" She stopped and shook her head. "No. I remember. Darian. The temple. Is it morning?"

He sat back to give her more space and nodded. "Late morning from what I can guess. We slept longer than I thought we would." He wasn't sorry for the extra rest, though his muscles ached from sleeping on the stone floor. "There's something going on outside. To be safe, I think we should go and see what's happening." He hadn't expected help to arrive for days, if not weeks. It would be a blessing if the messenger had found someone so close.

She nodded, pushing herself to her feet. She still wore the long, brown, belted robe he'd found which he found gratifying. He hadn't been sure she would accept any help from him. It was cleaner and thicker than the clothing she'd worn before, though it smelled of dust and age. Her feet were still bare, and very pale against the stone floor, which astounded him. He couldn't imagine how that could be comfortable, but at the moment there were more pressing issues than a wild girl's footwear.

He stood and, after dusting himself off, made his way to the main door, hearing her follow with only a whisper of sound – that was one advantage of being barefooted. It wasn't any easier to open the door this time, even though he'd only wrenched it partially closed. The effort strained already sore muscles, making Darian swear under his breath. It would take someone replacing the warped hinges and the damaged door to make the temple fully accessible again.

Outside people were in a hurry, talking to each other and wandering toward the main gate. The witch of the hills and the outsider that had questioned the Mayor were forgotten in the rush of someone new. Once they were out of the temple, Darian kept out of the main crush of the crowd, motioning toward the gate.

"It's a lot faster than I expected, but it's possible my brethren are the cause of this commotion."

"Maybe." Ephema watched the people rush by, a wry amusement in her eyes. "Certainly someone is at the gate. It may be your friends, or a wagon of tinkers. Either is exciting, especially so near to the white of winter."

Her tone was light, almost humorous, and Darian missed a step in surprise. She was a remarkably adaptable person, perhaps she'd already forgiven him his trespasses of only a few days ago. "Do tinkers come this way often? It seems far out of the way of the main roads." He fell in step beside her, letting her guide him through the town. She didn't avoid other people, but they seemed to instinctively move out of her way without incident.

"It could be tinkers, yes, but it is not very likely. They usually come in the fall and spring, bringing whatever they could not sell to others and collecting whatever the town has to be taken to the bigger cities." She paused as they got a glimpse of the open gates through the crowd and pushed a piece of hair out of her eyes. "It is not tinkers today. I see black armor, and I smell magic."

"Smell magic?" Darian had heard of people who could feel a magical presence. Higher Priests in his order had divine insight or could foresee a small degree into the future, but he'd never heard any claim they could smell magic. Then again, if you didn't have formal training how would you describe what divine power felt like? Smell might be as descriptive as anything.

Before Darian could question her further, two men broke through the crowd and strode directly toward them. The men led enormous war horses that looked like they'd been ridden hard, their nostrils flared and red rimmed from the exertion, sweat glistening on their sides. All eyes were on the Knights, and no one tried to stop them from going anywhere they liked. There might have been doubts as to Darian's association with the Knights of Osephetin, but there could be no doubt with these new visitors.

The men wore full field plate armor adorned from helmet to boot with various bits of polished human bone. Their helmets were wrapped in elongated skulls, the shoulder pieces enhanced with skulls and jagged edges of broken bone. Each joint of the armor was reinforced with stacks of layered bone and the more vulnerable sections studded with more bone wrapped in black iron.

One Knight carried a large kite shield that was ringed with finger bones. Two skeletal hands grasped each other around a thick iron spike in the center of the shield. At his waist he carried a heavy, curved spiked hammer that was also layered in strips of bone, sometimes pulled so thin it could be seen through.

The other Knight carried a massive two-handed maul with a shaft assembled out of tibia and fibula sections, fused together with dark strips of metal. Even in the wan light of day the weapons glowed blue, tiny sparks of divine power occasionally spitting from the enchanted bone. The unknowing might expect the bone weapons and armor would splinter and shatter, as most bone did; but these were sworn Knights of the Dark Lord and these were the bones of their fallen brethren. The metal would fail before the consecrated bone.

As they approached, Darian dropped to one knee, bowing his head. He recognized both Knights and thanked Osephetin in silent prayer that they were the ones who were closest. Not that he couldn't have explained the situation to any of the faithful, but the familiarity put him at greater ease. Especially since some of what he had to explain was at the edge of belief. "It is my honor to see you, my brothers. I am glad you came so quickly."

"We were not far as the raven flies." The larger of the two, a Knight named Tabor, offered his hand, hauling Darian to his feet with easy strength. "We were dispatched to accompany your convoy, but arrived too late. We found those who remained."

His voice was thick, and Darian knew they'd discovered the fallen and sanctified or destroyed those who had risen or might have risen. Unlike the sworn Knights or fully trained Disciples, the journeymen were vulnerable to the Lich's power over the land. Those who were unsworn would have risen as the soul-less undead. Darian knew now who had accomplished that terrible task, and was grateful it wasn't something he'd been asked to do, though the gratitude came with guilt he did his best to push away.

Tabor cleared his throat and continued. "We were surprised to receive your raven and learn you had survived. We thought all lost and their task with them."

"None were more surprised at my survival, than I, Knight Tabor." Darian sighed, pushing back the complicated mixture of anger and sorrow that came with remembering his fallen comrades. He knew the crowd was listening, but he reported anyway. Maybe it would be good for them to be reminded of what evils the Knights faced. "We were beset by a type of undead I've never seen before. The creatures came at us at a full run down the side of a mountain. They were upon us before the alarm could be raised. They were stronger than anything I've ever heard of, much less encountered. Knight Jagor, our Knight in attendance, was cut down first."

Darian shook his head as though he could shake away the terrible memories. "They knew, Sir. They focused all their efforts on him from the beginning. He fought so hard and destroyed many, but they just kept coming and things went sour very fast after that. Bishop Ton told Journeyman Iara and I to run, to do what we could to complete the mission, but Iara was intercepted soon after we broke from the convoy. The Priest called down Osephetin's fire on the scourge, but it only slowed them."

Tabor listened attentively as Darian spoke, his dark eyes attentive and piercing. He nodded at Ephema. "And this woman with you. Was she in the convoy as well?"

Darian stood slightly to the side so the Knights could see Ephema better. "No. This is Ephema. Without her I would be dead, too. She sheltered me from the undead and took care… of my wounds." He motioned to the town. "As I recovered, she informed me that this town was without disciples and the Temple was unattended. People claiming to be Followers of Osephetin were here a few months ago and made a mockery of our Lord before being cast out. I came to speak to the Mayor about it and other concerns. He didn't like that very much. Any of it."

"There are, indeed, many things we should speak about then." Tabor's dark features clouded, and he looked over the crowd before his gaze came back to Darian. "Where is the Knight in Residence?"

"Gone, Sir. From what I've learned, the last Knight was called from here several years ago. Most of the disciples left soon after, and the last Priest in residence died here. His body is still residing where he passed. I have not the training to give him the proper passing rites, but as he retains Osephetin's blessing, he can wait a little longer. I do not know why no one was sent in the interim."

The smaller, though only in comparison to Knight Tabor, Knight sighed. "I've been to this town before, and I remember the Priest in Residence well. He was a kind man and a stalwart follower. I hope his trip to the Hall of the Faithful was painless."

"I believe it was, Knight Ianel." Darian motioned in the direction of the temple, though he knew they couldn't see it. "When we found his body, he was knelt in prayer. It appears the false followers came sometime after the temple had fallen into ruin. The doors are damaged from someone trying to force them, but the temple was protected. They are the ones who have made the people of the town leery of the true Disciples, but the blame falls on us all."

"Then he left this life as any of us would wish. Now then," Knight Ianel turned to the gathered folks with a grim frown. "What governing council has allowed the Sanctuary to remain unmanned and unguarded? Who blames the true Knights for the actions of imposters? Where shall the judgement fall?"

"I think I can help you, sir." A young man strode out of the crowd, which parted for his coming. He was dressed in the colors of the town guard, though the closer he came the less confident he seemed. He stopped a few feet away from the Knights, nervously shifting his attention between the two men. "Er. My a…apologies, good sirs. I've never been this close to a true Knight before."

"Only the corrupt or the undead need fear the Knights of Osephetin." Knight Tabor's deep gaze hung on the young man before the corner of his lips quirked ever so slightly. "Speak your answers that the Truth might be witnessed by all."

"The words aren't mine, but I am a messenger sent to the temple this morning. Sergeant Markany is prepared to address everything in the main meeting hall, good sir." The guardsman managed to keep his wits about him. "He has interrogated the Mayor on a number of concerns and made some additional arrests last night that would be of interest to you. He thanks the Knights for giving him opportunity to serve the town as he was sworn to."

Knight Tabor inclined his head, a spark of blue light skipping along the top of his helmet from one unseeing eye socket to the other. The light made his dark skin seem even darker. "It seems to me that your Sergeant Markany is well on the path to restoring justice, but Knight Ianel will accompany you in your search for Truth. I do not believe this issue will require the rest of us. Brother Darian, you may show me to the Temple and complete your report."

Darian nodded, grateful to be able to return his focus to the mission. He believed helping the town was the right thing to do, but he needed to return to Hawthan and deliver the precious cargo he carried even more. "You might regret not assigning Knight Ianel to the Sanctuary, Knight Tabor. The door is jammed, and I'm not sure you'll be able to get inside."

Tabor snorted and tapped the pommel of his maul. "I suspect we can manage just fine, Journeyman Darian." He saluted Ianel as the crowd, faintly disappointed that the questioning had been moved out of sight, started to disperse. Knight Tabor gathered the reins of the warhorses and looked at Darian. "Lead on."

CHAPTER FOUR

Darian's concerns about the temple door had not been without merit. It had been easy to get lodgings for the horses at the Tapper, but opening the entrance wide enough for a man of Tabor's size seemed impossible. Darian and Tabor tried to free the hinges so they could lift the door down, but when that failed a few strikes of Tabor's maul sped up the process. With a sigh and a crash, the door folded to the ground, finally giving up the fight to the invaders. It had done all it was designed to do, only this time it faced a force its builders had never imagined.

Once inside, Knight and Journeyman both shed the bulk of their armor, sweat dripping as they sat in the outer chamber, regaining their strength. Ephema disappeared into the back of the sanctuary, returning with a wide basin full of water. She walked carefully, to keep it from sloshing onto the floor. A little water wouldn't do any harm to the worn stone surface, but it would make everything very slick. She set the basin and a wad of fabric where the two men could reach them before settling on the floor nearby.

Darian nodded his thanks, looking toward the outer door with a sigh. "I wish we hadn't had to do that."

Tabor grabbed one of the rags, dipping it into the water and rubbing it across his face and brow. "My thanks. Once the Temple is staffed and ready to function again, we'll worry about it. We can brace the inner chambers when we leave. That gods' damned door can stay in a pile for all I care." He sighed in relief as the cool water dripped out of his very short, curly hair and down his back. "That is better. Now, Darian, I assume there is far more to the story that I need to know than what you told back there. Let's start at the beginning."

"Of course." Darian ignored the water for the moment. He was tired, but he hadn't been the one swinging the maul. "You know what our mission was, yes? The things that happened before the ambush?"

"Yes. We know what you went seeking for and that at least the first stages of that seeking were successful. What happened then?"

Darian sighed, leaning back on his hands and closing his eyes. He'd not looked closely into his memories to this point, focusing on going forward, but it was time to tell all and hope Knight Tabor might see something in the telling that would help them. He was silent for a time, putting his thoughts in order, before he opened his eyes and began. "The night was still young when we were attacked. Knight Jagor was on watch duty with Journeyman Lanna. I was sitting near the fire and could hear them clearly; he was instructing her on some of the finer points of advanced combat. She was supposed to take her oaths when we got back. Several of us were." He swallowed, his throat tightening. "That's when we heard the first howls."

"Where did the howling come from, do you remember?" Tabor watched Darian carefully as he asked his questions.

"I do. It wasn't one source, but three. They came all at once from three different places." Darian sat up straight and motioned as he explained. "There was a ridgeline above the camp, about forty feet above and to the right. There. Then it echoed immediately farther to the right, this time only about ten feet above us. The third call was nearly atop us, and behind us to the left. The attack was coordinated. I'm certain of it." He shook, remembering the surge of fear and adrenaline the attack had caused and trying to remain calm now. "The span of time between the three was less time than it takes for me to clap my hands twice, my Brother. They were so fast, so certain."

"That is troubling, indeed." Tabor stood after dipping the cloth into the water again. He began to pace the hall, listening to Darian talk as he did so. "Continue. Did you get a good look at the attacking creatures? Did they retain any flesh, or were they fully skeletal?"

"I'm not sure. I couldn't see them very well. They wore scraps of armor and some carried weapons in addition to their claws. Weapons! The undead just… They don't carry arms and armor except in stories." Darian shook his head, his hair flopping into his eyes. "It's impossible, but I swear it's true. I ran to defend Bishop Ton with Journeyman Iara, as I'd been instructed to do upon any threat. When I turned around, Journeyman Lanna had already been killed, and Knight Jagor was fighting like a man possessed, but there were just so many of them. He couldn't get ahead of the surge. Then the torches went out. All of them at once.

"Bishop Ton ordered Journeyman Iana and I to escape. He pressed the scroll into my hands and told me to guard it with my life. I… I heard him calling on Osephetin's might and then, after the explosion, there was nothing, only silence as we ran. We went without a light to try to keep the undead from tracking us, but it didn't stop them.

"They picked up our trail quickly and Iana split off to try to divert their attention from me. I did not witness her death, but I heard it." He swallowed hard, staring down at his hands. He didn't want to see sympathy in Tabor's face. He just wanted to get the story out. "I managed to evade the monsters for a while thanks to her diversion, though I took a gash to the leg which slowed me far too much. I went as fast as I could, but they found me soon enough. I've never heard of a pursuit lasting so long. Every time I thought they were gone it was not so."

Tabor's voice was gentle as he spoke, encouraging Darian's tale. "And then?"

"Then things get a bit hazy." Darian glanced at Ephema, who didn't quite meet his gaze, though her cheeks were flushed. "They found me again and attacked. I clearly remember taking a claw across my face. I fought back. The stone around me crumbled, and I fell. That's when Ephema found me. I hit hard, and I'm certain my leg was broken. They should have killed me. I should not be standing before you, whole and healthy, yet I am. I can't explain how it is possible, but Ephema healed me. She called on magics that have been lost for over a century, and the healing Goddess answered her."

Both of the men looked at her, and Ephema rubbed her hands together, raising her gaze to look beyond them to the fallen door. "You are not wrong. I saw you fall. When I found you, you were gravely injured. My parents raised me to help others, even as they told me to keep my gift from the Mother secret. It is very difficult to do both of these things at once."

Tabor frowned, his brow furrowing until he looked like he was much older than his true age, nearly twice Darian's own. Darian could almost see the same shock and doubt going through the older Knight's mind as had gone through his. Healing wasn't possible. The Daughters of the Mother were insane, all of them. But Ephema sat there before them, calm and not in any way mad. Simple perhaps, but not mad.

Tabor drew a knife from his belt and studied it in his hands. "Our Lord trusts us to have Faith." He muttered. Darian half rose, worried Tabor might turn the weapon on Ephema, but the Knight made no move toward the woman. Instead, with a grim, determined look, Tabor slashed a line down his forearm. The cut was deep and blood immediately welled from the gash, dripping down his dark skin. He thrust the arm before Ephema whose eyes were wide with shock. "Show me." He didn't yell, but his voice was raised in suffocated pain and demand.

Ephema shot a look at Darian, filled with uncertainty, but it didn't last. She pushed quickly to her feet and gathered Tabor's bleeding arm between her hands, ignoring the blood that dripped down her arms and clothes and onto the ground. She closed her eyes and whispered divine words over the wound, the incantation almost a song as it fell from her lips. A soft white glow ran over Tabor's flesh and the Knight let out a surprised gasp. Over several minutes, the glow pulsated rapidly, then slowed and dimmed until it was gone. Sweat showed on Ephema's brow, but she didn't blot it away; instead she released Tabor long enough to wet another rag. Gently she wiped the blood from Tabor's arm. The gash was completely gone, leaving not even a scar behind.

Tabor's dark eyes widened as he whispered. "Dark One's blood!" He pulled away from Ephema, knocking her from her feet in his haste. He strode from where she fell to the door, rubbing his arm and touching his stomach as though it bothered him. He seemed unaware of Ephema's fall, focused only inward. Darian understood the feeling, though he put himself between Ephema and Tabor, just in case the man took the truth badly.

"As you can see, Brother. Healing. True, honest to Goddess healing. I, too, was rather stunned when she helped me. It's… like nothing I can describe."

"This is impossible. She didn't just…" He waved at his wrist. "I broke that eight years gone now, and it feels like new. I broke a rib ten days back and it no longer pains me. Much less the cut." Tabor's knees shook, and he dropped to the ground, staring at his newly healed skin. "No one can do this. They're all… How is this possible?"

Ephema stayed on the floor, though she picked up another rag, wiping Tabor's blood from her fingers. "My mother." She offered quietly. "And hers. We have always heard the voice of the Mother. Father says…said…that a divine bloodline and the mountain protected them, and his blood would protect me no matter where I placed my feet."

"Always heard the voice." Tabor shook his head, trying to clear his thoughts. "That's just…huh. Bloodline." He finally raised his head and looked her straight in the eyes again. Darian could almost feel the tension between the two. "Bloodlines are important, but that doesn't explain how you've managed to avoid the madness that's affected every other worshipper of the Mother Goddess of Life, Ephema. The

Goddess Lianna was driven mad by her battle with the Lich, and all of those in contact with her are immortal and insane. New worshippers cannot swear to her without losing their senses as well. Now, it's forbidden to even try. The Sisters are a blight nearly as bad as the Lich. So how is it you are not mad?"

"I don't know." She shrugged, sitting cross-legged and keeping Darian between herself and the Knight. "My mother wasn't insane, and no one ever told me that I should be. They just told me I had a gift and that it was important. I know everyone is taught the Mother is mad, but the voice I hear is just lonely."

Darian moved to sit beside her, stretching out on the stone floor as he didn't have the same flexibility she did. "Ephema, we're not just taught that they're mad. We see it. I've personally encountered Sisters of the Mother twice since my training began. The first time, they…" He paused, opening and closing his mouth. These memories were almost as hard as the memories of the convoy.

"They what?" Ephema rubbed the cloth at the stain on her skirt. "I need to understand."

Darian sighed. "There were three of them. They had come across some travelers. They'd chained them and taken turns carving agonizing curses into the travelers' bodies. By the time the Sisters grew bored and left, any trace of humanity was gone in those poor twisted souls. One of them literally melted away as we watched, his body turning into paste. He was still screaming until his face was gone and he couldn't. I still remember that scream."

He shuddered and continued. "The other two we were able to put out of their misery quickly enough to ease their pain and keep them from rising. The next time I met the

Sisters, it was a cleaner encounter. They attacked a caravan I was accompanying. They took the guards first, and two of our Knights held them back, but you can't kill the Sisters. The best you can do is distract them. The Knights gave us the time we needed to escape before they died."

Ephema's face paled as she listened, but she didn't try to stop him from telling the grisly tale. She twisted the cloth between her hands until her knuckles went white. "I see."

Tabor nodded, still rubbing his arm. "He speaks true. I've seen similar and worse from the Sisters. I hate them worse than the undead. At least the undead you can lay to rest."

"You keep saying Sisters. I was told we were Daughters of the Mother. Maybe…" She took in a breath, loosening the cloth. "Maybe that's the difference. Maybe the Sisters are someone else."

"The Sisters are simply what the Daughters are called now, Ephema." Darian's voice was quiet. "Few survive contact with those that call favor to your Goddess. Before the Lich destroyed so many of the Gods, the Daughters were the healers to the world. The other gods and goddesses focused on other aspects of duty; the Mother Goddess of Life gave healing to her disciples. They were blessed and then she went mad. No one has been gifted with divine healing for at least a century. No one, that is, but you."

"But, my mother could." She swallowed, dashing tears from her eyes. "That's not how it should be." She scrambled to her feet, leaving the rag behind. "I need…I need to think." She dashed away, slipping through the doors into the chapel where her footsteps grew silent.

Tabor rose, glancing at Darian. "We can't lose her, not knowing this. And she can't stay here. We need to take her and that scroll to the Great Temple in Hawthan. There's more going on here than we can handle ourselves without further guidance." He opened and closed his hand, then rubbed his arm. "The possibility that healing could be returned to the world, I never thought I would see it in my day."

"It's amazing, but restoring the power would take a lot more than just one woman, right? The Goddess would still have to be healed." Darian stood and dusted himself off. "Is that even possible?" Without waiting for an answer, he walked in the direction Ephema had fled. "I'll go see where she went, but I'm not going to force her to do anything she doesn't want to do, not yet. Because you're right," he glanced at Tabor. "There's far too much at stake right now. I think it will be better if she goes where she needs to be willingly."

"I understand your concern, young brother, but remember that our first oath is, and must always be, to Osephetin. If she is required to fulfill his will then I will see that she comes with us, even if I must carry her." He shrugged, and his tone softened. "Convince her, Darian. I agree it will be better that way. I will see to our Brother here and send a message that they require a new Knight in Residence and disciples to restore this place fully. My instincts say we should not linger. Not given what you carry, and not knowing what we've seen today."

"I understand." And he did understand, even if he didn't agree. Ephema was a person. Osephetin didn't accept oaths under duress, Tabor couldn't possibly mean that the Knights should take Ephema from her home if she didn't want to leave. Could he?

The courtyard behind the Temple was small, featuring overgrown stone paths that led between three small doors entering the building at different points. One could not reach the road directly from here, making it a bastion of silence against the world. A stone well sat in the center of the clearing, the edges crusted with soft moss. Darian had found a functional bucket in one of the storage rooms, and it now sat to one side of the well. The walls surrounding the courtyard were too steep to allow the sunlight in, save for when it was directly overhead.

Ephema sat several feet beyond the well, the thick grasses rising up around her. She had removed her mother's necklace and now clenched the globe so hard she thought her bones might crack around it. She wanted to deny what she'd been told. She wanted to believe the followers of the Mother were too strong in her light to partake in such atrocities, but some part of her knew the men were telling the truth. Her mother had always told Ephema that she was different, that they were different. There were reasons they'd kept her away from everyone high in the mountain, but she'd been too young, only fourteen turns of the seasons, when they'd left to ask the questions which flooded her mind now.

She tried to murmur a prayer seeking comfort, but nothing came to her lips except a pleading for the families of those the Sisters had murdered.

Footfalls against the stone pathway caught her attention. She recognized the pattern of the steps; Darian had already come to find her. A part of her wanted to hide, to flee back into the hills, vanish into her cave and just wait until all of this passed into distant memory. But the cave, despite being her home, held no answers to her questions.

The Knights might, and that changed everything.

She didn't look up as Darian approached, though she flinched when he placed a gentle hand on her shoulder and scooted away. Human contact felt odd after so many years alone even if she was mostly over her fear of him. His voice was soft as he spoke. "Ephema? Are you all right?"

Ephema shook her head, rubbing the globe in her hands. "I'm not sure. Maybe not. You've told me things I think I need to know, but I don't want to know." She sighed and finally looked at him. His eyes were kind, and his kindness gave her courage to continue. "When I healed you, you looked at me and you were just thankful. At least after you attacked me." Wryness touched her voice. "The Knight in there... he looked at me, and I don't think he saw me. He just saw what I'd done and his own hopes for what it meant."

"Tabor hadn't just had a caravan of twenty people slaughtered before his eyes and his own life nearly snuffed out, not a few minutes prior. I wasn't sure what or who you were. And, in my own defense, I didn't know exactly what happened or where I was." Darian sat next to her, keeping just enough distance for her to be comfortable, but close enough not to have to raise their voices to be heard. "My last memory before you woke me was claws in my face and rolling down a mountain. I don't even understand how you got me into the cave. I'm sure you're strong, given how you live, but I'm not a small man. You can't have carried me."

She smiled faintly, unable to help herself as she thought of that night. "I healed you some. Then I rolled you onto my blanket, hooked it to my shoulders, and pulled you up the hill like a load of wood. It took a while, and you might have bounced on some rocks, but that seemed better than leaving you."

Darian opened his mouth to speak, then closed it, then opened it again, then closed it. Finally, he laughed, a deep belly laugh that made him shake. He leaned back on his elbows, the laughter unlocking something inside of him and erasing some of the lines of strain from his face. It didn't seem like he laughed often enough, and Ephema smiled in return. There were many types of healing and this one didn't even require an incantation. "You were easiest to drag by your feet." She put her necklace back on, letting the globe rest against her shirt. She fell silent, letting his laughter run its course.

He shook his head, looking up at the sky. "My mother would be proud of you. It's not often I'm reduced to speechlessness." He took a deep, cleansing breath. "Praise Osephetin, it's been a while since I laughed that hard. I'm almost dizzy."

"Laughter is good for you. It lightens the body and the soul." She considered her questions and discarded them all, choosing something else to talk about. "You mentioned your mother. Is she living?" It wasn't an odd question these days, especially for those who followed Osephetin. Many Knights came from families broken by the undead.

Darian nodded. "The last time I heard from her, she was, yes. My family lives in Hawthan, the capital city off to the southwest. My father and most of his family were born there, as was I. My mother came there when she was assigned to the High Temple as part of her duties to Osephetin."

"Duties?" Ephema raised an eyebrow in surprise. "Is she a priest?"

"No." Darian smiled. "She is a Knight, and more. She is the Knight Proctor, one of the highest-ranking members of the order. I follow in her shoes, not my father's. I'm no fisherman. No matter how hard my father tried to get me to learn the family business, I just wasn't good at it. I swim well enough, but I don't have the patience for fishing trips. Plus, being surrounded by the smell of the deep ocean for weeks is not to my taste." He looked wistful for a moment. "My father was taken by the ocean, a few years back during a storm. A blessing, in a way, since the Lich's reach does not go under the water, but I miss him. It took a long time for me to accept that his death was not a punishment for anything we'd done wrong, but an act of the natural cycle which is part of our Lord's purpose."

She listened, leaning closer as she took in his story. She'd heard the name of the city of Hawthan, the home of the High Temple, but she couldn't picture it any more than any other city. She'd never gone beyond Aserian's borders, though she knew the surrounding mountains well. His talk of the ocean was like something out of a story from her childhood. She simply couldn't imagine a place with so much water. "Do you have brothers and sisters?"

"I have two. An older sister and a younger brother. My sister married young, found the man sleeping with the innkeeper's daughter, kicked her husband out on his heel, and after some negotiation with the innkeeper...now co-owns the inn. Turns out her ex-husband hadn't been honest with the innkeeper's daughter either, and he was run out of town. She ended up happily remarried to one of the bouncers and has three kids she's raising within the boundaries of the tavern."

Ephema blinked and covered a laugh. She knew about the various taverns in town, but she'd never stayed at one. She only visited to sell herbs, and sometimes she bartered for an old blanket or other supplies. "Your sister sounds interesting."

"She is that. She's nothing if not her mother's daughter. Honestly, the tavern's done considerably better now that she's running it. She has a really good head for business and since our mother is the Knight Proctor, the Knights frequent the tavern regularly, and the quality of the rest of the patrons has gone up. It's bringing in more coin than ever."

"And your brother?"

"He's a librarian for the sages in the Temple. The man has an unholy love for books. He's happiest when he hasn't seen the light of day for weeks on end and is covered in ink. If my sister didn't demand he come and visit at least weekly, we'd probably find his corpse sitting there, still reading, one skeletal hand turning the pages. No Lich could keep him from his duty, that's for sure."

"It is an odd thing to think of, to be surrounded by so many people." Her amusement waned as the smell of wood smoke drifted out to them. "I only had my parents. We came to town a few times a year, but not often enough to really have friends. And then they left, and it is just me."

Darian pushed up so he was sitting upright. "Do you know what happened to them? Any idea at all? How long have they been gone?"

"Father was…" She hesitated, trying to decide how much to tell him of what little she knew. "Father was a Knight. He and mother left when the other Knights were called away. Father promised they would be back when the snow melted and the first snowdrops bloomed. He said he and Mother were going to help his Brothers make everything right again. That when they came back, we wouldn't have to live in the cave any longer. I watch for them every year when the seasons turn, but… Five springs have gone by, and I think…" She drifted off, unable to state what she was certain of. She didn't think they were coming back, but if she said it then it would be real.

"I'm sorry." Darian let the silence sit for a time before he stood. "Come." He held his hand out to her to help her to her feet. "The past is what it is. What matters is the next morning. I, for one, am curious about the future. And I'd like to know what Knight Ianel learned about the Mayor. Shall we?"

Ephema looked at his hand for a moment before she accepted it and let him draw her upright. His grip was strong and warm, giving her strength, even though the contact was brief. Her stomach said she was more interested in food than in the Mayor. She used a lot of energy when she healed someone, and she was starving, but even that could wait. "All right." She followed in Darian's steps back toward the small door that led to the chapel. "Thank you. For talking to me."

Darian held the door open, letting her pass him by. He met her gaze and smiled. "I don't have your gift for healing, but conversation is something I can do. I would be happy to talk to you anytime, m'lady."

CHAPTER FIVE

As they stepped into the chapel Ephema and Darian found the temperature had increased several degrees. The gentle warmth was pleasant after the coolness of the outdoors. A small pyre burned in the fire pit, set well back from the hearth. It was obvious the pit for the Eternal Flame was designed to hold much more than this pitiful flame, but for now this was all that was needed. The remains of the priest could be seen in the flickering flames, and Ephema turned away from the sight. Though she knew it was a ritual all in the world came to, she wanted to remember the gentle old man she had known as he'd been while alive.

Ianel had joined Tabor in their absence, and he nodded at the pair as they entered. "Welcome, you two. Tabor filled me in during your absence as we assisted the good Bishop here." He shook his head, eyeing one of the old benches before sitting on it. It creaked a protest, but held. "It turns out that there were many wrongs the Mayor was involved in. The issues surrounding him attacking Darian and denying him sanctuary were minor among them, but it was enough that his lies came tumbling around him. He and four of the council members were in cahoots with the false followers that were cast from the town. It's a complicated matter involving theft and selling goods to the bandits that haunt the roads between here and the larger cities beyond, and that's the most minor of his problems. The folk are not pleased with their Mayor and his friends and are open to true Disciples returning to the Temple."

Tabor nodded, his gaze moving to Ephema and then Darian before returning his attention to feeding the flame. The fire burned nearly white, contained but much hotter than any fire outside a temple could ever be. "The Sergeant is a good sort. The guilty will be stripped of their positions and required to make reparations. It seems some of the remaining council are of the opinion the men should be turned out to the wild. I can't say they don't deserve it, but it seems a foolishness to me. Vengeful men should be kept close where they can do no harm, or killed cleanly if that's what the law calls for. But that is for them to decide. Hopefully, they'll be more cautious with their officials in the future."

Ianel rubbed a cloth across the armor he'd pulled onto his lap, removing the soil of combat and travel from the bone and steel. "Either way, that's no longer our concern. I've sent messages to the two closest temples who will take on the job of restoring this place and manning it again, at least for the short term. We need to report the loss of the caravan to the Bishop in Tallet and then move on toward the High Temple as soon as possible."

"Will you come with us to Tallet, Ephema?" Darian's voice was gentle. "It's not the largest of our temples by any means, but it's a stepping stone on the way to the coast and where our convoy was supposed to check in and resupply. They will be able to help us, and maybe they will know more about your parents."

Ephema curled onto one of the more stable benches, the question shaking her out of her contemplation. Her gaze rested heavily on Darian before she nodded. "I… I think I will. I have waited five years for their return. It is time I stop waiting and begin searching."

Ianel glanced at Tabor in question, but whatever comments the knight might have had about the new addition to their traveling party he left unasked. Darian caught the look, though he made no mention of it. He knew Ianel and Tabor had taken their oaths only months apart, but Ianel still looked to Tabor as his superior as well as his traveling companion.

Inwardly, he frowned. He'd assumed Tabor had explained Ephema's healing abilities to his fellow knight, but the sideways look made him doubt his assumption. There probably hadn't been much time, and what Ephema's powers suggested was unbelievable. It was probably just as well that not everyone knew her abilities, as he wasn't certain Ephema would be willing to show her gift to every Knight they happened upon. They needed to know more about her, and, more importantly in his mind, they needed to keep her safe. The Sisters and the Lich aside, there was no shortage of people in this world that would be willing to use her gifts for their own gain. If they couldn't protect her from such abuses, they had no right to take her away from the safety of her mountain home.

"It is too late to leave today. We would only find ourselves on the road at dark, and I would rather be behind walls." Tabor rumbled. "It's just as well if we stay a little longer and move about the town so our presence is not forgotten. We will purchase supplies and mounts for you two today, and leave at sunrise."

A grin spread across Ianel's face. "I agree, Brother. I've heard it rumored the innkeeper at the Tapper makes a solid brew, and it's been too long since we've eaten anything that wasn't trail rations. We can spread the good will of Osephetin with some coin and catch up on a few hours of sleep. It will almost be like a vacation."

"Perhaps a little, Brother, but remember we have a cause we must be about. I agree our presence may do some good, but not too much brew." Tabor's lean face stretched into a grin. "I'd rather not have to tie you to your horse to keep you aboard, Ianel. It bothers Star, and he's particular in temperament without irritating him further."

Ianel snorted, setting his cleaning rag aside. "That only happened once, and it was very good brew." He stood and stretched. "No time to waste then!"

The townsfolk were more than happy to accommodate the needs of the Knights, and their coin. The council had declared the Knights be supplied, but other than the first round of ale at the Tapper, Tabor insisted that they paid fair prices for their goods. Knights of Osephetin did not need handouts. Two steeds in good condition were paid for and brought to the stables late in the afternoon. They were far from war horses, but they were of a solid stock and good runners built for travel.

As the day waned, more and more of the townsfolk came to see the Knights as the initial fear and surprise of their arrival turned to wonderment. Those who were already quiet followers of Osephetin now readily showed their faith and promised to assist in rebuilding the temple. Children whom had never seen a Knight before stood nearby, some shyly and others fearful, until either their friends convinced them to approach, or their parents called them back home.

Not everyone was happy, and some who walked by made signs against evil or flashed necklaces dedicated to Neikan to show their new dedications, but no one was foolish enough to confront the Knights outright.

The evening found the quartet making their way back to the Temple. True to his word Ianel had not over-indulged and walked in a mostly straight line. He had a large rib bone in one hand, gnawing the last of the meat away from it with happy hunger, and a large wine skin in the other which he insisted was for 'later'. Despite knowing they needed to get the scroll to the High Temple and couldn't tarry, Darian found himself relaxing in the presence of the Knights. He was well aware that the dangers he'd encountered weren't defeated, far from it, but those dangers were hard to remember as he ate with his Brothers and listened to Ianel's ribald stories. He decided to consider the peace a blessing from Osephetin. Who knew what the morning would bring?

Dawn crept into the city, sliding between the buildings and painting the streets in pale light. It was a quiet start to the day, making it hard to think about the howls of the undead and the screams of the dying which had pierced the night. The air was crisp with the promise of snow and dark clouds gathered on the mountaintops, poised to sweep into the valley at the whim of the wind.

Ephema stood near the head of one of the horses, out of the way of the Knights as they packed supplies into saddlebags and strapped themselves into their armor. Ianel's eyes might be red-rimmed from drinking, but he made no fuss about the early rise and took on his share of the work without complaint. Even when Tabor made it a point to speak louder than was strictly necessary or to slap his fellow Knight on the shoulder and test his balance.

The horse shifted, nudging Ephema's shoulder, and she raised a hand to rest on its soft nose. The horse was a dappled grey gelding with a gentle look to its brown eyes. Ephema had never owned horses, but she liked them. Snelson's wife, a lovely woman, had shown up at the temple before the dawn and pressed a bundle of herbs and fresh clothing on Ephema. Ephema wasn't sure what Snelson had told his wife, but whatever it had been, her mothering instincts were in high gear as she tried to assure herself Ephema would be safe and well cared for.

Ephema appreciated the care, even if she didn't fully understand its origin. She liked the clothing and had quickly changed, leaving both the scavenged temple clothes and her old clothing behind. It felt something like shedding her old life and preparing for something new. Now she wore traveling clothes, a long-sleeved shirt topped with a heavier tunic and pants which were a little too big, but could be cinched up with a belt easily enough. She'd bundled the offered shoes with everything else and put it in the saddlebag. No one seemed to notice, or if they did, they didn't push the point. The horse nudged her again, pulling her out of her thoughts, leaning around her hand to catch her hair cloth and chew on it.

She pulled the cloth and her hair away. "Stop that. I know you have been fed. You have no need to eat my clothing."

The jingle of tack and armor caught Ephema's attention. She watched Tabor and Ianel mount, wondering how they managed with the weight of the armor. Maybe their horses were just that much stronger than her own mount. Darian approached her, and she offered him a soft smile. His presence, frightening only a couple of days ago, now brought a warmth to her heart that she didn't understand.

He placed a hand on her horse. "We're ready. The doors are sealed until other disciples can come to restore the temple. I wasn't sure if you knew how to mount."

Ephema looked at the saddle and its assortment of straps and hanging stirrups. "I understand the idea. I haven't ever tried."

To her surprise, and faint embarrassment, Darian dropped to one knee, creating a step out of his other leg. "We can teach you to mount on your own as we go, but for now this will be easier. Grab the sides of the saddle, step up, and pull yourself up. Don't grab the reins, or you'll confuse the poor fellow."

Warmth touched her cheeks at the unexpected kindness, but she nodded and moved away from the horse. She stepped as lightly as she could onto Darian's leg, using the boost he provided to clamber onto the saddle. For a moment, a memory tugged at her, sitting at this height with her Father's arms around her tiny body as the horse walked, keeping her balanced. She remembered his laughter and the brightness of the sun on a summer day. She pushed the memory away, though she held onto the laughter, and looked down as Darian rose. "Thank you. I will try to learn quickly. You should not have to kneel in the dirt for me."

Darian laughed, his eyes echoing the sound. "I don't mind. It won't take you long to learn. It takes a few times to get the idea, but soon enough it'll come naturally. It helps that you've got a calm horse." Darian stood and brushed the dust off of his knee. "It's more difficult while wearing armor, but I daresay you won't have to worry about that." He moved to his horse, turning it so she could watch him. "Your foot goes here and then you use your arms and a little momentum to swing up." He suited actions to words, but she could see that despite his reassurances that the added weight from his armor and weapons made it much harder, even with his strength. She was glad not to be so encumbered.

"Yes. She'll never have to worry about armor. I do not believe it is her fate to join the Knighthood." Tabor brought his war horse, who he'd introduced as Valor, around so he could face the rest of the group. "We ride with Ephema between the Knights. Journeyman Darian, you station yourself behind her to and to the right. There is a way station between here and Tallet. We should reach it by late afternoon and will stay over there unless we find reason to push on. Unless we discover bandits or the like along the way, I doubt we have too much to worry about this fine morning."

Ianel snorted. "From your mouth to Lord Osephetin's ears, Brother." He patted his horse on the neck, muttering just loudly enough that Ephema heard him. "Not that it's ever worked before."

Ephema smiled. She liked Ianel. He was straightforward and said what was on his mind. He was easier to talk to than Tabor was, though he didn't hold her gaze like Darian did. Tabor had told Ianel about her abilities last night. Perhaps it was because he had been drinking, but he took the news with little more than a shrug and an eyebrow raise. It was very odd to be so suddenly surrounded. She gathered up the reins, mimicking the others, and hoping that even if she didn't really know what she was doing the horse did. Tabor led the way through town, and when the others picked up speed, her mount kept up, stepping out nicely along the battered road. A few people waved at the little party as they made their way to the gate and slipped out into the morning.

No one talked much as they rode, the sound of hooves and the distance between them meaning they would have had to shout to converse. Ephema didn't mind, accustomed to the silence and enjoying the experience of seeing her world from this vantage. She couldn't help occasionally looking over her shoulder at the mountain home she was leaving behind. Going back for her few belongings had seemed foolish once she'd decided to join the Knights. They would be there when she returned, or not, it was too late to worry about it now.

The clouds gathered thickly around the peak of her mountain, and if she'd been home, she would have been inside, huddled against the snow and the cold. Here the sun was waning as the clouds crept down the mountain, and Ephema shivered, promising herself to find another layer of clothing when they stopped for the day.

The opportunity came sooner than she expected when Ianel slowed his mount, pointing toward a patch of tangled brush at the side of the road. He was the merrier of the Knights, but now his expressive face was grim. "We've a fresh kill. Poor bastard must have got caught on the road last night." He urged his horse, Star, a little farther down the road before dismounting.

Ephema blinked and glanced toward the brush, but she didn't approach it. She didn't want to see what remained of the man. She'd seen enough of the undead's kills over the years, and it was never an easy experience. "Is there something we should do? Won't he rise at dark?"

"Yes, and no." Tabor didn't bother looking at the corpse, urging Valor to join Star before he too dismounted. "It'll be a day or two, depending on when he was killed and by what, before he rises again. If we weren't here, the hope would be that someone would put him to the flame or an animal would scatter the corpse to delay his servitude to the unholy. But we have time and another option for dealing with the remains."

Ephema frowned a little, looking between the men. "You're not going to…" She waved vaguely at their weapons. "umm…scatter him, are you?" If they were going to destroy the body, she wasn't sure she wanted to watch. It was one thing when she saw an animal carrying a bone away, that was natural, but it felt wrong for the Knights to take the body apart.

Darian shook his head. "No. They can sanctify it." He hesitated before slowly admitting, "Though there have been times when scattering was the best we could do. It's not pretty, but it delays the rise, often long enough to come back and properly deal with a body."

A shudder ran through Ephema at the admission. There was a certain logic to it. The man was dead. It made sense not to allow his body to be used for evil, but she was glad there was another option than dismemberment. She nodded, letting Darian guide their horses to join the others. He dismounted, but she did not, deciding she could watch more easily from where she was, and she didn't want to get in the way.

The two Knights drew their weapons and pushed their way into the tangle, moving the brush aside or tramping it down until they could face each other over the corpse. Darian didn't join them, but knelt on one knee on the side of the road. He unsheathed his mace and set the head on the ground, holding the grip and bowing his head.

Ephema's gaze moved from him to watch the Knights. The forest around them was still as though even the little birds didn't want to interrupt the service the Knights were performing. Each man held his arms out flat, balancing their weapons across their open palms.

Tabor murmured softly. "Lord Osephetin, guide me." Blue fire gathered on the head of his maul, racing down the shaft until the entire weapon was engulfed, though it didn't burn. Ianel echoed the word, and his weapon too burst into divine flame.

Together they spoke again. The fire flared and each Knight dropped to one knee, slamming the head of their weapon into the ground. Fire surged around them, burning a perfect circle in the dirt and brush and racing inward over the corpse. From where she sat Ephema could hear the crackle of burning brush, though there was no smell of smoke or burning wood or flesh.

Now all three men spoke, but the words made no sense to Ephema. All she knew was they were words of power, similar to her prayers to the Goddess, but different. She felt the power in their words, the call on the divine, but that was all.

The moments dragged out, and she saw the strain on Darian's face. Ianel's knee dropped, both of his hands wrapping tight around the hilt of his hammer.

Tabor snapped something that sounded like a command, and the fire lashed forward, bursting into a bright star of power that extinguished itself from the center out in a whoosh of ash and a crack that felt like a physical blow to Ephema. The horses shifted uncomfortably, but none bolted, which Ephema was grateful for. She wasn't certain she could have stopped her own horse in a panic, much less the huge warhorses.

The silence held for another breath and then a questioning chirp came from one tree, answered by another bird farther away and another. Slowly, the Knights rose and shook the dust from their weapons. Nothing remained in the circle but ash, and the men moved as though they were old and stiff. Tabor stopped where Darian knelt and pulled the young journeyman to his feet.

"Come, Brother."

Darian shook his head, rubbing his hand over his eyes. "Right." He tried to sheath his mace, but it took twice before he caught the thong. He staggered to the horses, and Ephema stared at him in worry.

"Are you all right? That did not look easy."

"I…" Darian sighed, resting his head against the horse. "Sanctification is cleaner than destruction, but it takes a lot of effort. We'll be fine. That was just a lot harder than it should have been."

"Why?"

Tabor attached his maul to his saddle and, with far more effort than Ephema'd seen before, pulled himself aboard. "I don't know. Mount, Brothers, we need to ride, and quickly."

Ianel grunted and made a rude gesture at Tabor. He pressed his hand against Star's shoulder and the stallion obediently lowered himself, making it much easier for Ianel to mount.

Darian sighed, watching the display. "That's…not fair." He pulled himself into his saddle with the same weariness the other men showed. Ephema wasn't certain he would have managed if he'd been wearing heavier armor, and once aboard he still sagged.

Tabor checked on them all and nodded, taking the lead. "Onward."

It took nearly a half hour for the men to recover. No one spoke, but Ephema noticed them riding higher and with more control. They fell into a mile-eating pace which was easy for the horses, but after a few hours it became punishing for Ephema. She was accustomed to many hours walking or running, but riding was much more awkward. She hoped they might stop for lunch, but they only paused while Tabor handed out chunks of bread and apples and passed around a waterskin. The only real stops were for emptying their bladders, and Ephema's legs shook so hard she barely made it several feet off the road.

Darian assisted her in mounting again, his face no longer so pale as it had been. She murmured her thanks, certain that without his help she never would have managed. He offered her a wan smile, patting her leg. "We're not too far out now."

The wind whipped his words away, and Ephema shivered. "I am glad. It's more tiring to ride than I thought."

He moved to one of the saddlebags and produced a spare cloak. "Here. This will help block the wind. I agree it's tiring, but just hold on a little longer, and we'll be at the way station."

Ephema nodded, slipping the cloak around her shoulders while he remounted. The weight of the thickly woven fabric was welcome, easing her shivers. The horses began to move again and she pulled her feet up to try to shift the draw on her aching muscles and held on. As the day waned, Ephema found herself almost in a trance, staring at the road in front of her horse's ears and clinging to the reins with numb fingers. When they turned off the road, it was only the horse's instincts and desire to stay with the herd that kept them with the group. They slowed to a walk, coming upon a low building which served as a way station between the towns as the last glow of day retreated.

The long building was stiffly made of thick wooden poles reinforced with stone and mortar. The windows were no more than slits and the roof was a flat, grim, slab of slate. The back half of the building served as a stable and was built just as solidly as the front. For all that the undead ignored livestock, there were still brigands to consider and those tending to the animals to keep safe.

As they came to a stop, Ianel stood in his stirrups, getting a good look around. "Looks like we're the only visitors tonight, but I'll go around back and double check while you take the building." He made a clicking noise, and Star trotted around the corner of the station, leaving the rest of them to dismount and unload.

Ephema pulled her leg across the saddle and slid to the ground, or at least that was her intention. The results were much less graceful as her shaking legs gave way, and she ended up sitting next to her horse. With a heavy sigh, she decided it was a perfectly fine place to sit, and she stayed there, rubbing the feeling back into her calves while the horse nosed her hair.

Darian appeared with an open hand, an offer to help her to her feet which she took gratefully. Once Ianel returned with news that they were, indeed, alone, the men sent Ephema inside while they stabled the horses and unpacked the saddlebags. She was grateful, not trying to argue her ability to be helpful with those chores. They weren't things she was familiar with, and there were other ways she could be of use.

She entered the low building and busied herself by getting familiar with what few supplies and amenities there were. The interior was very plain. Nothing hung on the walls, and the only furniture was a long, empty table and a line of stiff cots.

A large fireplace was set in one wall and kindling sat in the center of it, awaiting flame. Her nose led her to a small closet where there was a bench with a hole in the middle and stained bucket under the hole. The last visitors had not cleaned the necessary very well, and she pushed the door closed again hoping not to have to use that facility. There were no other sundries or supplies left behind, save for a large stack of cordwood.

Once the horses were secured, the Knights brought the gear inside and barred the heavy doors against the deepening night. The sound of the heavy iron bar sliding in place seemed to bring a sense of relief to the men. Tabor assigned a night watch rotation, and they settled to wait, the sounds of night insects drifting into the hall.

Dinner was much the same as lunch had been, everyone too tired to bother with anything more complex. The men gathered together to apply cloth and oil to their armor and weaponry while Ephema curled up on one of the cots, covered by her borrowed cloak. Lulled by the soft whisper of conversation and evening prayer, she quickly fell into an exhausted sleep.

She woke only once during the night, a deep moaning and scratching pulling her out of the stillness of her dreams. Her gaze sought the door, but before she could panic, she saw Tabor sitting near the fire. His maul rested across his lap, tiny blue sparks fluttering across the weapon. He touched his lips, his voice a soft murmur. "Sleep, Daughter of the Mother. The door is thick, and your rest is guarded."

Comforted by his presence, Ephema rolled over and returned to sleep.

CHAPTER SIX

The next day began much as the first, with an early rise and cold breakfast. Darian noticed Ephema's stiffness and empathized, but there wasn't much he could do to help her with the pain. He wasn't overly comfortable himself despite having ridden much of his life. He remembered his first week in the saddle had been much worse, but the only way to make it better was to keep riding. He wondered if stiffness was something which could be healed, but asking about it felt far too much like asking her to expend unnecessary energy to fix something that was simply inconvenient.

Despite the urge to get on the road, they took the time to leave the way station prepared for the next travelers: setting kindling for the fire, splitting logs, and hauling in wood to replace that which they had burned. The horses were in a fine spirit, and Darian helped Ephema mount, doing his best to ignore the thick new scratches on the way station walls. It was odd to see the new scratches; most way stations were rarely bothered by the undead. The thick walls and small numbers inside weren't usually worth the effort, but the undead had come last night.

The feeling of being hunted put tension into Darian's shoulders, and as they returned to the road, he had a hard time not resting his hand on his mace hilt. His horse, noting his rider's inattention, continually set about trying to set its own path and speed, and soon enough Darian's attention was back on the reins. He noticed that Tabor, too, seemed especially driven, pushing them at a faster pace toward Tallet. Everyone wanted to be behind tall walls before darkness fell. Even the horses sensed the urgency and stepped out at a much faster pace than the previous day, quickly putting the way station behind them.

Once again lunch was taken in the saddle. It felt like they were racing the daylight as they pushed quickly into midday. The clouds which had been chasing them from the mountains were thicker and darker now, blocking the pale rays of the sun and threatening them with the promise of wintery weather. The wind mocked them, whipping clothing and hair, and stealing warmth with a harshness that disregarded clothing and armor alike.

By late afternoon pale flecks appeared in the air, and the riders could see their breath. Darian opened his mouth to comment on the falling snow when the scent of woodsmoke hit him, and he took a closer look at the flakes as they landed on his hands. He paled and whispered, "By the Dark One… ashes." He urged his mount forward until he drew up even with Tabor, the odor of pine smoke now clouding the wind. "Tabor! Ashes!"

"I know! Whatever is burning is big."

Whatever is burning is big. The words hit Darian like a punch. Only two things were close enough and large enough that burning would create so much ash. Either the forest was burning, or Tallet itself was on fire. He fell back to his position in the group, caught between the instinct to ride forward and find out what was happening and to stay back to protect the scroll and Ephema. Tabor leaned forward, pushing Valor into a full gallop that other horses strove to match. As they continued toward the city, Darian let his mind go blank; too much depended on him having a clear head to be clouded with possibilities and conflict. He had to take each step as it came, and he prayed to Osephetin it would be enough.

Within an hour Darian could see a red-yellow glow on the horizon and the smoke grew thick enough that he pulled a fold of his cloak across his mouth. A man lunged out from the brush, nearly falling under Valor's hooves, but the trained warhorse danced aside. The man's eyes widened when he realized whom he'd bumped up against and hope flared in his expression where once only fear grew. "Knights! Thank Osepehtin! You have to help us! The Temple has fallen! The undead are in the city!" The words came out in a hoarse shout, tumbling over each other like a panicked waterfall.

"Undead?" Ianel brought Star around, staring at the man from under the thick bones of his helmet. "You must be mistaken. It is still light."

"By the soul of the Eternal Father, I swear it. Undead are ravaging the city as we speak." With a shaky hand, the man gestured toward the brightness on the horizon. "Dozens of them. They've cut down the Knight in Residence, slaughtered the brethren, and routed most of the guardsmen already! The city's been put to the torch!"

Darian frowned, having to spin his horse in a tight circle to stop it from fidgeting. "Who put it to the torch? Fire takes too long to destroy active undead. They're not afraid of it, and they don't wield it themselves."

The man shook his head. "There was a man. I thought he was a guardsman, but I'm not sure now. He suggested that the undead could be brought to bear with a mixture of flammable tar and other stuff. It stuck to them, but it didn't kill them, and they spread the flame. If it was only fire or the undead, we'd be fine, but not both! And these undead... Sir, I'm not a coward. I did my stint in the guard, and I've fought the walking, but these were nothing like I've seen before."

Tabor frowned, glancing over his shoulder at Ianel and Darian. "Hunters." His gaze went back to the frightened man. "Where were you going?"

He swallowed hard and gestured to the west. "We have a logging post on the river. It's not far. If they haven't been attacked, I thought it might be a safe place to evacuate whatever women and children we can."

"Go then. Evacuate anyone you can, and hold through the night. We'll join those in the city and bring an end to the undead. The fire will need the hands of your folk to be extinguished." Without another word, he put his heels to his mount, and Valor leapt forward, drawing on new reserves of energy as he pounded down the road.

Neither Darian nor Ianel questioned their superior, but followed him down the road sweeping Ephema along with them. Snow mixed with the ash until the sky was spitting an odd muddy mash down on them, the wind biting and brutal. It wasn't long before the road opened up to reveal the burning city. Thick stone walls etched with hand-carved images encircled the tall buildings within, though many were now crumbling and cracking under the heat of fire and age. The fire was mostly on the eastern side of the city, the containment a small mercy.

As they approached, a skeletal shape stood in the broken gate, backlit by the hell of the inferno beyond. Tabor didn't slow his horse. With one smooth motion, he freed his maul from where he'd secured it and dropped his reins, trusting Valor's training. He swung the massive weapon around, using the momentum of the horse to increase the power of the attack. The maul's head slammed into the side of the creature, breaking it into two separate pieces and sending splinters of bone to the four winds.

"Ephema! Stay close!" It never occurred to Darian that they should send Ephema with the evacuees, only that if she stayed near enough, they could protect her. He drew his mace as he pulled his horse in close, letting the two Knights take the lead into the city. Tabor had used the word 'Hunters,' and the thought filled Darian with dread. He had heard of Hunter undead before, but only from his mother's stories; undead that walked in the daylight, dangerous, powerful creatures that were rarely encountered, and even then, only in the great wastelands left by the Fall of the Gods. Older Knights told stories of the Hunters and the beasts that commanded them.

But for them to be here, in a random city on the edge of civilization? It made little sense. Unless…unless they were the undead who had chased him across the mountains. The thought hadn't occurred to him until this moment, seeming too much a fire tale, and it filled him with dread.

"Darian! Ianel!" Tabor's voice brought Darian from his thoughts, ringing through empty city streets, backed by the crackle of flames. "We'll fight our way to the Temple and search for any survivors there first. Don't get separated, no matter the temptation."

Finding their way through the city was morbidly simple. All they had to do was follow the corpses. The undead had assaulted the front gates in broad daylight, when no one expected resistance. The slaughter of both guardsmen and innocents was savage and bloody, but it left a definitive trail for the Knights to follow straight to the burning Temple. There was no question this had been the undead's primary goal.

It wasn't long before they reached the stonework of a once proud Temple of Osephetin, though the damage here was done by attack and not by the power of time as had felled the temple in Aserian. Flame spread under two of the eaves, roaring with hunger. Darian heard the sounds of combat from within, and Tabor threw himself from the saddle, shouting a battle cry as he ran up the steps.

The thick doors were shut, and when he hit them with his shoulder, they held solid, wedged firm against his attack. Flames licked at the frame and he frowned, before bellowing, "Ianel! With me! Darian, Ephema, stay with the horses. Watch for survivors to come from the flame. Destroy the undead, do not hesitate!"

He growled a word, a deep tone that rang hollow and echoed in the air. His maul glowed a deep blue with the divine magic of the soul weapon. He raised the maul with both hands and brought it crashing down on the center of the door. Even stuck as it was, the door could not withstand the blow and folded inward, taking flame, wood, metal, and debris with it. He didn't look behind to see if Ianel was following and charged inside.

As Ianel dismounted, another battle cry came from inside the building. A tremendous impact shook the ground and a section of wall shuddered. Ianel shot a snarky grin at Ephema and Darian. "I'd better get moving before there's nothing left for me to fight!" He pulled the grinning skull of his helm down over his face and sprinted into the ruined Temple. "Osephetin! Guide me!"

Darian slid off his horse, shaking his head. "We're not all insane, I promise." He shrugged, waiting for Ephema. "Just most of us."

Ephema shrugged, directing her horse to a safer spot before looking up at the burning building. "I am not in a position to judge." She dropped to the ground, then blinked, her gaze narrowing. She gestured at the top of the building. "Is that a person?"

Darian followed her gesture to the roof, where a figure moved about in the haze and smoke. "It's definitely something. If it's a person they'd have to be desperate to be on the roof." He put himself ahead of Ephema, his mace held at the ready.

The figure on the top of the temple staggered forward, even as slate tiles slid out from under its feet. It reached the edge of the roof and stepped into oblivion, landing near a patch of burning timber. Without hesitation, the creature rose back to its full height. It turned toward Ephema and Darian.

The creature had been human, once. Now, no trace of flesh remained, but tendrils of shadowy magical essence echoed motions once created by living muscles and ligaments. In skeletal hands, it gripped a large hand axe; its grip sure around the pommel. Pools of orange magic reflected from the empty eye sockets of the grinning skull as it stared at the pair. It shouldn't have been possible to assign an emotion to the bony face, but Darian felt the hunger and rage the creature carried. A swath of burning pitch clung to the side of the creature's skull, and flame licked across the side of its bony pate with each advancing step.

"Stay behind me." Darian commanded, shifting his position to keep himself between the healer and the undead. As long as it was just the one, keeping her safe shouldn't be a problem. He tried to remember what his Mother had said about Hunters. They were faster than regular undead and more cunning. She'd not mentioned they could use weaponry beyond their claws and teeth, but there it was. And they could walk in daylight. And chase him down a mountain at the pace of a grown man's spring. He stopped thinking about all the things the stories didn't tell and charged the creature instead.

The first strike of his mace bounced off the hand axe which the skeleton raised in defense. That was also different – the undead never defended themselves – and Darian shifted his grip, driving his mace into his foe's ribs as he continued past. He felt more than saw Ephema dart around the side of the building, well out of the range of the combat, but also too far for him to protect if she encountered another one. The rap of the hand axe deflecting off his shoulder armor returned his attention to the fight in front of him. Ephema would have to be all right on her own.

The skeleton lurched forward with a wide overhand swing, but Darian drove under the blow and shoved his shoulder into his enemy's broken ribcage. They tumbled to the ground in a tangle of limbs and armor, the skeleton's jaws snapping as it tried to bite him. Darian rolled away and sprang back to his feet. He smashed the mace onto the skeleton's writhing body, shattering and splintering bone and evil magic. He moved to the rest of the body, tossing larger chunks of bone as far as he could, letting them fall where they might. Claws raked his shins, pulling at his greaves, but they were unable to penetrate the thick hide.

A few swings later, the Hunter's skull cracked under the blows, and its motions came to a stop. Darian rubbed the sweat from his forehead on the back of his arm and took a deep breath. He turned to follow where Ephema had gone and a sword slid past his guard, biting into his arm, digging nearly to the bone. Darian cursed in pain and swung wildly, knocking the sword away from a second Hunter. He hadn't heard it approach, but that came as little surprise. He'd been too intent on his first foe to remember to watch for a second.

The skeleton, its balance askew from loss of the sword, windmilled for a moment before it regained its balance. Darian's hand felt numb, aching from his grip on the mace. He turned his body and rammed the skeleton's sternum, sending it sailing toward the horses. Valor needed no other prompting; a warhorse of a Knight of Osephetin knew exactly what to do about the undead. A whinny and an avalanche of iron shod hooves fell, sending one more Hunter to an eternal rest.

Blood ran down Darian's arm, hot and metallic, but a quick inspection of the wound told Darian that it wasn't a fatal cut. Just a rookie mistake. He grimaced, grateful the cut was on his off hand, then went to find Ephema.

EPHEMA BLINKED the tears from her eyes, the risking smoke and heat from the flames licking at her skin. She got her hands more firmly under the priest's shoulders and pulled hard. His face was black with burnt skin, but she felt the pulse of his life through her fingertips. He could be saved if she could get him away from the fire. She pulled him foot by agonizing foot until she could lay him next to another unconscious man, who had managed to get himself out of the building but had fallen before she got to him.

Ephema glanced around, making sure she was alone. She

knelt between the men, lowering her head and whispering her incantations, praying to the Mother for mercy. Despite the Knight's insistence that the Goddess was lost, Ephema felt the warmth of the Mother's power. White wisps of power slid down her arms, and she rested her fingertips on each man's shoulder.

She felt the draw of energy leaving her body, even as she was filled with healing power. She knew she had the strength to restore them both to full health, but hesitated to use so much energy until she knew how many others were hurt. She had limits and pushing past them would be painful. As her power washed over them, blackened skin fell away from their hands and faces, showing the healthy pink of new skin below.

The man on her right started to wake, and Ephema lifted her hands, pushing to her feet and stumbling to the well to draw a bucket of water. She returned to the men, pouring water over their hands and faces. Darian came around the corner of the building, his lips pursed in a frown that made her feel guilty. He had told her to stay close, but she'd seen movement, and it had seemed a better idea to help. As he drew closer, she saw the sleeve of his right arm was bright with blood, slashed open just beneath where the thick leather covered his shoulder and upper arm.

He walked over and knelt down by the men, looking them over. "Survivors? Good. Have you found any others, or seen or heard from the Knights?"

She shook her head as another crash echoed from inside. "I've only seen these two, and I've heard the noises from the Knights. I worry the building might fall down if they continue like this." She shifted her position and touched Darian's arm, his blood cold on her fingers. She extended her prayer, and the white glow wrapped around his arm like a wisp of mist. The stain remained on his clothing, but within an instant the flesh below was made whole.

"You didn't have to do that." Darian smiled his thanks anyway. He looked up as dust and burning bits of roof fell from the building. "I see what you mean. I have only trained with Knights Tabor and Ianel, I've yet to see them in combat, but they are not subtle. We should get these two farther away in case the walls do not hold."

Despite the gloves covering his hands, Ephema felt warm from his touch. She disagreed with his insistence that she shouldn't heal him. Her father said sometimes the best healing was preventing other injuries from happening. If Darian could not defend himself, more damage would be done to him, and he could not defend others. She rubbed more ash off her face and nodded. "I agree."

One of the wounded men began to cough, and she slipped away from Darian, moving to the man's side. "Come. We must get away from here. It will be easier if you can stand."

"Wha…who?" The man groggily opened bloodshot eyes and tried to focus on the two before him. "Where am I?"

"You're outside the temple, my friend, but it's burning. We have to move now." Darian knelt and got an arm around the man, helping him to his feet. "Up you come."

"Who are you?"

"Darian, Journeyman of Osephetin. Two Knights are here as well."

"Journeyman…oh praise be to Osephetin." The man steadied himself, still weak but able to stand without Darian's help. "We thought we were done for! They came from…" He was unable to continue as a coughing fit wracked his body.

"Later. For now, let's get out of the smoke."

Ephema nodded, slipping her shoulder under the priest's

arm and nodding at his companion. "Darian, you will have to carry the other. I am not strong enough." She pulled on the priest, starting him toward the road. Even if the temple remained standing, the smoke wasn't good for anyone and unless someone doused the fire, the burning would continue until nothing remained but the stone foundations.

Darian secured his mace and hefted the unconscious man over his shoulder. It wasn't easy, but between their efforts, they reached the street a few minutes later. The horses still waited there, though they'd moved back from the burning building, showing more common sense than many people. Ephema helped the priest to sit on the side of the road. "Breathe deeply now. You will feel better if you breathe out all the smoke." Not that the danger wasn't still present here, but the thickest smoke was being drawn up into the wind and the touch of the snow was soothing.

"Thank you, m'lady." The man sat down, weary but with gratitude in his expression. He took a few minutes, breathing in deeply and coughing to clear his lungs. "Where did you come from? You are not locals to the city."

Darian settled the unconscious man into a comfortable position and stood, one hand never too far from his weapons. His gaze darted around as he spoke. They were far from safe. "No. We're not. I was part of a convoy that was supposed to stop here on our way to Hawthan, but we were ambushed. The Knights inside found me along the way. Ephema has joined us for reasons of her own. We saw the fire and came to help."

The man perked up as he listened. "The convoy! We have been waiting for you. Do you have the scroll? Tell me that the seal has not been broken and it remains safe!"

"I do. It is safe and sealed, though I am surprised you know about it."

"Thank the Dark One. Some good may yet come out of this day." He sighed and continued. "We have been watching for you for nearly a week. I was one of those who helped discover the existence of the scroll and thus knew what you were seeking. Forgive me for not standing, my child. I am Bishop Lam, formerly of the Temple of Tallet. But I can no longer say that, I suppose, seeing as how it's burning before us."

"Walls can be rebuilt, sir. Lives cannot." Darian looked up as Tabor and Ianel emerged. Relief filled him now that they were out of the burning building and seemed none the worse for wear. "It looks like they've cleared the undead, sir, but we should be wary. More may still be about, and the temple is still burning. Usually, the temples serve as places to gather the people in such emergencies. As this one is a loss, I don't know where else to go."

"There are other large buildings, my son. Depending on where the fires burned and what was spared, we can use them." He frowned deeply. "I do not know how many of our brothers survived, but they will return here when they can."

Darian nodded, waiting to continue until Tabor and Ianel joined them. Both men were covered in soot and ash and a long scratch marred the front of Ianel's breastplate, digging into the metal, though the enchanted bone remained in one piece. Darian saluted them with a hand across his chest. "Two of those Hunter undead came while you were inside. I defeated one, but had a lot of help from Valor on the second. You'll find the remains under his hooves. Ephema found these two survivors, Bishop Lam and…umm… I don't know the name of the other Brother yet. We found no others. Your orders?"

"Relax, Darian. My orders, at the moment, are to stand down. I'm confident that's all of the undead here." Tabor frowned. "These undead were Hunters and yet they weren't, not really. Hunters always operate under a chain of command. It is where they get their power. Hunters under a Commander are deadly opponents. These?" He ran a hand along his maul, checking for nicks. "Stronger than regular night walkers, but only barely. These were the stragglers. Otherwise, we'd still be fighting."

"But why were they here in the first place?" Ianel worried at his hammer, trying to dislodge a piece of skull which was wedged atop the weapon. Fractures spiraled out from the point of impact, but the bone held tight to the bone-studded metal.

"Once the fires are out and the whole town is secure, we will find out." Tabor looked around the road with a practiced eye before nodding to himself. "Come. There are a few buildings that way which are untouched by flame. We will gather the wounded there. Darian, carry our injured Brother. Ianel, help Ephema with the horses, not that they will need much direction. Bishop Lam, please accompany us. You will need to be the voice of the temple in this crisis, and we will be your hands." He offered Bishop Lam his hand, which the man accepted, and pulled him to his feet. "We have much to do."

CHAPTER SEVEN

Despite Tabor's assurance they would rest, it was long in coming. Led by the remaining guardsmen, and assured the Knights would destroy any other undead, the townfolk were quick to return to the defense of their city. Darian found himself assigned to a team to gather folks from the outlying areas while Tabor and Ianel assisted in repairing the gates and extinguishing the flames. The undamaged buildings, most of which were on the western side of town, became focal points to gather the injured and to bring supplies for survivors and those with no home no return to. The sense of camaraderie wouldn't last, but for now, everyone was doing their part to help. Bishop Lam and his fortunate counterpart, a young acolyte by the name of Timmon, made space for the wounded in a large storage shed and offered prayers of sanctification for the dead. Neither man seemed to realize that their condition was a matter of healing, and not divine intervention of the Dark Lord, which Darian decided was just as well.

Ephema wandered the makeshift aid station, speaking

softly to the injured and helping with bandaging and bringing food and water. Darian never witnessed her actively using her healing abilities, but wherever she went the injured recovered faster. As the hours passed and darkness fully fell, he and Ianel had to convince her to retire to one of the cots and sleep, otherwise she would have tended to the wounded until she collapsed. Darian was certain that his plea for her well-being wasn't nearly as convincing as Ianel's threat to put her on the cot and sit on her.

Darian lost track of time as the night crept on. The gates, as hastily repaired as they were, held steady against the encroach of the nightly undead, which were few, but there were many other tasks that called for a strong back and willing hands. Every time he tried to sit down and rest, someone else called for more help. He managed to doze here and there, but true sleep eluded him. As daylight broke, he found a spot at a table in the busy inn. He sat down, intent on sitting for just a moment, but woke up over an hour later when Tabor sat next to him and slapped his shoulder by way of greeting.

"Wake up, Journeyman." Tabor grinned as Darian jerked awake. "We still have lots to do today, and little time to do it in." The big knight startled some of the other patrons when he dropped the head of his maul to the ground with a loud thud and pulled it closer, letting it sit upside down on the floor beside him.

"Uh!" Darian nearly came out of his seat at the force of the slap combined with his sudden return to wakefulness. "I'm awake! Osephetin's blood, Knight Tabor, do you ever sleep?"

"I slept for about two hours this morning. That's plenty. Have you spoken to Bishop Lam, yet? He's asked about you twice."

"I have not." Darian grimaced. "He knows something

about the scroll and can verify its authenticity, but every time I go to see him, he's been far too busy seeing to the needs of his people. Which is really as it should be."

Tabor nodded, learning back in his chair. His weight brought a protest from the wood, but it held. "Understandable. Many need his guidance and comfort and his temple staff has been reduced to a handful of people. He will require assistance in completing the rites for our Brethren and the other deceased from the city. We have, of course, volunteered our services to assist the dead to gain safe passage to Osephetin's Halls."

"Of course." Inwardly, Darian groaned. The next few days were not going to be any shorter than this one had been, and he felt the weight of his mission to return the scroll to the High Temple, but it would be foolish to strike off on his own. The rites they could use were different with the priests present. They would not be difficult, especially for non-disciples, if they were done quickly after death, but they could be time consuming. Especially if the numbers were high. "Do we know how many perished?"

Tabor adjusted the position of his giant maul, the bone squealing against the floor. Many of the inn's patrons gave the Knight a curious glance, which he ignored. Darian supposed a Knight got accustomed to being started at. Eventually. "We do not have a final count, and more could still die from their wounds. Right now, it appears there were around thirty lost among the guards and the people with an additional nine perishing at the temple either in battle or the fire. This included Knight Pyina, but her death did not come cheap."

Darian's stomach grumbled, the gurgling interrupting Tabor's accounting. Darian flagged down one of the tavern maidens, a pretty girl carrying a large tray of empty plates and mugs. "M'lady, is there something more to eat for two hungry men?"

She smiled shyly. "We do indeed. Our stores were fortunate to be spared in the chaos." Her gaze flicked to Tabor, "And for you, good Knight? On the house, of course. Wouldn't be a city left without you Knights."

Tabor snorted, not correcting her as to their efforts. "Anything will do, girl. Empty stomachs aren't overly picky. Though I'd be obliged if a full tankard came with it."

The tavern maiden curtseyed without tipping her tray and hurried away. Darian shook his head, trying to clear the last of the cobwebs of sleep. "How many did it take to down Knight Pyina? I remember her from my early training. She was a very dedicated woman, and she was insanely dangerous with a battle axe."

"Aye. She was a beast. It's hard to tell how many she killed from the piles of debris that we found her body in. I would guess at least a dozen. She called on Osephetin's grace in the end. Bishop Lam told me that's what set the Temple on fire and not the burning pitch on some of the skeletons." Tabor was quiet for a moment after that, both men paying a moment of silence in honor of the fallen. Finally, Tabor's gaze rose to the people of the tavern. "Darian, why would Hunters attack here? These are uncommon beasts. What is so alluring about some little city that's barely above a town on the edge of nowhere?"

Darian took in the soft question, pitched under the chatter of the morning crowd. The weight of the bone and metal case at his side was heavier than he'd remembered it being. "This is the first place with a decent sized temple that I've seen since we left the temple at Winter Spire and came south. Bishop Lam knows something about what I carry, and the undead focused mostly on the temple here. You can see it in the damage patterns. They could have destroyed more of the city, but they didn't. That can't really be a coincidence, can it?"

"I don't believe in such coincidences." Tabor met Darian's gaze across the table. "I think we need to get that case to Bishop Lam. He told me he received a message entreating him to assist the convoy when you got here. I want to know what else he was told." He paused, shrugging. "After we've gotten some food in our bellies, naturally. I don't think another half hour is going to make much difference, but then we must make him make time for us. We need the answers he can provide in order to take our next steps. We need to know if the plan to journey straight to Hawthan is still a solid one." He frowned, rubbing his jaw, his fingers rasping against the bristles of his short beard. "Or we need a new plan, before something worse than Hunters arrives at our doorstep."

"I can't see how there's much worse than…" Darian stopped himself. "You don't really think…" He couldn't force himself to speak the thought out loud, as though saying it might make it happen. No Knight had seen the Lich in living memory. They had only fought his minions, and those were bad enough.

"I don't know. Just because it hasn't happened before now doesn't mean it can't. I don't know enough about that trinket you're carrying, but I know things are changing. Something in the air is different. It is harder to draw power than it used to be. And if we have to defend against more than Hunters, I'd rather do it with the power of the High Temple and more of our Brethren for back up." Tabor paused and allowed a grin. "Not that Ianel and I didn't enjoy the work out, but we were lucky what was left was weak and already coming apart. We can't count on that luck to sustain us.

"And I wasn't referring to the Lich. I don't think he has any need to deal with us himself, at least not at our current strength. We see only the least of his powers when the dead rise. His Hunters and Commanders serve much as Journeyman Knights might, but there's more, Darian. I've seen them. Once, a long time ago when I was only a journeyman, myself. Those…those he might send. We call them the Corrupted."

"Corrupted?" Even the sound of the word sent chills down Darian's spine, and he found himself gripping his mace as though he might have to spring into action. "Dare I ask what those are?" And whatever they were, why hadn't he been told about them before now? Even Hunters hadn't been part of his training; he'd only heard about them in stories from more experienced Knights like his mother. Between undead that could run at the pace of a man and others that could walk in the light of the day, it appeared there was much that hadn't been covered. Things he thought even a Journeyman deserved to know.

"There are many types of undead, Darian. You have been taught that if one of Osephetin's faithful dies, the Lich's magic cannot affect the corpse like our Brother in that small temple." He nodded at the tavern maiden as she brought the food and drink, accepting the heavy tray and setting it on the table between he and Darian. "Ah, this will hit the spot. Thank you."

The maid left, and Tabor handed some of the bread, which was a dark color and spread with soft cheese, and a flagon of mead to Darian before he continued. "Well, there have been very rare times when one of the faithful has died in the actual presence of the Lich and has not been able to call on Osephetin's grace. These fallen Brothers become the

Corrupted. Their souls do not move on to Osephetin's Halls, and their bodies become the worst of undead monsters. This is why we are sworn to take our own lives before allowing ourselves to be captured by the Lich's minions. The Corrupted retain their skills and knowledge from life, bound to eternal servitude to the Lich's whims. There is no rest for the Corrupted, only rage and blood as they slaughter those who are as they once were."

"That's horrific. Why…why is this the first time I'm being told about this?" Darian bit mechanically into the bread. Ordinarily, it would have been a delicious start to the morning. The bread was dense with a nutty taste and the cheese soft and salty, but after everything he'd just learned, it tasted flat, and he ate out of obligation rather than hunger. "There seems to be a lot about our foe that isn't mentioned in our training."

"That's by design." Tabor took a large swig of his mead, eating and drinking neatly though quickly. "Hunters, Commanders, and especially the Corrupted are exceedingly rare. I've been hunting the undead for over a decade, and this is only the third time I've encountered Hunters. I've only ever seen a Commander once, and a Corrupted at a distance as we ran like hell. The vast majority of your service will be against the garden variety of undead that roam the face of the world. There is no sense worrying about something you may never see, and once the thought is planted in your head, you'll think you're seeing worse monsters everywhere. So, you learn when you need to know. I've decided you need to know."

Darian sighed and took another bite, ripping the crust from the bread and setting it aside to eat last. "I can see the argument, but right now I wish I'd known. I might have been better prepared."

Tabor laughed, chasing a bite of bread with another swig.

"You've got a good head on your shoulders. I personally think the training should be expanded to cover all the possibilities that we are aware of, but I'm not in charge of training."

Darian snorted. "As long as my head remains on my shoulders, I can keep serving Lord Osephetin properly, which is exactly why I'm going to complain to the training staff when we get home." Darian let the conversation drop as the two men bent to the meal in earnest.

Ephema sat on the edge of a cot, far away enough from the bustle of the aid station to have some peace and quiet, but close enough to assist if there was an emergency. She was beyond exhausted, but still too wound up to sleep, though the Knights had insisted she try. She didn't think Ianel would truly sit on her, but the teasing threat had been enough to get his point across. The kindly Bishop Lam had drafted her as soon as the wounded began coming in to wrap wounds and apply compresses, and while drifting between patients, she had healed everyone she could without being too obvious. It was difficult, but she was managing to keep the light of her healing magics hidden.

She sighed and scooted back so she could lean against the wall, drifting into a near doze until a figure took a seat next to her. It took several blinks for her eyes to focus enough to recognize the slight form of Bishop Lam. He held a tray on his lap that held a small bowl filled with something that smelled delicious.

"You should get some sleep, young lady. But I thought you might want something to eat first."

Ephema nodded, pushing herself up right and accepting a

chunk of bread and the bowl from the priest. The broth was thin with a few chunks of root vegetables floating in it, and the smell brought a grumble from her stomach. "Thank you."

"You've earned it." He paused, watching her eat before adding. "Young healer."

She startled at the naming, the warm broth splashing up the side of the bowl. Ephema wiped her mouth with her sleeve, swallowing to clear her throat. It was one thing to show the Knights what she could do, but she was so certain she'd been careful around everyone else. "I…I don't know what you mean."

"Of course, you do." The man's smile was gentle, and his voice quiet enough that no one else would overhear him. "I'm not fool enough not to know what the possibilities were inside that fire. Myself and my scribe should be dead. I know for a fact I should have savage burns on my leg. I remember a burning timber landed on it. I couldn't stand. I thought it was broken." He touched his leg, shaking his head before looking at her again. "In addition, you have your mother's eyes, and your expression at this moment is just like hers when she was flustered. It's amazing how things are passed among family."

Ephema tightened her grip on the bowl, the ceramic solid and warm under her fingers. She took a deep breath before lifting it to her lips and drinking the broth down, leaving the chunks for last. It smelled better than it tasted, but it eased the gnawing in her stomach. "You met them when they left?"

He patted her knee before sitting back and beginning on his own scant meal. "I knew them before that even. I trained with your father before deciding the path of the priesthood was for me. When he came east, I traveled with him as a strong arm and spiritual advisor, though I remained here when he journeyed on. They were good people. I miss them both terribly. I wondered how long it would be before you followed in their footsteps."

She lowered the bowl, setting it on her lap. "I just want to know if they're still alive out there somewhere. They promised, but they never came back."

"Merciful Osephetin. They didn't tell you more than that?" Bishop Lam's eyes were pained. "Osephetin's blood, Anceil, you idiot. You left it to me to break this news?" He pushed the food away and took Ephema's hands in his, sighing heavily. "There is no easy way to explain, but I can spare you a fruitless search. There never was much of a chance their quest was going to succeed. We all hoped it would, but… they were lost to us."

Ephema closed her eyes and then opened them again, looking away from the priest. She'd suspected for a while that her parents weren't coming back, but she'd clung to a shred of hope because she didn't want to face the truth of being alone. "What happened?" She needed to know, but that wasn't going to make it easier to hear.

Bishop Lam stood and paced to a low window, watching the people outside in silence. Finally, without turning around, he began. "Do you know what the Rite of Rebirth is?"

"No. I don't."

"I didn't think so, but there was always a chance." He sighed, bowing his head. She saw his eyes were closed, though he continued speaking. "I suppose I'm not entirely surprised that Anceil never told you what he and your mother were attempting to do. Disappointed, but not surprised. It was very dangerous and chances were slim they would succeed." He turned and opened his eyes again, meeting Ephema's gaze. "But you have the right to know.

"It started before your birth, Ephema. Your father, Knight

Anceil, was one of our greatest knights and my closest friend. One summer, he returned to the High Temple from a mission from deep in the heart of the Dejected Lands far to the east. A man of deep devotion, Anceil asked for guidance as to his next assignment. One of the higher ranked bishops entered into meditation on Anceil's behalf and received a vision from Osephetin. A vision that seemed so unbelievable he was reluctant to tell it. Three more times he appealed to the Dark Lord, and three times he dreamed the same dream.

"In the vision, the Dark One bade Anceil to find a living, sane Daughter of the Mother, a woman who could heal and who would undertake the Rite of Rebirth and bring peace to Lianna, the maddened Goddess of Life. It was hard to believe that this was Anceil's calling as everyone knew the Daughters of the Mother no longer existed, and approaching the Sisters was a path of insanity and death. The Bishop had been given such firm direction and had been gifted with proven visions in the past, but it was so very hard to imagine the message was true.

"But your father believed. I think he may have had dreams of his own that drove him, though I never asked. He never questioned, and I went with him when he rode away to follow the guidance he'd been given. We searched for close to two years with little success beyond hearing the occasional rumor and fighting the Sisters wherever we found them.

"When we reached Tallet, the Bishop here was on his deathbed, and there was no one to take his place. I'd taken a hip wound a few weeks earlier that made riding more and more difficult, and I felt compelled to stay and help the city. Your father understood, but he could not be stopped in his quest. It was three more years before I saw him again."

He chuckled softly, the memory bringing warmth to his

expression. "That's when I first met you, Ephema, though you do not remember it. Anceil and Elaina arrived one afternoon out of the blue. They revealed that the Bishop's vision was accurate. They had found each other and in doing so, they'd also found love in this forsaken land. Anceil held a tiny bundle in his powerful arms, proof he'd fallen in love twice. Your mother may have held his heart, but you, my dear child, were his joy.

"Anceil and Elaina visited often in those early days. They were a spark of light and hope to the Brethren, and they loved life and each other dearly, but your father was plagued with dreams and couldn't rest. His oaths drove and tortured him and, once you'd come of an age where he thought you could be safe without them, they came to me. We discussed the Bishop's vision again. Bringing peace to the Goddess of Life would radically alter life on this world and open the path to destroying the Lich. They felt it was worth the cost to try. They wanted a better world. For you."

He sighed, the lines returning to his face. He looked older now. Tired. "We…have known about the Rite of Rebirth for a generation. It was discovered shortly after the Fall of the Gods, but until Elaina, there was never a hope of the Rite working. And even with your mother, as powerful as she was…" He shook his head. "Maybe we should have known better.

"But they both thought any chance, no matter how slight, made it worth risking everything. Because, as your father often reminded me, what if it worked?" Bishop Lam let out a soft breath, rubbing the tears from his cheeks. "Your father was nothing if not stubborn. I decided if I could not change their minds, it would be best if I accompanied them to the Eye of the Goddess, deep in the Southern Lands. That was the second hardest journey of my life."

"Why?"

"Why?" His voice was soft. "Ephema, the priestess doesn't survive the Rite of Rebirth. It demands a sacrifice to rejuvenate what was lost. I was journeying to witness the death of my best friend's wife. Even if we won, we were going to lose."

"No. That's... That's not possible. My mother wouldn't have gone just to die. There had to be..." Ephema's voice broke. "There had to be another way."

Bishop Lam sighed deeply. "If she knew of one, she didn't speak of it to me, and it wouldn't have mattered anyway. We had only just begun the Rite when the Lich attacked. Your father and four other Knights did all they could to hold off the waves of undead, and the lashing of the monster's magic, but even with their skills, there were just so many foes. I saw your father call on the Dark Lord and bear the Lich to the ground, but no matter how they struck him - the undead king would not die. In the end, Anceil..." He paused, seeming unable to continue.

"What? What happened?" Ephema barely managed the words, the painting of her parents' last moments horrific, tearing into her as though she was being struck.

"Your father wasn't allowed to die. It would have been better if he had been. While he was focused on the Lich one of his followers got through Anceil's guard and pinned him to the wall with a spear. As he strove to call on Osephetin's grace the Lich did something. I don't know what it was, but the thing that stepped away from that wall was no longer the man I knew. My best friend, your father, now walks the land in servitude as a Corrupted."

"No."

The Bishop continued as though he didn't hear her agonized denial. "Your Mother was spared that, at least. The interruption of the Rite broke her mind. Incapacitated like that, she was an easy target. What few of us were left managed to escape, carrying her with us, but she succumbed to her wounds within a few hours. I think, perhaps, if Anceil had been there she would have survived, but without him to anchor her she slipped away. Coming home to report our failure, and the loss of my friends. To report that all hope was lost? That was the hardest journey in my life."

Ephema felt the tears running down her cheeks, the remains of her meal forgotten, dripping onto the floor. She felt numb. These were all of her fears laid out before her, and worse. There wouldn't be a happy homecoming. Not now. Not ever.

For a time, neither spoke, the silence stretching out painfully between them. Finally, in a small voice, she asked. "Why?"

"Hmm?" Bishop Lam recrossed the small space, sitting beside her and placing his hands over hers. "Why what, my dear?"

"My parents left five years ago. If they died then, why didn't anyone come looking for me?" She couldn't meet his eyes. "I was little more than a child, left alone! Why didn't anyone tell me what had happened? Why did I have to come here now to get answers?"

"I tried, Ephema, I really did." He sighed, his shoulders slumping under the weight of guilt. "Anceil told me he and your mother lived somewhere in the mountains above the town of Aserian, but he never told me exactly where. There was a geas placed on your home to protect it, so that no one could find it – or you – without having been shown the way. I looked for months, but I never found you."

He frowned deeply. "I left instructions with the local

Bishop, Cerenus, to take care of you if he saw you in town and give you instructions to contact me. When I didn't hear from you, or him, I assumed the worst. I felt it was my penance to serve as long and as well as I could in Tallet in memory of my friends. When I first saw you in the temple garden, I was sure you were your mother in spirit, and I was dead."

"Cerenus…died. The Aserian Temple has long been abandoned. We found his…body…there. He passed before he could tell me anything."

"Oh. Oh my." Bishop Lam suddenly pulled her into a gentle hug. The weave of his robes was coarse, but the gesture brought Ephema comfort. "I'm so, so sorry, Ephema. I had no idea."

"It's all right." Ephema rubbed her fingers over her cheeks, drying her tears. "So, what am I supposed to do now?"

"That's a question only you can answer. But, whatever you choose, I will support you in it." He leaned back, smiling. "Though I think, if you can, the first thing to do is rest. Plans and questions will wait for a little longer."

Ephema wasn't sure how she would be able to sleep now, but she nodded. "Thank you."

CHAPTER EIGHT

The funeral pyres of Tallet burned high for two days, thick black smoke competing with the blowing snow to block out the cloudy skies. The mood in the city was somber; the loss of so many of Osephetin's faithful as well as the citizens and guardsmen had darkened the arrival of the season's first snowfall, usually a celebrated event.

Bishop Lam and the newly-promoted Bishop Timmon guided the Rites, keeping Ianel, Tabor, and Darian busy from, as far as Darian could tell, the moment they woke until they collapsed. Finally, on the third day, the last deceased member of the populace was given rites, their flesh consumed by sanctified fire and the dust that remained given to the cemetery. As Darian sought his bed, he was grateful they could return to their journey south. He knew why they had remained, but the pressure to move on was always in the back of his mind.

The house of a deceased guard had been selected to lodge the visiting defenders. In the small room that he'd been loaned, Darian sat with his back to the wall, lightly napping with his mace across his lap and a large hand axe by his side. A knock came at his door, waking him. The knock was too soft to be either Tabor or Ianel; both had a tendency to bang loudly and open the door as they were knocking. Darian looked up from his nap and yawned. "It's open."

The door swung open on heavy hinges, and Ephema peeked into the room with undisguised curiosity. In the last few days Darian hadn't seen much of her, their assignments keeping them on opposite schedules in various parts of town. He was surprised at how happy he was to see her, then again, they'd been through more adventures in a week than many of the people he'd trained with. She offered him her little, crooked smile. "Did I wake you? I know it is early still."

"It's all right. I've had more sleep today than in the last few days." He set the mace aside on the cot, stood and stretched. Ianel and Tabor had proper beds, two smaller ones lashed together in Tabor's case, but Darian wasn't about to complain about his cot. It was heaped high with blankets and far more comfortable than anywhere he'd stayed since leaving Hawthan. He eyed Ephema, noting the dark marks under her eyes. "You look like you should still be in bed, yourself. Bishop Lam is keeping you far too busy."

A flush touched her cheeks, and she shrugged, not leaving his doorway, but he could see the tension leaving her body as they spoke. "There is so much need. People need help and a home and healing. Winter is on the doorstep and there is so much to fix. The library behind the temple did not burn as much. We have been cleaning it when there are not the hurting to care for. I have never seen so many books at once."

"You should see the archives in the High Temple. My brother's made it his life's mission to read everything there, even though it's going to take a dozen of his lifetimes to even make a dent." Darian chuckled at the thought. He and Fressin were very different in personality and didn't always get along, but he could appreciate his brother's passion. Getting back with the scroll was the most important reason for returning to Hawthan, but Darian privately admitted he was looking forward to seeing his family. "The Knights and I will be leaving in the morning, Ephema. I spoke with Bishop Lam yesterday, at length. He was able to confirm that the scroll was the correct one, and urged us to get it back to Hawthan as quickly as possible. I'm sure Fressin will jump at the chance to work on it. If he can't translate it, no one can."

He paused for a moment, keeping in mind Tabor's plan to take Ephema with them willingly or unwillingly. "Have you decided what you wish to do? Bishop Lam said he'd spoken to you and that the search for your parents was…umm…ended. I'm sure he can arrange for safe passage back to Aserian, or you could, perhaps, stay here under his tutelage. It would be good for you not to be alone."

Ephema looked down, studying her dirty toes before looking back at him. "He offered me a place here, but he suggested I should go with you to Hawthan. I think he is right. With my parents gone…" She shook her head and cleared her throat. "With them gone, what is there for me in Aserian, but a dirty cave?" She leaned against the doorframe, though she managed another little smile. "Also, I overheard Tabor talking to Ianel about tying me to Valor if I refused to join you. I don't think he would do so any more than Ianel would sit on me to get me to rest, but he very much wants me to talk to the High Priest in the city. I do not want to fight with him."

Darian snorted, busying himself with folding the bedding and setting the room to rights. "Tabor is about as subtle as his choice of soul weapon, but there is wisdom in his words, if not his methods. I know he wouldn't hurt you, but he might be... er...impolite about getting his way. High Priest Calinin is a very wise man, and he can help you figure out what you want to do with your gift." He smiled, looking for a way to encourage her without resorting to threats, empty or otherwise. He didn't agree with such things. "My sister would love to meet you, and would lavish all sorts of sweetmeats on you. She's been writing me for months, though I only get the letters occasionally."

Ephema's smile lessened with confusion. "Sweetmeats?" She asked, interrupting him and making a funny face. "I don't know what those are. I have never tasted sweet meat, and I do not think it sounds good."

"Oh, it's not really a meat. I don't know why it's called that, honestly. It's more a really sweet bread. But Alloyna's cooking is really amazing and the bread winds up sticky and nutty, like honey. In fact, I think there's honey in it."

"Oh." She pondered the information, absently running her fingers along the doorframe. He found himself watching her hands move, her fingers long and delicate against the rough wood. "I guess that is okay then. You do not mind if I keep traveling with you? I know I am not a good rider yet, and I do not fight well. Knight Tabor is very reassuring, but also... big. And Ianel is...loud. I do not always know what to make of them, but despite how we met, you are a kind man."

"A pretty lady like you would be considerably more pleasant company than those two." Darian winked, though he was only partially joking. "You saved my life, and in return I nearly killed you. I can't forget or forgive myself for that, but I can protect you as best I can and help you to find your way. I would be happy to journey with you to Hawthan, and show you around once we get there. Maybe, if you wanted, I can even show you how bad of a fisherman I really am, though fish is the one thing I can cook well. You'll understand why I chose to become a Knight instead of following my father to the sea."

"I think I would like that. I've seen fish, but never eaten one. The river is the biggest body of water I have ever seen. Knight Tabor and Bishop Lam said the journey to Hawthan would require travel on a boat. It is somehow better than a horse."

"Better than isn't exactly right. It's just that the road over land takes three to four weeks of travel and exposes us to constant attacks by the undead at night. It's hard travel, and there aren't nearly enough way stations or towns to stay in. Going by boat will take a week to a week and a half depending on the wind. And since the undead have no means to attack by sea, it's as close to a vacation as a Knight can take." He held up four fingers. "It will take us four days to get to Eoth from here. There is a large port there where we can catch a trawler for sure, and a steamer if we are lucky. We just have to go that long without becoming fodder for the undead in well-traveled lands. Simple."

Ephema opened her mouth and then closed it again, her brows furrowing. He gave her an encouraging look, and she sighed. "That is a long time. What if we meet strong undead creatures like the ones here? They can't have gone far."

"Then our weapons and skills will get a work out." Ianel came down the hall with an easy stride, interjecting himself into their conversation without a hint of shame. "You will be in the company of two Knights and a Journeyman in service to Osephetin. Royalty couldn't ask for a better vanguard." He glanced at Darian and smiled. "It's good that you're awake. Bishop Lam wants to see everyone at the earliest opportunity.

And, ah," He laughed good naturedly. "Knight Tabor has declared our earliest opportunity would be right now."

"Of course." Darian picked up his mace, running his thumb over one flange where the metal was missing a chunk. This weapon had seen more action than it had been built for. He'd picked up the hand axe to go with the mace, for now, but he was anxious to get to a city big enough to have the weapon properly repaired. He secured both weapons and joined Ephema and Ianel at the door. "We'd better not keep Knight Tabor waiting. If he gets impatient who knows what trouble he'll get us into?"

Ianel grinned, the wan light from the hallway glinting on the small gold stud he wore in one ear. He stepped back, gesturing for Darian and Ephema to proceed him. "Even so, Brother. Even so."

THE ROOM IANEL led them to was in the same building and not much bigger than the chamber where Darian had slept. A much-used map was spread on a small square table over which Tabor loomed, marking locations with a small charcoal stick that looked ridiculous in his large hands. He didn't bother with a greeting, tapping a spot on the map as he spoke to Bishop Lam. "The convoy was ambushed here. If they're working the trail back it won't take long for them to circle around. I don't know why they went around Aserian, and I don't much care as long as we're good and gone before they come back this way. Not for our own sakes, but if we assume they are following the scroll, we need to draw them away from these outlying towns."

He traced the road to Eoth with the stained tip of his finger. "Taking the tinker road is the fastest and has the benefit of established way stations. It's also obvious and much easier to run undead down than going across country. We exchange speed for risk."

Ianel snorted. "It wouldn't be the first, nor last, time. We should take the road." He glanced at Ephema with a grin. "Though we'd do better to take Knight Pyina's war horse and have that one ride double if we're going to make the kind of time I know you're thinking we should. Pyina has no use for the animal in the Halls of the Faithful. Journeyman Darian should start practicing with a heavier mount anyway."

Darian leaned against the wall and crossed his arms over his chest. He was surprised at Ianel's suggestion, but saw the sense in it. "That would work. In addition, the war horse has training the other horses do not. I don't see a problem with another undead stomping horse." He grinned. "I can arrange the sale of the two horses and have the coin brought to here to be used to help restore the temple, if that's agreeable for you, Bishop."

"There's no need, my son. You keep any profit for your needs. The attackers might have nearly demolished the temple, but our coin was stored elsewhere and our coffers are well-stocked. We will rebuild." Bishop Lam turned to Ephema. "Will that suit you? Or would you prefer your own steed?"

Ephema blinked, looking surprised at being brought into the conversation. She shrugged and glanced at Darian. "I am not an experienced rider, as the Knights have seen. I do not mind riding with someone."

Tabor snorted, waving at Darian. "You'll ride with him. With his lighter armor, it makes the most sense for the two of you to ride double. If things get bad, we will protect your escape. Journeyman, you will continue to carry the scroll, and her life is under your protection. She is your first and utmost priority above all others. You will see her and the scroll to the Great Temple. Is that clear?"

"Crystal." Darian tried to meet Ephema's gaze across the room, but she looked away, her cheeks touched with a pink flush.

"Good. We'll leave within the hour. Pack up whatever you've got. We have distance to make before dark."

Much to Ephema's surprise the first two days of travel went smoothly – or at least as smoothly as possible. Riding behind Darian was its own challenge compared to riding a horse on her own. She didn't mind the company, and they rode much faster, but the war horse was wide-backed and she always felt a little like she was falling. Darian's repaired armor posed a problem as well. The leather and metal protected him, but it wasn't easy to hold onto and dug into her when the horse moved unexpectedly. As a result, the ride was never really comfortable and left her aching every time they stopped, though she did her best not to complain.

The forest grew thicker as they continued south, though it was a forest like Ephema had never seen before. Her mountain home had been a place of granite and stone, dotted with scattered evergreens that emitted a continual crisp scent. Here the trees grew close with broader leaves and thick limbs that often tangled together. The cloying scent of moisture and rotting leaves heralded the end of the season and weighed heavy on the air and in her nose. She didn't like it. She used all of her senses to feel the life and the magic surrounding her, and this scent was so pungent she felt almost nose-blind, though no one else seemed to notice.

Each night was an exercise in caution, despite the presence of way stations. None were as big or as well built as the first one they'd stayed in. They went without a fire, and slept close with one guard at all hours. The cries of the undead were heard hunting every night, but they were either lucky or just too small of a group to attract attention. The first way station was reached without incident, as was the second. They had left the snow behind in the mountains, but rain dogged their steps from Tallet onward. As the morning of the third day dawned grey, it looked to be no different from the previous days. Thick, nearly black storm clouds hugged the sky where it could be seen above the canopy. They held their watery load for the moment, but that would change as soon as the rising sun hit them.

Ephema didn't mind being cold nearly as much as being wet, and the nights with no fire had not been long enough to dry out from the day's riding; as a result, she always felt slightly damp. As they began the morning journey, she pulled her cloak tighter around herself and leaned closer against Darian's back. The weather was making it hard to travel as fast as Tabor wanted, making the usually easy-going Knight snappish. He started them off earlier each morning, and they still had to ride later than he wanted to reach the next way station. His complaints led Ianel to declare the way stations should simply be closer together.

The morning hours slipped by in near silence, even the birdsong and other forest noises dimmed by the wind and the heavy threat of rain. Ephema felt like she was breathing in water, and she almost didn't notice the moment when the few sounds came to a stop, but the dimming light caught her attention. She frowned, peering up at the trees. "Darian…" She sniffed, trying to push her senses out to determine what was bothering her. "Something." Her frown deepened, and she sat up straighter. "We are not alone."

Darian didn't respond with words, though he brought the horse around slowly until its nose pointed toward the woods and away from the road. All three men came to a stop and looked into the trees beyond, a strange look on each face. None of the men's hands went to a weapon; they all just stared listlessly into the trees, their expressions becoming more contorted as the seconds ticked away.

Ephema pushed herself up higher on the extended saddle so she could see over Darian's shoulder. She didn't see whatever they were seeing, though she felt a thick, strange pressure around them. The air grew dark around them as though night were falling despite the hour. Thunder rumbled once and then again, drawing closer. Ephema shook Darian's shoulder, her fingers brushing the skin at his neck. "Darian... wake up! We need to ride!"

Darian blinked like he was coming out of a deep sleep. "What?" He grimaced and rubbed his hand over his brow. "Oh hells. Sisters."

"I..." Ephema narrowed her eyes, a figure clad in ratty grey robes becoming visible among the trees as she searched. She swung her head around and found more, counting under her breath. "Four. I think. Why is no one moving?"

"Because the Sisters don't want us to move. I don't know why we can." His gaze darted between the shapes in the trees and his Brethren. He cursed under his breath and dropped his hand to his mace. "Damnit. Okay. Ephema, you have to try to bring the Knights' visors down. The armor helps against the Sisters, but it needs to be locked. It's the best chance we have. I'll see if I can hold them off while you help Tabor and Ianel."

Ephema chewed her lower lip and nodded, gathering her

feet up so she could jump off the horse. It didn't seem like a great idea, but if he was going to fight, she needed to get away and help the others. She took a deep breath and prepared to jump. "Be careful."

She half jumped and half slid down the side of the horse, rolling ungracefully away and scrambling to her feet. The ground was soft under her feet, slick and cold. The moment she left contact with Darian, his hand relaxed on his mace and his arm went slack against his side.

One of the cloaked figures crouched as Ephema moved, hissing with hatred. It spat words into the air, but if it was intelligible language, Ephema's couldn't tell. The other three cloaked figures dropped as well and, as one, they skuttled toward the group moving on their hands and feet like oddly jointed spiders, kicking up leaves and debris as they approached.

Ephema saw the Sisters clearly and choked on a scream. Nothing natural should move like that. It was like they were jointed in all the wrong places and all of the men were just sitting there, letting the monsters come. "DARIAN!" She screamed, then remembered what he'd said about the visors and the soul armor. Their only protection.

She didn't fully understand, but there was no time for wondering. She ran for Tabor, yelling his name as she went. His mount was so high, but she managed to wrap one hand in Valor's mane and step onto Tabor's foot where it rode in the stirrup. She pulled herself up, grabbing at him as her balance shifted.

With the Sisters screaming in her ears, Ephema reached over Tabor and caught the front of his helmet. As Darian had done, the moment Ephema touched him, Tabor blinked as though he was coming out of a deep sleep. "Wha… Dark

Lord protect!" Ignoring his outburst, she grabbed the visor and slammed it down over his face. The moment the bone clamped down around his jaw, blue ethereal magic wrapped around Tabor's head, and Ephema understood; Osephetin's power protected his Knights through their armor, including their minds. But only when the armor was fully in place, and the visors were hard to see through and doubly so in the rain, so they'd left them up.

There were no words spoken. Tabor took stock of the situation and formulated a plan immediately. He caught Ephema up and tossed her bodily over to Ianel's horse, Star. She landed behind the motionless knight with a startled yelp, scrambling to stay on the horse's back. Then, with a deep battle cry, Tabor wheeled Valor around and pulled his maul from its sheath in a single motion. He glanced at the narrow pathway and swore, spinning Valor on his hind legs. There just wasn't enough room for the warhorse to maneuver, and Tabor dropped to the ground, exchanging one advantage for another. "Come, you heathens! Let's see you weave your foul magics now!"

The Sisters reared up, and Ephema recoiled. Their faces, once human, were now a grotesque mash-up of plant and human features, equal parts growing and screaming. As they moved, human parts meshed and formed with plants, again and again, a horrible cackling and muttering coming in unison from the four creatures.

The nearest Sister hissed and swung a clawed hand at Tabor's leg, her nails black and fetid with debris. A thin trail of black magic trailed through the air behind her strike, but the edge of Tabor's maul intercepted her hand before it touched him. A heavy thud, and the body of the Sister convulsed underneath Tabor's maul. To Ephema's horror, the creature was still moving, refusing to die.

Ephema tried not to gawk at the violence, pulling herself up to where she could reach Ianel's helmet. He too started sputtering and blinking the moment she touched him. She fumbled the visor around his face, pointing at Tabor and the Sisters. "Ianel! Help!"

He snarled and drew his hammer. "Off!"

It was the only warning Ephema got before Star reared up, making a terrible noise. She tumbled off the animal's back and tried to get out of the way. She could see why Tabor had dismounted. As powerful as the Knights were on their horses, this spot was just too narrow for the horses to be used effectively. The road widened ahead, but this was a perfect place for the ambush they'd tumbled into. Ianel cursed and dismounted, sending Star to follow Valor to the wider road.

Darian's horse followed after the other two, with Darian still transfixed in the saddle. Two more Sisters emerged from the brush, already skittering on hands and feet. They took off after the horses, while the three remaining Sisters continued to circle Ianel and Tabor, snapping their teeth like maddened dogs.

Ephema got to her feet, her head spinning from the rough landing and the fighting happening around her. Tabor and Ianel knew what they were doing and engaged with confidence, now that their minds were again their own. Darian had no such protection. It seemed like a terrible oversight to Ephema, but she knew very little about the process of becoming a Knight besides what little Darian had told her. She just wanted everyone to survive. She chased after Darian and the horses, afraid they had outpaced her, but they hadn't gone far, just around a bend.

There Ephema saw one of the Sisters pinned by Star, who was stomping and biting the creature as though he was possessed. The second had a hold of Darian's leg, dragging him from his saddle as his war horse bucked and reared. Smoke rose where her claws dug into Darian's leg, ripping through his armor as though it wasn't there. The smell of seared flesh hung acrid in the air, but Darian didn't defend himself. Somewhere in the flight his mace had fallen from his horse and lay on the ground between Ephema and the two Sisters.

Darian crashed awkwardly from the saddle to the ground, making no effort to catch himself. The Sister leaped on his chest, clawing his armor into ribbons. Darian made a terrible strangled noise and then started screaming. It wasn't a scream of fear, but of utter anguish.

Ephema threw herself forward, not knowing what she was going to do, but desperate to make his pain stop. Her foot caught on his mace as she ran, and she stumbled, caught herself, and looked down. The glint of the hard flange edges held her gaze. She picked the weapon up, surprised at how heavy it was. It almost fell from her hands, until Darian screamed again and her grip tightened. She wasn't going to lose her friend to those monsters.

She ran to Darian and swung the mace into the Sister's side. The creature wailed, and Ephema wrenched the mace free and swung it again. The stroke knocked the Sister off of Darian, the ripped robes rippling like mist.

]The thunder boomed again and rain pelted from the sky. An unfamiliar rage ran through Ephema's body. She gritted her teeth and gold-white light poured down her arms and into the mace. She ran past Darian, screaming out her wrath, seeing nothing but the writhing Sister. It was a blight on the world. Its existence was wrong. She needed it to die. Ephema swung the mace over and over, blood and other materials splattering her clothing and skin. In moments, what was left of the creature wasn't moving any more, the bits seeming to melt in the downpour.

A hiss turned Ephema's attention, and she spun around. The other Sister had broken away from Star's attacks and ran at her, leaping into the fray with a second hiss of hatred. The creature's claws raked at Ephema's face, catching one cheek, but Ephema felt no pain, only burning heat. The Sister skidded to a stop a few steps away and reared up, drawing dark smokey magic around itself. Ephema didn't hesitate. With a grunt she swung the mace wide. It slammed into the monster with a meaty, terrible sound. The Sister skidded across the muddy ground and lay motionless, but Ephema hit it again until she was sure it was dead.

Ephema let the head of the mace rest on the ground, her arms feeling leaden from lifting the heavy weapon. The glow died away while she stared at the bubbling remains.

Ianel skidded around the bend and came to a quick stop. He looked over the scene, his expression hidden under his helmet, but he stood still for a long moment and made a soft whistling noise. "Dark Lord protect." He gave himself a shake and sprinted to Darian. "Come on, warrior girl. We need to ride. The Sisters will reform quickly." He got his arms under Darian, lifting the Journeyman as though he were an infant. Ianel's gaze darted to the remains of the Sisters Ephema had left. "Well, maybe not those two, but the rest of them will. Unless you want to do to them whatever you did here."

Tabor limped behind Ianel, his maul over his shoulder. "Damnation, where did they come from?" He frowned when he saw the field and the injured. "By the Holy One's blood, this day's getting better and better. Put him on his horse. We ride while we still can. Will he live?"

Ephema's fingers were numb, but she managed to keep a hold of the mace as she staggered over to Darian's horse. It took three tries to get the weapon into the loop where Darian carried it. "He's going to live. I'm not going to let him die." She heard the savage note in her own voice and took a deep breath. "Just...just bring him here and give me a minute."

Ianel shrugged, carrying Darian to the horse. "Can you heal on the move?"

"I've never tried."

"No better time to find out, then. He's bleeding like a sacrificial hog." Ianel draped Darian's body across the front of the horse, then helped Ephema up behind him. "The Sister's magic still holds him in thrall. That'll end soon, and the pain might finish what they started. He deserves saving." He met her eyes through the gap in his visor, which glistened with raindrops. "Good luck."

CHAPTER NINE

The return to consciousness was a long, slow climb for Darian. It felt like there was something blocking him from waking and, though he tried, he couldn't push through it. He relaxed, floating in a numb state. Finally, whatever was preventing him dissipated, and light played along his eyelids, bringing him out of the dark. He shivered, but couldn't remember why he would be cold. He remembered the beat of rain. The road. Something had happened. Pain.

He groaned and tried to sit up, but moving was nearly impossible no matter how he tried. His entire body was stiff and sore, and he quickly became aware that he had been stripped of his armor and clothing save for his under breeches. A light blanket was spread over him, but it wasn't enough to push back the chill. He opened his eyes, blinking until they focused right. His gaze traced the ceiling beams above him and then darted around the room, realizing he knew where he was. The way station they'd stayed in last night.

He rolled onto his side and saw Ephema asleep on a cot

beside him. She was curled into a ball as though she too were cold, her brow creased, her fingers bloodstained where they rested under her cheek. A few feet away, the Knights were inspecting something by the light of a roaring fire and talking softly between themselves, oblivious to the fact he'd awakened.

Darian laid back and tried to think. He remembered leaving the way station this morning, but everything beyond that was a blur of confusing images. He grimaced and sighed. "Osephetin's blood, what happened?"

Ephema stirred slightly at the sound of his voice, but she didn't wake. She was pale, her skin almost grey in the low light. Her face and her clothing were stained with blood he hoped wasn't hers.

He frowned and swung his legs around to stand. It was a slower process than he expected it to be. Darian's gaze came to rest on his leg where a long pink line of newly healed flesh showed where at least some of the blood had come from. His chest ached, and he rubbed the skin gently finding more signs of the healing he'd been given. It itched and was tender, but he couldn't imagine what it would look like if Ephema hadn't been there. She'd saved him again.

"Ephema?"

"Let her rest, Journeyman. She's the only reason you live, and she's exhausted." Tabor's voice was low and he motioned for Darian to join them. "Come, you should eat and you need to see something."

Darian slowly got to his feet, being careful not to disturb Ephema as he shuffled his way over to Tabor and Ianel. He wobbled with every step, but no one came to help him, and he didn't want them to. He had to know he could stand on his own, or he would be a liability. "I remember... a battle against something, I think."

Ianel snorted, stretching his neck until it cracked. He sat on one of the cots, his hammer next to his hand. "Something is an understatement. They were Sisters."

Darian's stomach dropped, and he lowered himself to another empty cot before his leg gave out. He closed his eyes. The memories of twisted grey shapes and agony returned. "How many were there? How did we get here?"

"Six. It's the biggest damn grouping I've ever heard of." Ianel leaned down and grabbed an apple from his pack, handing it to Darian. "And be honest, Tabor, she didn't just save Darian; she saved us all both in battle and healing up the aftermath."

"Aye. That she did. I never realized how important the visor was to completing the Dark Lord's protections. Proof that you are never too old to learn. We are fortunate we have the chance to try again." Tabor clapped Darian on the shoulder, bringing a wince from the younger man. "Lucky for all of us the Sisters' magics don't work on a true Daughter of Lianna. She broke the thrall. If she hadn't, we'd all be tucking in at the Hall of the Faithful by now."

Darian grimaced. "And since I'm not a full Knight yet, my armor did nothing useful at all. I remember pain in my leg and…" He dropped his hand to his torso. "Chest."

"Yes. They peeled open your armor like a fruit. It will do you no good now."

"A shame; I'd just gotten that chest piece to fit right." Darian sighed, pushing his hair back from his eyes. He'd been too long without a haircut, not that it was of much importance now. "What did you want me to see?"

"This." Ianel casually tossed Darian's mace to him, which Darian caught on reflex with a wince. Even in the crackling light of the small fire, the weapon shimmered with white-gold light. The damage that had been done to it in the past was gone, pieces of stone which looked like smoky quartz filled in the gaps while unknown runes glittered down the shaft of the mace. The runes pulsated occasionally with golden sparks similar to the blue sheen of Osephetin's divine will. The mace vibrated under Darian's grip and somehow felt lighter, stronger, and more right than ever before. The thoughts he'd had of getting a new weapon for his soul weapon were immediately banished.

"Whoa!" Darian stared at the mace with wonder, feeling somewhat like he did on his birthday or Midwinter's Feasting when he'd received a particularly meaningful gift. "When? How? What did this?"

Ianel gestured at the sleeping healer. "She took exception to the Sisters trying to kill you and borrowed your mace. She didn't leave much of them behind. It's the first time I've seen Sisters die and stay dead." He dug a cloth from his saddle bag, grunting with approval. "I didn't think she had it in her."

Tabor shook his head, his gaze set on the fire. "It makes me wonder what else she's capable of, though that is likely a question for wiser men than I. And I have the feeling that she doesn't know her limits either. We have removed her from her sheltered life, and the world is forcing her to adapt quickly."

"This is incredible." Darian glanced at Ephema, who continued to sleep as the conversation flowed around her. "That's twice she's saved my life in as many weeks. I'm starting to wonder if I'm worthy of being a Knight at all, given that…"

Tabor looked away from the fire, raising his eyebrows. He snorted. "Given what? That you survived an undead ambush and brought the scroll back? That you found the last healer in the world? That you sacrificed yourself to the Sisters so that she could help us? Which of your great failures should we highlight when we return to the High Temple? Let me know, and I'll tell your mother."

"The scroll isn't back yet. I could still fail at that before all is said and done." Darian leaned to the side to dodge the stick that Tabor threw at him and grinned. "But your point is taken. I will follow the path Osephetin provides, wherever he takes me, faithfully."

"Good lad." Tabor tossed a wad of clothes onto Darian's lap. "Now get dressed. It's still a few hours until dawn, but we'll leave as soon as we can."

Ephema rolled over, awareness returning all at once. Her head throbbed in time with her heartbeat, and she thought she might throw up but there was too little in her stomach for that. Her gaze came to rest on the cot where Darian should be. It was empty and panic flared in her heart.

She pushed herself up on her hands, ignoring spinning nausea as she peered around the room. Tabor and Ianel were sitting near the fire, talking idly amongst themselves. Darian sat on another cot, the various beds really the only furniture in the station. He was dressed and seemed to be trying to salvage pieces of his ruined armor.

All of her Knights were safe and whole. Comforted by that thought, she sat all the way up, testing her stomach and her head. Both seemed content to let her move, for now. The way station was lit only by the little fire, and she wondered how long she'd slept.

Rain pounded on the roof, thumping along the wood and stone, yet under the thundering rain drops howled the distant cry of the undead. Those sounds meant it was night time, though she still wasn't sure how close they were to dawn. Ephema pulled her knees up to her chest and listened to the rain. Her thoughts went back to her little cave, and how, on a night like this, she would be curled up in front of her fire.

Safe.

But alone.

Safe, but so very alone. How very different things were since she'd followed Darian to what she thought was his certain death in Aserian. She wondered if she regretted it. Her gaze went to the two Knights, then lingered on Darian. No. She was certain she didn't regret following him, even if she didn't know what was to come.

Darian turned at her movement and smiled. The expression warmed Ephema's heart and relieved her. He'd been so hurt, and she had feared that she would never see his smile again.

"Good, you're awake. Looks like I owe you another debt of thanks." He moved over to her cot, settling down carefully beside her. "I'm still pretty stiff and sore, but the Knights tell me that's considerably better than the alternative. Thank you."

"We are friends now, yes? So, there is no debt between us." She gave him a weary half-smile. "You are making me work hard at my healing. Maybe that is good for me."

"If I were better at my job, maybe you wouldn't need to heal me so much." Darian laughed quietly, shaking his head. "I didn't realize how sheltered the trainees really are. I've never personally faced foes as terrible as the Sisters, only the remains of their work as I told you. I thought I would have at least a minute or two, but I had no defense. The soul magic of the Knights protected them, but even that can be worn away if you fight Sisters for too long. A fast attack and retreat while the Sisters reform has been our only defense. Thank Osephetin their powers didn't work against you. I wonder if that's because, in a way, their powers are from the same source as yours even if they work in the opposite direction."

"I guess so. It seems to make sense." She stared at her hands, rubbing at the dry blood. "I do not like them. Their magic feels cold and prickly, but familiar – like a scene I know, but cannot name. Will they find us here?"

"No." Darian shook his head. "The Sisters do not track like the undead might. Even though the Sisters are more deadly than, well, most of the undead, if you can get away from them, they generally won't follow. They mostly haunt certain areas and driving them out is difficult. Once we reach Eoth, we'll have to warn them that this path needs to be avoided. The High Temple might be able to send senior Knights to try and drive them out, since they can't kill them permanently."

"I…" Ephema clenched her fingers. It was as though she could feel the weight of the mace and the hot splatter of blood on her skin all over again. "I do not think the ones I hit will return, but I do not wish to hunt them."

"I don't want to hunt them either. Even after I get my soul armor. Though if we meet them again, I think whatever you did to my mace will make a difference." He removed the weapon from his belt and placed it on her lap. "Did you know you could do that?"

She touched the shaft of the mace and the light, which had almost dimmed to nothing, surged, glowing with a fierce, joyful intensity before ebbing again. "I don't know what I did. I remember I was very angry, and I had to help you. This is the first weapon I have held besides my father's morning star."

"Ah. Shame. Ianel was fully prepared to ask you to, what

did he say? 'Pretty up his hammer something good.' But if you don't know what you did, I guess that's not meant to be." Darian chuckled and lifted the mace from her hands. He held it level with his eyes, staring at the runes. "Even if it's not something you can repeat, it's incredible. Do you know what these runes say? I don't recognize the language."

Ephema shrugged, shaking her head. She had already told him she wasn't good at reading, and these markings were even more foreign to her. "I do not know. My mother taught me to read, but I only remember a little bit. We didn't have many books to practice with."

"That's right. I'm sorry. I forgot. Well, if we have some time, I would be happy to help you remember some of it." He smiled gently. "There are so many stories to read. My father insisted we all learn to read as soon as we could, though I never fell in love with it like Fressin did. I do have favorite books, and I can help you if you want to learn."

"Maybe there will be time when we float across the water." She sighed and rubbed her head, finding a tender spot on her scalp though she didn't remember being hurt. She wanted something from Darian, but she wasn't sure what that something was. Comfort, maybe? Knowledge that she was doing the right thing, that she would not regret leaving her home? These were things he couldn't give her.

"We'll certainly have downtime on the boat. We should have some in Hawthan as well; the city affords a level of protection you've never had out here. Some say it rivals the cities of old from before the Lich, and many of our Brethren are there. If nothing else, I can assure you of one thing…it's no cave."

THE POUNDING rain stopped shortly before dawn. As the hours drew on Tabor produced their borrowed map and searched for a way around the area where the Sisters had attacked, planning a wide half-circle on their way to Eoth. Ephema could see he wasn't happy with the detour. The Knights argued the benefits of seeking out the Sisters and seeing if Darian's mace would be as effective in his hands as it had been in Ephema's. If it weren't for the need to get the scroll back, and her own presence, she thought they would have taken the battle to the Sisters, but they decided they couldn't take the risk. They would ride on, warn the next city and hope the Sisters would move on before anyone else encountered them.

The travel that day was soggy. The roads were caked with mud and grime, and the paths they were driven to were worse, leaving thick burrs in clothing and horse manes and tails. The war horses bore the rough terrain without complaining, but Ephema still felt bad for them. She was grateful when they finally reached the last way station before the city, and fed her share of apples to the tired mounts.

The morning when they would finally reach Eoth, Tabor allowed everyone to sleep in an extra hour. The ride was only a half-day's effort, and even with the additional rest, they hoped to make it to the city by noon.

As they crested the last hills leading into the plains of Kathaaw, the forest gave way and blessed them with a fantastic view. The harbor town was in sight, standing tall against what looked like the end of the world. They came around another small bend and the ocean came into view, glimmering in the sunlight with ships showing as distant shadows traveling up and down the coastline.

Ephema's breath caught, and she leaned around Darian to get a better look at the glittering expanse as they descended toward the city. A variety of expressions played over her face, somewhere between awe and fear. "It's like the world just ends. Is that where the edge is? Is there nothing beyond but the water?"

Darian laughed and waved his hand wide to cross the expanse that they could see. He had grown up with the ocean at his doorstep, and he always forgot how overwhelming it could be to those who hadn't been soothed to sleep by the sound of the waves. "No one really knows if there is an edge, but there are lands far beyond that water. Ships come into port cities like Eoth and Hawthan from far, far to the west carrying trade goods and sometimes people unlike any who live in our cities. When I was a young, my father and I would sometimes sail for five or six days straight out until we couldn't see the land anymore, just the waves and the ocean."

His voice took on a wistful tone. "He'd tell tales of creatures that lived in the water; creatures big enough to eat the boat in one bite, but so gentle they'd simply swim on past. Pods of huge fish would swim right up to us, making this squeaking noise that you could hear above the water. They'd be chasing smaller fish, and would leap out of the water and come crashing down, like they were playing. They were always good luck."

She made an odd noise, almost a squeak of her own. "You went where you couldn't see the land anymore, and where there were giant monsters? And with only a wooden boat between you and them? WHY?" She shook her head, looking away from the glittering sea. "That is a lot of water, Darian. A very lot of water. I am not sure this is a good idea."

"People travel across the waters every day." Ianel brought his horse up beside them, matching their speed. "And at least the power of the Lich doesn't expand to the waters. His forces cannot swim, though they can capsize a boat in shallow enough waters, so the docks are well protected. If a person dies aboard ship, they won't rise, though we never bring someone back from the sea. The waves are as safe as fire for carrying the dead to Osephetin's Halls. Everything about water travel is safe. As long as you don't get caught in a storm, there is little to fear."

Ephema arched her eyebrows at him and took a deep breath. "If you say so. It seems very big and flat and wet to me. I miss the mountains." She glanced back at the forest, and Darian felt sorry for her. He kept forgetting just how many new things she'd encountered in so few days. Knights and soon-to-be Knights were trained to be flexible and traveled all over the lands. He couldn't imagine staying for so many years in one place. She tugged her cloak tighter around her, as though she needed the protection in the quickly warming day. "I guess it is too far and too late for regrets or returns. So, we must look forward."

"Indeed." Darian reached back and touched her knee before the sound of a loud horn echoed from the city below them. "That's a good sign. That horn means all is well. It's used by many of the coastal cities to alert those approaching that the guardsmen on the city walls do not have any undead threats in sight. In other words, no Hunters here."

"At least not yet." Ianel grinned, taking any fatalism out of the words. Sometimes Darian wondered if Ianel was truly serious about anything. The Knight stretched, looking out over the city. "I'm looking forward to a night in a proper bed, at a proper inn, with a proper wench to keep me warm. It's been far too long."

Tabor snorted from behind them. "Priorities, Ianel. Priorities."

Ianel laughed and put his heels to Star's side, leading them down the road.

As they drew within visual distance of the city, a set of guards clad in brown and yellow rode out to meet them. The guardsmen greeted Osephetin's warriors warmly, inquiring about their travel and the purpose in Eoth. Darian didn't speak, leaving it to Tabor to decide how much information to share. Talk of the scroll and Ephema's presence never came up, but warning of the Sisters did.

"Aye, Sir. We're well aware of the encroachment. They've been haunting that area for the last few months."

"We heard nothing in Tallet or the other cities beyond."

The leader of the men shrugged. "I don't know that any messages were sent beyond. The council has brought the issue up several times, but without conclusion."

Tabor snorted, cocking his head, a look made menacing by the helm and visor which covered his dark features. "Sending a message that the problem exists is the first step and not one which should be difficult to agree upon. There are tinkers and merchants who need that road."

"Well above my pay scale, Sir, though I'll relay the message that they're still there to the Captain. Too bad there ain't a way to just kill the beasties and be done with it."

Darian glanced at Ephema, but said nothing. He was certain the Sister's she'd killed weren't coming back, but they had more important things to address, and he didn't want the city to try to convince them to go back to the ambush point. Maybe if she could enchant other weapons it would be different, but given she didn't know what she'd done it wasn't worth mentioning.

"Will you be staying in Eoth, or moving through?"

Tabor grunted, but answered the question readily enough.

"We'll be in the city a day or two at best. We're looking to book passage to Hawthan."

"Ah. A bit of a bumpy voyage this time of year, Sir Knight, but doable. There's always a ship or two headed that way. Trade waits for no storm."

"Bumpy. Lovely." Grumbling, Tabor let the conversation lapse.

Darian peered at his Brother, unable to help himself from poking at the issue. "Don't like the sea, Knight Tabor?"

"No, Journeyman. I do not." Tabor harrumphed in displeasure. "Besides the fact that the smell of the sea is wretched, this armor ensures that I would sink straight to the bottom were I to fall in. Though I yearn to serve the Lord Osephetin in his halls for eternity, I would prefer that my journey to him not be completed through drowning."

Ephema shuddered, nodding her head in emphatic agreement. "Are we sure the ride across land isn't a better idea?"

One of the guardsmen gave her a sharp look. "Nay, m'lady. The journey south is a horrible idea by land. The city is fortified well enough, but there is wilderness between here and Hawthan. We've been hearin' reports of something new, some new kind of undead freak no one's seen before chasing merchant trains that dare that path. I talked to one survivor. He said it's worse than Sisters."

"Worse than the Sisters?" Darian leaned forward in the saddle; his gaze intense. "Worse? How exactly can something be worse than those monsters?"

"I don't know for sure. There have only been a few survivors. Whole caravans who have made it through despite the challenges before have been slaughtered. A Knight went with the last one, but he never came back." The guard motioned to the waves in the distance. "Bumpy or no, this way is the safest and the fastest."

Ianel frowned at the news, tilting his helm slightly and gazing out across the valley. "It's probably best not to put too much stock into rumor. There is a large temple here. The Brothers will know what is truth and what is exaggeration." He shrugged, settling back into his saddle. "Either way my seat thinks it's time to get off the road."

"Let's go." Tabor nudged Valor and with a motion to everyone, they were on their way.

CHAPTER TEN

Eoth was the largest city Ephema had seen, bigger than Tallet and many times the size of Aserian. It was a sprawling mecca that appeared to have been laid out by two toddlers arguing over a large mass of building block toys. There seemed to be no rhyme or reason to how the city streets and buildings were arranged. Roads and streets ended abruptly and started elsewhere on a whim. Shops and marketplaces were strewn almost accidentally in corners, sometimes stacked on each other with stairs or simple ladders leading to the shops that were in higher locations. When the world couldn't build out, it built up.

The walls of the city were the one thing which had been planned and cared for to the last stone. The fortifications were well-built and tall enough that any approaching undead would have to reach fifteen feet up to breach the top. It was thanks to these walls and the access to the ocean that Eoth prospered as a city for trade; the port here was an important hub for travel both north and south from the coastline, and for larger boats heading west that didn't want to stop in Hawthan further south. So, the city enjoyed a level of prosperity and luxury not often seen elsewhere in the world.

Once they passed the main gates, the guardsmen left the Knights to their own business. They rode into the city, the horses picking their way slowly through the crowd. They were surrounded by the sound of commerce. Shouting people hawked their wares, though from the calls and smells in the air most of the goods in this part of the city were fish and cooked foods. People milled about, looking over various products and haggling on prices in loud voices that were met by even louder arguments from the shopkeepers. It seemed to Ephema the winner had much more to do with who was loudest than who was in the right.

Ianel grinned as they rode down the main road. "I've missed this place. It is always good to come home."

Ephema glanced at him, but her gaze didn't linger, too busy trying to take in all of the city at once. The noises and smells were overwhelming, even as the bright colors adorning people and buildings drew her attention. She was curious, but the chaos scraped on her nerves, and the pull of the living essence around her was already playing havoc with her innate senses. Even in the height of celebrations, things were never this loud in Aserian. Someone grabbed her leg, thrusting a string of smoked fish where the riders could see the catch. It smelled burned, and Ephema jerked her leg back, grabbing onto Darian to keep from falling and shaking her head until the man let go, looking for an easier sale.

Ephema ducked her head, taking in a deep breath. Darian's cloak smelled of earth and rain and his unique scent, all of which she found comforting. "I don't like this. There's too much to see and hear."

Darian placed a hand on her leg, the gesture comforting and strong. He wouldn't let anything happen to her if he could help it. "Hawthan isn't nearly this bad, I promise. Eoth is a bit…what's the word I'm looking for?"

"Barbaric." Tabor waved off another vendor as he snarled. "That's the word you're looking for. Why they don't have a proper market and contain this is beyond me." His voice rose. "No! Dammit! I do not want any fish!"

"In all fairness, it's probably fresh caught and might be quite tasty. If we buy something, they may stop trying so hard."

"Then *you* buy it, Journeyman. I am not carrying fish, raw or cooked, around with me."

"I will." Darian motioned to the vendor and held up two fingers. The man happily wrapped two large fish and handed them over in exchange for a few copper coins. "Once we find a place to stay, I'll see if they'll let me cook these up. If not, I'm sure the local temple will appreciate the donation."

Ephema wrinkled her nose at the smell of the bundles he handed to her. It was a strange smell, even if the fish was freshly caught. She peered through the tangle of people, men and women and children all involved in their own business, hoping to see the local temple and a refuge from the onslaught. "How many people will be on the ship? It won't be like this will it?" She hoped not.

"Depends on what vessel we can find that's headed south." Darian patted the war horse on the neck, the animal seeming as antsy as Ephema felt. "There are common transports that run between the ports routinely, but they tend to be pretty crowded and hard to book passengers and horses on at short notice. We might be able to find a transport schooner, which would be a safer bet for the horses and considerably less crowded."

"And uncomfortable as the nine hells." Ianel grimaced, turning in his saddle to look at them. Ephema wasn't sure how he'd heard the conversation at all. "If we can avoid it, I'd prefer not riding in one of those death traps, even if they'd have space for the horses."

Darian nodded in agreement. "I hate to say it, but Ianel's right. A transport schooner in heavy weather wouldn't be as safe. Our best bet would be a steamer. If one happens to be at dock. Those are less expensive for Faithful since the travel fires are lit from the Eternal Flame at the High Temple."

Tabor cupped his head over his eyes and looked to the sky. "We will hope for that then. There may even be time to go to the docks tonight. We have a few hours still before sunset." He gestured off to the left where a dark grey marble towner jutted into the sky. "There's Eoth's temple."

Ephema's gaze locked on that spire as a guiding point, and a hope for quiet and safety.

IT TOOK LONGER than one would have guessed to arrive at the Eoth Temple. The spire – easily seen from anywhere in the city – was much more difficult to reach in the tangle of streets and people than it looked. Things had changed since either of the Knights had last been to the city, and they kept coming to dead ends. Tabor finally resorted to paying for directions, and their impromptu guide swung up onto Star and led them to their destination in a mostly direct way.

The Temple's towers stretched high into the sky, the stonework adorned with the skeletal artwork typical of

Osephetin architecture. Bits of bone and silver were worked into the façade, many of the faithful donating shards of departed loved ones as a sign of their devotion. One tall pillar smoked faithfully away -- the Eternal Fire within dutifully burning the city's dead. The Temple was extremely busy, and the doors of the place of worship never closed.

As they approached, an elderly woman hobbled down the seven steps of the temple. Wisps of grey hair escaped the bun at the back of her head, but her hands were clean and her eyes kind. She drew her hands across her body in a complicated formation which was at once greetings and blessings, ending with a deep bow. "Greetings to the faithful of our Lord Osephetin. I am Bishop Lisse. I pray your journey has been much blessed by our Lord, and your hands dedicated to his righteous calling."

Tabor bowed from the saddle, and even Ianel didn't smart off, both of their faces touched with a soft reverence. The rites to attain the Priesthood of Osephetin were difficult and exhausting. There were many women who achieved Knighthood, but fewer who became Bishops and Temple leaders. Those that obtained those heights were revered for their kindness and knowledge.

Darien remembered his mother explaining once that Lord Osephetin held a special fondness for women because they were closest to him. Each time they walked the path to create life, they stepped into the valley of death to do so. Choosing death, even for a moment, to ensure life continued was at the very core of Osephetin's teaching.

"How can the Temple serve you today?"

"We're looking for lodgings, Bishop Lisse." Tabor explained. "Just for a few days until we can book passage on a steamer."

The aging Bishop slowly shook her head. "We've a large family staying in the temple at the moment. They have petitioned to stay with us until they can catch a deep-sea ship, based on the wishes of their father to have his ashes given to the sea. That, along with the arrival of the winter celebration, means our rooms are unfortunately full. Our stables, however, have much space. Your mounts would be welcome there, and prone to do a lot less damage than they might do in the small stalls at the local inns. You would be welcome if you wanted to sleep in the stalls, but it is not exactly comfortable for Knights." A humored smile touched her wizened face. "Personally, I would recommend the Half-Full Tankard down the street. They are close. Their beds are comfortable with no rodents, and their wine is excellent."

Ianel grinned and inclined his head. "That sounds right up our alley, good Bishop."

Tabor nodded, absently thumping Valor on the side of the neck. "That will be our lodging then, and we will leave the horses here. You are sure they will be no trouble?"

"Bah. They will be as gentle as lambs, at least for me." Bishop Lisse winked at Ephema. "It's been years since I worked in the stables, but I remember how, and we have a full staff with time on their hands. Your mounts will be fine. Spoiled, in fact, if I do not miss my guess."

The men dismounted, Darian pausing to help Ephema, though she mounted and dismounted better now than she had just a few days ago. He enjoyed assisting her. It seemed odd that it had only been a few days over a week since all of this had begun. He felt like they'd been on the road forever.

Bishop Lisse glanced at the doors of the Temple where two junior priests waited. At her nod, the young men came swiftly down the stairs and took the reins of the trio of warhorses, leading them down a large alleyway on the side of the Temple and back to their stables. They exchanged a few further pleasantries and promised to return later in the evening to discuss issues of the faith and receive any updates Bishop Lisse had for them.

It was not difficult to find the Half-Full Tankard. The building itself was nearly as wide as the temple, though not as tall with only two large floors. The crowd of people flocking to the Tankard rivaled one of the festival crowds at Aserian. The building itself was rather plain, with only a large barrel of ale half-spilled emblazoned on a large sign over the doorway to give indication as to the purpose of the business; the patrons stumbling out, well in their cups, left little doubt as to the goings-on inside.

Darian caught the nervous look on Ephema's face as they approached the crowd. She kept her head held high, but he could tell she was uncomfortable and offered his hand. "Here. Take my hand, I'll steer you through the crush. We'll follow along behind Tabor. He'll be able to plow us a path. No one will stay in his way for long, right?"

Ephema smiled at that and took his hand. It was hard to remember that she'd shied from his touch not so long ago. He'd removed his gloves and her fingers were cool despite the warmth of the day. Here by the sea the memories of the winter storms just a few day's travel north were almost forgotten. Not that it was balmy weather, but the breeze off the sea kept the coast temperate until much later in the season.

"I hope we will not stay here long. I do not like the feel of this city." She watched the people stumbling from the tavern as Tabor pushed his way through. "I do not think Tabor likes it here either."

"No, he doesn't." Darian guided them after the large

Knight, keeping half an eye on the crowd and making sure he didn't lose his coin purse, not that there was much inside to take. "Ianel grew up here after his parents passed and fits in naturally, but this isn't Tabor's and my kind of town. I've visited here before, but all I remember was not liking it much then, either. My father would come here to sell his fish sometimes depending on how far north he'd been fishing. I'd come with him to help."

He squeezed her hand, his grip strong and firm, but he was careful not to hurt her. Her touch brought a stirring to his heart, but he didn't say anything about it. "I came to prefer the fish over the people here, but the dockhands were friendly enough. Once Father died, there was never a real reason for my mother to return, at least not one where she would bring her children. It's been a few years since I saw this place as anything more than a quick stop on the road north."

Ephema nodded, falling into place as the Knights broke a path to the inn. She gripped Darian's hand more tightly as a rotund man brushed past them, stinking of alcohol and knocking into her shoulder. Finally, they made it to the bar and attracted the attention of the innkeeper long enough to rent out the remaining room which held a pair of bunks in it. The good news that came with the room was that a steamer was in port and leaving in two days.

EPHEMA LAY BACK on the hard, wooden bunk, trying not to shift around and wake anyone else. For all that the beds sported what the innkeeper had assured them were new rushes and hand crafted, well-sewn quilts, she struggled to get comfortable. Ianel had found his own lodging with a degree of laughter and teasing between the three men that Ephema didn't fully understand.

Tabor and Darian shared the room with her, though, given their weights, it was decided it would be wise if they took the bottom bunks. Their sleeping sounds had become familiar over the last several days; Tabor always on the verge of a heavy snore, while Darian's breath came slow and even.

She rubbed her hand over her forehead, trying to ignore the sounds of merrymaking which still rose from the taproom below. She wondered if it would go on all night, or if at some point the noise would die and the doors close. Perhaps when there was no more drink to be had. Darian had mentioned these types of places typically had massive storerooms though, so she doubted it would end before dawn.

Searching for distraction, she stared out the small round window. The moon was very nearly full, tomorrow it would rise in complete fullness, but the difference in brightness wouldn't be too different. Ephema loved high moon nights. They were times when her mountain home took on a new light, and she felt most alive with the silvery light wrapped around her.

The moonbeams touched her bed, and the globe resting at her neck flared. Ephema threw up her hand to shield her eyes as the light filled the room. She sat up, blinking against the brightness. Tentatively, she whispered, "Darian?"

She knew she'd spoken. She heard the echo of her voice, but there was no answer save for the continued slow breaths of her companions. A pearlescent ball hung before her bed as though a small piece of the moon had drifted into the room. Unable to help herself, Ephema leaned forward to get a better look, seeing an echo of her own face reflected in the pearly surface. She stretched her hand toward the globe, but it drifted just out of reach.

She glanced at Tabor's maul, where it lay within reach of his slumbering form. The heavy weapon emitted a slim blue light, the blessing of Osephetin given to his Knights; but when the light of the floating globe flickered, the weapon echoed the glow, intensifying and bathing the corner where the Knight slumbered with a bluish tint.

The ball spun slowly, and Ephema caught a glimpse of another face. It was a familiar face, much like her own, but older, wiser. Her mother's name hung on Ephema's lips, but she didn't speak. The visage clouded and drifted away, replaced by her father, but not as she had known him. This man's face was twisted in agony and an orange glow seeping through his face, showing the stark outline of the bones within. He turned toward her and his skin split, brilliant streaks of red liquid pouring down his skin, peeling back the flesh from his bones.

Ephema choked on her breath, backing up until her back hit the wall. The globe drifted closer, trapping her. The images swirled faster, coming in glimpses so rapid they hardly made sense, but she couldn't tear her gaze away. She saw men in twisted, bloody armor marching down from dark ships, though she didn't recognize either the ships or the armor. Women and children lay slaughtered in the streets of Eoth, their corpses thrown haphazardly against the closed door of the temple or simply left where they fell, trampled underfoot.

The globe tilted the view to show the temple spire where the body of Bishop Lisse dangled, caught around the neck with a chain which glittered cold and silver in the icy light. As the globe whirled faster, more scenes filled Ephema's mind, some of them familiar places razed to the ground with hardly a stone left standing. Other locations were completely foreign to her, but the results were the same; marching troops, no survivors, blood in the streets, Sisters crawling through broken lives and feeding on what remained, while the undead rose from the discarded corpses.

The deluge of vision was too much, and Ephema closed her eyes, scrambling to get away. She reached the head of the bunk and felt the lack of substance beneath her fingers only when it was too late to stop herself from falling. The hard landing on the wooden floor ripped out the scream she'd been holding in. The globe of light shattered, flooding the room with its light one final time before fading away.

Ephema curled into a ball between the bed and the wall, pressing her head to her knees as sobs wracked her frame. In the darkness the glow from the maul continued to throb, and the Knights slept on in enchanted slumber.

"By the Dark Lord!" Darian yawned widely and sat up, careful not to crack his head on the bed above him. He rolled his head from side to side, the muscles in his shoulders feeling loose and relaxed. "That innkeeper wasn't kidding about the quality of these beds. I can't remember a time I've slept so well."

Tabor grumbled in response, stretching and making his bed squeak in protest. "Nor I. And that's very unusual." He sat up and casually inspected his maul, a little frown playing over his face. "I can't remember a time I've slept an entire night. Still, I suppose I shouldn't look a gift horse in the mouth." He stood and began to sort through his clothing. The inn had a washroom for their laundry and everyone intended to take advantage of it.

"Did you sleep well, Ephema?" Darian looked to the bed where Ephema had been, and raised an eyebrow at finding it empty. He tried to convince himself that she'd just gone to relieve herself, but he couldn't help the concern that filled him. "Ephema?"

A quick look around the room found the woman wedged between the wall and the bunk, asleep but with a strange, pained look on her face and dried tears on her skin. Her cheek sported a large bruise that he couldn't explain any more than her position. He knelt and touched her on the shoulder. "Ephema?"

Ephema started at his touch, banging her head against the wall with a dull thud. There was simply no room for much movement. She blinked, looking as though she hadn't slept at all, her green eyes sunken and red rimmed. "Huh? Darian!"

"What in the world are you doing down here?" He helped her to her feet, surprised at her awkwardness as she rose. She was always unconsciously graceful, but now she moved like he did after a hard sparring session. "Have you been down there all night?"

She rubbed her head, knocking the hair cover she wore hanging askew. Scattered white locks showed against the dark mass of her hair, an oddity he didn't remember from the day before. "I don't know. Something happened, but..." Her brows creased in confusion. "I can't remember."

"Something?" Darian frowned, worried for her and more worried that whatever had happened he'd slept through it. How could he protect her from something that kept him from waking? "Something like what?"

"There was a light...and the moon...and..." She shook

her head, pressing her hands to her temples as though she was holding her head together. "I don't remember. It hurts to try."

"Then don't try." Darian gently took her hands off her head, squeezing them between his hands. "Maybe it was just a dream, though I don't know how you ended up on the floor without waking us. Tabor and I were here the entire night. Let's get you something to eat, and explore the town a little. Maybe that will help you truly wake up."

Ephema nodded, though she shot an uncertain look around the room. "I… okay. A dream."

As Darian guided her to the door, he saw the look on Tabor's face. It was obvious the older Knight didn't believe that it was nothing more than a dream. Darian didn't believe it either.

CHAPTER ELEVEN

Darian took a deep breath, the salty brine in the air a familiar touch. He released his breath all at once and smiled at Ephema from where he stood at the edge of the docks. "It's funny. You never quite realize how much you miss certain smells until you've been away for a long time. Even if it's a smell you don't always like." He turned back toward the bay, where the smaller transport and hauling boats were moving aside in preparation for the arrival of the much larger steamer. "What do you think of the ocean, now that you're up closer to it?"

Ephema made a face, looking out over the waves. "It smells bad. Tabor says it tastes bad, too, though I have not tried. He says the water from the mountain comes down the river and mixes with the sea where it tastes bad." She shrugged. "It is warmer here. I like that."

"It's not a bad taste, really, just salty. You wouldn't want to try to survive off of it; it's not drinkable right from the ocean. You can boil it and capture the steam; it's a process I can show you one day if you want." He stopped himself and laughed. "And now I sound like my brother. You probably don't have any interest in reclaiming salt water."

She raised both eyebrows and finally laughed, tucking her hair back behind her ears. "Not really, but that is mostly because I don't understand what you mean."

"You just need the right cloth." He motioned at the boats moving around in the bay. "This is probably more interesting though. They're moving out of the way so the steamer can dock. Steamers are special ships, built in only three locations around the nation. Hawthan is one of those locations, with Port Ithath to the far west, and Mukklan even farther to the south being the other two. All of these locations are also hosts to large Temples to Osephetin. That isn't a coincidence."

He pulled his mace off of his belt and held it up. "A steamer is, in essence, nothing more than a regular steam ship. A large one, no doubt, but still a ship. But like you've enhanced my mace to be more effective, the same goes with the steamer. It's a regular ship that's been enhanced with three Eternal Flames of Osephetin."

Ephema held up her hands. "Wait. You keep referring to the Eternal Flame, but I'm not sure of the difference between an Eternal Flame and any other flame. Bishop Lam kept talking about it in Tallet, but there was never time to understand."

"Oh." Darian blinked. He shook his head, embarrassed at the omission. Ephema fit in so naturally with the Knights he sometimes forgot how much she didn't know that he'd learned at his mother's knee. "There are many flames that are used by the Priests and Knights, but the Eternal Flame is different. It's a sanctified flame. The stories say that the Eternal Flame was a gift to the very first High Priest of Osephetin, a man named

Nummera. It was in the early days when there were only a few roving priests and the Knights hadn't been organized. Nummera went to the mountains to commune with the Dark Lord. When he returned, he brought with him the tenants of our religion and a bowl filled with burning stones, the heart of the Eternal Flame."

"Burning stones? How can you burn stones?"

Darian laughed and shrugged. "I asked my mother the same thing and she didn't know either. I suppose when you are a God you can do that kind of thing."

"Huh. Then what happened?"

"He took the Eternal Flame to the small shrine in Hawthan which would one day become the High Temple. The stones still burn there. When a new Temple is dedicated fire is brought from the stones and set there to light the temple flame. This is meant to shine Osephetin's light into dark places."

Ephema poked at one of the ropes wrapped around a post on the dock. She tilted her head to the side, thoughtful. "But… we saw temples with the fire gone out. If it is eternal wouldn't it keep burning?"

"The stones themselves are Osephetin's Eternal Flame. The flames lit from the source are often also referred to as Eternal Flames. They have to be fed like a normal fire with wood, but you also keep it alight with prayers and devotions. In temples like Aserian the flame died because there was no one there to tend to it. When there isn't an Eternal Flame, we do the best we can with normal fire, but it's different. The Eternal Flame burns more purely and there are some rituals that require it, but that's usually the realm of a priest, not a Knight."

"Huh. So, they put those fires in the ships. Isn't that dangerous?"

Darian peered into the distance where he could see the huge steamer making its approach. "It's contained within special metal chambers, so not much more than any fire on a ship, really. There are pipes inside of it that pull water from the ocean. The water is heated and compressed and the ship moves. It has sails for when it might be too delicate or dangerous to use the flame. The magic is very forceful so it shaves days off of travel, but it requires a priest continually in attendance to maintain it, and when a steamer breaks down it's dangerous and hard to fix."

"How do you know all of that?"

Darian pulled his gaze from the ship back to Ephema and grinned. "Because I was curious and I nagged my mother about it until she told me to go talk to my brother. Fressin studies everything, and I do mean everything. So, he explained what he could and told me to get out of his face, which is typical of Fressin. But the biggest point is that steamer travel is faster and there is plenty of room for the horses. We may even find more of our Brethren and see what they know, and we can protect the steamer in case of attack."

"What would attack a steamer? You said there were monsters in the deeps, but would they attack such a large ship?"

"Not often, but the undead have on occasion and pirates."

Ephema shook her head, her eyes widening. She shot a look out over the ocean, then back to the dock. He noticed she kept glancing at the waters, but didn't watch them for long. "But undead aren't in the sea. You keep saying this. That's why we're traveling on a boat."

"They aren't, but sometimes your passage might take you under something they can leap down from." Darian pointed to the north. "There used to be a natural rock bridge between two large towns far to the north. It was heavily patrolled, but about a decade ago it was swarmed when there was a steamer underneath. They were trying to help the towns, but hadn't expected the undead to drop onto the boat. As a last resort the priest on board overheated the system, and the engine exploded. The explosion was so great it took out part of the cliff and the bridge collapsed taking everyone, dead and living, into the waters. It was a good idea, because now something like that could never happen again, but it came at a terrible cost."

Ephema blinked slowly, her gaze moving from Darian to the speck on the horizon that was the incoming steamer.

A familiar deep voice rumbled from behind them. "Don't let him scare you." Tabor stepped up next to Darian, his steps shaking the boards of the dock. "These days the steamers all have a compliment of three priests to see to the flame. Our trip to Hawthan won't cross under any stone bridges, tresses, nothing of the sort, and pirates are rare in these patrolled waters. We will keep you safe."

Darian nodded, feeling a little sheepish. He'd been so intent on answering Ephema's questions and trying to help her feel excited about the upcoming voyage, he hadn't realized the color had been draining from her face as he talked. Scaring her hadn't been his intention, but his enthusiasm had gotten the best of him. Lately, whenever he spoke to Ephema, it was like he just couldn't stop talking. He wanted her to love his world and not return to her cave. The thought struck him, and he stood very still, thinking about it.

He wanted her to stay. He tried to consider what that feeling meant, but was shaken from his thoughts as Tabor slapped him on the back. "It nears. We should all step back."

The steamer grew in size as it cut a swath through the

water, leaving a trail of rich grey smoke that floated over the wake behind it. As it drew closer, a sharp whistle cut through the air, a piercing warning call from the deck that warned folks to stay away from the edges of the docks where they might be in danger.

A chorus of voices rang out from the waiting docks. "Steamer incoming! Ahoy! Ready dockhands! Ropes ahoy! Prepare yourselves!" The call quickly raced through those waiting, echoed over and over.

At a set distance, a pair of whistles sounded, and a second sound cut through the air. A deep gurgling rumbled from the depths of the steamer and the ship lurched and bobbed as the water stopped traveling through the pipes. A trio of sails emblazoned with the skull and crossed hammers of Osephetin's followers unfurled from the ship's masts, catching the wind and giving the ship the momentum it needed to dock, but slowing it enough so it didn't do any damage.

Darian always forgot how big the steamers were until he saw them close up. The sleek ship towered above them, the modified berth the only way it could get so close to the docks proper while making way for the deep bottom. Steamers only came fully to dock in a few ports where the sea floor fell off quickly and deeply. The sunlight glittered on the ship's sealant, painting the steamer a dark, rich, red the color of drying blood. His father had told him the wood cured naturally to that coloration and the sealant oils were actually clear, but Darian suspected the wood was specifically chosen for the color. The sails snapped in the morning breeze and, for a moment, Darian was a child again, waiting for his mother to ride home on the stately steamers.

As the ship settled into place, the men aboard tossed down lines as thick as Darian's wrists to the men waiting on the dock.

The moment the ship was secured, openings in the rail were rotated to the side and large planks lowered, allowing for the offload of cargo and passengers. Above it all the grey smoke continued to billow, drifting off into the pale blue autumn sky.

Darian watched as the dock workers bent to their work and sighed. "It will be a few hours until they allow passengers to come aboard. We won't be able to get near it while they're unloading cargo."

Ephema raised her hand to shield her eyes from the sun, watching as the cargo was moved from the ship. Some of the boxes were placed on planks and slid into the waiting arms of the men below. Other huge loads were lifted from the interior of the ship using an array of pulleys and ropes drifting through the air like oddly shaped birds. Sea birds would drop to the rails for a moment, pecking at the shining finish before flying away.

She tilted her head as a figure came to the top of the passenger way, though they didn't disembark. The figure was armored and stood to one side, watching the same proceedings that they were. Ephema motioned at the person. "Is that a Knight?"

Tabor followed her finger to where she was pointing. "I think so, yes, though I cannot say who from this distance. It is not a surprise. It would be odd if we were the only ones going to the High Temple. Come, you two. Let's go confirm our passage."

"Welcome to the Waveskimmer." The man, who had introduced himself as Captain Aham, bowed low, his deep brown eyes sweeping over the four people in front of him with a practiced eye. His skin was a heavy bronze color, pockmarked with many years of life on the sea, but he carried himself with the air of one who was in love with his work. "Two Knights for certain. I daresay you're a Journeyman if I don't miss my guess, and you, m'dear, are a mystery to me." His eyes twinkled. "And I love me a good mystery. You have all booked proper passage south, I presume?"

"We have, indeed." Tabor presented the writ he'd purchased from the harbor stall the day prior. Knights traveled cheaply on the steamers as a way to compensate the faith for the use of their priests, but they still had to pay for rations and their mounts. "Passage for the four of us and three war horses."

"Ah, those are your lot in the loading stable, then. Right solid, those. They should weather the trip well." He glanced at the writ. "A single cabin? I suppose if you insist, but we've space to spare this trip. The lass could probably stay with one of the other ladies aboard. We have two female Knights traveling with us and there are empty beds in their quarters."

Ephema heard Darian suck in a quick breath, and she raised her eyebrows, not sure what was bothering him. "I have not been away from my friends much. I do not know what is right on a ship." She glanced up at the large vessel, which they hadn't boarded yet, fighting down the fluttering in her stomach. It would be okay.

"Journeyman Darian!" A loud voice interrupted her thoughts as a Knight shouted down at them from the top of the gangplank. She wore armor, though it was lighter than what Tabor and Ianel bore. Instead of thick plates of metal and bone it was created of overlapping scales of bone over leather with steel grommets. She carried a large staff that was a fusion of bone and metal. At either tip, a skull gracefully capped off the ends, and Ephema saw a faint blue essence wrapped down the length of the staff.

The woman wasn't wearing a helmet, though one bounced at her hip. Her features were sharp, her greying blonde hair bound in a straight plait down her back. As she descended the gangplank, her attention was fully on Darian. "Journeyman Darian! I do believe I told you that I was not to see you again until you were prepared to take your oaths as a full Knight, was this not correct? Where is your Training Master?"

Darian dropped immediately to one knee with his head bowed and did not answer.

Tabor shook his head, crossing his arms over his chest. "Hello, Knight Proctor Lauret. It's nice to see you as well. To answer your question, something happened to the Journeyman's caravan and, of course, we'd be happy to tell you about it, when the time is right, and we're not standing on a dock waiting to board."

Her head swiveled to the large Knight, and she snorted, looking between the Captain and the small party. "Fine. We will talk more later then. Captain, they are with me. I would appreciate it if you assigned them to my area. How many are in your party?"

Ianel cleared his throat, though he had a pinched look, and Ephema thought he was trying not to laugh. "Ah, four of us, ma'am."

"Four. Good. Very good. Two Knights, a Journeyman and…you." Her gaze came to rest on Ephema, and her features softened as she caught sight of Ephema's concerned expression. "Goodness. You're not a Knight at all. Oh dear, I'm sorry, I do apologize for my behavior! I did not expect to see these three here."

Ephema glanced at Darian and the Knights, trying to urge

someone else to speak before her gaze went back to the sharp woman. She wasn't afraid of the Knight, but she didn't know what to think of her either. "I…no." She cleared her throat. "I am not a Knight. I am traveling with them though. They are my friends and have…" Her mind spun as she considered the right phrases, echoes of words she'd heard the Knights say. "Offered me protection in my travels."

"Well of course they have." She offered her hand to Ephema, palm upward. "We are Knights of Osephetin, after all. You travel with some fine company. Knights Tabor and Ianel are well known for being capable defenders, and my son is likely learning much from them, though last I heard he had been assigned to another trainer. These two do not train journeymen."

Ephema looked at Lauret's offered hand for a moment before extending her own. Her palm touched the Knight's and a white spark jumped between them, sending a quick flash of heat up Ephema's arm. "I have seen them fight the undead and the Sisters. They are very effective." Her voice died off as she took in the rest of what the Knight had said. "You are his *mother*? But, I thought his family was in the city?"

"His sister and brother are." The woman released Ephema's hand. If she'd noticed the spark of power, she said nothing. "I find it very difficult to stay in one spot for very long, not when there is work to be done in bringing peace to this world." She smiled, and it took some of the harshness from her features. "I actually haven't seen any of my family in over a year, so running into this knucklehead on the way home, though a complete surprise, is a pleasant one."

"Does that mean I can stand up now?" Darian's voice was quiet and respectful, but with a bemused undertone.

"I didn't say that. I still don't have answers to my questions surrounding your presence here."

"Please?" Ephema shifted, her feet rubbing against the warming planks of the docks. If Lauret was upset with her son, it made sense to draw her attention to someone else. "I think we're supposed to be getting on the ship." She tried for a little smile, trying to figure out this woman before her. "I do not think Knight Tabor would be happy to carry him."

Lauret snorted again and shook her head. "Perhaps not. Given you asked so nicely on his behalf, I can be patient." Lauret looked down at her son. "Journeyman Darian, please stand and resume your duties guarding this lovely," she paused for emphasis, "daughter, on her journey. Once we are away from dock, I would like to see all four of you in my quarters."

Tabor nodded, nudging Darian who scrambled to his feet. "We will do that, Knight Proctor."

The Captain, who had remained silent through most of the conversation, tucked the writ into his belt and gestured toward the long passenger plank. "After you." He gave Ephema and the Knight Proctor a half bow.

Ephema's stomach tightened, hearing the emphasis on the word daughter. The woman knew. She had to, or she wouldn't have said that. But why would she know? And how?

She was a Knight. She was Darian's mother. Why shouldn't she know? Keeping the secret of her powers was so second nature to Ephema, the thought of someone guessing filled her with misgivings. She swallowed and nodded, deciding she wouldn't know where to run even if she tried. It seemed that, again, the only way to go was forward. She stepped onto the wooden plank and made her way up into the ship.

∼

Darian remained on deck for as long as he could, not because he was worried about what his mother would say to him, but because this was his favorite part of the journey. He loved the push away from land, watching it retreat in the distance as divine magic hummed through the ship, and the Eternal Flame replaced the wind in driving the ship over and through the waves.

Sea birds cried as the waves crashed behind them, and Eoth fell into the distance.

Once they were far enough away, a second burst of power flushed through the system, pushing more energy into the engine, and the steamer gained full speed. Darian faced into the wind with his eyes closed and smiled. This. This is what he'd missed. The wind from the ocean on his face, the smell of the sea, the brine. It brought back so many memories of his family and his father in particular, in a different time, and in a much smaller boat.

He felt more than heard a person come up behind him, though he did not turn around. Gently, a hand touched his shoulder. Knight Proctor Lauret's voice was soft. "I figured I'd find you out here, Darian."

"Yes." He didn't turn around, not yet. For a time, they stood side by side, until Darian spoke again. "I know we'll see him again, but I can't help but miss him."

"I know." Lauret moved beside Darian and leaned over the railing, looking down at the water. "Every time I go out on the water, I think about him. He's out there, waiting patiently I'm sure, and will be there beside Osephetin once we've finished our journeys."

After another few minutes of silence, Darian sighed.

"Indeed. Enough of this. I'm sure you want to know what's going on."

"Of course, I do. I need your report." She stood fully and turned away from the rail. "But I also wanted to make sure that my son was all right. I am allowed to worry, you know." She frowned, her gaze darting over him. "And one question you're going to have to answer now is where in the seven hells you've misplaced your armor. Here you are, wandering around with a Daughter of Lianna – yes, I know what she is, though I don't know how it's possible – and you don't even have your Journeyman armor to protect yourself with!"

Darian made a face, chagrinned. "Those two things are connected. My armor was destroyed during the journey. It was weakened when my convoy was lost and ripped apart when we had a run in with the Sisters. Ephema was able to return my hide to one piece in both instances, but she can't do anything for steel and leather."

Lauret's gaze sharpened. She looked him over again as though she could look through his clothing and spot any wounds he wasn't telling her about. "I think I need to hear this story in order." She gestured toward the interior of the ship and the berths they had all been assigned. "This way."

EPHEMA DID her best to stay out of the way, perching on a chair in the Knight Proctor's quarters. The story of the fallen convoy, Darian's arrival at her cave and the subsequent travel, first to Aserian, then Tallet, and Eoth, passed between the men almost seamlessly. She answered questions that were directly asked of her, but didn't add much to the narrative otherwise. The Knight Proctor was intent in her questioning, and

Ephema was just as happy not to be the subject of sharp questions, not to mention her head and stomach were spinning in time with the swaying ship. She hadn't realized just how much the deck would rock beneath her feet.

The conversation fell quiet, and Ephema felt the weight of four pairs of eyes on her. It was obvious someone had asked a question, but she'd missed it. She blinked and rubbed a crease from her forehead. "What?"

Lauret sighed. "I said, you're looking a bit green, my dear. Are you feeling alright?" She paused, glancing between Ephema and the men. "This is your first time on a ship, isn't it?" It was a statement, not a question, realization spreading across her face.

Ephema nodded, but slowly. She was afraid to move her head too fast. "I think I do not like sailing." She rolled her shoulders to try to loosen the tension in her muscles. "There is always an earthquake beneath my feet."

"I suppose neither the Knights nor my son warned you that it takes time for your body to adjust to being on the sea. In a day or two, you'll hardly notice the movement anymore." She glared at the men and rose, crossing the room to dig through a chest which was chained to the floor.

She pulled a small bag out of the chest and brought it to Ephema. "Here. This is ginger root. It has a very unique taste. If you chew on small pieces of it, it will help with your seasickness. Keep it on hand. It'll help."

Ephema tilted her head, regretting the movement immediately. "It's not their fault." She muttered before looking at the root Lauret offered. She knew a lot about roots and herbs, but this one looked different from the ones she was familiar with. She took it and rubbed her fingers against the papery skin. It came away at her touch, and she smelled the root underneath cautiously. Even the smell was soothing, and she nodded her thanks before nibbling on the end of the ginger. It was an odd flavor, burning inside of her mouth, but it made her stomach hold still.

Tabor ran his fingers along the head of his maul, then cleared his throat. "There is one thing we've not spoken of, and I think now is the time. Ephema, when we were at the inn you had a dream, or a vision, of some kind. I think you should tell us whatever you can."

Ephema frowned, and Tabor held up a hand before she could voice her protest. "I know you said it was hard to remember, but that was when it was new and when it was just us. Knight Proctor Lauret has experience with visions, and she may be able to help draw the memory to the surface of your mind. You would not have been sent a vision if it was not important that we know about it."

Lauret sat down beside Ephema, taking one of Ephema's hands into both of hers. "All you need to do is let your mind drift. Then just say whatever comes to mind, whatever you remember, even the smallest of details. Don't try to force it into an order or make sense of it. Just talk it through."

Ephema's frown eased as she focused on Lauret and her instructions. For all that the woman was sharp and intimidating, there was another, softer, side to her that reminded Ephema of her mother. There was confidence in Lauret's gaze that said everything would be all right and that helped Ephema relax. She was beginning to understand where Darian's empathy came from. With a sigh, Ephema closed her eyes and cast her memory back to the night at the inn. She forced herself to explore the feeling of lying on the bed and thought about the bright glow of the moon on her skin. She shuddered.

Her lips moved, and she whispered. "I saw my parents. When they died. How they died. Black ships coming across the water. Men in black armor, twisted armor that bled. Broken towns, burning. Death. Bishop Lisse hanging from the spire of the Temple. Sisters in the ruins of Eoth eating the fallen." Her voice cracked, and she swallowed. The thump of her heartbeat was loud and too fast in her ears, fear flooding through her body and making her tremble. "A flag. Black with red swords beneath a strange crown. The doors to the Temple are closed. The Knights are fallen." Tears touched her cheeks, and she jerked her hand away from Lauret as she leaned away from the Knight. "I…I can't. I don't want to remember anymore."

The room was silent as the Knights watched Lauret's reaction to the vision, but she simply studied Ephema's face, her expression neutral. Tabor frowned, crossing to stand at Ephema's side as though he thought she needed protection from the Knight Proctor. "Lauret, is everything all right?"

Lauret did not look at Tabor as she said, "That, good Knight, depends on quite a lot of things." She patted Ephema's knee and stood with a determined look. "Give me a moment." She spun on her heel and strode out of the room.

Darian brought a small mug of water to Ephema, holding it until she stopped shaking enough to take it from his hands. "I don't know where she went, but she's always this way. She'll be back and explain, umm, something. I'm sure."

Lauret returned with a carefully wrapped parcel under her arm. She crossed the room and knelt before Ephema. "I wish to show you something." At her nod, Lauret unwrapped the parcel to reveal a torn, bloody ship's standard.

The standard's background was black, adorned with two wickedly curved swords stitched in white thread that dropped blood made from silk strings sewn to their tips. They crossed over top of a white, ragged crown of thorns, worn by a skull with an arrow drawn through the left eye socket. "Did it look like this?"

The sight of the flag made Ephema's skin crawl, and she very carefully didn't touch it as though it might infect her with something if she did. She cleared her throat, wanting to look away, but she couldn't. "Yes."

Lauret leaned back on her haunches, crossing her arms over her chest. "And you've never seen it before now, except in vision?"

Ephema shook her head, managing to tear her gaze away from the scarlet and black fabric. She drank from the mug, trying to ground herself in something that felt real. "No. Only in the dream."

"Damnit."

CHAPTER TWELVE

"Bosun! Sound the alarm! We are under attack!"

The shout echoed across the ship, picked up by the sailors and passed along. A clanging bell followed, waking anyone who had managed to sleep through the shouts.

Darian startled awake, trying to get out of the hammock he'd slept in and wishing he'd followed Tabor's example and rested on the floor. He pulled himself free and yanked on his boots while the other Knights donned their armor. Without armor to worry about, Darian only had to grab his mace as he ran out of the berth and raced to the ladders that lead to the deck.

When he emerged above, the mace began to vibrate. He glanced down and saw the runes flickering and snapping with brilliant white light. He grimaced. "That's not a good sign, is it?" But there was no one to answer.

Men ran around the deck, some keeping the ship steady in her course and others tying down anything they could to keep it from flying about as the boat rose and dipped. One of the top sails was ablaze, far too high for anyone to get to easily, though the men were trying, scrambling up the ropes like clever rodents. The wind whipped the ruined sail and thick rain splattered on the ship as a volley of burning tar flew in from the darkness.

Darian held a hand over his eyes just as a flash of lightning illuminated a large war ship approaching the steamer at speed, though it wasn't on a collision course. The angle of travel would bring it alongside the steamer. They'd timed it perfectly for when the full power of the engines couldn't be used in a narrow strait.

"Why are they not trying to ram…" He paled as the realization hit. "Osephetin's Blood, they're going to board!"

Sinking a steamer would be catastrophic, capturing one maybe even more so. Darian ignored the bits of flaming tar that were scattered around the deck as he ran to the railing nearest where he'd seen the ship.

Another flash of light tore the sky, and Darian growled. Men hung from the rigging of the enemy vessel, waiting for the ship to get close enough that they could cross the distance, clad in armor that wasn't familiar to him. From the rigging above came the call to arms as the first raiders swung into the gap.

The captain managed to keep the ships from colliding, but the maneuvering he had to do cost them more speed and made it simple for the raiders to drop between the ships. They were met with violence by the Knights, joined by the ship's hands that weren't busy dealing with fire. The Knights were trained for battle, but no one was going to stand aside and simply let the ship be taken.

One of the invaders landed beside Darian, dropping to a half crouch to absorb the force of his landing. The sailor on

Darian's other side startled and drew a sharp nasty curved knife, more designed for use against ropes and tackle than an armored enemy. Before Darian could stop him, the sailor lunged at the enemy, but the man's armor turned the sharp blade.

Sneering, the invader dodged and shoved his sword deep into the sailor's side as though he was gutting a pig. The sailor dropped heavily, dead before he landed. Darian was no stranger to combat, but the speed of the violence was stunning even to him.

His shock nearly cost him his life as the enemy spun from one attack to the next, and it was luck and training as much as skill that put Darian's mace between himself and the edge of the attacker's blade.

The mace flashed as white as the raging lightning. The black steel sword shattered, one of the metal shards skipping along Darian's forearm. The pain was swift, but minor and before the stunned invader could react, Darian slammed the mace into the man's exposed face with all his might. The sickening crunch of flesh and bone could be heard even over the wailing winds. The man fell, bleeding out onto the deck.

Darian stared at the corpse, though he knew better than to lose his focus again. This was the first time he'd killed a living human. Even in the dark of the storm, light from the shielded lanterns glimmered in the dying man's blood as it pooled on the shifting deck. The undead didn't bleed.

He grimaced and spun away. More invaders were swarming the deck, the rain pelting down as though it too were on the attack. There would be time to deal with the emotions rolling through his guts later. For now, there was only survival.

The sound of the bells sent Ephema scrambling to her feet in time to see the back of the Knight Proctor as the woman sprinted out of the room they shared. She followed, not knowing what the alarm meant, but recognizing the danger. The rungs of the ladder were slick with rain water, but she scampered up it without slipping.

She emerged to the pounding rain and the chaos of battle. The shifting lantern lights and flashes of lightning made it difficult to tell friend from foe, but wherever the Knights of Osephetin fought the pale blue light of Osephetin's divine magic followed them. The urge to flee filled Ephema's body, warring with the desire to help. But these were her friends, and they were in danger. Courage won out, and she threw herself forward onto the rocking deck.

Outside of the safety of below decks, the noise was deafening. The sounds of the waves and the weather was joined by the cries of combat and the screams of the dying. A flash of light illuminated one of the enemy bodies, and her breath caught in her throat. She recognized the armor from her dream.

Not her dream. Her vision.

A scream from above her made Ephema jerk to one side, a body narrowly missing her as a man dropped to the deck. She ran to his side, her feet struggling to find purchase on the slippery wood. The man drew in a shaky breath, alive, but only barely, broken and burned. She sent a whispered prayer to the Mother and rested her fingers against the side of his face. Power raced through her hands and into his broken form. She didn't have time to fix everything that was wrong, but she did what she could as quickly as possible. He gasped and clutched his chest, breathing in rain. She rolled him to his side, letting him cough until his breath evened out. His eyes were wide, and she grabbed his shoulder, yelling in his ear to be heard over the din.

"You have to get up!"

He blinked, and his face screwed up in confusion. "But… I fell. I remember." His hand pressed against his ribs, and he hissed softly at the remaining pain. "Are you an angel?"

Ephema shook her head and pushed to her feet. "Just a friend. Go on."

A flash of eldritch light and movement caught her gaze, and Ephema turned. What she saw made her breath catch in her throat, but whether it was from fear, awe, or some combination of the two she didn't know. Five of the invaders had advanced on the Knight Proctor, though two of them were already sprawled on the deck, bleeding and twitching. The other three warily looked for an opening in the deadly dance created by the knight and the staff that spun so quickly in her hands, creating wide circles of light.

Where Tabor was a force of nature, destroying everything in his path, the Knight Proctor's movements were so delicate and graceful it hardly made sense they were also deadly. She parried their attacks almost effortlessly, slapping them with breaking force on exposed wrists, hands, and necks at each opportunity.

Enraged with her onslaught, one of the men launched an impassioned attack that pushed through her whirling defenses. A thin line of blood rose from a small cut on her arm, and she glanced at it, unperturbed.

Her voice was calm against the rage of the storm, and clearly audible. "Very well. May Osephetin have mercy on your souls, for I will not! Lord Osephetin, guide me!" She spat, the words of power echoing against the booming thunder. Her bone staff flashed with magic and moved under her hands as the three attackers stepped back involuntarily.

With a snap, metal and bone moved outward from each end of the staff at a right angle, forming a double-bladed scythe. Divine magic dripped from the weapon, not the pale blue light Ephema had seen before, but darkness so deep it was like liquid shadow. She lunged and though her opponent raised his sword to the defense, his arm tumbled to the deck uselessly. He shrieked and stared at the severed limb as Lauret kicked him, sending him backward over the ship's railing.

Ephema shook herself out of her stupor. It felt like she'd been watching forever, but only a few seconds had passed. She saw a few men charging up the stairs to where the Captain stood at the ship's wheel and shouted, trying to draw Lauret's attention. It was useless as the wind whipped her voice away.

She didn't know much about ships, but the captain had shown them around yesterday. He said the ship's wheel directed where the ship went. If the invaders took control of it, they had control of the ship. Someone had to help him, and Ephema ran for the stairs.

As she ran, her gaze caught on one of the long fishing spears kept on deck. While the steamer wasn't designed as a fishing vessel, that didn't mean the crew didn't enjoy fishing when there was occasion. She stooped in her run, catching up the spear which had come loose from its ties. It was shorter than she had guessed, but the wooden shaft felt good in her hands. Much better than charging the enemy with nothing but her fists and her magic.

She reached the top of the stairs as the invaders threw themselves on the captain's men. Captain Aham clung to the wheel despite the blood running down his face from a long gash across his forehead. A sailor fell heavily to the deck, sliding off of an invader's sword. Ephema hesitated, her attention pulled to the injured and dying. Another man approached the captain, but Darian landed in front of him, dropping from somewhere above. He pushed the attacker back, taking the stroke meant for the captain on his mace and kicking the man away.

Ephema was surprised by Darian's arrival, but it shook her from her shock. She ran into one of the men, holding the spear tightly. The multi-headed fishing spear hit his armor, and the barbs bent uselessly, meant to pierce fish scales not metal. But it turned his attention from the captain.

She saw only the bottom of his face, which was mostly covered by a coarse shaggy beard, his eyes shadowed by his helmet. He sneered and slashed at her with a sword as broad as her arm. Instinctively, she threw the spear up to block the swing.

The sea-aged wood didn't stand a chance against forged metal, but when the two met white light poured from her fingers into the weapon. The spear took the blow and exploded, throwing both combatants backward. The man landed, stunned, at the captain's feet and the first mate stabbed the invader in the throat.

Ephema flew back, knocked from her feet. She landed on her hip and skidded across the rain-soaked deck as the ship dipped wildly. She grabbed for the deck, but felt nothing as she slipped through a broken piece of rail. The rain pelted her as she tumbled, and she caught her breath and lost it again as she crashed into the sea.

~

THE FLASH of light on deck distracted Darian's enemy long enough that he smashed his mace into his opponent's knee, crushing the armor and sending him to the deck where a nearby sailor finished him off. Darian nodded his thanks, trying to spot his next opponent.

"The girl went overboard!"

The shout was close enough Darian heard it over the rain. He spun, searching the deck for Ephema, but she was nowhere to be seen. "Which way?"

The deckhand waved toward the shattered railing on the starboard side of the ship. "There!"

"Osephetin's Blood!" Darian raced to the railing, the sounds of combat around him suddenly less important to his ears. The waves below raged, black and thick, but about fifteen yards from the ship a thin light bobbed in the water. "I see her!"

"You see who?" A voice at his elbow drew his attention, and he turned to see his mother looking at him with cold curiosity. Her bone staff-scythe dripped with blood and darkness. "What are you doing? Inattention will get you killed, Journeyman!"

"Here!" Darian shoved his mace at her. He wished he had time to unlace his boots, but wet as the laces were, it would take too long. He wasn't going to lose Ephema now. He'd promised to protect her and that she'd be safe.

Lauret caught the mace, puzzlement breaking through her expression. "What are you doing, Darian?"

"I can't let her drown, Mother."

She stared as he sprang off of the edge of the ship, throwing himself out as far as he could before he plunged into the waters below. Hitting the water was like taking a punch to the jaw, but he was prepared for it and shook off the impact, pushing himself to the surface and reorienting again.

He identified the mass of the ship and put it behind him, pushing along the waves toward where he'd seen the light. As fierce as the storm was, it was nearly impossible to make progress, but Darian refused to give up. He'd find her, or Oesphetin would take him, there were no other options.

"Please, Lord Osephetin." He didn't speak the prayer aloud, nor was there much substance beyond pleading. Where was she?

Another flash of lightning, this one close and low in the sky, lit up the seas illuminating the boats, combatants, and a bobbing form just beyond him.

He swam to her as quickly as possible, dragged back by his boots and clothing, letting the waves do much of the work. Once he was close enough, he could hear her struggling to stay afloat. "Ephema! I'm here! Come this way!"

A response floated over the crash of the waves, a shout of wordless terror. The choking cry of someone being pulled under the waters. He'd heard that agonizing sound many times on the shores of Hawthan while learning to swim; not everyone that sailed should. His direction now firm, he kicked and pulled himself through the water until the splashing and choking cries brought him to her.

As he reached her, Ephema slipped under the water, but Darian wasn't about to let her go. He knew it wasn't her time to join Osephetin, or Lianna. Not while he drew breath. He followed her down, grabbing her from behind and kicking for the surface. A moment later, they breached again, and he gasped for air.

Ephema sucked in a gargling breath, coughing as she began to struggle again in earnest. She fought the waves, and lashed out at his grip, throwing off his stroke. Darian rolled onto his back, doing his best to keep their heads above water.

"Ephema!" His shout was garbled by the water splashing his face, and he had to yell a second time before her terrified eyes focused on him. "Stop fighting! I've got you!"

She stared at him until his words made their way through her terror. The globe hanging against her chest took on a silvery white glow, and Darian felt warmth rush through his limbs bringing him extra strength he hadn't had before. Ephema stopped thrashing, but she grabbed onto him, still too much in his way.

Darian thanked Osephetin and Lianna and anyone else that might be listening and pushed Ephema to her back, throwing an arm across her chest so he could protect them both. She latched onto his arm, but he could handle that.

Darian treaded water as he tried to figure out how to get them back to the ship, the thoughts of battle overwhelmed by those of survival.

A loud whistle blast from the enemy vessel interrupted his thoughts. It was followed by a second whistle and men jumped between the ships, scuttling for their home territory as the vessels parted.

Retreat.

They'd won.

GRUNTING AND HEAVING, the assembled men pulled the dinghy up the side of the ship. The storm had eased, though rain still pelted the deck, and the small boat bounced as it was raised. Once it was secured, the sailors helped their soggy passengers back aboard the steamer.

Knight Proctor Lauret waited patiently as Darian and Ephema sloshed their way across the deck. "I must say, you could have picked a better time and place for a swim, but no matter." She smacked Darian none-to-gently on the back of the head. "Don't scare me like that again."

"I'm sorry, Mother. But there wasn't time."

"I understand." Lauret nodded and handed him his mace. "You'll need this again, I'm sure." She glanced at Ephema. "I've never seen a weapon shatter blades and cleave through armor as this does. It's very curious."

"Did you use it?" Darian accepted the mace, holding it in his hands given how wet his belt was.

"Indeed. I think the first time it broke a blade, I was as surprised as the enemy. You could have warned me."

Darian heard his mother's tone relaxing under the absent chatter. He knew they'd worried her, but she would never show it. He shrugged a little, repeating himself. "There wasn't time for that either."

"No. There wasn't, was there?" She turned to Ephema, her tones gentle. "Are you all right, my dear? How did you end up down there?"

Ephema tried to answer but she was shivering too hard. She wrapped her arms around herself, huddling in her wet clothes and tried again. "Captain…in danger…try…tried to help."

Lauret shook her head. "Bah, I'm a fool." Lauret gently took Ephema by the hand. "Questions can wait. Let's get you inside into something dry and warm." She nodded at Darian. "Come, you too."

∾

Once in the Knight Proctor's quarters, Lauret moved with the speed of a mother on a mission. Ensuring all the men were forbidden from entering, she helped Ephema out of her ripped, wet clothing. The only other clothes she had on hand were her own, which were too big, but would do for the time being.

Lauret threw the doors open and bustled Darian, who had also changed, inside before calling for blankets and something hot to eat. Only then did she take the time to shed her armor and change her own wet clothing.

Ephema leaned back against the wall, huddling in a blanket. There had been a moment in the tossing sea when she thought she would never be warm again, but the blankets were thick and the thin broth – the only thing the galley had hot on demand – was warming her from the inside. She looked at Darian, huddled in his own blankets and found a faint smile. He was here. They were safe. Everything was going to be all right. "Now, I owe you."

"I am still behind, if we're keeping track." Darian smiled, though he looked exhausted. "Next time, we should choose warmer waters. It's been a long time since I had to swim in water this cold. It's still not fun."

"I'd prefer neither of you swimming in the near future, thank you." Lauret looked over as Ianel and Tabor entered the room. While Ianel was unharmed, Tabor was nursing a deep stab on his arm that he'd covered with a bandage of cloth and canvas. "Good to see you two made it."

Ianel's smile was wide and gleeful. "It was fun. It's been years since I've participated in ship-to-ship combat. Whomever those attackers were, they were skilled. I pulled out some attacks I haven't had the opportunity to practice in a long time."

"Be sure to tell the families of those who died how elated you are to have been involved in their defense." Tabor's voice was dry, his words harsh. The smile melted off of Ianel's face, but Tabor didn't allow him to respond. Tabor's gaze moved to Lauret. "I saw the flag. It was the same as you showed us, Knight Proctor."

"The very same."

"I got aboard their ship during the fight. It's not a design I'm familiar with, but I'll sketch down what I can remember."

Ephema's gaze caught on the blood-soaked bandage. She felt bad she hadn't done more to help the Knights and the sailors. Maybe she should have stayed away from the fighting and healed them instead? She still wasn't sure what was the right thing to do. She opened her mouth to offer to heal Tabor's arm, but realized she was too tired, and she couldn't form the words.

Sleep wrapped around her, though her mind resisted. There was too much activity, both in the room and in the whirling recesses of her choices. The day's events kept playing over and over in her thoughts, until her gaze came to rest on Darian. He had come for her, just like he promised. The thought was calming and finally she relaxed as darkness came.

CHAPTER THIRTEEN

It had long been argued that the great city of Hawthan, a sprawling metropolis surrounded by thick walls to guard the city, was best viewed from horseback. Many claimed that the only proper way to experience the full beauty and strength of the massive city was to approach from the main gates with the twenty-foot-tall walls pressing down on you as the expanse of the interior was laid bare to the wondering eyes of fresh visitors. The first and greatest city built after the Fall of the Gods, Hawthan was meticulously planned, the city streets straight and wide, every building in its place as though set by the hands of the gods themselves. It was a masterpiece.

Those people, Darian mused, were missing out on what was truly the best way to experience the majesty of Hawthan. From the vast bay leading out to the ocean, the city was not hidden by walls, but protected by a wide semi-circle of natural cliffs. They had passed through the narrows and now from where he stood, he could see every east and west facing street all at once. The city population was abuzz with a hive of activity, people moving about their daily lives. Smoke from chimneys filled the air, collecting together in lazy clouds before the winds higher up tore them apart.

The harbor came into view, and everything was much as Darian remembered it. Nearly a hundred ships stretched before him, in all shapes and sizes, with more coming and going just like they were. To the far side of the harbor, the bay where new ships were launched was full; a newly-constructed steamer was set to sail soon, and people were gathered to see the vessel take to the waves.

As he watched the city unfold before him, Darian couldn't help but smile. It had been nearly two years since he'd been home between training and his assignment to the convoy, but coming home always felt both new and familiar at the same time.

Soft footsteps approached from behind him, footsteps he recognized immediately from the lack of the click of a wooden heel or brush of a leather sole. Even now Ephema refused to wear shoes, much to his mother's horror. There were many things his mother could command men and women to do, but making the healer protect her feet didn't seem to be one of them. Watching Ephema wordlessly stare his mother down at the very suggestion was a memory Darian would always cherish.

She came to a stop at his side, staring out at the approaching city. They hadn't had much time to talk in the days since the attack on the ship. Her resources had been put into caring for and healing the wounded wherever she could without being noticed. His efforts had gone to being part of the watch in case there was another attack, and helping to rebuild and shore up damaged parts of the vessel. The at-sea repairs weren't as good as what could be done at dock, but they made sure the steamer made it through the remaining days of travel.

Ephema rested her hands on the rail before them, tapping her fingers slowly against the wood. Finally, she spoke. "I thought Eoth was big, but this is… I have never seen anything like it. Like a beehive full of people."

"Beautiful, isn't it?" He motioned to the eastern side of the dock. "Over there is where our family fishing boat used to be moored. And that big building, the one over on the far side? That's where these steamers are built and sanctified." He spent a few more minutes pointing out other details of the dock before he stopped himself. "Sorry. It's been a while since I've been home, and I'm more excited about the prospect than I'd thought I would be."

"I do not think you need to be sorry for that. Isn't it always good to go home?" She didn't look at him, and he wondered if she was thinking of her own home in the distant hills. It was nothing like the sprawling city before them.

"Not always, no. I'm lucky. Many don't have a home to return to." Darian moved closer to her and placed his hand over hers on the rail. Her skin was soft and warm beneath his calloused fingers. "I know this is a big city, Ephema, but I promise it won't be that bad. And when all of this is done, you have my word, I'll make sure you get home safe and sound. If that's what you want." He smiled and shrugged. "Hopefully, with fewer battles on the way there."

She didn't move her hand away, her fingers pressing softly against his. "I don't expect to return to the cave again. There is nothing there for me anymore. My family is not returning home, and that was the reason I stayed."

"Then I'll escort you wherever you wish to go." Darian's voice was quiet against the backdrop of the steamer starting its docking procedures. "It's a big world out there. I'm sure we can find somewhere you'll be happy."

Ephema still didn't look at him, though he wished she would, her gaze stuck on the docks and the great city beyond. "My mother once told me that it wasn't the place, but the people that made you happy. She could live in a cave or a palace and be contented, as long as we were there." Her clear gaze turned to him, the wind toying with locks of her hair. Her hair covering had been lost to the sea, leaving her dark locks with their odd streaks of white visible and loose. Darian realized, for the first time he could put words to it that she was beautiful, but it was more than her physical beauty that drew his eye. "I think I understand what she meant, now."

It took Darian a moment to find his voice. "She was a wise woman." He fell silent, his hand remaining on hers as the steamer pulled into port. He only released her once they'd fully moored and were beginning to disembark. He wished the moment didn't have to end, but the other Knights would be looking for them soon. There was work to be done. "Guess we'd better head down to join the others."

"I suppose." She paused and shook her head, a little smile – the familiar one he liked seeing – touching her face. "Is a rocking ship on the water or a huge city more to worry about?"

"I don't know. But there is less chance of pirates in town."

He led the way to where the passenger gangplank had been lowered to touch the dock. In the distance the High Temple was clearly visible to all who entered the city. The building stood head and shoulders above the others; an impressive feat given how tall some of the merchant centers were. Twin stone towers stretched to the heavens at each corner. Even at a distance the dark stone shone, the detail work in the engraving obvious and meticulous. Darian pointed to draw Ephema's attention. "That's Hawthan's High Temple. It's where we'll need to go first. Where I must take the scroll."

"And where you'll go through your ceremony to become one of us." Ianel interrupted as he approached, giving a friendly nod to the pair. "I daresay there will be little doubt in the Elders' minds as to your readiness, after the successful journey you've had. Are you ready for it?"

"It's not my place to guess what the Elders will say, but if they allow me the chance, I'm as ready as I'll ever be." Daria caught Ephema's eye again and smiled. "I have someone rather important to defend now. I'll do that more thoroughly as a Knight."

"Hah. Indeed, you do." Ianel laughed heartily and clapped Darian on the arm. "Good man. Well, I have a report to make and wenches to impress. It's been good to journey with you, Journeyman Darian. And you, m'lady healer." Ianel bowed low to Ephema. "I'm glad we were able to bring you this far."

Ephema inclined her head to Ianel as regally as any queen. "Thank you, Knight Ianel. I am glad we met. Maybe we will meet again, at least if you can be found in this forest of buildings."

"I'm sure I can be. To the Eternal Rest, my friends." The Knight saluted and walked down the dock planks.

Almost as fast as Ianel left, Tabor brushed past them and disembarked the steamer, joining the other Knight on the dock. A few words were exchanged, then they clasped hands. Tabor pulled Ianel forward and grasped the other man's arm with his hand, then nodded as he released him.

He turned and waited for Darian and Ephema to join him, inclining his head as they reached him. "And thus our journey, at least this part of it, ends." He nodded at Darian.

"It has been a pleasure to serve beside you, Journeyman. You'll make a damn fine Knight one day, and Osephetin willing, I'll be there to speak for you when the time comes for your Trial of Ascension. I'll take Ephema to the High Temple, now, and stay with her until she can speak to the High Priest."

"After she's been introduced at the High Temple, I'd like to show Ephema around Hawthan." Darian gestured broadly toward the city. "It is my home, after all, and…"

"If the High Priest allows, I am sure that can be arranged." Tabor gripped Darian's arm and slapped him on the shoulder. "Complete your mission, Journeyman. Though it will wait just long enough for you to report to Knight Proctor Lauret first. She said something about a homecoming ceremony."

Darian nodded, flustered. He'd forgotten the ceremony, which wasn't really a formal ceremony at all as much as a remembering. He hadn't done it for years, but it was important to his mother. "Yes, Sir." He turned to Ephema and suddenly felt like he didn't know what to do with his hands, or how to say goodbye, even if it was only for a while. He hadn't been away from her side for long for nearly a month. Finally, he bowed low and said, "Knight Tabor will guard you well. I'll see you soon."

She nodded, looking between Tabor and Darian. She started to step forward, then retreated as he turned, her voice chasing him as he walked away. "I hope so."

"Took you long enough, my son." There was no venom in Lauret's teasing words. She glanced down the dock, watching as Tabor escorted Ephema away into the city. "I was beginning to think I had been replaced by a pretty face."

"I'm not sure what you mean." Darian also watched as the pair walked away, his gaze lingering on Ephema.

She chuckled, shaking her head. "Of course, you do. You spent every moment that you could with the shoeless Daughter of an insane Goddess, and your smile got brighter every time she entered the room. You're fond of her, not that there's anything wrong with that."

"I suppose I am. But I'm not sure that means anything to her, or means anything besides friendship. It's not as though our time together has been remotely normal."

Lauret raised both of her brows, her smile warm. "You could ask her."

Darian snorted softly. "I think she has enough to think about right now."

"Just remember that if I'd waited to talk to your father about these things, none of you would exist. He was so sure a Knight of Osephetin wouldn't look twice at a poor fisherman, even when he was the kindest and most handsome man I'd ever laid eyes on."

As they walked, they veered toward the end of the dock where a large stall that sold flowers and other sundries was doing a brisk trade. Lauret glanced at Darian, shifting the subject. "Would you like to do the ceremony today or shall I?"

Darian sighed heavily. The ceremony for those lost at sea was an old tradition in Hawthan. He understood it was rooted in tradition and well-meant emotion, but it had never really appealed to him. He liked remembering his father as a doting, jovial man, not focusing on how they'd lost him. However, he wasn't going to deny her whatever comfort she drew from it. "Would you? I think it means more that way."

"I suppose." Lauret approached the stall, looking over the flowers and trinkets. The man who ran the little shop, a rotund, balding man by the name of Kel, immediately turned his attention to them.

"Ah, Knight Proctor! And young Darian. It's been quite some time since you two have graced me with your honorable presence." His voice was gravely, the voice of a man who'd spent far too much time by the sea and pulling on his tobacco, but he spoke with a smile. He pulled a row of flowers out from the wall behind him, moving them into the pale sunlight. "If I remember right, and I always remember my best customers, you prefer the simple lily, m'lady Knight."

"Your mind is as sharp as ever, Kel." Lauret picked through the lilies, selecting one with a dark blue heart and bright yellow stamens. "And, I'm assuming, you're going to refuse payment for this one as well? You've never once let me pay."

Kel interrupted her with a scoff. "Bah! You're a Knight of Lord Osephetin, m'lady! Your service to the people of this world is payment enough for a simple flower! I will not accept your coin today, or ever!"

"You're a good man."

"Tell my former wife that. Hah!"

Darian waved a goodbye to the man as they walked to the end of the dock, away from the largest crowd of people. A few people were doing the same as they were, holding their own little ceremonies to give thanks for safe passage or honor those lost to the waves. He saw a few familiar faces, but he'd been gone from Hawthan long enough that many faces were lost to him now. "Is this far enough?"

"Yes, this will do." Lauret sat down on the dock, setting her staff to her side, her legs dangling over the water as she gazed out over the ocean. She waited until Darian sat beside her to speak. She closed her eyes and lifted her head to the heavens. "It has been years since you left me, but the love is still there."

Darian closed his eyes as well and clasped his hands in his lap.

Lauret murmured softly. "Our children have grown up to be fine young people, walking their own paths, guided by your hand from afar." Her voice cracked, but she continued. "I have trod a lonely path without you by my side as my strength, but the fire of my love has never waned."

She fell quiet for a time, then spoke in a whisper. "I miss you. I know one day we will be together again, and I look forward to that day." She extended her hands, the lily resting on her palms for an instant before she released it. The flower fell toward the water, but a quick breeze sprang up and lifted it back into the air. It spun as it rose, turning and tossing before lazily drifting back down and settling on the waves.

Lauret's eyes shone with unshed tears, but a smile touched her lips. She pulled Darian into a sideways hug. "Welcome home."

Together they stared out across the water, enjoying the peace as mother and son. Soon they would return to being Knight Proctor and Journeyman Knight with work to do. But for now, all was quiet.

EPHEMA DIDN'T LOOK over her shoulder as Darian and Lauret left, but only because Tabor's bulk blocked her view. The large Knight smiled, guiding her down the docks with a touch on her shoulder. It didn't take much guidance to keep her moving.

She expected questions from Tabor, or at least conversation as they walked the roads of the city, but he surprised her with his silence. She started to break the quiet between them, heavens knew there was no silence around them, but before she could speak a man emerged from the crowd, steering unerringly toward Tabor.

The man was dressed in the long, dark robes Ephema knew meant he was a religious disciple of Osephetin, but not a Knight or a Journeyman. However, his robes were brown and unadorned so he did not yet have rank among his brethren. Ephema was proud of herself for realizing all of these things, but the emotion was short-lived, replaced by shock as the man skidded to a halt in front of Tabor and grabbed the Knight's hand, pressing it to his lips.

"Tabor! I mean…Knight Tabor! High Priest Calinin saw you would be returning today. He sent me to wait for the steamer, but you managed to go one way while I went the other. Isn't that just the story of our lives?" He grinned and ran a hand through his long, thick hair, setting the pale locks fluttering around his face. Ephema was surprised at how white his hair was, as he didn't look old. Without missing a beat, he turned to Ephema and bowed deeply enough that the wide sleeved cuffs of his robe brushed the ground. "And you must be the honored guest Calinin saw. How could you be anything else? You're far too lovely to be one of the Knightly hangers-ons that Knight Ianel is so fond of and Knight Tabor so annoyed by."

His words tumbled after each other in their hurry to get out of his mouth, tangling together into a merry accent she'd never experienced before. Ephema blinked, having a difficult time following everything he was saying. She looked up at Tabor and caught an odd, fond expression on the Knight's face before he covered it. He held up his hand, stopping the priest's chatter.

"Ephema, allow me to introduce you to Brother Adaman. Given a chance he will talk your ear off, but forgive him that, and you'll see he is a good sort." He turned to Adaman. "Brother, this is Ephema. She has a message for High Priest Calinin at the Temple."

Ephema inclined her head to Adaman though she was puzzled at the introduction. She didn't really have a message for the High Priest, unless he meant the vison that still made her shudder when she thought too deeply about it. Mostly she had questions, but she wasn't sure why Knight Tabor was saying so little. They hadn't hesitated to tell the Knight Proctor everything, but maybe it was different here, especially standing in the middle of the street.

Adaman nodded with a self-effacing smile. "It's true what he says good lady…" For the first time since they'd met, his gaze met Ephema's full on. She felt something strange pass between them, a sensation that made the hairs on her arms and the back of her neck prickle. It didn't seem dangerous, but it was like he was reading her down to the very soul. His eyes grew wide and his voice fell to a whisper as he muttered, "Holy Dark Father, Daughter of Light." He made an odd noise and dropped to the ground, pressing his forehead to the cobble in front of her feet, ignoring the dust and the growing heat of the day. "My Lady."

Ephema was startled by his drop and stepped back, nearly knocking into a merchant cart piled high with colorful blankets. "Tabor? What…What is he doing?"

Tabor studied Adaman for a moment, not hurrying to make him get up. "Adaman has a gift. With his sight, he is able to see into a person and help guide them down their path without error. Adaman has been blessed by the Dark One to see a person or an object's potential, at least to a degree." A wisp of a smile tugged at his face. "I believe you've terrified him."

He bent down and grabbed Adaman's robe and, with little effort, hauled the man to his feet. Tabor gave Adaman a little shake to get his attention. "Now, Brother Adaman, stop making our guest uncomfortable. You will stop making a scene in public. This is not the time or place. Am I clear?" There was no malice in his voice, but a firm finality.

Adaman shook his head, blinking a few times and finally focusing his gaze on Tabor. "I…but…she's…I…"

"By the Dark One." A full smile creased Tabor's face. "Ephema, you've done something I've never seen before." He turned and patted her on the shoulder, careful not to knock her off balance. "You've made Adaman speechless."

Adaman scowled and rubbed at a spot of dirt on his forehead. Ephema thought he meant to rub it off, but all he managed was to spread the dirt around. "You tease. She's… this changes everything."

Tabor's smiled eased, and he nodded. "It's why we brought her here. The High Priest needs to know."

"You think?!" Admana burst into laughter, shaking his head which made it look like he was in the center of a whispy snow storm. "That is quite the message. The best I've heard in ages! The High Priest is an old man. He may not survive the experience. Come, come, both of you. I'll find the most direct way there!"

The rest of the trip through the city was a much noisier affair. Adaman recovered from his shock and kept up a running commentary as they walked. Unlike Tabor's general view of the city, Adaman knew almost everything about

Hawthan and rambled on as though he couldn't stop himself from sharing his knowledge. He pointed out everything, big and little: a small garden planted in an alleyway, a fish monger to avoid because he used strange bait, a small bakery he required them to stop at because they had 'divine' biscuits, and other unique oddities that gave the city a new and distinct depth in Ephema's eyes.

Ephema didn't know if the biscuits were actually heavenly, but she had to admit they were amazing. The vendor must have expected Adaman, as he had a package of pastries at hand when the priest approached. Adaman opened the package right there and demanded Ephema try one in front of the rotund baker. She'd done so, and pleased him with her delighted expression. The biscuit was light and delicate, studded with little berries that popped on her tongue in a delightful way.

She was licking the last of the berry juice off of her fingers when Adaman directed them down a side alley. She hesitated, looking between the men and the spires of the High Temple, which they were turning away from. Her gaze fastened on Tabor. "Wait. Isn't the building we want over there?"

"Indeed, it is." Tabor pointed down the alley with the last bite of his sweetroll in hand. "However, entering by the front door at this hour would take us far too long as we made introductions, gave explanations, endured Brother Adaman's jokes..."

"Hey!"

"...and other interruptions that would take far too much time." Tabor's eyes twinkled with mirth, the first time Ephema had seen that expression in all the time she'd known him. He seemed to take great delight in teasing Adaman.

Tabor continued, as though Adaman wasn't huffing like a

steamer. "So, we're going to enter through a back door, avoiding all the noise and bustle, and quietly make our way to the High Priest. I do not know if he will be available now or we will have to wait, but waiting inside will be more comfortable. It is the route we would have taken, even if we had not been joined by such esteemed company."

Adaman settled at the title 'esteemed' and nodded, leaving Ephema wondering if the word applied to her or him. "It's wisest. When this oaf returns home there is no end to his popularity. If he walked through the main doors with a young woman in tow, regardless of your actual situation, chaos would break loose." A grin spread over his face, and he walked backward for several steps as they went. "While that would be fun, I am more interested in seeing you stand before the High Priest. I knew change was coming. I've been telling them so since the last rise of the full moon."

Ephema's brow furrowed as she listened and tried to follow his words. There were so many levels to the conversation, she was sure she was missing something. Though she wasn't sure what she should ask, even if she wanted to. "I see."

The path took them in a slow arc around the back of the High Temple to a courtyard Ephema recognized as being similar to those in Aserian and Tallet. She concluded they must base all of the small temple designs on this big one, at least where there was space to copy the construction.

Adaman stopped them at the well, drawing water so they could drink and remove any remaining stickiness from their hands and faces. He straightened the front of his robe and looked Ephema and Tabor over as though making sure they looked presentable enough to enter the temple. He nodded and strode to a small back door, rapping smartly on the wood with the attached knocker. The thick door swung back to show the face of a wizened older woman, who squinted up at him in the morning light.

"Good morning, dear Yazza. If you'll just scoot there to one side, I have Knight Tabor and a guest to see the High Priest. I'll just take them to his antechamber to wait. I know the way. He's going to want to meet this young woman as soon as possible."

The skin around her eyes wrinkled, and Yazza rubbed her nose. "This time of morning? Even for Knight Tabor it'd take some time." Her gaze landed on Ephema, and her eyes widened. She gave a soft shriek, pressing her hands over her heart. "Dark Father…Elaina… You, you're alive! You've come back to us!"

"No, Yazza. Not Elaina, but you're close." Tabor's voice was gentle as he pushed the door fully open, careful not to harm the old woman, and gestured for Ephema to go in. "But please let the High Priest know that Elaina's daughter, Ephema, has come to visit, and she would very much like to speak with him at his earliest opportunity."

Tears streaked the woman's cheeks, and she blotted at them and sniffed deeply. "A-At once!"

CHAPTER FOURTEEN

Yazza ushered the little group through the back hallways of the High Temple, which were lit by widely spaced sconces burning low pots of oil that had a soft musky scent to them. They seemed to be as much for the scent as for any light they might produce as wide windows set much higher into the wall lit the temple during the day, and covered lanterns burned at night.

There were many people moving through these hallways, all in robes or armor, but the hall was wide enough that there was never a feeling of being crowded; it was the largest building Ephema had ever been inside, and she found it beautiful and terrifying all at once. Unlike her cave, which had been close and comfortable, this space felt like it might all come down on her at once. She wasn't sure she liked it and moved closer to Tabor.

He noticed the small adjustment and smiled a reassuring smile. "Don't worry. This is the safest place for leagues in any direction."

Ephema shook her head and pushed loose hair back from her face. "It's just... It's like a hollow mountain, but it doesn't..." She searched for the words, aware that both Yazza and Adaman were listening even if they didn't look directly at her. "It feels dead."

"Well, of course it's dead." Tabor gestured to the skulls adorning his armor and bone maul. "We serve the God of the Afterlife, after all. We serve the living by helping their souls reach their proper place after they pass. You are the only one here that serves the Goddess of the Living."

Yazza's eyes widened at the statement, and the old woman's mouth moved soundlessly before she turned away, moving to push a door open leading into a central chamber. It was at the back of the temple, in the sections where the Brethren went about their work closed off from the daily visits of the faithful.

Ephema made a face at Tabor, though her shoulders relaxed slightly. "That is not what I meant. I will try not to fear."

"That's all I ask. Many things are changing for you, but it does not have to be a bad thing." Tabor's words were kind, though his pace was still quicker than his normal stride, making Ephema stretch to keep up. He held the door open for her, Adaman, and Yazza before entering last.

Two people looked up as the small group entered. The man bore a striking resemblance to Darian, though younger and with a much thinner build. His face seemed etched with a permanent frown, one which deepened in displeasure at the interruption that had entered the chamber. His voice carried nearly the same inflection as he grumbled. "Interruptions. Why is there always something interrupting?"

The woman, an older woman with silver in her hair and

time etched on her face, smiled disarmingly. "Don't mind Fressin, please. Welcome back, Knight Tabor, Brother Adaman, and esteemed visitor. To what do we owe this delightful excuse to stop staring at these interesting, but very dusty tomes?"

Fressin snarled, his brows gathering between his eyes. His thick eyebrows almost seemed to bristle as though he were an angry boar. "Don't insult the tomes! The answer's in here, I know it! We just have to keep looking. We will find a solution."

"Looking at words that move as you read might excite you, Fressin, but it makes my head hurt after the first six hours." The woman stretched, rubbing her back and nodded to Tabor and Ephema. "I am Priestess Sian, and welcome to the Hawthan Temple." Sian glanced at Ephema and her eyes narrowed in thought. "And you, my dear, look familiar. Have we met?"

Ephema blinked, the question drawing her attention away from the man who looked so much like Darian, but acted nothing like him. She remembered Darian had spoken of his family and a younger brother who loved books, but this wasn't what she'd pictured. In her mental picture Fressin had been plump and charming with spectacles, not angular and crabby.

"No. I do not think we could have met. This is my first time here." Ephema spoke up when Tabor let the silence draw out. "But, my father was a Knight. Maybe you knew him."

Sian sized Ephema up with a glance. "Mm, well, you look a bit small to be volunteering to follow in his footsteps, so you must be here for some other purpose then." Her smile took on a disarming charm. "There are, of course, plenty of other ways to serve our Lord Osephetin. Fressin here, for example, is one of our temple scholars."

"Beg your pardon, Priestess, but I don't think a Daughter

of the Eternal Mother would volunteer to join in servitude to Lord Osephetin." Tabor smiled at the look that crossed Sian's face. "She's already bound to one Goddess; I doubt she's in a position to swear fealty to another."

"What? But that's impossible. The old gods are lost, save for our Lord Osephetin."

Ephema blew a puff of air out, blowing a lock of hair away from her face. "That wasn't nice, Knight Tabor." She scolded, feeling her stomach tighten. She had kept the secret so long that it was odd hearing him share it. And what if they shared it with the wrong person? It was obvious not everyone would welcome or trust a Daughter after all that had happened with the Sisters. How would most people even know the difference?

Adaman waved a hand toward Ephema, his eyes lighting with excitement. "Oh, come now, my dear, Sian. Impossible is hardly a word a Priestess of Osephetin should be using! We deal with the impossible nearly every day of our lives. Look at her with your inner sight, with the eyes of Osephetin, and you'll see Knight Tabor's truth. Not that we should be telling just anyone, but the news will not be quiet for long among the upper echelon."

Wary, Sian's gaze went to Adaman, then to Tabor, then to Ephema and back again. "This is all very unusual, but all right. If you could look directly at me, please, my dear?" When Ephema did so, Sian looked deep into her eyes. Sian's gaze went unfocused, and, after a second, she stepped backwards with a gasp of shock, her face going pale.

"By the Dark One! An honest to the gods Daughter!" She strode forward and knelt before Ephema, taking Ephema's hands and grasping them so hard Ephema had to bite her lip to keep from crying out in pain. "Forgive me for doubting you, but given how many of your Sisters are…how do I put this?"

Sardonically, Fressin piped up from behind her, not nearly as impressed by the announcement. "Out of their minds? Twisted bitches? Lethally crazy? Am I getting close yet?"

"Well, yes. Those things. Not how I'd put it, but apt, I suppose."

Ephema glanced at Fressin, raising her eyebrows at the near accusation in his voice. "I know. We fought some on the road. They are warped. The touch of the Mother in them is tainted. It is terrible, and very sad."

"You claim you fought them? And you survived?" The disdain dripped from Fressin's voice as he crossed his arms and leaned back in his chair. "Color me doubtful, but I'd be hard pressed to see how any of you made it out of there. Unless you had lots of sacrificial friends to throw behind you as you ran away."

Tabor glared at Fressin, but the withering look had little effect on the wiry man. "We fought them, yes, though we did not defeat them. We escaped. Ephema killed two with your brother's mace before we retreated to safety."

"She did not. You can't kill those things." Fressin motioned at Tabor with his thumb. "But, you agree you fled, right?"

"Think what you will, but do not insult my truth again, or we will have more than words between us, Librarian. You'd have fared worse against their kind."

"Of course, I would have, I'm no fighter. But, I'm also not fool enough to have gone up against a group of Sisters in the first place." Fressin stood up, the noise of his chair masking the sound of the door opening in the far wall. As he talked, Darian and Lauret entered from the far side of the room behind him and walked toward the group.

"All of you are going to wind up getting yourselves killed one of these days." Fressin continued, his angry gaze trying to bore a hole through Tabor. "Whether it be from the Sisters or some of these roaming undead, I don't know, but mark my words, every single one of you is going to wind up on a slab somewhere, and it's going to be me left to perform your rites. There is nothing to be gained from all this violence. These foolhardy missions. Gah!"

He threw up his hands in disgust and shook his head. "They make me sick. The only good thing about them is all the new information you Knights keep somehow finding. But no scroll's worth losing all of these people." He slammed his fist down on the research table, looking much like his brother for an instant. "And the more information we find, the more active the Lich gets. If my mother or my brother falls on one of these missions, I'm holding each of you responsible. I swear it!"

Ephema stepped forward before anyone else could. The room felt increasingly crowded, but the anger and pain in Fressin called to her. She remembered Darian's stories about their lost father. Fressin would have been so young, and to live in a place where his family continually ventured out into danger, and he didn't know if they would come back was far too close to her own memories. She knew something of the pain of loss.

Ephema touched his hand where it rested on the table, the knuckles red with the beginnings of a bruise. With a silent prayer, soft healing magic flowed from her fingertips, wrapping around the injury. Her voice was low, and she was aware that all eyes in the room were watching her as she said, "The Lich is active because he fears your brother and his brethren. He fears what they find. He fears what someone like you will learn. So, he creates fear in others and feeds on it to help himself. Your brother and your mother would not fight so hard if they thought it was useless."

"I find it hard to believe anyone fears my brother." Fressin watched as her magic worked on his hand. "Handy, that. Is that why you survived the Sisters?"

"That's one reason. This is another." From behind him, Darian loosed his mace and placed it across Fressin's shoulder, hilt-first, so the runes were easily visible. "Her magic enchanted my mace, and made it able to kill them. Despite the odds. Can you read these symbols as well as the others you've studied?"

"Oh, you're back are you?" Fressin snipped, his cheeks turning pink with the realization he may have been overheard. He tried to focus on the shaft in front of him. "To answer your question, I certainly can't from this angle."

"Then grab it, and look at it at whatever angle you need." There was amusement in Darian's voice. "And good to hear you aren't afraid of me and care so much. Didn't know you had it in you."

"Humph." Fressin snatched the mace as Darian released it, grunting at the weight. "You moron, you could have waited until I had a better grip on it!"

"No. No, I think he released it at the right time." Lauret crossed the room and pulled Fressin into a solid hug, still wearing her full armor. She ignored his grimace and grinned at Ephema. "Don't let his sour mug fool you, Ephema. Fressin cares deeply. It just all comes out as ire."

Ephema nodded, stepping away as the family surrounded their own. It was good that they had each other, but it was a visible reminder that she would never have such a reunion with her own kin. She stood at Tabor's side, murmuring softly. "He does not believe."

"It's hard for people to believe after so long, Ephema." Tabor placed a reassuring hand on her shoulder, suppressing a chuckle at the scene before them. "For a hundred years there have been no Daughters, only the Sisters, and you saw what they are. After a while, hope for redemption has to face reality. Given what we learned in Tallet, you may meet older people here who knew your parents, but don't assume everyone will accept you and who you are, no matter how true."

Fressin pulled away from his mother, his expression shifting between irritable and pleased. He lifted the mace, not holding it like the weapon it was, but as a curiosity. He held the shaft so close to his face his nose nearly touched it. "Hrm. It's certainly enchanted, but not with Osephetin's power. I've never seen something like this. It vibrates." He glanced at Darian, stating with the finality of all younger siblings who had acquired something they wanted from a family member, "I'm keeping this."

"Wait, you are not." The tone of Adaman's voice caused everyone to stop and stare at the thin man, whose eyes were fixated on the mace in Fressin's hands. With three wide strides, he stepped forward and grabbed the mace, though he was unable to wrest it free. "By the Holy Dark Father himself, release that mace at once! I must see it!"

Fressin blinked at the sudden assault on what he had rightfully stolen. "No! Not until I've figured out the script. These are old runes, older maybe than the Fall. They should be in the library, or it'll at least point me in the right direction. Now let go!"

"Boy, you do not have the sight. You cannot see the bright power flowing out of this weapon. The sheer intensity. It shines in your hand like a beacon!" Adaman tugged at the mace ineffectually. Fressin was stronger than he looked. "Release it at once!"

"Let me play tie breaker here." Lauret reached between them and calmly took the weapon from her son, who reluctantly relinquished it. No one in their right mind would try to wrest a weapon from the High Proctor. "It is Darian's mace, so it's proper for *him* to retain it. If he offers to allow either of you to study it, you will return it to him when asked, and you will thank him. Am I clear?"

"Yes, ma'am." Fressin nodded in well-practiced habit.

"Of course, High Proctor." Adaman licked his lips and bowed low, though his gaze followed the mace as it returned to Darian's keeping. "I would never dare to question otherwise."

"Good."

Ephema shook her head as she watched the discussion. Sometimes she truly did not understand people. She opened her mouth to say something and then stopped when she noticed another door open near the back of the room. An old man who seemed so frail it was a wonder he could stand on his own waited in the entry. He touched a finger to his lips and gestured for her to come to him.

She hesitated, then saw that Tabor, too, had noticed the newcomer. The large Knight nodded and gave her a tiny push, stepping between her and the others and effectively blocking her from their sight. She didn't entirely understand, but decided it wouldn't hurt to see what the old man wanted, especially since Tabor knew who he was and seemed to trust him.

When she got to the door the man gestured her through into an adjoining room. He smiled once the door was fully closed and pulled her into an unexpected embrace. "Oh, my dear child, it is so good to see you again. It has been many,

many years since I last saw you. You've grown into a beautiful young woman." He broke the contact and looked at her face for a long moment. "You've got Elaina's eyes."

Ephema wasn't certain what to make of the greeting, stiffening at first, but the embrace felt familiar – similar to the last time she'd seen her parents and hugged them goodbye. When he spoke her mother's name she sighed, looking down to steady herself before returning his clear-eyed gaze. "That's what my father always said." She tried to smile, but it was a small thing. "I'm sorry. I don't remember you."

"I wouldn't think you would. The last time we met, you were barely four years of age, if that, and we were in a small temple many days' journey from here." The old man chuckled and led her to two comfortable chairs in a seating arrangement before a small fire. "Come. Sit." As he sat, he sighed deeply. "I know you have many questions, let me start with the easy ones. My name is Calinin. My official title here at the High Temple is that of High Priest, but I do very little in that role anymore; I'm afraid I'm not too long from my walk down the Halls of the Faithful. It keeps me from being too much help to the people these days." He smiled, wrinkles forming around his eyes. "Your father, Anceil, and my son were the best of friends. I watched the two of them grow up together."

"My...you..." Ephema stopped herself from speaking, tilting her head as she thought. "Bishop Lam. He is your son? I met him on the road. He told me about..." She cleared her throat. "He told me my parents weren't returning."

"He is, yes." Calinin motioned in the general direction of the road to Tallet. "At one point he and Anceil were going to be Knights together, but the position of a warrior never truly suited Lam. He had the ability, but was too gentle hearted. Once Anceil took up the mantle of a Knight, Lam followed my path and eventually took over the Temple in Tallet. I believe that it was Lam's decision to stay in Tallet that eventually led to Anceil's discovery of your mother. Our Lord works in mysterious ways, many which seem nothing more than coincidence at the time. But I find there are very few true coincidences in our lives." His smile came again, easy and warm. "The rest of that story you likely know very well."

Ephema watched Calinin as he spoke, his voice playing with her memories, stirring up glimpses of a past meeting she barely remembered. She nodded, meeting his gaze. "Tabor… Knight Tabor said I should leave home and come to the Temple now. When we met, Bishop Lam told me how my parents died. I wanted to go home, but it feels like there is something I should do, but I don't know." She paused, rubbing her hands over her face. "Maybe I don't want to know what it is. If I know what the world wants of me, I can't go back. Can I?"

Calinin didn't answer immediately, but after a moment he asked softly. "My son may have told you how they died, but did he tell you what your parents were trying to do?"

"A rite to make the world better."

"Yes, but that's only the beginning. There lies the real story. I wish…" He sighed and his shoulders slumped. "So many lives were lost along the way, unnecessarily and wasteful in their loss. Hindsight is a horrible mistress, Ephema."

He glanced at the door as the sounds of voices got louder again. "Still, you're here now. We cannot make the past right, but we can plan for a better future. And we will, once the din has calmed down. You are staying for a few days, yes?"

"I don't know, but I think so. My whole goal has just been to get this far, not what comes next. But, I think it would like to stay, at least for a while."

"You are traveling with young Darian and Knight Tabor. I am certain you will be here for some time. Journeyman Darian has something very important coming up, and I believe you should be there."

A soft knock came at the door. "Excuse me, High Priest. Journeyman Darian has brought the scroll and is ready to report to the council."

The High Priest sighed and nodded. "We'll continue to our discussion at a later, calmer, date, my dear. There is more you should know, however, I must meet with the council. Your arrival is welcome, but comes at a time when we are under pressure as the attacks from the undead have grown more vicious, and there is much that must be done in a short period of time."

Her gaze was drawn to the door, as the robed messenger She nodded. "What do I call you? High Priest Calinin?"

"In public that would be for the best, yes, or just High Priest as most here are want to do." He gripped her shoulder once in reassurance, though his grip was so soft she almost couldn't feel it through her shirt, then moved to open the door. "When we are in more comfortable surroundings, you may call me Calinin."

As Calinin opened the door for Ephema, he looked down and his thin eyebrows rose. "My dear, forgive me for asking, but where are your shoes?"

CHAPTER FIFTEEN

Darian stood on the steps of the High Temple, enjoying the warmth of the day and the breeze coming off of the sea. Yesterday, he'd turned over the scroll and given his report to the High Priest and the council. He'd tried to do justice to his fallen comrades and to remember every detail he could. The questions the High Priest had asked had been searching, and Darian feared he'd been found wanting, but he'd done the best he could. Now the scroll was in the hands of the Priests and the scholars. Hopefully, it held the direction they all hoped it would.

He'd hoped the High Priest would talk to him about his Knighthood, but nothing had been said. He was trying not to be upset. They'd only just arrived.

"I'll meet you both later. Tabor, Ianel, and I have a few things to discuss with the High Priest, and they're above your rank, Journeyman." Lauret's voice broke through Darian's musings, pulling him to the moment. She chuckled and tousled

Darian's hair. "You're looking very shaggy, my son. Please see to that."

He shook away his worries and found a smile for her. "Is that an official order or a mother's directive?"

"Which is more likely to get it done without backtalk?"

"Yes, Mother." Darian bowed low. "By your leave, Knight Proctor."

"Granted." Lauret glanced at Ephema. "Try your best to keep him in line, will you?

Ephema raised her eyebrows, a small smile toying about her lips. "I will try. I have not had much luck in the past." She glanced at Darian, but her gaze didn't linger or meet his, and he wondered what she might be thinking. Not that he could ask while standing before his fellow Knights and his mother.

"True." Lauret dug a small parcel out of her belt pouch and placed it in Darian's hands. "Give this to your sister. I assume you will be visiting the inn."

Darian nodded, accepting the package without question. The parcel, though small, was heavy. "Still collecting, is she?"

"She is. I found her a nice one, though she'll need to be careful with it, some of the interior is loose. Now, you two shoo, there is work to be done."

"Come on, Ephema. You heard the Knight Proctor." Darian put the parcel into his pouch and led Ephema through the Temple doors. A few of the acolytes and journeymen waved as they passed, and soon enough they were outside of the main Temple grounds, where Darian visibly relaxed. "Ooof. Well, that went better than I expected."

Ephema pulled her attention from a flower which had pushed its way up between the cobblestones near the Temple steps. She blinked, falling into step with Darian. "What went better?"

"The whole process of returning and your first visit to the temple. In addition, my brother was in a good mood. If you catch Fressin in a foul mood it will ruin your whole week." Darian grinned, pulling his mace out and inspecting the runes as they walked. "He was quite interested in this though."

"That was a good mood?" The surprise in Ephema's voice caught his attention. Her expression was filled with disbelief. She sighed. "I wish to like your family, but your brother is not nice, and your mother is very intimidating." Her attention drifted to the mace, and she tugged absently on the end of her hair, twisting it around her fingers. "He didn't believe your mace could work as I told him it did. I don't think he will want to hear how it was made."

"You'd be surprised. Fressin likes taking a mystery apart, and that means he needs facts. A lot of them." Darian put the mace away, looking up as someone called his name. He waved hello to the shopkeeper, an old family friend. "Afternoon, Jarston!"

His attention returned to Ephema. "As I was saying, Fressin will eke every detail out of you if you let him. He's a good person, just very rough around the edges. I don't know the best way to put it, but he takes the entire world as it is as a personal affront to his sensibilities, and he's made it his mission to bring down everything he sees as being wrong with it." He shrugged. "He doesn't like the idea of faith and thinks he can find the answer to every question sooner or later in a long-lost tome or scroll somewhere. That scroll I returned with will be his new passion project, I'm sure. I hope something on it will give us some concrete answers."

"Faith isn't easy for everyone. I hope he can find direction, both for himself and for others." She shuddered, as if a chill had run through her. "The High Temple feels like the mountains before a storm. Heavy with anticipation of something about to burst. No one is talking about it, but everyone feels it."

Darian blinked, shocked at the insight. "Yes. It has felt that way for months, since the Lich's attacks in the field began to grow in frequency and violence. For all that he professes that his age makes him useless, the High Priest is very blessed. Our Lord Osephetin speaks to him through his dreams, and tells him things no one could possibly know. It is a rare skill for any of His followers to have and once High Priest Calinin has gone to walk the Halls, we will miss his guidance."

Darian stopped at a fruit stand to purchase a small yellow fruit that looked like it was covered with spikes. When Ephema indicated she didn't want one, he tossed the stand owner a coin and continued. "I understand what you mean about the feeling, though I doubt I sensed it as astutely as you did. There is an underlying tone there. The priests are under far more stress than usual. I don't remember it being like that before I left. I think things have happened we're not yet being told about."

He took a bite of the fruit, pulling the spikey peel back with his teeth before biting into the fruit's flesh. The sweet taste on his tongue reminded him long it'd been since he'd had any. He chewed absently. "I wonder if it has to do with those pirates that attacked us on the way here. Undead attacking is one thing, we've been dealing with that for years. Living attackers is another issue altogether. I don't know if any of our cities is truly fortified against the living."

Ephema cast her gaze around the large buildings and raised both eyebrows. "Tall walls and heavy weaponry seem a good defense against either. They worked on the ship." She paused as she dodged a cart coming down the road with a clatter of wheels on stone, then continued with a frown, "Though I was not much use there."

Darian shouted at the driver and steadied Ephema after the cart passed. "You are not trained in warfare, Ephema. It was impressive you managed as much as you did. The walls were designed for undead. They attack and attack and attack, over and over, in straight waves. They don't normally vary their attacks much, though we've seen a few lately that challenge that. For the most part, even a force of a thousand skeletons will simply throw themselves on a barrier time and again.

"Human forces won't do that. They will go around a wall, or over it, or under it, or burn it down. The walls are effective for slowing down an intelligent attacker, but I wouldn't trust the walls to slow the foes we faced at sea much at all. They know what they are doing."

"Huh. Maybe so, but they were still beaten on the ship."

"Yes, but that was a small force, and even with your help, we lost many good men."

Ephema sighed and nodded, but she didn't continue to press the issue. She gestured toward the package he carried, changing the subject. "What did your mother give you?"

It took Darian an instant to realize what she was talking about, his thoughts still on the tall ship and the warriors they'd faced. He gave himself a little shake and chuckled. When she was curious Ephema didn't hesitate to ask about anything. He removed the fist-sized package from his pouch and unwrapped it. After a few layers, a large, dull stone was revealed, and he held it up to the light. "Alloyna asked my mother and I to keep an eye out for stones like these in our travels. I haven't seen any that weren't in a shop, but my mother's got the family luck and finds one nearly every trip."

Ephema's head cocked to one side, looking vaguely bird-like in her curiosity. She glanced at him for permission, then touched the stone, running her fingers along the ragged seam that ran around it. Her little smile finally appeared, and she laughed. "I know what this is. Crystal stone!"

"My sister calls them geodes, but it sounds like the same idea." Darian carefully manipulated the stone along the crease, and pulled it in two, splitting where Lauret had broken it apart earlier. Inside the stone, a mass of brilliant purple crystals glimmered, its beauty mesmerizing against the start dullness of the surrounding stone even though a couple of the crystals were loose. "Alloyna absolutely adores these, and she's been working for years to decorate the inn with them. Most places consider them a worthless bauble, but she doesn't let that deter her. You'll see; she's got the whole place bedecked with them. When the light is right, it's spectacular."

Ephema raised her brows and shook her head. "She is wiser than you think. The Mother's touch is in crystal rocks. My mother said they offer her protection. There were some in my cave." She murmured a soft incantation, drawing a tiny spark of power to her fingertips, the white glow he was becoming accustomed to paling her skin. She touched the crystal, blowing across the stone at the same time. It flared, warming in his hand while giving off a soft purple light.

"Well, that's new." He inspected the crystals with a smile, then capped the stones back together and wrapped it back up. "Though she doesn't have the capabilities you do, remember? She just likes them because they are pretty."

Ephema frowned and started to retort, then stopped as a feminine voice from nearby interrupted. Darian turned to see a middle-aged woman walking by, carrying her daily shopping. She smiled and repeated his name. "Darian!"

"Hey, Marana! It's good to see you! How's the husband?" He dropped the stone into his pouch, tying it off as he talked.

"Doing well. Kids are happy. Hope things are going well with your family." The woman nodded at Ephema without comment and continued walking. The groceries in her arms were large, and it was obvious she was only willing to talk while she could continue on her way.

"Same as they always are." Darian shook his head in bemusement as the woman walked away. "Take care!"

"You too, young man."

As she turned a corner, he chuckled. "This place never really changes, you know?"

Ephema watched the woman go, then returned to walking. "I do not know. Though I suppose Aserian rarely changed between my visits either. Perhaps that is similar." She glanced around with a soft sigh. "I do not think I can stay here long." She brushed her toes over the thick cobbles, the grey dust coloring her skin. "It is so big and busy."

"It's much bigger than Aserian, I'll admit, but it's not so bad. Maybe you just need to give it a little time." He pointed at a large building at the end of the block. It was a towering structure, easily two stories taller than the other buildings around it, though still smaller than the High Temple and the market buildings nearer the docks. People streamed in and out of the colorfully-painted tavern in a steady flow of movement, like an ocean of humanity. The doors were propped open as the weather was pleasant which kept them from banging open and shut constantly. "There's our destination, provided we can push our way through."

His words were interrupted by a high-pitched squeal of delight. "Darian!" A young child launched herself from a nearby stall and latched onto Darian's leg. "Darian! You're home!"

"Hah, Tanata! Yes, yes, I am." Darian scooped up the young girl, who looked to be six or seven years of age. The family resemblance was certain, as she looked more and more like her grandmother every time he saw her. The girl squealed and gripped Darian's neck in a massive hug. He grinned. "Careful. I have to be able to breathe!" He waved at Ephema. "Ephema, meet Tanata, one of Alloyna's daughters. Tanata, this is my friend Ephema, she's visiting the city for a few days."

Ephema raised her hand and wiggled her fingers in greeting. "Hello, Tanata." She pushed her hair back from her face, tucking the errant locks back under a new cloth wrap, though the mix of brown and white was still visible at her hairline and where the tips flowed out of the wrap. "How many children does your sister have?"

Tanata grinned widely at Ephema. "I have a sister and a brother. And they're both mean! So don't listen to them, okay?"

"Oh, don't be like that. Your Uncle Fressin is the grumpy one in the family. You don't need to act like him." Darian lifted Tanata up onto his shoulders. "She's the youngest of the three, and a bit wild, as you might guess. The other two usually help out around the inn, whereas this one likes to disappear into the town when no one's looking. Like I bet she did today. Again."

"The inn is boooring."

Ephema gave him the look he was beginning to recognize as meaning he'd said something she didn't understand. "She is not meant for life at an inn."

"Oh, she's not. Four walls won't contain her for long. But it does worry her mother when she vanishes." Darian waved at another townsperson. "It's not for me to decide her future, of course, given I'm not her parent, but I'm fairly certain being an innkeeper or shopkeeper wouldn't suit her at all. Would it, Tanata?"

She stuck out her tongue in disgust. "No way! Boring, boring, boring. I'm going to be a Knight! Just like Grandmama."

"You know she hates being called Grandmama, don't you?"

"But she is my Grandmama. What else should I call her?"

"Well, if you become a Knight, you'll call her Knight Proctor Lauret."

Tanata laughed. "Knight Proctor Grandmama!"

Ephema chuckled softly, peering up at the child. "If you are a Knight you must be respectful."

Tanata sighed, resting her chin on the top of her uncle's head. It was amazing how pointy a child's chin could be. "I know. I know. Everyone tells me that." She looked down at Darian from her perch. "Did you bring me anything, Uncle Darian? I saw you put something in your pouch."

"I was a little too busy for gift shopping, so no I didn't. That's a present for your mother."

"Oooh, is it a stone?" Tanata leaned over, peering down with childhood curiosity and threatening his balance. He shifted her so he wouldn't stumble. "She's got so many, but they're all pretty! What color is it inside? I hope it's green! We don't have any green ones!"

Darian adjusted his position again. "Stop wiggling or you will have to get down. And I'm sorry to disappoint you, but it's a light purple stone. It's still really pretty. Also, before you ask, I didn't find this one. Your Grandmother and her keen eye did, so she's ahead of me by like a thousand to my measly two."

"Momma says you bought your two at a market."

"Your momma's too smart for her own good, and certainly too smart for me." Darian winked at Ephema. "Because I did exactly that."

Ephema shifted to one side, stepping around someone before starting up the steps to the tavern and inn. "I have seen the green ones in my mountains." She looked away, glancing at the rising doors of the inn. "My mother told me they come from deep underground and are forced to the surface by great heats or shifting earth. They would not be found by a living sea."

"Can I give it to momma?" Tanata's voice was quiet as they approached the inn. "I snuck away before doing my chores this morning. She's gonna be mad."

"Well, Ephema is our guest, so maybe the pretty lady should decide that." Darian shrugged enthusiastically, jostling the little girl about and making her giggle. "But she's a really nice lady, so I think you've got a good chance."

Tanata turned to Ephema and screwed up her face into the best sorrowful look a little girl could know. She said, "Please? Please pretty lady, Ephema? Can I give the stone to momma?"

Ephema flushed at the compliments, and she laughed softly. "You will have to come down from there, little squirrel, and use both hands. It is not too large, but it is very heavy. I also think that an apology would do more than a stone."

Tanata was moving before Ephema finished speaking, climbing down Darian like the squirrel Ephema named her. She landed on the ground with little effort and grinned up at Ephema, both hands held up before her.

Ephema inclined her head and Darian handed the stone to her. She checked that the stone was secure in its wrappings and placed it into Tanata's hands. The little girl was off like a shot, ducking inside and weaving through the crowd of people faster than a couple of adults could hope to manage. Ephema raised her gaze to Darian, shifting out of the way as more patrons entered and exited the building. "Now what?"

"Now?" Darian waited until the way was clear and bowed to her. "Now, we enter. After you."

As they entered, the din of conversation was like walking into a wall made of sound. People were milling about, waiting for tables to be cleared by the throng of staff that moved expertly between patrons. Each table was adorned with at least two or three geode stones, broken in half and arranged to display their crystals in all their beauty. Other small geodes were settled on every window panel, sending multicolored rainbows dancing along the ceiling.

Against the far wall, a large wooden bar was surrounded by constant motion as a large, older man took orders and barked instructions to his people. His apron was well-used but clean, and the hair on his arms as silvered as that on his head. His hands still showed skill and strength as he popped open barrels and slung mugs of dark beer and pale ales for the patrons. Beside him, a younger woman that also bore a resemblance to Darian gave assistance, removing empty cups from the bar and shuttling food from the kitchen to the barmaids.

Ephema came to a stop a few feet into the room, her green eyes wide as the noise crashed around them. Her gaze darted around, and her breath caught. "It's…" Her voice was almost lost, and Darian leaned closer to her. "It's so loud. This is a bad idea."

"It's all right, Ephema." Darin slipped an arm around her shoulders. "It's loud, but I promise you are safe." Inwardly, he swore. He'd hoped the place wouldn't have been so busy, just this once. He wanted her to like it, but he should have known that so much noise and so many people in an enclosed space would make her uncomfortable. "If we just get across the way, there's a room in the back that will be quieter. Can you do that or do you want to go back? Maybe we can meet Alloyna later."

She looked up at him and took a deep breath, her shoulders straightening. "A room. Yes. I can do that. I just can't stay in the crowd. I hear their words, their hearts, their breathing, their lives."

Darian nodded and gave a little smile, reluctantly releasing her. "Just stay next to me and I'll make a path." He offered his arm which she grabbed onto, her grip showing her discomfort more than anything else about her. He admired her courage and squeezed her hand where it rested on his arm, then plunged into the crowd, nodding at familiar faces, but not pausing until he reached the bar. Darian waved at Alloyna, but kept going, past the bar toward a storage room where he knew it'd be quieter.

Alloyna gave him a curious look, waving over someone to take her position and opening the door for Darian and Ephema. She followed them into the storeroom, carefully setting aside a few discarded food items that had fallen off the shelves. "Well, this is new. Welcome home, Darian, and hello to whomever this is?"

Ephema took a deep breath and let go of Darian's arm, leaning back against one of the shelves. "I'm sorry. Each city we have come to has been bigger and louder, but not so confined like this." She shook her head. "And all the stones, so pretty, but I hear echoes of heartbeats and breath and words through them."

She made herself stop and look at Alloyna, her brow creasing as she studied Darian's sister. Another geode on a nearby shelf flared, casting a pale blue shadow. Ephema sank down onto an unopened bag of wheat. "And you are two."

"I am what now?" Alloyna blinked as the geode flared, raising her hand to shield her eyes. "Oh! Darian, who is this woman you've brought to us? I didn't think a Priestess of Osephetin could affect geodes. Come to think of it I didn't know geodes could do that."

"A Priestess of Osephetin can't." He paused, considering all he knew about his sister before offering softly. "But a Daughter of the Eternal Mother can. She says the Mother's touch is in geodes, and they seem to amplify her usual senses." He watched Ephema settle. "That would explain what you're hearing and why it's hitting you so hard."

Alloyna's eyes widened in disbelief tinged with hope. "That is not possible. A Daughter? And not a Sister? How are you not affected with the madness?" She knelt, placing her hands on Ephema's knees. "There are many that still try to follow our Lady's ways, even if we dare not worship Her. My brother gave me a few tomes about our poor Goddess and the path of worship. It's such a shame what has happened. How is it that you escaped? You are too young to have been alive when the Goddess went mad."

Ephema's hands closed over Alloyna's, and the stone on the shelf sparked again, vibrating against the wood. "I was born this way, protected by my parents and a mountain." She tilted her head, watching Darian's sister for a long moment before she spoke again. "You may know more about the Goddess than I do, at least what tomes and book learnings might say. I know only the stories my mother told and the truths that whisper in my heart."

Alloyna sighed. "There are many that would love to hear her as you do. But none of us dare try a formal prayer or ritual. We can't. All that have ever tried to contact the Mother end up dead -- or worse." She frowned. "The Lich took so much from her, and her faithful still want to help. We feel her in our hearts, but we just… there's nothing we can do. It's so frustrating."

"I understand." The whispered words caught Darian's attention, and he stared as the glow he associated with her divine magic rose along Ephema's hands and danced down along his sister's skin. Ephema blinked, the color drawn away from the irises of her eyes, making her look as though she'd gone blind. When she spoke it was her voice, but yet not, reinforced by a second, deeper voice that he heard in his mind as well as his ears. "Alloyna, you are blessed with the heart of a believer. I accept your worship, and I bless you with my grace."

"Blessed Mother." Alloyna turned her face toward Ephema's, her voice trembling almost as much as her hands.

"You may not have been able to worship me as you should. None of you have. But I have remained in your thoughts, in your lives, your deeds, and your hearts. Your belief has sustained me when nothing else has." Ephema smiled at Alloyna. Darian was certain it wasn't his friend, but the Goddess herself speaking. "Continue as you have. Watch to the dawn for my light. The day will soon come when I will call upon the faithful for their strength. Prepare the way."

Alloyna nodded, unable to speak as tears streamed down her face.

The glow eased, and Ephema sagged on the sack, which threatened to dump her on the floor. She pulled her hands away from Alloyna, pressing them to her temples. "Darian. My head hurts. What just happened?"

Darian released his breath, only then realizing he'd been

holding it. "As far as I can tell, the Goddess spoke to Alloyna through you. Lord Osephetin uses some of his followers as his mouthpiece from time to time, but I didn't think the Goddess would be strong enough to do so through you, even if she wanted to. But maybe there is something about this place, or about Alloyna that allowed it to happen." He crouched beside Ephema and placed a hand on her leg in reassurance. "Are you all right? Do you need anything? It's pretty draining when that happens to one of our faithful."

"I'm very tired, and my head hurts." She patted the still kneeling Alloyna's hair before covering Darian's hand with hers. "Water. And can I lay down somewhere? Just for a minute?"

"There are rooms upstairs reserved for the staff and family." Darian glanced at Alloyna, whose face was still wet with weeping. "Can I take her there?" When she nodded, still not speaking, he sighed. "Come on, snap out of it, Alloyna. I know this is a big deal, but I need you to help me get her upstairs so she can rest. Please?"

"Yes. I can do that." Still stunned, Alloyna rose on unsteady feet to help. Soon enough, the trio made their way up the wide staircase, the siblings leaving Ephema in a quiet room where she dropped into slumber as soon as her head found a pillow.

CHAPTER SIXTEEN

"In the mountains. Seriously." Alloyna shook her head and took another swig of ale. The traffic in the common room had slowed now that they were between mealtime rushes, and she and Darian were catching up on everything that had happened. "And you just fell into her cave?"

"Not quite. I fell near her cave, and she rescued me from some undead that I'd been fighting. I'm still not sure why they turned away from us, because they had me dead to rights. I think it's because there was something sacred about her home, but I've never really taken the chance to talk to her about it." Darian shrugged, picking up the last of the biscuits from his plate and biting into it. His sister's biscuits were delicious; warm and flakey with little bits of ground spices. "We've had a lot going on, and I'm not sure the 'why' is as important as the fact they stopped and I survived."

"Yeah. I bet." Alloyna slapped Darian gently on the shoulder. "No matter how it happened, I'm glad you survived and that you found her. It's nothing short of a miracle."

"A timely miracle, at that." Lauret's voice started Darian, as she approached from behind, slipping into a nearby stool.

Alloyna leaned across the counter and gave Lauret a hug. "I'm glad to see you're home and in one piece."

"You and me both. Had a few scares along the way, though your brother proved to be helpful. Him and the girl, Ephema." Lauret looked up as someone called her name, and caught the mug of ale that slid down the bar. "Thanks, Karlton! You're a good man, no matter what my daughter says about you."

"Hah!" The older man grinned, showing a missing tooth, but the lack didn't make his smile any less welcoming. "It better not be nothin' good, if she knows what's good for her! I gotta reputation to keep up."

Lauret laughed and saluted the big man. "Indeed." She took a big swallow of the ale and set the mug down with a satisfied sound. "So, what are we talking about?"

"Ephema." Darian jerked a thumb toward Alloyna. "She and Alloyna had a bit of a chat earlier."

"Oh, I hoped you would." Lauret leaned in and continued, "I hadn't told her that you were looking for ways to follow her Goddess, but I thought you'd have a lot to discuss."

"Yes. Well, you could say that." Alloyna shot a knowing look at Darian. "I'm still trying to piece through everything she said. Especially that first bit. She said, 'and you are two' when she first met me. That's got me thinking…"

Lauret's brows rose. "No. She didn't!" She pulled the ale mug out of Alloyna's hands, setting it next to her own. "Between you and that husband of yours, we'll never run out of new recruits! Though you shouldn't feel like you have to repopulate the world all on your own."

Alloyna blinked and glanced at the purloined mug, looking confused for another instant before realization flooded her expression. She pressed her hand to her flat stomach. "But, I'm not late."

Darian shrugged, taking his sister's mug from his mother and draining it. "Do you want to argue that point with a Daughter of the Goddess of Life? She could hear people's heartbeats in here. If I was a betting man, I'd put my coin on Ephema being right on the mark, and start thinking of names."

"I…" Alloyna rubbed the middle of her forehead. "I told Oerin that I had a surprise for him. This was not what I meant. Though I don't think he'll be unhappy." She smiled widely as the anticipation of the future set in. "Oh, I hope it's a boy! He's always wanted another son."

A soft squeak came from the floorboards as Ephema descended the stairs. While she had rested for nearly an hour, she still appeared tired to Darian. He jumped up, pulling out a stool for her. Once she was seated, he retook his seat and said, "Feeling any better?" Darian motioned toward Karlton. "Need me to order you anything to eat or drink? The food here is fantastic, even the stuff my sister cooks, honest."

Alloyna swatted Darian's head. "You stop that, or I'll have you on dish duty for a week."

"Oh no, not dishes." Darian pantomimed fear with his hands near his head. "I've faced the undead and pirates, even the Sisters, but not the dishes! You evil woman, you."

Ephema leaned heavily against the counter, shaking her head as she watched the interplay of the siblings. "Food. Yes. Food would be welcome. If there is bread, I would like that." She rubbed her eyes, giving herself a shake. "It has been an odd day."

"I'll get you something." Alloyna squeezed Ephema's hand

and, after a final mock glare at Darian, disappeared into the back kitchen.

Lauret took a large draw of the ale. "Mmm. I've missed that burn. So, Ephema, what are your plans now? I know you want to speak to the High Priest again, and that he has words for you."

"I do not know. There are things I wish to talk about, yes, but…" She ran her fingers along the table, watching the way the light moved on the polished wood. "I cannot stay here. I did not leave my home merely to find a new one, but because Tabor was convinced that I was needed here. I need to figure out why."

"That makes sense. But you will be here for a few days, yes?" When she nodded, Lauret smiled. "Good. There's something you'll want to observe tomorrow. On the same note, Darian, the High Priest has a very important matter he'd like to discuss with you this evening."

"There is?" Darian pulled his attention away from Ephema. "If it's about the scroll I don't know that I have much more to say. I gave them my report and turned the scroll over to Fressin. I'm sure he's working on deciphering it as we speak. I doubt I'll be much help there. That's always been his expertise, not mine."

"It is about the scroll, but it's also about many other things. And I shall say nothing else except that I am very proud of you." Lauret's smile brightened, and she lifted her mug in salute.

Darian's mind spun, latching onto the possibility he almost didn't dare hope for despite the assurances he'd received from Ianel and Tabor. Was it possible his days as a Journeyman of Osephetin were finally at an end?

Ephema sat on the narrow cot in her borrowed room, leaning her head against the wall and listening to the silence of the Temple. Alloyna had offered her a room at the inn, but Ephema had chosen to return to the High Temple with Darian. Alloyna was a very kind woman, however, the inn was so full of noise and people that even walls didn't cut the din enough. The way the woman looked at Ephema was also more than a little embarrassing. It was as though she expected the Goddess to speak again at any moment, or for Ephema to do something amazing, and Ephema didn't have anything to offer. She didn't know how the first amazing thing had happened.

As nice as it was, it was also strange to be surrounded by so much silence. It didn't feel like there had been many moments of peace since she'd first found Darian outside her cave. He and his fellow Knights had changed her life. She was mostly certain this was a good thing, despite the moments which had been frightening or difficult. One thing for certain, she knew she couldn't ever go back.

The bells in the tower chimed, the sound distant though they were housed in the Temple too. She counted under her breath. Six bells. It was still very early. She should be sleeping, but sleep eluded her, and she didn't know why.

She'd been able to speak to High Priest Calinin for a moment before he'd taken Darian into his chambers, but it hadn't been enough. He had promised he would make more time to talk to her about her parents and, more importantly in Ephema's mind, about what she should do next. He must have something in mind, but there hadn't been an opportunity to spend more than a moment with the man. If he sent her away somewhere would Darian and Tabor come with her? Or would she go alone? Would there be someone else entirely to work with? And what would they have her do anyway? She didn't know how such things were arranged, and she didn't want to travel with strangers. But she felt too restless to just stay at the High Temple.

She slipped off the cot and paced the small room. She wished she had a better understanding of what was happening in the world, and her place in it. It felt like she was walking while blindfolded, and while she'd been glad enough to keep moving toward Tabor's goal of the High Temple, but now that they were here, she wasn't satisfied with stumbling along. She just didn't know how to change it.

A soft knock came at the door, and Ephema stopped pacing, surprised. "Yes?"

The door opened, and Priestess Sian entered with another younger woman in tow. She smiled gently at Ephema. "Good morning, Ephema. This is Priestess Kadama. Did you sleep well last night?"

Ephema nodded to both of the women, wondering why they were here so early. "Good morning. I think so. The beds are very nice." She cocked her head to the side, maybe the High Priest had time to speak to her. It wouldn't surprise her to learn he rose early. "Is there a reason you are here? That is…I was not expecting anyone."

"Not expecting." Sian blinked, touching her fingers to her lips. "Oh, my dear, did no one tell you what was happening today?"

"No. What is happening?"

"It is Journeyman Darian's Knighting ceremony, and you are among the few invited to attend. I thought Knight Proctor Lauret would have told you."

"I haven't seen her since last night. She said there was

something I should see, but nothing more." Ephema rubbed her hands together, not sure whether to be worried or excited. Darian, Tabor, and Ianel had spoken about him being knighted, but never gone into detail about what that meant or exactly when it would happen.

Kadama settled on the bed with a deep sigh. She peered out from underneath her crimson hair, which fell over her eyes, and grimaced. "I don't like watching these things, myself. They're creepy. Are you sure I can't return to the library and help Fressin instead? That scroll he's working on is the most important thing the High Priest has asked of us. I should be there instead of at another knighting."

Sian sighed, and Ephema decided they had been having this argument all morning. "No, Kadama, it's important we attend. We are there as witnesses of Lord Osephetin's will, and to support the Knight Proctor in her son's ascension to a Knight. You know this."

"Just in case. I know."

Ephema's brow creased at the interplay, confusion welling up in her. "In case of what? It is just a ceremony, yes? The High Priest will ask questions. Darian will answer, and he will be given his armor and Knighted."

Kadama laughed, and the look of contempt on her face made Ephema decide she didn't like the woman. "A bit of an innocent, are you? We serve the God of the Dead, little girl." She stood and sighed, wringing her hands. "Lord Osephetin is a just god, but do not let that deceive you into thinking he is a nice god. Those that tread on His path know that His will is both that of Justice and Vengeance."

She glanced at Ephema. "I'm guessing that you've never even heard about the Knighting Ceremony. Journeymen that go into the ceremony with the proper respect, preparation, and dedication become Knights. Journeymen that go into the ceremony that are not true to the path go on to meet Osephetin himself to answer for their failures."

The woman's tone struck at Ephema's heart, drawing not fear, but a protective anger she had only felt during the battle with the Sisters. She stepped up to Kadama until they were very nearly touching. "Then it is a good thing Journeyman Darian is well prepared. And a better thing that you have no need to be there." Her gaze darted to Sian. "She should return to the library if that is what she wants. I will serve in whatever way might be needed."

Sian's smile turned sharp. Ephema thought she was enjoying the shocked look on Kadama's face. "Much as it would please me to let my sister go play with the books, her presence is required as much by tradition as by necessity. The Ceremony will draw from all of the Faithful present, and though she might squawk, I assure you Priestess Kadama's faith is unshakable."

She gently took Ephema's hand. "Your presence there will be a remarkable one, but your invitation is extended as a guest, not as a participant. It would be inappropriate to involve you further, and I have to warn you that you will not be allowed to interfere." Her long fingers squeezed Ephema's. "I know the Knight Proctor's son very well, and any that know him don't have any doubts about today's ceremony. Some people simply would do well to spend time with members of the Knight Proctor's family beyond Fressin."

Ephema pulled her hands away, not ready to be mollified. The sense of disturbance in her grew, and it took effort to beat back anger and impatience. She took a few steps away, closing her eyes and wrapping her hand around the globe that hung at her neck. She breathed in and out, seeking calm. She knew she would be of little good to Darian if she stood at his Knighting filled with anger. A whispered prayer passed her lips and warmth filled her body. She opened her eyes and inclined her head to the Priestesses of the Death God. "Lead the way."

∽

"ENTER, JOURNEYMAN DARIAN!" The voices echoed and roared, heard almost from within the mind and not from outside, though they touched his ears too. Wordlessly, Darian walked down the short hallway, his new armor gleaming in the flicker of torchlight. The fitted plates clung to him, though their weight and flexibility was still as yet unfamiliar. This armor was not the armor of a trainee; this was the intricate, jointed armor of a full-fledged Knight of Osephetin, though no bone yet adorned the dark plates. His mace was strapped firmly to his waist, the runes sparking faintly in the low light. He entered the ceremonial chamber and walked through the ankle-deep sand to the center of the room, where a single dark stone pedestal shot through with silver veins stood raised to chest height, waiting for him.

On top of the stone, a single finger bone lay on a square of black velvet, glowing faintly blue with eldritch energy and pulsating with magical life. The voice continued, "Journeyman Darian, you wish to become a Knight of Osephetin, to swear yourself to his service until your bones return to the dust from whence they came?"

"I do." The response wasn't necessary, but Darian spoke anyway. He'd spent the morning in meditation and cleansing, using every second since the High Priest had told him it was time to begin.

"Are you prepared to be judged in body and soul?"

"I am." Darian's voice, calm and firm, echoed through the enormous chamber. He'd been preparing for this day for years, and the events of the last few weeks had only strengthened his resolve. There was so much evil in the world. He wanted to fight it, and he needed the additional strength and power of being a full Knight. He had never been more ready than he was now.

Dark shadows crept through the open arena, setting the high torches to flickering, their golden light dimming to echo the blue of Oesphetin's divine power. A Knight, shrouded in armor that showed nothing of his or her skin or eyes, strode from the tunnel, approaching with steady steps. Darian swallowed hard and drew the mace from its place at his waist, flexing his fingers around the shaft as it vibrated in his hand.

The Knight didn't speak, but swung a thick baton studded with metal bits, warming up. Darian turned away from the pillar with a silent prayer, facing the Knight who would test his skills. He had no chance of winning this spar, that wasn't the point. It was a test to see what he'd learned, not to see if he would win.

There were no words, no taunting, or elaborate explanation or instruction. The Knight attacked with full force and power, his baton slamming into Darian's mace and bouncing off his armor with each punishing strike. Like any good teacher, the Knight knew all of Darian's strengths and weaknesses. He highlighted the former and punished the latter, driving Darian around the chamber without mercy. Darian struck back as often as he could, but in general it was all he could do to keep himself from taking too much damage, each impact painful. The baton didn't rip and slice like a sword, but it jarred bones, bruised flesh, and put dents into the armor which had been new just minutes ago.

Darian didn't know how long the fight went on, caught in the rhythm of dodge, parry, and attack. He felt like he was at least holding his own until a misstep opened his stance, and the Knight swept Darian's feet out from under him. He landed badly one arm trapped beneath his body. He tried to swing with the other, but the Knight knocked his mace aside and swung at Darian's face.

Darian braced himself from the pain he knew was coming, but didn't look away.

The blow stopped a fraction of an inch from his head as the voice filled the chamber again.

"Enough! The applicant has been found: Worthy."

His opponent stepped back, bowing before offering Darian a hand and pulling him to his feet. Darian wished he could tell who was behind the armor and the eye veil, but it was forbidden to ask or even attempt to find out. The Knight left as he had come, leaving Darian alone in the chamber.

He took a moment to catch his breath before again approaching the pillar. Everything hurt, but he did his best not to show it. He couldn't stop now, even though his legs shook from pain and exertion. If he asked to stop, his trial would be over. He would fail.

As he approached, seven matching pedestals rose soundlessly from the sands around him, surrounding him in a perfect circle. Upon each stone lay another single finger bone, and each bone pulsed with the same divine energy.

Once all eight pedestals had ceased moving, the voice spoke again. "What is your place in this world?"

The question boomed through his ears and mind. The answer was standard, but the test wasn't about the words he spoke, but the path they opened into his heart. Without hesitation, he barked, "To give my life in servitude to Osephetin, our

Lord of Death, that I may be his hands in the struggle for balance between life and death in this world of chaos. So I might be his scythe, his hammer, his hand, and his shield in this time of need, and when I die, to carry on his fight in the afterlife at his side for eternity."

"So it has been spoke, so you will be judged." The voice dropped low, and before Darian, the eight finger bones moved. Each bone shook violently until, with a snarl of magic, they snapped in two. A gust of wind picked up, pulling a cloud of dust off of the floor and obscuring the stones. It only lasted a few seconds and when the wind died, there were now two complete finger bones on each velvet drape, glowing more brightly than before.

The voice returned. "You are found: Honest. What do you stand for in this world?"

Again, a common question. He knew the answer. Darian replied in the same tone as before, fighting down the butterflies that wanted to escape his stomach. He could not doubt, or he would fail. "I stand for the people. I stand for those who cannot stand for themselves. I give voice to those that cannot or will not speak for themselves. I will be the oasis, the refuge, the last to fall, the first to rise. I am the candle in the dark to lead the people back into the light. I stand for the Will of Osephetin."

An electric burst of power and pain shot up from the ground through his feet all the way to his head. He stumbled, but forced iron into his legs and spine so he wouldn't fall.

"So you are judged." As before, the finger bones trembled, more violently this time. When they shattered, they fragmented into thousands of pieces, scattering off of the stones and into the sand below. The wind returned, lifting the sand into the air, obscuring his vision completely.

Darian fought to breathe, squinting against the stinging sand as it abraded the skin on his face. When the wind abated, eight fully-formed skeletal knights stood in a circle around Darian, their pedestals gone.

Each knight wore the soul armor of the Knights of Osephetin that they'd worn in life, grasping soul weapons in their hands. A circle of the past, come to judge the future. They stood silently, dark magic with flickering sparks of brighter blue dripping from their eye sockets and vanishing as they fell. The silence drew out and finally the voice intoned, "You are judged: Committed. What is your motivation?"

This was the question all potential Knights knew and feared. A simple question, but one which required soul seeking. Answering without total honesty and openness would result in death. Darian met the eye sockets of the skeleton that stood before him with a steady gaze. "Initially, my motivation was simple duty. I was following in my mother's footsteps, knowing how much she did to make life better for others. Like her, I felt a duty to protect the people of this land…then my convoy of friends and fellows was destroyed, and I burned with sorrow and guilt. The need to revenge my fallen comrades."

He glanced to where he hoped Ephema was watching, even if he couldn't see her. How could he explain everything that had happened so few weeks? "Now? Now my motivation is simpler. My motivation is to follow the will written on the surface of my heart. I am to guard she that could bring peace to our world, and through my life or death, ensure she is kept safe from all harm along her path whatever that may be. So my motivation is duty, a passion to protect, to do the will of our Lord, and to free our people from the tyranny of the Lich."

The last word echoed through the chamber, and Darian

felt magic infuse his being, a scorching power that dove deep into his soul, examining him with holy fire until he felt he might come apart. He shook so hard he nearly dropped his mace, and it was more than a full minute before the voice rose again. "So you are judged." The voice was quiet. The eight skeletons stared at Darian for a long time, unmoving; then, as one, they fell to one knee, a pose of respect. "The applicant is found…"

Darian held his breath, his fingers flexing inside the unfamiliar gloves. The muscles of his thighs spasmed, and he wanted desperately to just sit in the sand and recover.

"Worthy."

At the last word, the skeletal knights exploded, sending a shower of bone flying through the air. The bones circled Darian in an ever-tightening whirlwind, blue tendrils of magic arcing between the fragments. Lances of light shot out of his armor, snagging bone out of the air and pulling it in where it fused to the metal plates.

Smaller bones reinforced joint pieces and lined the edges of smooth plates. Larger bones spread across wider sections which were vulnerable to attack. Stretched kneecaps appeared high on his shoulders, and a large skull wrapped itself around Darian's helmet, dropping around his face to form the protective visor of a fully sworn Knight. Bone ringed Darian's kite shield, a pattern of knuckles embedding themselves around a thick spike.

Darian held out his right hand with the mace grasped firmly in it. The runes that Ephema had etched in it pulsated in time with the magic around him. To his amazement, the head of the mace melted away, the molten slag simply vanishing into the sands. Tendrils of magic snaked out of the runes nearest the top of the weapon and darted down into the sand, raising another skull.

The skull was screaming, its jaw hung slack, open and dripping with a mixture of blue and white eldritch energy. Deadly spikes grew through the skull at regular intervals, and the runners of magic wrapped around the bone securing it to the mace's hilt, seating it with one last flash of white energy. The magic began to withdraw, and Darian felt a surge of warmth move into his hand and through his body, filling him completely, taking away his pain and weariness. He had only a moment to realize he'd never seen another knight leave his ceremony healed. It usually took days for them to recover.

With his weapon and armor now formed, the ceremony wound to its end.

"Make your oath!"

Darian stripped the glove from his right hand as the main pillar rose again from the floor. This time there was no bone, but a carving of the complex sigil of Osephetin. It was ornate, but compact, no bigger than the palm of his hand. He took a deep breath and covered the carving with his hand. It flashed with blue flame, and his skin burned. The pain he'd known up to this point was nothing compared to the searing of his skin and soul.

"I...so...swear."

A DOOR OPENED in the far wall, and Darian strode out, confident his greeting on the other side would be a warm one. His helmet hung on a hook at his waist, making it easier to see. Knight Tabor and Knight Proctor Lauret approached with Ephema between them. Tabor smiled widely upon seeing

Darian, and he strode forward, gripping Darian's hand firmly. "I knew you'd make it, my friend. Never had a doubt."

"Thank you. I mostly worried about that last question." Darian smiled gently at Ephema. "That one actually turned out to be the easiest."

Ephema's answering smile was small, but warm. "You have a good heart and know your duty. Now everyone else knows that too." She shook her head. "Though I'm not sure I would ever want to watch that again. It was not comfortable."

Lauret chuckled. "Osephetin's ways take some getting used to for outsiders, I will admit that." She joined Darian, kissing his brow. "I know you had it in you. Your father is very proud of you. I hope you know that."

"I know." Darian went to say something else, but his stomach chose that moment to gurgle as the waning stress of the trial eased. He grinned sheepishly. "Sorry. There's not much eating during meditations."

"Just like your father, stomach forward." Lauret shook her head, but smiled fondly on her son. "Come on, Knight Darian. Let's get you something to eat."

"Yes, Ma'am!"

CHAPTER SEVENTEEN

Ephema made her way back to her small room at the Temple, feeling slow and heavy with too much food in her belly. She'd tried something Alloyna called hard cider, and even though she'd only had a few sips, it'd left her head feeling odd. Ephema couldn't say she had enjoyed the evening at the inn. It was too crowded and loud. She was certain Darian had a good time though, and that ultimately was what mattered. He was well known and loved by many in the city despite his time away training, and they were excited to see him take this step in his Knighthood. Ephema was…she paused to think about it. Proud was as good of a word as she could think of to describe her feelings. She had been certain Osephetin wouldn't reject Darian as a Knight. He was devout and dedicated and brave, all the things a good Knight should be.

He'd been in his element at the inn, juggling many conversations and giving time and a share of his attention to everyone. Ephema had watched from behind the bar, where she'd found some level of safe haven from the noise and the crush. So many people together set her on edge. She could feel them breathing, the blood racing through their bodies, the sounds of life adding to the chaos. She remembered sometimes feeling this way before, but it had never struck her as much as it did here and when it had been the worst, she had been able to retreat to her cave until it went away. Here there was little respite.

Darian had tried to draw her into the excitement of the evening, but she felt uncomfortable being in the middle of things. His family had wanted his attention, and she knew it was the right thing to let them have him. Privately, she admitted she didn't care for some of the attention he got from the girls who worked at the inn, especially the one who kept sitting on his lap. He didn't look comfortable with her, but it irritated Ephema all the same.

She sighed and sat on her cot, tucking her feet up under her. She was tired and yet wide awake all at once with an ache behind her eyes that promised to become a headache. With a little adjustment, she turned so that her back rested against the wall, and she wouldn't fall over. She didn't think she could lay down without triggering the threatening pain. She took off her necklace and cradled the globe in her hands, resting them in her lap. Ephema breathed in and out, closing her eyes and opening herself to the peace of her own breath and heartbeat.

Her mother had never taught Ephema formal worship, fearing it might bring unwanted attention, but this contemplation came close. It was all about calming yourself and opening your mind to the living world around you. With so many changes in her life, it had been too long since Ephema had really had much of a chance to even think about such things.

Usually, her winters were full of time to connect with herself and the Goddess, but here it didn't even snow and life tumbled on at a breakneck speed.

She rubbed her fingers along the silken stone, slowly turning the globe as she cleared her mind. She reached out, feeling for the life around her. She saw the twitching noses of the tiny mice that crept through the walls of the temples and felt the tapping legs of creeping spiders. On the rooftops, she heard the sleepy sighs of nesting swallows. She felt the whispering steps of the priests as they went about their duties, and the soft breath of those who slept. In the heart of the High Temple, the Eternal Flame called out to her, burning with a life of its own.

The globe between her fingers came to life, filling the room with white light and rising until it hovered a few inches above her hands. At first, the light was gentle, white ribbons caressing Ephema's skin and darting about the room, but it didn't stay that way. Her brow furrowed as the light grew hot and painful, and the calm of her meditation exploded with images she couldn't control. Soft whimpers escaped her lips, followed by screams.

DARIAN AWOKE from disturbing dreams he didn't remember to Tabor standing at his bedside. When Tabor spoke, his voice was deep and concerned. "Dress quickly. We are needed at the High Temple. Something has happened to Ephema."

Darian was up and moving before Tabor finished speaking. It took him a moment to get into the unfamiliar armor despite it being designed for quick donning, but Tabor helped him with the more unwieldy pieces and soon enough he was ready. He picked up his mace and grimaced. The runes on the mace glowed fiercely, light shining out of the eyes of the skull. "That's new."

Tabor shook his head, barely sparing a glance for the enchanted weapon. "It is touched by both the Goddess and by our Dark Lord now. I do not think we can guess how it will react to anything." He pushed the door open, the only other sounds in the inn the tick of shifting walls and the snap of the banked fire. Darian wondered briefly where Tabor had come from and how he'd gotten into the inn, but that seemed a foolish question right now. Tabor waited until they exited the building then broke into a trot, which was impressive for the large man, much like watching a draft horse gallop.

Darian kept pace easily, his new armor already starting to become comfortable and familiar. Osephtin's will reduced the weight of the armor, but it still was an adjustment. He couldn't fight the worry that surged through him with each step. "What happened, Tabor?"

"No one knows." Tabor kept up the pace, the High Temple a good distance from the inn even without the daytime crush of people and animals. "Priestess Sian heard her screaming. Now she will not wake."

Darian's gut clenched and he nodded, dropping the conversation so they could run faster. What few people were out this time of night gave the two Knights wide berth; it was obvious they were in a hurry, and it was never wise to step in front of an armored Knight at full steam.

When they arrived at the High Temple, the doors were already open for them. An acolyte stood by the door, waving them entry. Darian didn't so much as glance at the man as he pounded up the stairs, overtaking Tabor and passing him. He knew the way to the room where Ephema was housed, and Tabor would catch up.

Kadama stood by the door to Ephema's room, holding it open as Darian approached. He didn't stop until he stepped inside, skidding to a halt. Sian knelt by the bed, trying to rouse Ephema, but every time she touched the unconscious woman a bolt of white magic arched into her, making Sian yelp with pain.

Ephema's hands were closed into fists, her body twisting and writhing as though she were possessed. Though she was unconscious, she spoke a steady stream of words barely above a whisper, the words in a language Darian did not understand. Her face twisted into a contorted expression that was a combination of concern, pain, and fear. The orb that normally rested calmly around Ephema's neck hovered in the center of the room, nearly touching the ceiling, casting a pale white-blue light over everything.

Tabor stepped in after Darian, frowning at what he saw. "We need Adaman." The words were spoken only loud enough for Darian to hear before the Knight turned and left.

"Why do we need..." Darian turned, but the man was already gone. "Adaman. Priestess Sian, do you have any idea what's going on?"

Sian took in a deep breath as she rose and stepped back from the cot. "I have never seen anything like this, but I have seen priests in communion with our Lord Osephetin and there are some similarities. If it is the Goddess trying to tell her something, the message is not clear. She is hurting, and I fear for her. Perhaps this is what the beginnings of her Goddess's madness looks like." She paused, rubbing her hands together, the skin red and raw from her attempts to help. "Fetching Adaman may be a good idea. He has experience with Osephetin's visions and interpreting dreams."

"Madness. No, it can't be that." He looked up at Sian. "How long has she been like this?"

A look of shame touched the older woman's face. "Too long. Hours maybe. When I found her, she was screaming, but it had been so long she was hoarse and soon after she lost her voice. The whispers are all she has. The High Priest sensed there was something wrong and sent word, but it was not acted on quickly enough."

Darian crossed the room and sat beside Ephema, careful not to touch her. The globe flashed, its light warming faintly as the frenetic spinning slowed. Ephema's muttering continued, though he thought he heard her speak his name at least once.

Sian peered at the globe with interest. "It changed when you approached, that has to mean something. Careful. Don't touch her."

Darian nodded, slipping into silence as he watched Ephema's struggles. Though it seemed like an eternity, it wasn't long before the sound of footsteps echoed in the hall again, and he looked up as Tabor reentered the room, breathless.

"Did you find Adaman?"

Tabor was saved from answering the question by Adaman bustling into the room after him. The priest looked disheveled, dressed in a plain tan tunic and brown britches without the robes of his office. His white hair tangled around his face and shoulders in a way that made him look like he'd been struck by lightning. He pushed his way around Tabor and stood in front Sian, staring at the odd scene. "Oh my. Yes, this is a problem."

Darian stood and took three steps forward, stopping under

the hovering globe. "It is, yes. Tell me what I can do to help, and I'll do it. But hurry, this has gone on long enough."

Adaman shook his head. "There is no hurry with such things as this. We do it right, or we don't do it at all." He turned his attention to Tabor and Sian. "Dear lady, we will need food and water for when she wakes. Bring a cold compress for her brow and a glass of wine…for me." He touched her hands, looking at the little blisters there. "See to your hands, and then bring those things back if you'd be so very kind." He waved toward the door. "And you, oh oak tree, take the door. No one interrupts until someone from this room tells you we're done. No matter what happens."

Tabor's brows rose at the last statement. "No matter what happens? Adaman, that is never a good warning with you."

"It may be loud, possibly with a light show. It will all be all right. This is the Dark One's will, and maybe the Goddess's too, but I can't speak for her in the same way, at least not yet."

Tabor snorted and gripped Adaman's shoulder for an instant before he turned away, leading Sian out. He moved Kadama out of the way of the door. "You heard the man. Priestess Kadama, I'd suggest you go gather some folks and see if you can put together the food, some sort of bandages and herbs, maybe a room to put that all in."

"Yes, Knight Tabor." There was a sullen note to her voice, but Darian ignored her. Kadama got along well with his brother, but didn't seem to care much about anyone else.

Tabor took a position just outside the door and pulled it shut. Darian took in a deep breath. No one would move Tabor until he wanted to be moved. It was now up to Adaman and himself.

Adaman rubbed his hands together, his long fingers almost

spider-like in the motions. "You may want less armor for this, Darian. It may take a while, and it's going to get warm."

Darian wondered how Adaman knew, but he just nodded. "As you say." He removed his armor, setting the plate against the wall as the things Adaman had already said rang through his thoughts. Light show. Noise. No matter what happens. He wasn't sure what was going to happen, but his worries were all secondary to helping Ephema. Darian knew he had to do anything he could to help her. He hadn't misspoken when he'd sworn his vows. He would keep her safe by any and all means necessary.

He just hadn't expected to be tested so soon.

Adaman pulled a couple of stools up to the bed. Darian didn't remember the stools being in the room, but he hadn't really looked and wasn't going to question where they'd come from. He sat on one, watching Ephema with a sense of dread.

The globe above them continued to spin, sometimes so fast he could barely see it. When it slowed, sparks would fly. Throughout, Ephema continued whispering. Adaman smoothed the blanket near her, but went out of his way to avoid touching the woman. "To reassure your worries, I do at least have an idea what is happening. She is, for all intents and purposes, a creature of magic tied together in the body of a woman. Priestess for a mother. Knight for a father. The only living Daughter of the Goddess we've seen in a century. It's a wonder nothing has gone wrong before now."

Adaman continued, "I've been doing a bit of research, and Daughters draw their power from the life around them. Unlike a vampire that steals life from the living, a Daughter just kind of, well, she picks up what we cast off. The more intelligent and bigger the creature, the more magic we're talking about. So spiders, not so much magic, at least not in the household variety. People, we're big old pools of magic. That magic is what the divine touches when you make your oaths.

"Now, here we have a Priestess without others of her faith or ability to really teach her about what she's doing. It seems many of her actions are instinct. So she's been instinctively gathering power her whole life, but her home in the mountains would have given her a lot of protection from picking up too much magic. She probably didn't see many people on any given day, and the magic castings off of a deer aren't going to be hard to deal with.

"But you brought her to a city, and not just one but through several more. She's been building up a magical store, and only bleeding it off when actively healing someone, or when it naturally bleeds off on its own, which isn't quick enough. And then tonight, something happened, a connection with deity from the look of it, but she's got too much stored magic and there's ambient magic messing with the process."

"Ambient magic?"

Adamana shrugged. "Well, this is a major Temple to the Dark One. Osephetin has many Priests and acolytes in residence here. Between them and all you lovely Knights running around all over the place, his influence is everywhere. All those major sources of magic can't make it good for one lone Daughter to try to commune with her Goddess. She's just overwhelmed. To bring her back we're going to have to drain off some of that power. In a perfect world, we would have seen it coming and taken her to a healing house to help people. Healing is a really good focus for the excess, and probably why she didn't notice before given she was watching after three Knights. So, we'll have to do it the hard way. Clear as mud?"

"The hard way." Darian frowned. "What exactly is the hard way?"

The priest answered with a tight grin. "We're going to bleed it off through you. Me too, a little, but mostly you. She probably won't kill you. She might kill me."

"She?"

"Ephema, or the Goddess through her. The line between the two is a little strained right now. She wants help. She keeps asking for it. But she doesn't know the extent of the power she carries, so it's going to lash out until she brings it under control."

"Ah." Darian swallowed past the lump of concern in his throat, looked down at Ephema, and then back at Adaman. "Very well. What do I do?"

Adaman gestured at Ephema. "Just take her hands." He shifted his stool and put his hands on Darian's shoulders. "And hold on for the ride."

"That's it, huh?" Darian shook his head. "You make it sound as easy as one of Ianel's afternoon excursions." He held his hands near Ephema's, hearing a crackle of static as he did. The hairs on his hands and arms stood on end, sending a shiver through his body. Darian glanced at Adaman who nodded.

Darian hesitated a moment more, then grabbed Ephema's hands. It wasn't as gentle as he wanted, but if he was slow, he knew he would falter. His heart pounded with uncertainty, and he tensed, prepared for pain. There was an instant where nothing happened, her hands warm and soft in his. Then an odd, earthy scent filled his nose, like grass after a summer rain, followed by a bolt of light and pain. He'd felt pain when he'd taken his oaths, but this was a different kind of punishment, raw and aching and there was nothing he could do to make it ease.

"Osephetin's blood!" Gritting his teeth, Darian nearly let

go. His hands burned, the sensation riding through his body and straight through his back where Adaman held on. He heard an echoed hiss of pain from the Adaman, who tightened his grip. Darian grimaced and closed his eyes, trying to focus on the experience, to ignore everything other than not crushing Ephema's hands and to wait for the pain to stop.

Light flashed around their hands, so intense he could see other colors in it, and it left him all but blind. He heard screaming and it took Darian a moment to realize it wasn't in his ears, but something he heard in his mind. Ephema's fingers spasmed, but he didn't let go. The stench of burning flesh followed, and Darian realized it came from their joined hands. How long could this go on?

He closed his eyes and sent up a silent, fervent prayer to Osephetin, though he didn't pray for his own safety, but Ephema's and Adaman's. The light flashed again and again, and when he thought he'd never see again, the room went dark. He heard a soft clunk and clatter as the blank globe fell to the floor and rolled to the far wall.

Adaman's head rested against Darian's back, the priest breathing heavily, but at least he was breathing. Darian blinked, but it took several minutes before he could see clearly again. Ephema was still, her features finally calm though marked by her long struggle. Darian tried to speak, but his voice came out as a croak. He coughed, cleared his throat, then managed. "Is it over? Is she going to be okay?"

The dark silence drew out before Adaman responded. He pushed himself upright and released Darian's shoulders so he could hold his own head in his hands. "Yes. It's over. She's out of immediate danger, though more is to come. I must speak to the High Priest. I must…" Adaman half-rose from his stool and then sat back down, missed the stool and ended up on the floor. "Or this…this floor is nice."

Darian tried to help him and nearly fell over as well. His arms and back ached and burned, and even now the smell of burnt flesh and hair hung over the room. "Oh dammit. Just stay still, Adaman. I can't help you yet. I don't think…" He blinked as his vision swam. "Whoa. I don't think I should move either."

Ephema gasped softly, coming awake all at once and coughing. She rolled onto her side, her eyes finally open. Once the fit passed, she stared up at Darian. Her eyes shone with a silver light that pierced him to the core, then she blinked and the woman he knew peered out of her gaze. When she managed to speak it was barely more than a whisper. "Darian, you're hurt!"

Darian smiled weakly. He really wanted to fall down onto the bed face first, but Ephema was already there and moving sounded like it would hurt. "Yeah. I am, but it's not just me. Adaman is hurt as well. Help him first, if you can. He needs to go speak to the High Priest. I can wait."

Ephema frowned, sitting up slowly and then nearly falling off the cot to kneel between the men. She laid one hand on Darian's leg and the other on Adaman's shoulder, closing her eyes and whispering a prayer.

Nothing happened.

She clenched her fingers and tried again. And again. Slowly her hands fell away from the men, and she stared at them. "I can't. I don't feel any power."

Adaman lay back on the floor, his arm over his eyes. He laughed, a hoarse, thready sound. "Course not. We had to take it from you to get through to the Goddess and make the communion stop. I think you'll be fine in a few days, but until then we're on our own." He groaned. "I could really use that wine now."

Ephema attempted to scramble to her feet and nearly fell back over, her steps as unstable as a new colt even though she was still in better shape than Darian or Adaman. She half crawled, half stumbled to the door and pulled it open to Tabor and Sian's anxious expressions. "Help."

CHAPTER EIGHTEEN

Darian grimaced as he waited for Fressin and Kadama to finish puttering around in the makeshift infirmary. He wasn't sure why everyone in the Temple agreed that he and Ephema should stay here instead of going to the hospital, and why Fressin and Kadama were the go-to people to care for them. His brother had never been the type to give much concern for the physical well-being of his fellow man.

"Since when did you become a physician, Fressin?" Darian did what he could to relax, but it was difficult. Burns began at his fingertips and spread up his arms and across his back and shoulders, with particular spikes of pain at his elbows, wrists, and the joints of his hands. It was difficult to do much of anything, his thoughts clouded with pain.

"What? You're the only one allowed to be humanitarian? The function of the human body is fascinating." Fressin tossed a bandage to Kadama, who caught it easily. "And there are records of ways to increase healing that no one at the hospital wants to consider. This is a golden opportunity." He nodded to

Kadama. "Take that one to the Daughter, then see if there are any more in the cabinet over there."

"Of course." Kadama placed a few bundles of herbs she had been carrying on the table in front of Darian, carefully juggling the herbs and the armload of dressings.

"It's just a new side to you, that's all. It's not a bad thing." Darian winced as he shifted, not sure he liked the sound of being Fressin's golden opportunity. Shouldn't his brother have been more focused on the scroll than on healing methods? And why was it only Ephema and himself? Where was Adaman? "So what are you going to do?"

"We're going to start with Ephema." Fressin glanced at her. "You were only burned on your hands and wrists, correct?"

Ephema blinked as he spoke to her. It seemed to take her a moment to process what was being said, her gaze not moving much from her hands which bore the same burns and blisters Darian's did. "Yes. Only here."

"Good. That'll be easier to apply and monitor." Fressin snapped his fingers to get Kadama's attention, but the woman was already in motion, bringing him a bowl of greenish liquid. Fressin took up a second bowl and pestle and crushed herbs in it as he joined Ephema. He put the bowl down and accepted the liquid from Priestess Kadama then sat down on a chair. He produced a small brush from a pocket in his shirt. "I want you to turn your hands upward as best you can, and I'm going to brush this on it. I'll warn you now, it's going to be cold and sting, but that will go away very quickly. Do not get any of it in your mouth; it's poisonous."

Ephema frowned slightly, glancing at Darian before looking back to his brother. The globe necklace hung in place again, though it was dark now, the usually white stone reflecting grey. "I will not eat it." She agreed, holding her hands out.

Fressin dabbed the viscous concoction onto her hands, using the brush to spread an even coating of the liquid on her savaged skin. True to his word, Ephema gasped when the remedy touched her wounds, and she jerked her hands away. If she felt anything like he did, Darian wondered how she could feel any more pain. But, after a couple of moments, she relaxed and Fressin was able to finish the work. When he was done, he set the liquid aside and picked up the crushed herbs, sprinkling them liberally onto the goo on her hands. He turned her fingers this way and that to be sure the coverage was complete before he wrapped her hands loosely in clean bandages.

Darian watched with interest, though he wasn't looking forward to the process. "What is that stuff?"

"Which, the herbs or the poultice?" Kadama returned with more bandages and herb bundles, setting them up near Darian.

"Both. Though I'm more concerned about the goo."

Kadama snickered as she peeled herb leaves from their stalks. "I bet you are. The poultice is a mixture Fressin and I came up with after working with some of the locals and analyzing a herbology book. They needed something to dull the pain of injuries until they could be moved to the hospital. We found that a mixture of stinging nettle, a bit of poisonous mushroom, and some jellyfish stinger venom will dull pain for about three to four hours. It's not dangerous as long as you don't eat it."

Darian blinked, pulled from the painful haze he slipped into all too easily. "You're putting that on an open wound? Are you insane?"

Ephema closed her eyes, her fingers twitching as Fressin finished the bandaging. "It helps." She admitted softly. "Though it hurts a lot first. Now, it's numb."

"What about Adamana?" Darian protested. "He'll need this too. Where's he?"

"Nervous, little brother?" Fressin smirked as he gathered up the remnants of his work and moved everything to the table Kadama had set near Darian. "Adaman's wounds are nowhere as severe as yours and Ephema's. His can be healed with rest, time, and in his words, wine. Tabor has him under good care. He will be fine until the Daughter here has regained her magic." He peered at Darian's shoulders. "In the meantime, it's your turn."

Darian sighed. "Let's get this over with."

EPHEMA TUGGED at the bandages covering her hands, working at the complex knots. Two days of enduring Fressin's ministrations had been more than enough for her. She understood that he meant well, but he didn't seem to care that his cures hurt. His work on the scroll had been temporarily assigned to Sian, so he'd decided this was a chance for experimenting with his mixture and bothered both she and Darian multiple times a day to change their bandages and try something new. After the last time she had flat refused to allow him near her again, no matter how well meant his efforts were.

She put the stained bandages to the side, holding her hands up in front of her face. While Fressin's brew helped with pain, it did not truly heal. She needed her hands, and this morning as the dawn had come, she'd felt the warmth of healing power within her again. She'd never been able to heal her own wounds before, but no one else could do it for her, and she was determined to try again.

Ephema closed her eyes, feeling for the divine magic inside of her like a tiny, cool star. She'd been using her gifts almost continually since Darian had come to her doorstep, and with each healing she felt stronger and more confident in her abilities. The Goddess had blessed her with this gift, and her faith grew each time. Healing herself shouldn't be so difficult, unless the Goddess specifically didn't allow it, and she didn't know any way to find that out. It wasn't like the Goddess answered her prayers with words.

Brushing those thoughts aside, Ephema concentrated and prayed, focusing on turning her healing inward instead of outward. The magic inside of her resisted the new direction, and Ephema doubled her efforts, silently pleading with the Goddess to help her. Her hands throbbed in time with her heartbeat. "Please. Please." She felt like she was pushing with all her might against a stone wall, and just as her strength began to fail something popped inside of her. Cooling, healing power rushed through her body and over her skin, stealing her breath away.

She felt her hands healing, the new skin growing up under the ruined flesh and sloughing it off. It was like a puzzle where everything was wrong and the pulse of life slid the pieces around until they were right again. This time it was her own body that was the puzzle. The minutes stretched forth and finally the sensation eased. She opened her eyes, staring at her hands which were perfect and whole. Her fingers wrapped around the globe; the stone again warm to her touch. "Thank you."

She pushed to her feet, joy bubbling through her at the new turn of her abilities and the thought she could help

Darian now. Then she paused, pondering that thought more deeply. She and Darian hadn't really spoken since the incident. He'd been mostly confined to the makeshift infirmary, where Fressin and Kadama fussed over him day and night. For as much as she hated her bandage changes, he had to hate them ten times more. Did he blame her for his pain? Would he even want her to heal him?

Ephema gave herself a shake. Of course he would want to be healed, that would be much better than enduring Fressin's concoction, but would he want her around after this? After he'd seen how dangerous she could be? She hadn't meant for any of this to happen, but good intentions weren't a very strong argument. It shouldn't matter if he told her to leave him alone, but it mattered to her. He was her friend, and she couldn't imagine going a day without seeing him. He had to understand that she would never do him harm on purpose.

She flexed her hands, the newly healed skin still feeling tight, but she thought that would ease. She needed to heal Darian. Whatever happened after that she would face when it came. So decided, she made her way to the infirmary and knocked softly on the door.

It opened to Fressin's scowl, and Ephema did her best not to duck away from him. Behind him, Kadama poured more of the numbing agent into a container. "We're about to change his bandages again. It would be better if you come back later. Unless you need more."

Ephema shook her head. She acknowledged there was a nicer side to Fressin, but she still didn't like him very much. She held up her hands. "No more bandaging. I can help him now."

"Oh. Well, I guess that's encouraging. So, your magic's back then?" At her nod, he sighed. "No more testing, I guess.

Very well. I want to take another look at how much progress he's made before you heal him. Not everyone, okay, almost no one, has your capabilities just within arms' reach, and it's imperative we get this mixture as potent and effective as we can." His voice dropped, and she almost didn't hear his mutter. "At least it would be something useful I can do."

She glanced at the room beyond before answering. "That would be up to Darian. He…I…we both appreciate your efforts."

Fressin checked to see where Kadama was before he spoke again, his voice still low. "Just bring him back, all right? It's obvious he's not just going to stay safe, so wherever it is you two are directed next, or however many are going, I don't know…just, bring him back." He held the door open for her and stepped aside to allow her entry. "It'll be just as well to be done here. I need to go back to the scroll."

Ephema paused, the desperation in his voice catching her, making her dislike of him seem petty and small. She touched Fressin's shoulder, magic teasing her skin. "I promise. He'll come back." She wasn't sure if it was good to make such promises, but she did it anyway. If she had any say in it, Fressin wouldn't lose any more family.

"I'll hold you do that." Fressin cleared his throat. "Hey, lunkhead. You have a visitor."

Darian tried to turn around to see who had entered, but his back was to the door, and he was unable to move quickly due to the mass of bandages. "Well, all right. Come on in visitor. Just please don't bring stinging nettle with you. I don't think I can take any more of that today."

Ephema smiled, crossing the room silently, the stone smooth under her toes. "How about jellyfish stingers?"

"Osephetin's blood, not them either." Darian tried a smile,

but she could still see how uncomfortable he was. "Good to see you up and about, and with no bandages. Is that from their stuff, or did your magic return?" He shuddered. "Please tell me it is your magic, because I'm tired of the goo and herbs. I smell like I'm being prepared for roasting."

"Oh please, you big baby." Fressin shook his head. "It's not that bad."

"Stinging nettle on open wounds. Have you tried it?"

"I'm not rash enough to venture into a situation that would require me to need it." Fressin sniffed. "Before she heals you, allow Priestess Kadama and I to inspect how much healing your body did with the aid of our skills so we know what we can do in the future."

"Didn't you do that this morning?"

"I want a final look before she does her thing. We need to know."

Darian sighed and nodded. "Go ahead."

Ephema ducked around Fressin and Kadama to stand in front of Darian, caught between curiosity and fear that his burns would look as bad as they had days ago. Burns were awful.

Fressin and Kadama worked in unspoken harmony as they stripped away the bandages and placed them into bowls where they could be cleaned and reused, or burned depending on the stains. They were careful not to pull too hard, not wanting to cause any further damage.

Under the wraps, Darian's skin was still red and angry with paler edges where the lost skin met up with his darker, uninjured skin. Blood welled up to the surface in a couple of places, but they were fortunately few, the moisture from the mixture protecting the healing tissue and allowing new skin to begin to form. Ephema was surprised at the progress, given how extensive the burns had been. It had arguably been much more effective for Darian than herself, but he had been under more constant supervision.

Kadama arched her eyebrows, nodding with approval. "Oh yes, that last mixture has made a big difference."

"Very much so." Fressin bent close and peered at Darian's skin so close he almost touched it with his nose. "This section here was nearly charred, and there's new skin appearing here and here." He pointed to a few sections without touching Darian's body. "I think you were right to add crushed marigolds into the mix; that seems to be helping nicely."

"So am I done, please?" Darian grimaced. "Please tell me I'm done."

"Yes, you're done. The mixture was helping, no matter how much you griped about it." Fressin stood back from Darian and bowed low. "He's all yours."

Ephema was impressed by how much they'd accomplished. She briefly considered teasing Darian by threatening to leave him in their care, but that seemed mean. She inclined her head to Fressin and then laid her hands on either side of Darian's throat, just above the burns. The moment her prayer began, power surged through her fingers, but this time it was controlled, and the light that poured over him was tinted with a warm golden hue.

Ravaged flesh came together and skin formed, sloughing off the dead and burned remains. Even parts of his body that had been completely scorched were healed, and within a few minutes the light faded. Darian slowly moved his arms. "Oh! It feels good to be able to do that." He dusted off some of the flaking skin, stopping when Fressin stepped up with a wet rag and sponged it off. "Thanks." Darian cocked his head. "That's the first time your healing has left a mess behind."

It took time before Ephema replied, her eyes closed as she savored reconnecting with her Goddess and with what her power was meant to do. She blinked and looked down at the powdery pieces of skin. "It happened with Bishop Lam too, but you didn't see it. Burns are different. The skin is too ruined to knit back together. It's better just to replace it."

Kadama shook her head. "I'm still surprised that works." She tapped on the side of her head. "All of you are supposed to be crazy, but crazy or not your healing works."

Crazy. Ephema was growing weary of everyone reminding her about the fate of the Goddess's followers. And it was even more unwelcome from Kadama. Ephema was sure she wasn't crazy. Or wasn't crazy most of the time. She turned to Darian. "Feeling better?"

"Much better, yes, thanks to you." He made a wide sweep with his arms this time, testing his range of motion. "My skin feels kind of tight, but I guess that's normal since it's all new. Do we need to go see the High Priest, or can I eat first?"

"Here." Fressin tossed Darian a shirt. "Put that on and go eat. Everything else can probably wait." He looked over the room, his lip twisting with annoyance. "I'm going to go find a broom."

DESPITE DARIAN'S WILLINGNESS, the High Priest did not call for him for another full day, giving Darian more recovery time. Even with Ephema's healing, he was tired and sleep was welcome. Finally, the call came, and he joined Fressin, Ephema, and his mother in the antechamber near the High Priest's chambers.

A square table sat in the middle of the room, the scroll

parchment spread out on the surface and weighted at each corner.

"So this is it?" Darian peered at the parchment with a frown. It was yellowed and stained with age, but the words written across the page were clear and dark. They were also as illegible as if a child had written them while holding a brush with both hands. As he watched, the words swirled, coming back to rest in different locations from before, still clear but unreadable. He blinked twice, trying to steady his vision. "It's like seeing double. Words aren't supposed to move."

"Exactly." Fressin sighed, running his fingers across the bottom of the scroll. "I know there's something important here, especially given how dreadfully you were pursued, but I'm not sure I'm ever going to be able to decipher these runes." He rubbed his temples and sank into a nearby chair, clutching his hair in his frustration. "I've tried everything I can think of, as has Priestess Sian and Priestess Kadama and we haven't managed a word. It's maddening!"

Lauret raised a finger. "If I could point out, some of that time was spent working on Darian and Ephema's wounds."

"Yes, yes, I know that." Fressin waved the point aside angrily. "I was hoping the break would provide clarity, but by now I should have at least gotten somewhere with it. I'm no closer than when you came sailing into port."

Ephema cocked her head, sitting off to one side of the family members. "There is no one else who might be able to assist?"

"None that I'm aware of." Fressin slumped lower in her chair, visibly defeated. "There was another that was as skilled in deciphering languages as I am, a few years back. But he was ambushed by some of the Lich's forces and now walks among them, so I doubt he's of any help."

The door from the High Priest's chambers opened without notice, pushing wide to reveal Adaman a few steps ahead of the High Priest who was supported by Knight Tabor. Adaman bowed low to the assembled Knights and other parties. "Your friend might be unable to assist, but we do have an answer to the question, courtesy of Ephema's communion, and His Holiness's expertise in dream interpretation."

Darian rose from his chair and hurried to help Tabor as they guided the High Priest to a seat. He was fragile these days, his health fading with each passing dawn. "Dream interpretation? You managed to get something out of what happened, Adaman? All I felt or saw was light and pain."

Adaman laughed, a noise that seemed to dart around the room and peer into the corners. "With assistance, yes. There was a message for us." He waited until everyone had settled before continuing. "The Goddess knows about the scroll and has a solution which she managed to share, if in a very confused fashion. The High Priest put the question to Lord Osephetin and we gathered more pieces of the puzzle." He sobered for only an instant before a twinkle lit his eyes. "So, it's praise to the gods, though if you want to sing my praises too, I shall be happy to listen."

"The gods are what got us into this mess in the first place. I'm not sure how many praises they've earned." Fressin muttered. "But it seems anything's better than where we are right now, so let's hear it. How do we read the scroll?"

Tabor drew in a breath to speak, his expression indignant, but High Priest Calinin held up his wrinkled hands. "No, Knight Tabor, the young man is right. In many ways the Gods' own foolishness is what brought us here." He sighed as he settled into the chair, and curled his gnarled hands around each other. "They were not prepared for a force such as the

Lich, and by the time they began to consider him a threat, it was too late to stop him. So now, it's up to us mortals to make up for that failure, and the deific power that remains will do all they can to assist."

He turned to Tabor. "Knight, do you have the book I asked you to bring?"

Tabor nodded, offering an old, thick, tattered tome. He made sure the High Priest had a good grip on the volume before releasing it.

High Priest Calinin guided the book to the table with a resounding thud as it came to rest. "This book is from an age long past. It predates everyone in this room, myself included. A few of these volumes still remain, kept away from prying eyes, stored and preserved as best we can as a reminder of the before times."

"I haven't seen that book!" Fressin protested, jerking forward before stopping himself. Darian was certain Fressin wanted to take the book from the High Priest's hands, but no one would dare go that far. Not even Fressin.

High Priest Calinin raised a brow. "That is true. A talented scholar you may be, young man, but that does not give you access to every book in the temple. There are many things your faith is not ready for."

He carefully opened the book and turned it so the people near the table could see it. Despite the gentle rebuke, Fressin pushed forward, so he got the best view. Darian considered pulling his brother back, but decided it was just as well if he read first.

Fressin read several paragraphs and then blinked. "Who is Whilpow? I've never heard of this god before."

"You wouldn't have, though you would like him." The High Priest leaned back in his chair, his gaze moving to the ceiling as he thought. "He vanished early in the Lich's culling of the gods. He was the God of the spoken word, languages, and the arts of diplomacy. Every kingdom once had a few of his disciples on retainer, especially as translators and diplomats."

Darian raised an eyebrow, nudging Fressin aside enough to share the reading. "It says here his fate is unknown."

The High Priest nodded. "No one knows for certain how a God lives or dies, my son. It's not as though they leave corporeal bodies behind. We know he vanished about the time the Lich was looking for him, so the writers of this tome assumed he was killed and his essence absorbed by the Lich."

"But since he was the god of languages, do you think his followers survived and might be able to help?"

"No. We are not aware of any followers, and even if they survived, they no longer had a deity to follow. Whilpow would have been easy prey for the Lich, as he was not a God of battles or weaponry. The stories say his followers did their best to take messages between those who fought the Lich and were hunted down and destroyed for their assistance."

"Which probably also says something about the Gods and the way things used to be, but that's one of those philosophical discussions which could take a lifetime." Adaman tried to pace, but with so many people in the room there simply wasn't space for it. "However, this particular God also loved devices and puzzles, which is what the Goddess pointed us at. There is a device which we think will make the scroll clear. It's described as being a decoder for the unreadable, provided we can lay hands on it, which isn't the easy part."

"What is the easy part then?" Lauret moved away from the table and tried to find a spot against the wall where she'd be out of the way.

Adaman smiled tightly. "It's easy to use and you don't need a connection with the deity, just an understanding of reading and language."

"So that means the hard part is getting it?"

Adaman glanced at the High Priest who gestured for him to continue. "Yeah, that's the hard part. There are ruins of Whilpow's one and only temple only about a week's journey away. But…erm…it's at least week into the wildlands, and the ruins are most assuredly overrun by bad things. And, because of the God's love for puzzles, it's not like it's just going to be sitting there with a sign that says 'ancient reading glass' on it." He took two steps, nearly tripped on Tabor's feet and stopped himself again. "The venture is Goddess blessed though, so that should help as long as you take Ephema with you."

"I'm going then." Darian stood with a nod. "Getting the scroll was my quest, so this is more of the same. And I oathed to keep Ephema safe, which means staying close to her."

"As am I." Lauret jerked a thumb at the door. "I can be ready in…"

"No, Knight Proctor." The High Priest shook his head. "I need you here. We have a new batch of recruits arriving in three days from Lethor, and they're to start their Journeyman training as soon as they arrive. I need you to oversee that while Knights Ianel, Tabor, and Darian escort Ephema to Whilpow's temple. They have traveled with her before and have shown they can be trusted with such a mission. More ships like the one that attacked your steamer have been spotted, and our defenses must be increased. We need you here."

Lauret looked like she was going to protest. Darian understood exactly how she felt, but the idea of more of those fighters coming across the sea made him glad she would be training more help. She swallowed and nodded, short wispy hair falling across her brow. "As you say, High Priest."

"Adaman has maps for your use and will assist with what information we know. The sooner the Knights can leave the better."

Tabor gave a hard little smile. "Then I see no reason not to pack now."

Lauret bowed to the High Priest as the meeting ended. She turned to Darian. "Knights Darian and Tabor, could you meet me in the hallway, please, while Ephema gets the maps and other information from Adaman?" She pivoted and strode from the room, her tone of voice leaving no question of obedience from either Knight or son.

Darian cocked an eyebrow at Tabor, who shrugged. They both followed after Lauret, who shut the door and addressed them the minute the door was shut. "You know what I am going to say, don't you?"

Darian nodded, running his hand through his hair. "We're to guard Ephema with our lives, and bring her back safely at all costs."

"Good boy." Lauret sighed, her shoulders slumping as she tried to roll the tension out of them. "With just the four of you, it should be easy to stay out of sight and avoid trouble, but I'm not counting on that. Tabor, you're the senior Knight, so you're the commanding Knight. Keep an eye on him, and…"

Tabor raised his brows, his heavy arms crossed over his chest. He interrupted her. "Lauret." His voice was gentle. "He is a Knight of Osephentin, and not a boy. I am as old as you are, and you are not my commander or my mother. Ephema is as important to both of us as she is to you. Trust us to know what we are about. We will return before the end of the month."

"Yes. Of course." Lauret's voice cracked once, and she composed herself. Darian had never seen his mother so worried. "Right. All right then, Knights. Your first duty before you leave is to go find Knight Ianel."

"I'll do it." Darian volunteered. "I'll shake the brothels until he falls out of one."

Tabor clapped Lauret on the shoulder then nodded to Darian. "Start with the one nearest the docks with the pink paint job. He has a steady girl there and often stays with her when we are in Hawthan. I will requisition supplies, review the map, and we will leave at first light."

"Yes, Knight Tabor."

CHAPTER NINETEEN

The morning sun, wan with winter's kiss, rose as Darian and fourteen other Knights hit full gallop out of the gates of Hawthan, racing along the well-traveled road to the northeast. Tabor and Ianel were in line beside him, with Ephema hanging on safely behind him. He smiled at the noise and dust they were producing. Any enemy for miles would be attracted to the sound and would come to investigate. The idea was that the other Knights would lead off anything that came hunting, opening an opportunity for the smaller party to slip away unharassed.

A few miles down the road, when the lead Knight allowed the horses to slow down somewhat, Tabor pulled his horse up even with Darian's and motioned back to Hawthan. "I did not see the Knight Proctor this morning. Did she see you off, Darian?"

Darian barely heard Tabor over the noise and through his new helmet, but he caught enough of the question to reply and shook his head. "She did not. She never watches me leave.

She's seen me return nearly every time, but never watches me go. She did the same with my father. I think it bothers her too much, the possibility she's seeing me for the last time."

Tabor shrugged, his armor showing signs of cleaning and repairs which had been undertaken during their time in the city. It didn't shine, that would be foolish, but it rode in perfect synch with his movements, the joints oiled and plates fitted snuggly. "Perhaps. We all leave behind those we are close to with no promise of return. Everyone finds their own way to deal with that uncertainty."

"I suppose." Darian tapped on Ephema's leg. "Are you holding up back there? We have a long way to go before we stop to rest."

Ephema shifted a little, but not enough to upset their shared mount, who probably didn't even notice her. The warhorse from Tallet had become Darian's official mount as a Knight. No one knew the horse's previous name, and everyone had an opinion about what it should be called until Darian finally settled on Raven. Ephema wore a thick leather vest at the insistence of the High Priest. Otherwise, she went unarmored and barefoot, though she had given in to carrying a long knife. "I am fine. I'm hoping it won't rain. I remember the smell of wet horse."

"Ugh, I do too." Darian let the conversation drop as the pace picked up.

By the early afternoon, the large outpost that was their first night's stop was well in view, and they were ensconced within its walls before night fell. The next day was much the same, an early rise and a long ride to another outpost, their last before they would go their separate ways.

The party rose on the third day to a dusky morning and a crisp breeze. As they rode, the riders' and horses' breaths left a trail in the air behind them. They'd nearly reached the foothills and the mild weather of the sea port was behind them. Darian had always marveled at the wonder of cold weather. As a child, he'd played with the steam that came out of his mouth in winter; now, watching a crowd of Knights and horses smoke like chimneys, he found the effect alarming.

In the middle of the day, they crossed the invisible line between the Wildlands and the settled territories. Once the Wildlands had been a place of cities and towns and bustling industry, but all of that had been lost during the Fall of the Gods, and now only the desperate or the insane ventured into these places. Those that wandered into the Wildlands rarely returned, and it was here they parted ways.

The Knights that rode with them handed off their excess supplies and wished them well. Darian knew they, to a man or woman, wanted to accompany the smaller party to their destination, but orders were orders. A full team of Knights would be too visible to roving undead as well as any other enemy in these lands. The undead weren't the only creatures freed in the clash of magics and faith, just the most numerous. A team of three horses could move faster and quieter and escape with greater ease. So, with cautious optimism, the Knights bid the trio of their Brethren and the Daughter a fond farewell.

Darian saluted the other Knights and watched as they rode off. He removed one of his waterskins from the saddle and held it over his shoulder for Ephema. "Thirsty?"

She didn't answer immediately, her gaze for the road – such as it was – ahead. A delicate shudder ran through her, one Darian knew about only because of the pressure of her body against his. She took the waterskin, murmuring. "Thank you. This place smells odd. I smell rot on the breeze."

"Not surprising." Ianel motioned to a nearby bush, where

a large congregation of flies buzzed about merrily. "Things, especially people, die out here without proper rites or even burials. Who is there to take care of such things? The days will be dangerous and the nights even more so."

Ephema shuddered and took a drink from the waterskin before handing it back to Darian.

Tabor pulled on the reins of his horse and turned north. "I don't want to look any closer at that, though my instinct says it's animal not man. We have at least three days ahead of us before we arrive at Whilpow's temple. Let's move."

"Horses coming, Tabor." Darian motioned to the movement he'd spotted, off to the east. "Looks like about a dozen." Last night had been unexpectedly peaceful. Though the undead had roamed, their hunting cries had remained far away from their encampment, and Darian had entertained the thought that, perhaps, this trip wouldn't be so bad. Now, with unknowns bearing down on them at a fast clip, that thought fled.

Tabor followed Darian's gesture and grimaced. "Coming fast, all right. Our horses are bred for battle, not evasion or a pitched chase. We won't be able to outrun them, even if we were so inclined." He lowered his visor and nodded to Ianel. "Take left. Darian, in the center. I have the right. We'll wait right here for them, and hopefully they will pass on. If not, we will make them wish they had."

Ianel grinned as he pulled his shield free from Star's saddle, strapping it into place on his arm. "I kind of hope they don't. It's been a while since I had a good scrap."

"Got fat and lazy cooling your heels at the brothel."

Tabor's comments were off-handed, touched with humor, not vitriol. He shifted slightly, his gaze never leaving the approaching force. "They are lightly armored or not at all. Mostly mismatches. Their horses have been ridden hard and aren't well fed. I do not think they're riding for help."

"Bandits then, most likely." Darian shook his head. "Desperate ones to live out here. They won't find us easy prey."

"Indeed not."

The horses came upon them quickly, pulling up in a loose circle. Most of the twelve riders were weathered and thin, with sharp eyes and darting looks that filled with nervousness upon seeing the waiting Knights. Two of the men were thicker in girth and carried weapons of much higher quality than their fellows. Their weapons were ringed in bone, though what little armor the men bore showed no other sign of Osephetin's grace.

Tabor held his maul in a casual, wary guard, keeping it between himself and the largest of the men in the group. He frowned, his expression barely visible beneath his visor. "It would be best if you move on. Whatever you might seek, I doubt you'll find it here."

One of the thinner men hissed, "Blood of the dead, Nararul, they're blasted Knights. Blasted friggin' Knights!"

The largest of the bandits, kicked his companion high on his leg. "Shut your gob. I know exactly what they is." He turned his greedy gaze on Tabor. "We's not unreasonable, Knight. We's seen you approach and knowed ya might need some protecting. These ain't nice places. Not like your big cities and all. Someone could get hurt out here. 'Specially a pretty little thing like that girly there."

"She is accompanied by Knights of Osephetin. I believe she has plenty of protection." Darian crossed his arms over his chest and studied the men. Most of them looked nervous, shifting on their horses and exchanging uncertain glances. Only Nararul and the other bigger man of the group showed any ease. "I expect your 'protection' leaves a lot to be desired."

Nararul grinned, showing a gap on one side of his mouth and a gold glint on the remaining teeth. "Ain't had no one complain yet. This don't have to get ugly, boys. Jus' pay up a bit so we can continue keeping these roads safe, and ya can wander on however ya like."

Tabor snorted. "None of us happened to remember to bring extra coin with us. Shame that." Blue essence flickered to life along the edges of his bone maul, highlighting the menace in his tone.

Nararul's grin faltered, showing the snarl beneath. "We'll take the flit in trade, then. She's probably good fer a tumble or two." His grip tightened on the thick flail he carried. "Shame if this has ta get ugly."

"It will be far uglier for you than it will for us." Tabor murmured a soft chant and the head of the maul crackled with divine magic. "However, maybe we should make this more fair. Your other compatriots don't seem nearly as enthralled by the idea of a fight."

"They'll do what I tells them to." Nararul didn't even look at his scruffy band. "I ain't afraid of you, and I gives them safety. You think yer so tough with your shiny weapons." He patted the flail. "I gots me my own magic right here."

"I see that. So you stole some dead Knight's flail. Congratulations, that's so brave of you. That doesn't mean Lord Osephetin answers your calls." Tabor snarled under his visor. "But by all means, pull your magic up, friend. Take a swing. Let's see what you've got."

Nararul's face creased, the only hint that he thought he

might be making a mistake. He gripped the flail tighter and hissed an unfamiliar word. A single red symbol on the haft of the weapon flared to life.

Darian heard Ephema gasp, and she gripped his waist as though she might fall off without him. But there was no time to do anything for her before Nararul set his horse toward Tabor, screaming a battle cry. The horses around them made space, and steel hissed as the riders drew weapons, not content to let only their leader fight.

Tabor pulled some dust out of a pouch at his belt. Blue essence flared to life on his maul, and he threw the powder into the air. Ianel and Darian both wheeled their horses away from Tabor as the powder floated lazily through the air, looking almost like snow before it burst into a crick crack pop of explosions.

The bandits' untrained horses reached to the explosions with explosions of their own. All but a few panicked, bucking and rearing, trying to escape. Some managed to throw their riders, and others took off with their passengers clinging for dear life.

Nararul's horse was too committed to the charge to fully disengage, but it didn't like the explosion and veered to one side of Tabor. Nararul snarled and swung his flail. He wasn't anywhere close enough to be effective, and Tabor and Valor side stepped him. "Bastard!"

"Just felt like I'd even the odds a bit." Tabor glanced over his shoulder as the remaining bandits surged forward. "You two have them handled?"

"On it!" Ianel flicked Star's reins and clicked his tongue. The horse needed no other guidance, secure in his training. The bandits that had fallen were quick to learn that a Knight's steed was just as dangerous as its rider. One fell to a vicious kick before he could regain his footing, and another rolled to safety only to be smashed by Ianel's hammer as he tried to rise.

Darian signaled Raven with his heels and the beast spun, lashing out with its back hooves in a wicked kick. The movement threw Ephema forward and she collided with him, a harsh reminder that though he was trained for this, she was not and his training wasn't for two on a horse. Belatedly, he called out, "Hang on, Ephema!" as he loosed his mace, essence freely flowing out of the skull's eye sockets.

"I'm trying, but you are all edges." He barely heard her over the crash of combat, but she clung close, trying to avoid being thrown and trampled like their enemies.

Darian swung his mace at a bandit who'd managed to remain mounted. He lifted his sword to defend himself, but the blade flew from his hand under the impact of Darian's mace. Without a word, the bandit turned his horse around and kicked it into a full gallop. "Tabor! Two dead, seven routed. Three left, including your friend there."

Tabor didn't answer, though Darian was certain he'd heard the report. For all of his bluff, Nararul wasn't only bluster, showing skill with his flail that kept Tabor and Valor on the move. As the two enchanted weapons collided, bright sparks shot into the air, the red aura of Nararul's flail plucking at Tabor's maul, searching for weakness in weapon or man. The thick, cloying scent of decay rent the air, intermingling with the smells of blood and dust.

Distracted by the fight between Tabor and Nararul, Darian nearly lost his seat and his head as a horse plowed into his. Ephema pushed him in the back, forcing them both to duck, the bandit's club whistling overhead by mere inches.

The runes on Darian's mace flared as he swung wildly, directing Raven with his legs and trying to create distance between the two mounts. He swung upward to deflect a second blow and nearly lost his mace as the glowing spikes cut cleanly through the thick wood of the club, sending shards scattering. There had been no resistance at all.

Ephema yelped, throwing her weight counter to his. The intention was the right one, but their combined lack of experience threatened to over balance them, and as the next attack came, she simply dropped from Raven's back and scrambled away. Darian had no free hand to reach for her, having no choice but to trust her to stay out from underfoot.

He grimaced and directed Raven away from Ephema, pushing hard into the large bandit's mount and shoving it back. "Care to finish this, friend? I've already shortened your club. Let's see how much closer to your hand I can shave it."

The bandit snarled and reached to his waist, pulling a short sword and dropping the club stump. "Come dance, Death Lover. I make a new club from your leg."

He charged, and Darian prepared to meet him, hearing Ephema's voice in the background of his awareness. There was no panic to it, but a sing-song quality he'd heard frequently enough in her prayers. The words didn't make sense, but bright light wreathed him, adding strength to his arm and sharpness to his sight. That was new.

When the bandit closed the distance, Darian blocked his sword high and then drove his mace down in a savage attack. The mace connected with the man's leg, and the eyes of the skull flashed as the bandit's leg went limp, the bone shattered. He shrieked in pain, a cry that was silenced when Darain pulled the mace free and swung it into the man's chest, sending his lifeless body to the ground.

Darian stared down at the body as it twitched. It was one thing to kill the undead, even the Sisters, but fighting the living was still a new concept to him. They were men, like him, often desperate, sometimes evil, but still men, which meant they had more in common than those risen by foul magic.

From behind Darian, Ianel's voice rang out in a curse. "You misbegotten son of a one-legged whore and a bastard goat!"

Concerned, Darian pulled his horse around to offer aid, but while Ianel was shouting, it didn't appear that he was in any need of help. He drove his enemies back with stroke after stroke of his hammer like a smith at a forge. Where his strokes landed man and animal broke before him, until only Ianel and Star stood tall.

Tabor's opponent fell only seconds later, the great flail missing a large chunk and sparking odd red magic until the moment its wielder ceased breathing. As Nararul fell, Ianel let out a victory whoop, but Tabor remained quiet, staring at the dead man and his enchanted weapon.

Darian maneuvered Raven up alongside Ephema and offered his hand to help her up. "Come on. Let's get you back up here before their companions think to return."

Ephema shivered, rubbing her hands along her arms. She stared at the fallen bodies for a long time then took Darian's hand and mounted behind him. "So much waste. I don't understand."

"They believe they can be stronger than the world, I guess. Just like some of us feel like we can change things with kindness and passion, some people think they can change it with cruelty, selfishness, and violence. To give them credit, they managed to stay alive in the wilds for this long, so they weren't utter fools." Darian waited until Ephema had settled then turned to Tabor. He raised an eyebrow when he found the big man still staring at the body of the bandit leader. "Tabor? Everything all right?"

Tabor shook his head and pushed back his visor. His expression was troubled. He nudged the fallen flail with his maul. As the glow died, the weapon went from looking nearly new to ruined, covered in rust, dents, and dings. "Nothing so wrong as to stop us, but a lot to be wary of. That wasn't just some enchanted weapon left in the wild lands. It tugged at my faith, at my very connection to the Dark Lord. That thing is the weapon of a Corrupted."

"What do we do with it?" Ianel spit off to the side as he rode up, glaring at the weapon as though he could melt it with his stare. "If it is a Corrupted weapon, the Dark Lord knows none of us should touch it."

"We leave it with the corpses." Tabor flicked Valor's reins, directing the tall warhorse back to the battered path. "It holds no power now, unless an actual Corrupted were to find it again. How that bandit knew to draw on it, even in such a small way, I don't know, but I doubt he shared the secret with any of his companions. If the survivors want it that badly they can try to return before the corpses rise. We've not the time or resources to put them to final rest. In the meantime, we need to make some distance before nightfall."

CHAPTER TWENTY

Ephema jerked in her bedroll, coming again into wakefulness. She shivered, a reaction that was only partially due to the cold. The night had passed badly for all of them, and Ephema regretted not being allowed to take a turn on watch. She was awake most of the time anyway, and when she slept, she dreamed horrible dreams. Not that she remembered exactly what the dreams were about, only that they disturbed her sleep and made her restless and uneasy. She was anxious to get away from this place, and they were still several hours ride from their final destination.

The eastern sky had only just begun to lighten to a pale grey. Usually pinks and golds would follow the dawn, but not here. Here in the wildlands the sky was always various shades of grey, greater and lesser. The lack of color was another thing in a long list of things she hated about this place.

Deciding that she wasn't doing anything but getting colder, Ephema slipped to her feet and wrapped her new cloak around her. It was heavy and thick, something Knight Proctor

Lauret had insisted on, even if she'd lost the argument about getting Ephema into boots. Ephema didn't know why her clothing choices were of such interest to everyone but her.

Tabor glanced at her from his position on watch, but he didn't speak, his brows furrowed and his thoughts turned inward. Not in the mood to initiate conversation if the Knight didn't, Ephema walked over to the horses instead. She didn't understand them the way the Knights did, but she found it soothing to take care of the horses, especially to brush their tangled manes. She'd taken to doing so each morning. The first morning they'd looked at her with uncertain eyes, but now there was eagerness when she took up the brush. It probably helped that she carried wilted carrots or apple cores in her pockets to offer as treats.

Ianel's horse, Star, shared his rider's exuberant personality, and he was always the first to greet her when she came near. Today was no different, and he pressed his nose up against her shoulder, whickering lightly before sniffing her, searching for a snack.

Ephema shook her head, fishing out a carrot for him before rubbing her fingers into his forelock. "I think you are the only one who is calm out here. A life of searching for carrots, and being brushed sounds nice." She chuckled very softly. "Though carrying a Knight in full armor is probably a lot of work."

Star took the carrot and munched happily, his nose and whiskers soft against her hand as he chewed. She moved to Star's side, running her fingers over the thick muscle that supported the saddle and his Knight, making sure he didn't show any soreness. She didn't know much about horses, but her senses that told her when a person was hurt seemed to work just as well on the large beasts.

With the exception of a few bug bites, he was in fine condition, and as she moved her way around him Star grabbed her by the cloak. She felt the tug and glanced at him. She considered pulling it away, but gave up on the idea. If chewing on a bit of fabric and leather made him happy, who was she to complain? She scratched his shoulder, removing a bit of dried mud. "Just another couple of days and this will be over. I hope."

The horse's ear flicked toward the camp as Tabor roused the other two knights. Ianel spoke, and Star nearly bowled Ephema over as he twisted around, looking over her head to try and see Ianel. The Knight rose and muttered something to Tabor that was unintelligible from this distance, and Star whinnied happily.

Ephema laughed, grateful for something worth laughing over. "I can feed you carrots, and pet your nose, but you will always love Knight Ianel best."

While the Knights worked on breakfast and packing, Ephema checked on Raven and Valor, grateful none of them had been injured by the bandits. She was fairly confident she could heal a horse, but she'd never tried and wasn't sure she wanted to try out here. They were so much bigger that it might be too hard or leave her too tired to help the Knights. As much as she never wanted to choose, if it came down to it, the Knights were her priority.

After a quick breakfast of trail rations and an apple split between the four of them, they were back on the move. The road through this part of the wildlands had not been traveled in a very long time, but at one point had been well-kept. Cobblestone, now overgrown with weeds and grasses, clattered underneath the horses' hooves as they rode. The hours passed in a haze of wan light and the music of hoof beats.

Early in the afternoon they rode into the ruins of a long dead city.

Ephema kept looking around her, feeling more and more like they were being surrounded as the trees gave way to piles of stone and warped, cracked timber. The half circle of a well or an occasional shattered foundation showed where there had been a farmstead here and there, but those only lasted for a short time before they drew up into a series of what must have been shops and centers of living. Ephema heard echoes of voices carried just beneath the breeze and what seemed like laughter at the edge of her hearing, drifting around her and beneath the pounding of hooves. She kept catching glimpses of something in the shadows, but when she looked straight into the darkness, whatever it was would be gone. She had no description to give Darian, save her sense that 'something' was there.

What they couldn't see, the horses could definitely sense. All three horses slowed their pace the farther into the ruins they went. Evan Valor, the most solid of the three, shied and started to take mincing steps until he refused to go any farther. To Ephema's relief, they had come almost to the temple street they'd been told to watch for. Darian helped her down from Raven's broad back before he joined her. He removed his shield from the side of the horse, slinging it over his back.

"Well, I suppose this is where we want to be. Awful place."

Ephema closed her hand around the globe at her neck, her fingers trembling though she tried to stop them. The chill that had begun before the dawn still haunted her, making it impossible to get warm no matter how she huddled in her thick clothing. "It looks very sad. We should hurry if we can. It would be bad to be here when the sun sets."

"Nowhere in the wildlands is a good place to be when the

sun sets, but I agree." Darian's voice was calm, but Ephema knew he was as unsettled as she was. His hand rested on his mace, and his eyes constantly moved as they walked away from Raven, searching shadow and fallen stone. "Come. Let's get this over with."

No one argued. They didn't hobble the horses – horses like these had no need for it. They would wait until their masters returned or until they died, whichever came first. Tabor took the lead, Ephema walking behind him with the other two Knights to either side and slightly behind her. Tabor had been given general directions to the building they were looking for, though it took a few missed turns and backtracks before he came to a true stop.

"I believe we are here."

The structure before them had been beautiful, once upon a time. Tall rose colored stone towers which must have once reached toward the heavens lay strewn in every direction, crumbled and smashed. An archway that showed the way into the depths of the shattered and desecrated temple was partially covered by more collapsed stone. One ruined door frame was still visible, the wooden door mostly rotted away.

Tabor paced to the door and grimaced. "That's not much room. Ianel, come. Give me a hand here." He started to shove, and between him and Ianel, they shifted the debris enough to allow passage while Darian and Ephema completed a check of the courtyard, finding only more rot and overgrowth. Tabor brushed the dust off his hands and carefully pulled his maul in behind him as he entered first. "Dark as pitch in here. Everyone be cautious. Osephetin, guide me." He murmured, and the head of his maul flared to life, illuminating the hallway beyond with a pale blue glow.

Darian nodded to Ephema, gesturing at the arch. "Go on

ahead. I'll be right behind you. Better to have two of us back here if anything starts to shift around."

Ephema held back her fears, trying not to let them show in her expression, though she didn't know if she succeeded. She wasn't good at hiding what she felt or thought, but it seemed wrong to make things worse for the Knights. She tried a smile that felt fragile. "I wish we knew exactly where to look and what we were looking for. Though, it can't be that big, can it?"

"Hard to say. We're looking for something that's been missing for at least a hundred years. Some sort of reading device. I wish we knew if it would work. We just don't have another lead to follow." Darian paused and then snorted. "I'm starting to sound like my brother now. I'm sorry."

Tabor's voice echoed back to them. "The Dark Lord and the Lady Goddess have given us this direction. We must have faith."

"I have faith in the Dark Lord. What I don't have as much faith in is my own ability to know what it is He wants us to find here." Darian murmured his own prayer, and his mace too glowed as he fell in step behind Ephema. "All of these exterior rooms have collapsed. Hopefully what we're looking for isn't in any of them. It would take weeks to move that much stone."

"Adaman said that the device was part of a puzzle and that it was important. If it was just in one of these outer rooms someone would have found it by now."

"Huh. I hadn't thought of that." Darian lapsed into silence as they carefully picked their way through the rubble and into the main building of the temple. The tunnel opened up into a proper hallway, and they found other rooms branching off into more recognizable chambers framed by rotted wood and cracked stone. Living chambers stood to one side, but had been gutted by fire, long ago. They found a dining area that vandals had cleared, though they found a crumbling table and a scattered handful of rough iron forks. In one large room, the walls and ceiling stood proudly and the ruined remains of a library loomed, a vast storehouse of knowledge lost to the march of time and decay.

Darian picked up a tome and opened it, grimacing as the pages turned to dust in his hands. "Such a waste. I'm glad we didn't bring Fressin. He'd have a heart attack and try to figure out a way to reconstitute the paper dust. Anyone find anything worth keeping?"

Ianel called from where he was removing books from an old, lopsided shelf. "Nothing." He sounded bored, which Ephema thought was probably the case. These were Knights, not librarians.

She walked around the room, prickles of more than cold running along her skin. It wasn't the heightened sensation of danger, or the overwhelming presence of evil she had felt before. This was like catching the warm draft from a fire, but not knowing the source. As she walked, she felt the flooring under her foot shift slightly, as though she had stepped on a loose tile.

Ephema stopped and crouched to touch the wobbly stone. She stepped back, cocking her head, then dragged her foot over several of the tiles to push the dust and dirt back. There were lots of small tiles in different colors and textures, like a picture. Or maybe a pattern?

She knelt down and brushed back more dirt, trying to count how many colors there were, but it was too hard to see. "Is there a way to make more light? There are colors here."

"There is." Tabor moved to the center of the room. "Dark Lord, I pray, light my way." The light from his maul flared brighter. The light changed from blue to a pale, constant white. "This is as bright as I can make it for you. Where do you need it?"

"I don't know yet." She ran to the north-most point of the room, trying to see out over the floor. It wasn't enough, and she looked for a higher vantage point, finding an old window casement she thought she could climb to. She scrambled up a few stones, digging her fingers into gaps in the wall and pulling herself up step by step. The glass was long gone and greenery filled in the gap. Tiny pieces of slick stone shifted under her hands and feet, and she did her best to stand without starting any further collapse. She wedged herself in place, peering out over the room.

Her eyes narrowed as she tried to identify the colored stones and find some sense to it. She rose up on her toes. "There are…maybe it is letters. I am not sure. It's something though. Something purposeful."

Ianel knelt and inspected the floor. "I can see something, but it's hard under the dirt and debris. Even close up." He sneezed. "Anyone bring a broom along?"

"Of course not." Tabor shook his head. "We need to clear the way. Ianel, Darian, go back out and find long sticks and grasses. Lash them together as best you can. There is twine in my saddlebags. Ephema and I will move what we can." He released the maul, though it remained standing where he left it.

It didn't take Darian and Ianel long to return with the supplies. They had created impromptu brooms, though the workmanship left much to be desired. When they returned, they bent to the task of helping Tabor and Ephema move the remains of furnishings to the edges of the room.

With concentrated effort, the floor was cleared enough that they could see the tiles beneath their feet. After a short argument over safety, Ephema climbed back into the remains of the window. Darian handed her a piece of parchment and a charcoal stick.

She carefully leaned back against the broken frame, holding the paper in one hand and drawing rough lines as she studied the floor. "There are two symbols, I think. Darker and lighter and they're all tangled up." She squinted, trying to get higher and see more. "Darian, I can't see everything. Your light is brightest. Can you take it to the middle and put the others on the edges?"

"Sure thing. Ianel, you take the west. Tabor the east. That should shed as much light on the pattern as we can." Darian walked to the center of the room while the other Knights moved to the corners. Between the three holy weapons, the room was illuminated nearly as well as daylight. The symbols crisscrossed the room, covering nearly every piece of flooring and running through each other, creating a pattern that repeated itself every dozen steps.

Ephema kept drawing, having to work to keep herself from falling and drawing all at once. She chewed her bottom lip, trying to figure out what the pattern was. It was like words, but not, and it was familiar, like something she'd seen before, but she couldn't place from where.

She sketched in another square then held the paper at arm's length, squinting at it. She almost had it. If only... She turned the paper, looking at it on its side and the familiarity soared. She knew where she'd seen this pattern. It was on a wooden box that played music. Mother had kept it tucked deep in the cave and would bring it out sometimes when Ephema couldn't sleep. They had taken the box with them when they left.

The complex pattern on the lock looked like the drawing

on the paper, intertwined symbols with a keyhole in the middle. A keyhole. She looked up.

"Darian? Is there a hole in the middle? Where the black squares and the grey ones cross each other?"

Darian peered at the ground by his feet. "Not that I can see…or… wait." He scuffed at a suspicious clod of dirt with his foot. "Yes. Right here, though it's pretty full of dirt." He set his mace on the floor and cleared the hole out with his fingers. "It's not deep."

"Something should go in there." She frowned a little, thinking. "What does it look like? Maybe if it's a certain shape it will tell us what to look for."

Darian held his mace closer to the hole. "It's too dark to tell. I'll see if I can see into the hole. Maybe there's a latch or something." He touched his mace with his other hand, murmuring in prayer. The runes along the haft joined the head of the mace in glowing, bathing him in light.

Ephema nodded, putting a hand out to steady herself as the rocks around her shifted. It took her a second to realize it wasn't just a stone or two turning beneath her feet. The wall was vibrating. "Something is happening!"

Darian had no chance to respond as the stone squares in the floor flashed around him. The dark stone patterns pulsated with deep blue and the pale patterns in a brilliant, nearly-blinding white. It was more than light, showing angular runes on each tile, invisible to the naked eye until lit from within. The hole Darian had cleared flashed with both colors alternating, one after another.

The power erupting from the keyhole solidified into two magic tendrils, one dark blue and one bright white. They wrapped around the mace and pulled it hilt-first into the keyhole, the tiles around the edges breaking under the force.

The skull atop the mace turned skyward and screamed, a terrible wail that ran down Ephema's spine and nearly made her scream with it. Mercifully, the scream only lasted an instant, drowned in a clap of noise and a brilliant flash that left her momentarily blind. When the light dissipated, the mace was gone.

So was Darian.

Ephema half-jumped, half-fell from the window. "No! Where is he?"

Tabor and Ianel ran to the broken keyhole. Tabor's eyes filled with horror. "I don't know."

CHAPTER TWENTY-ONE

"What..." Darian blinked in surprised as he picked himself up off the floor. At least it was no longer shaking. As the light faded, he tried to get his bearings. He blinked, stunned. The temple around him had changed. It was no longer decayed, crumbling, and falling down around him. Instead, it appeared as it must have a hundred years ago.

The library was new, the bookcases shining with polish that showed their rich mahogany finish, with all the books ordered and stacked in pristine condition. The holes in the walls and ceiling had vanished, replaced with carved timber and etched masonry. The dust and dirt were gone, and sunlight poured through the small window showing the patterning on the floor, the colors as pure as the day the stone had been laid.

The changes were stunning in and of themselves, but the biggest problem Darian saw was that Ephema and the other Knights were missing. He tried to pick up his mace from where it was lodged in the floor, but it remained sealed tight no matter how he pulled. He grimaced in frustration; whatever had pulled him here wasn't going to release his weapon easily. He sighed and cleared his throat. "Hello? Ephema? Tabor? Ianel? Anyone?"

A calm voice from behind him chuckled. "No one can hear you, my boy. There's no one here but me, and it's been that way for a long time. So tell me, what is a Knight of the God of Death doing in my realm? Have you come to collect this old soul?"

Darian turned around as a man walked out of the hallway and into the library proper. The man was unremarkable. He was short, balding, obviously ate well and walked with a limp. What hair he had was grey, and he wore a small greying goatee that he pulled at idly as he studied Darian.

Darian raised an eyebrow. "What do you mean?"

The man shrugged. "Well, you must be here for a purpose, yes? As I remember soul gathering was one of the jobs Osephetin intended for you. Though I'm not sure how that applies in this case, even though I'm sure I have a soul. Quite the theological ponderation."

"I'm not taking anyone's soul. I…that's not something we do while alive." Darian's hand fell to where his mace should be, forgetting for an instant that the weapon was lodged in the floor. "I'm not even sure where I'm at. One minute, I'm standing in a destroyed temple, tracing a bunch of symbols on the ground and the next minute here I am."

"Destroyed temple?" The man sighed. "That damned Lich. He's killed them all then."

"Killed all who?"

"My disciples."

"Your what?"

Amusement flooded the man's face. "You don't know who I am, do you?"

Realization hit Darian like a hammer. "No. But if I had to guess," Darian ticked his fingers. "You mentioned this was 'your realm.' You said you've been here a century, but you don't look a century old, and there wasn't supposed to be anyone alive in this temple anyway. With all of that and talk of disciples, I'd guess you were Whilpow, the God of Languages."

"Right in one. It's gratifying to see they still teach young people to think." The man bowed low, his grey and pink robes rippling around him. "So, let's go back to the first question. What are you doing here?"

Darian sighed. "I don't rightly know the answer to that, m'lord. We came to your temple seeking something to assist with deciphering a scroll."

"Wait." Whilpow held up his hand, interrupting. "Let me stop you right there. Did you say, a scroll? One encased in silver and bone, I might guess?" When Darian nodded, the god's face broke into a wide smile. "Oh me. Oh, dear me. She did it. Bless my soul. Bless her. She did it."

"Did what?" Darian scratched his head, his hand coming away dirty and assuring him that he wasn't dreaming.

"What transported you here, my boy?" Whilpow ignored Darian's question, visibly excited as he rubbed his hands with glee. "I want to see it with my own hands. What activated the spell?"

"The spell? The runes on the floor reacted with my mace, if that is the same thing." He gestured at the head of the weapon where it was lodged in the floor. "There was some kind of keyhole, and magic came from it and pulled my weapon in. And well, now I'm here."

"Well, of course it did. That was its purpose, after all." Whilpow walked past Darian to the mace and nudged the skull with his foot. "Pointy thing, isn't it. Appropriate for one of

Osephetin's children." He held out his hand and the floor around the embedded mace hummed with power. The mace flew upward, and he caught it easily. The god turned the mace over and over, inspecting it with a practiced eye. "Oh my, yes. Yes. Right here." His fingers traced the runes across the hilt almost lovingly. "It brings a tear to my old eyes. She actually did it. You do know what you hold in your hands, don't you, my boy?"

"No. It's my soul weapon, but I'm sure you aren't referring to that." Darian folded his arms across his chest. "There's a lot that's been lost since you went away. Would you care to explain?" It was hard to fight back the impatience and uncertainty that filled Darian's thoughts and emotions. He seemed safe enough, but what about the others? They needed the information this man – no, this God – knew, but he was taking his time in revealing it.

"You serve the God of the Dead. All of your fellow Knights wield weapons blessed by Lord Osephetin. Though every soul weapon is unique to the wielder, yours is blessed beyond that." Whilpow offered Darian his mace. "Your mace is touched not only by the God of Death, but also by the Goddess of Life. Blessed by the last of her line if all has gone as we hoped it might. No other in recorded history has ever held a weapon blessed by two gods at the same time. It is only possible under very specific circumstances, you understand."

"That's interesting, Sir, but it does me very little good here."

"Knowledge always does you good, young Knight. It is the search for knowledge, after all, that brought you to my temple." The god walked over to one of the shelves and removed a thick tome. "You seek to destroy the Lich, do you not?"

"Yes. As I said, we came to your temple looking for something to help us with a mystical scroll. Your followers were well known for their ability to translate, and we were hoping there was something here that would help us decipher it."

"There was something in the temple, my boy. You found it. And by 'it', I mean me." Whilpow smiled, a twinkle in his eye. "I know the scroll very well. The Goddess of Life and I discussed its creation at length before I was hidden from your world and my knowledge with me." He opened the book and thumbed through to a page. "This is the scroll you're speaking of, yes?" He showed the page to Darian, where a diagram of a scroll was sketched.

Darian studied it. "That looks very similar to it, yes."

"Good. There are many mystical scrolls in the wide world. It is best we are sure we're talking about the same one. This scroll will help you. It contains, among other things, the location where Liana, the Goddess of Life, hid the Lich's phylactery." He closed the tome with a triumphant thump and slid it back into the bookcase. "Now, obviously, I can't tell you where it is, that was done after I came here. But, it was part of a plan that if she was able to lay hands on it, she would document what she'd done, and I would keep the key to reading that information safe for the right people. Wait here." He spun on his heel and strode out of the room with purpose, leaving Darian staring after him.

Darian sheathed his mace, pacing the length of the nearby bookshelf. His gaze traced the titles on the book spines, many of which he couldn't read as the languages were foreign to his eyes. He paced back and forth at least another half dozen times when the sound of approaching footsteps stopped him.

Whilpow returned with quick strides. "This will be what you need." He took Darian's hands and placed something cold and metallic into his palm. "Guard it well, for it is the only one of its kind. Such a thing has never existed before, nor will again."

"What is it?" Darian opened his hand, peering at the item. The necklace consisted of a heavy silver chain with a small circular bauble that looked like a tiny glass sheet bound in rose gold hanging from it. It appeared unremarkable, like a small monocle, except for the fact a literal god had handed it to him.

"That, my boy, is one of my translators, taken to another level for this very purpose. I'm afraid in your hands, as a servant of Osephetin, it's not going to do much. It'd take one of my disciples to make it function to its full ability. But even given that, it will be enough to allow your scholars to translate your scroll. Simply run the circle across the text and peer through it. The purpose of the reader and the text will be made clear." Whilpow clapped his hands. "I won't say this is the only way you could read the scroll, but it will be the most efficient and most timely. Now, let's see about getting you back home, shall we? You've spent far too much time here as it is. I expect your friends will be concerned and the activation of the lock may well have brought enemies. They know there is light and knowledge here, but have never had the means to reach for it."

Darian thought this all sounded a lot more complex than Whilpow seemed to think, but those thoughts were chased out of his head at the mention of enemies. "I have to go, then. Please."

"Spoken like a true Knight. Put the necklace around your head, and I shall reverse the lock. I have enjoyed meeting to you, Knight Darian. It's been nice to have someone to speak to after all this time."

"Thank you, m'lord." Darian moved to place the necklace

around his neck, but paused. "Wait. I didn't tell you my name."

Whilpow smiled. "No. You did not."

The necklace dropped around his neck and a flash of light blinded Darian, then darkness overtook his senses.

EPHEMA STARED at the spot where Darian and the mace had been, stunned. From outside, undead wails arose, familiar in their keening intensity. The walls bucked and shuddered, throwing Ephema from the casement. Tabor rushed to the doorway to the main hallway, holding his maul high to brace the gap. "Here! We have to get out before the room collapses!"

"But… Darian." Ephema protested, trying to get her feet under her.

Tabor shook his head. "He's lost. If we remain this will be our grave as well."

"But…" A stabbing pain ran through her chest, turning her stomach. She couldn't leave Darian behind. He'd been there since the beginning. How could she continue without him?

"No buts!" Ianel grabbed Ephema by the arm as he ran by, dragging her to her feet and pushing her in front of him. "Run, girl! I'm not dying in here. Darian, wherever he is, may be safer than we are."

Wherever he is. The words struck hope in Ephema's heart. It made sense. There wasn't a body. Darian had just gone… somewhere. He'd come back. He had to come back. She prayed he'd come back.

They ran through the building and dove into the long tunnel that led away from the ruins. It lurched and swayed around them, held back by the passage of the Knights and lit by the glow from their weapons. Ephema stumbled and tripped as they went, keeping to her feet only by Ianel's iron grip on her arm. She was going to have bruises, but she didn't care.

The darkness of the passageway seemed never ending until they stumbled out into the world, where night had fallen. It was late, the moonlight obscured by the clouds that never parted.

Ephema burst out of the tunnel, Ianel still pulling her along. She was tired of being dragged, even as she was grateful for the support. "How…" She sucked in a breath, still running. "How did it get dark so fast?"

"We took too long playing housekeeper and clearing the floor. Even if it was necessary." Tabor grimaced and stepped aside, allowing them to move past. He gripped his maul and his eyes focused on the horses where they stamped at the ground, fully alert. The night sounds were unfriendly, filled with the howls of the risen and something else. Something that shrieked above the wind. "Company! Ianel, to your left!"

Ianel spun, taking the blow that would have taken off his head by the shield which rode across his back. The impact sent the surprised Knight and Ephema sprawling as a large creature shrieked in fury from its landing perch on the wall. It was humanoid only as an afterthought, its muscular arms and legs carrying it down the wall like a spider. It leapt, filthy claws and wicked teeth seeking to rip into its prey.

Ephema's eyes widened, and she bit down on a shriek as she backed away. "What is that?"

"Wight! They sometimes nest near religious sites." Tabor shouted, even as he surged forward to bodycheck the wight and push it away from Ianel, buying the other knight time to get to his feet. "Watch our backs, there will be more!"

Despite the surprise of the attack, Ianel scrambled to his feet and turned right back to the fray, coming in low at the creature's belly as Tabor swung his maul over Ianel's head. The two worked in perfect concert, their actions part practice and part instinct as they beat the creature back, crushing bone and joint until it fell still.

True to Tabor's warning, more shapes detached themselves from the shattered stones, shrieking as they attacked.

"Lord Osephetin! Guide my strength!"

The enchanted weapons burst into flame that left traces in Ephema's vision. She put her back to a pile of rubble and gripped the globe at her throat. She prayed for her friends and protectors, pleading for their strength and safety. Light filled the space between her fingers, gathering into a tight sphere before shooting out to wreathe the fighters in the Goddess's light.

She couldn't help Darian, wherever she was, but she was determined to do her best to help Tabor and Ianel.

The wights threw themselves against the knights, who turned back-to-back to protect each other and the mound of stone where Ephema stood. Hammer and maul fell with a steady rhythm, clashing with the screams and hisses of the monsters. Beyond them, additional movement told a grim tale of other visitors, attracted by the sounds of battle. They were surrounded.

Tabor slammed one of the wights in the chest, knocking it back several paces. He whipped around and a sharp whistle made it past his visor. The response to his call was immediate as the three warhorses came charging in, kicking and biting their way through the enemy forces. The shrill cries of the wights combined with the screams of the warhorses tore into Ephema's ears, and she prayed harder, feeling like her bones might crack around the globe. She felt strength leaving her and saw claws slide off the pearly light around the knights and believed it was helping.

"Tabor!" Ianel's voice was ragged and rushed as another blow slammed into his shield. "More coming! I count... Damn you!" He crushed the claws of a wight as it slashed at him, leaving furrows on his armor. "Would you just die already? There's at least five more coming around the temple, and I swear I saw skeletons behind them."

"Get to the horses! We can outrun them."

Tabor's instructions were cut short as the ground shook beneath their feet. Wave after wave of motion curled over the broken landscape, doing further damage to the ruins and knocking friend and foe alike to the ground. A silvery light flashed, too bright to be looked at, and Ephema threw her arm up to shield her watering eyes, trying to gain her feet on ground that refused to stay still.

After another moment, the horrid motion ceased. Silence reigned, and Ephema wondered if she'd gone deaf to match the blinding spots that danced across her vision. She blinked, trying to clear them. In the center point of the earthquake she was certain she saw something, no, someone.

She squinted as the familiar form fully materialized, and her heart gave a joyful lurch. "Darian!"

Tabor lurched to his feet first, shaking his head as though he too was struggling to see straight. He grabbed for Valor's reins, the horses the only ones who seemed unbothered by the light show. "Mount up! Or none of us will see daylight again!"

Ephema scrambled to her feet, stumbling to Raven's side. She was near to bursting with questions, but knew this was no time for them. Darian met her at the horse, pulling himself aboard before reaching for her. Her fingers closed over his with a tingle of warmth, but her attention shot away as she heard Ianel scream and swear.

She spun around to horror as one of the creatures pulled its claws free of Ianel's body. He hammed it down, breaking bone and flesh into mush.

"Ianel!" Tabor shouted and spun his mount around, turning toward his companion.

"Too late!" Ianel set his feet, taking a firm grip on his hammer as he grimaced in pain. "Gut shot, I'm done. Ride! I'll cover your retreat."

"No!" Ephema tried to pull her hand away from Darian as the undead surged, encouraged by the waning light. "I can fix him!"

Darian refused to release her, his voice firm, his expression hidden under his visor. "There's no time, Ephema. If we save him, we'll be overrun."

"No! I can do this!" She thrashed against Darian's grip, the edges of his gauntlets digging into her skin and leaving long scratches that bled freely.

Ianel's eyes were bright with pain, but his voice was steady as he shouted. "It's been an honor! We will meet again! Come and get me you bastards!" Ianel howled a challenge as the undead circled, thrusting his curved hammer to the sky. "Lord Osephetin! Lend me thy grace! Your vessel awaits! With weapon held high, I come to thee!"

At his call, lightning illuminated the cloudy sky, racing toward Ianel in a web of silver and blue light. Eldritch essence raced across his broken body, running from his hammer down his armor. Blue light flashed at every joint as he turned toward the undead and charged.

Tabor rode alongside Darian and caught Ephema around the waist, hosting her onto Raven against her protests. "Ride! Damn you! We'll die! Don't make his sacrifice in vain!"

Ephema slammed against Darian's armored back, clamping down on her cries of pain and burying her head against his cloak so she couldn't see the pain she could hear. Darian kicked Raven into action, and they fled.

Behind them the lightning arced to the earth, illuminating Ianel's form as it struck over and over, answering his death cry. A thunderous explosion tore the earth asunder, burying wight and skeleton alike, utterly destroying the remains of the temple and leaving behind only charred earth and singed bone.

CHAPTER TWENTY-TWO

After a few miles, Tabor allowed their flight to ease, though he did not allow them to stop. He pushed the horses and their weary riders through the night, hour after hour, pausing only as the horses required and passing out small chunks of mold touched cheese and hard bread. No one spoke. There were no words to be spoken.

Darian knew he needed to tell them about the God, and about the device, but it seemed too little consolation against Ianel's death. Darian knew, better than many, the cost of being in Osephetin's service. He felt emptier than he had after his caravan had been decimated for the closeness of the loss. He knew glory awaited Ianel, and the sacrifice had saved them all, but it still felt unfair, too soon to lose the jovial Knight whom nothing had seemed to touch.

Ephema hadn't said a word since they'd fled, and he doubted she would until he broached the subject. Loss was something different to the Knights of Osephetin, and he couldn't remember if they'd ever really discussed it. Fleeing from the crater made by Ianel's corpse had hardly been the right time.

A sliver of light to the east caught his eye, the faintest lightening of the cloudy gloom, and Darian sighed in relief. Daybreak. Tabor kept them moving until full dawn, finally calling a halt near a muddy stream. "We'll camp here for a bit and let the horses recover, then push on. I want to be out of these accursed lands as quickly as possible."

Ephema slid off of Raven before Darian could help her, landing awkwardly and moving away from his offered hand. "At least you care about the horses." The soft words were sharp as she stomped over to Star and begin stripping his gear.

Tabor started to speak, but Darian held his hand up and shook his head. He took his time removing the gear from Raven, rubbing her down, and checking her hooves for stones. When he had nothing more he could do but let her graze and drink he thumped her affectionately and made his way to Ephema. He prayed he'd know what to say to ease her hurting, hoping it would make him feel better too.

She had already done the basics for Star, and now stood at his head, working a brush through his mane. Darian sighed softly standing back far enough that she couldn't hit him with the brush, though he didn't think that was likely. "So, do you think you could have saved him?"

"It wasn't a mortal wound. I could have fixed it." She didn't look up. The brush flew like a weapon in her hand, horse hair flying where the bristles passed. The weary warhorse didn't seem to mind, too tired to protest. "I was shielding him. If I hadn't stopped it would have helped him. I…You… you should have let me try!"

Darian kept his voice quiet, as though speaking to a wild thing. "Could you have saved us all?"

She rested her forehead against the broad neck in front of her. "We could have saved each other. We just needed a little more time."

"We were out of time, Ephema. There were more wights coming out of the neighboring buildings. Other undead too. It was a death trap." Darian placed his hand on her shoulder. "If we hadn't run, we would have been slaughtered."

"But..." The protest was light, her shoulders shaking as she wept. "It's not fair. It's not right. He did everything Osephetin asked of him, and he still died."

"Ephema." Darian turned her around gently to face him. "You're exactly right. Ianel did what Osephetin asked of him, up to and including dying in service to our Lord, defending his friends and our world. If he hadn't been true of heart and dedicated, his final call to the Dark Lord would not have been answered.

"Ianel was worthy, and will have a place of honor in the Halls of the Faithful. And because he perished this way, there is no possibility for him to return as undead. He's a martyr, forever sanctified. Knights rarely die of old age, Ephema. It is our honor to die in the service of the people and our Lord."

"But he's still dead!" She rubbed at the tear tracks on her cheeks, facing him, but not meeting his gaze directly. "Nothing about where he goes next will make me like it."

"I don't like it either." Darian released her, still standing close. "I've lost those close to me, but many in this world lose friends, lovers, sons, and daughters every day. This will keep happening until we put an end to the Lich." Darian looked back the way they had come. "Ianel knew this. We all do. This is why we fight, so that one day, we won't have to."

Ephema sighed softly. "Then... I guess it's why I need to fight too." She touched her necklace. "In my own way."

Silence drew out between them until Star nosed her shoulder, pushing her until Ephema fished out the remaining broken pieces of carrot from her pocket. She held them up to the stallion, letting him eat them off her hand. "What happened to you, Darian? When we were in the temple?"

Tabor looked up from where he was cleaning his maul. "I too would like to know the answer to that question."

Darian wordlessly removed the amulet from around his neck. "I met the god Whilpow, who gave me a device to translate the scroll." He held up the necklace in the wan morning light, letting the bauble on the end rotate for them to see. "This is what he gave me."

Ephema tilted her head, watching the disc spin. She sighed, stroking Star's nose. "I hope it is worth what it cost. Do you know what to do with it?"

"He said to run it across any text and peer through it, and the purpose would be made clear." Darian shrugged. He hadn't thought much on the device, certain Fressin and the others would figure it out faster than he could. "Other than that, no."

Ephema moved away from Star, letting him munch on the dried foliage. "I'm sure Fressin will like it." She glanced toward Tabor. "I am sorry I was angry. Can we sleep, or do we need to ride again?"

"I know why you were angry. I am angry too, but not at you. It wasn't your fault." Tabor ran his hand across his eyes. "You can sleep. Darian and I will keep watch. I have more questions for him."

Ephema nodded, dragging a blanket out of the supplies and finding a spot to curl up. Star followed her, settling in nearby, the other horses joining him to tear up anything they could, despite having been fed the grains and oats the knights carried for them.

Darian glanced after her, but decided it was best to let her rest. He joined Tabor closer to the roadside. The older knight looked like he had aged five years since the night before. Darian felt older and more wearied himself.

"So, you met a God. I thought he'd been killed a hundred years ago."

"He wasn't, though his disciples were." Darian rubbed his eyes, both yearning for and dreading sleep. He told Tabor everything that had happened from the moment he'd been pulled into Whilpow's realm until his release. He took his mace from his belt, studying it. "This was the key. It wouldn't have worked for any weapon that wasn't touched by both Gods. A feat that was thought almost impossible, thus the best way to protect the realm and Whilpow's information."

"I'm starting to think you've got a bit of luck to your soul, Darian." Tabor finished cleaning the ichor off of his maul. "Go rest. I will take the first shift, and I'll wake you in two hours to take a turn. We should not linger long."

Darian nodded, looking up at the grey sky and thick with unshed rain, which felt like it mourned Ianel too. "Agreed."

EPHEMA CLUNG to Star's reins, desperately trying to keep herself upright. She was beyond exhausted and muscles she didn't even know she had throbbed in time with each step. She missed riding behind Darian where she could doze against his back and shift against the rocking motion of the horse. It hadn't been her idea to ride Star, but without Ianel around, the stallion had taken to following her. After the third time he'd tried to pull her off Raven's back, Tabor insisted that she ride the warhorse to stop his games. If they had been forced to ride at speed, she would have fallen off, but at the pace Tabor kept she could manage, even if only barely.

Even though she wasn't angry anymore, Ephema still found it hard to talk to the Knights. She understood everything Darian had said about Ianel's death, but it still hurt. Other people had died before, between the people in Tallet and some of the sailors on the ship. She'd felt sad, but none of them had hurt her like losing Ianel. None of them had been her friends.

Ahead, the road to Hawthan stretched before them, the gates to the city walls clearly visible in the morning light. Even from this distance, she saw the gates open and a contingent of riders leave the city. The riders wasted no time in hitting full stride once they were outside the walls, and made a beeline for them.

Darian slowed Raven to a walk and turned in his saddle to face Tabor, frowning. "Tabor, do you see the colors? Those banners under the main flag."

Tabor held his hand up to his brow to shield some of the light and squinted. "I do, but I'm not familiar the meanings. I've only stayed in Hawthan on visits to the High Temple."

Darian turned back to the city; his expression troubled. "They mean there was an attack from the sea and the city is on high alert. There's more smoke than there should be for this time of day too, but I can't tell if some part of the city is burning or something else. Something happened while we were away."

Ephema chewed on her lower lip, then shrugged. "Whatever happened, it doesn't look like the city is closed. Riders just came out. Can't we keep going?"

"We can, and we will." Tabor turned Valor's head back to the road. "The riders are probably advance scouts of the guard, coming to ensure that we are friendlies. They can tell us what to expect at the city." He made a noise and Valor broke into a run, quickly followed by the other warhorses. Ephema bit down on a shriek as it felt like Star might run right out from under her. She tangled her fingers in the reins and gave him his head to follow his herd.

COMING HOME WAS ALWAYS a moment of reflection. Lately, it seemed to Darian that his returning trips to Hawthan were destined to be with fewer people than he left with. Darian looked up at the walls of the city, his weary eyes searching for signs of new damage. From this entry point, there appeared to be nothing substantial. Whatever attack the flags signified, this entrance hadn't been damaged.

The city guards that they rode with called out to the ones on the walls as they passed. As Tabor had surmised, they had been watching for riders and come to ensure their safe return. As it turned out, they weren't the only ones. Darian recognized the familiar sight of his mother and her warhorse approaching as they entered the gates.

Knight Proctor Lauret pulled her horse up to a halt beside Tabor and Darian, her eyes pained as she spotted Ephema on Ianel's horse. "He's gone, isn't he." It wasn't a question, and everyone knew it. She turned to Tabor. "We felt something at the Temple. A great loss. What happened?"

Tabor shook his head, pushing his visor away from his face. "Wights. A full nest of them centered on the ruined city. The biggest nest I've ever seen. We found the temple, but the full explanation should wait until we are off the road. For the short version, it took longer than we expected as one of us had to speak to a God. Ianel took a gut shot and called down Osephetin's Favor in order to save us."

"Dark Lord Protect." Lauret closed her eyes, a quick prayer crossing her lips. When she opened them again, she looked at Ephema. There was an attempt at humor in her voice as she said, "Most Knights' steeds as old as Star won't allow another on their back. Have you decided to pick up some training and cross over into Osephetin's service? Typically, we would have to put him through extensive training for a new Knight, or retire him to the breeding fields."

Ephema shifted in the saddle, running her fingers through Star's mane. "I do not wish to be a Knight. Star just wants a friend and kept trying to pull me off Darian's horse. We tried walking, but that's too slow." She shook her hair back from her face. "I think he misses Ianel and I have, or had, carrots."

"Well, they say the way to a man's heart is through his stomach. This applies to horses, too. We will arrange for a saddle and tack proper to your build. You have made yourself a new friend and with Ianel… With Ianel gone it would be cruel to take you away from him too." The hints of humor left Knight Proctor Lauret's voice. "Dammit. At least his place in the Halls is assured, and he is out of the sway of the Lich. That is a small blessing." She turned her horse and fell in stride beside Darian. "I am curious over who among you spoke to a God."

Darian half-smiled, though it took effort. Smiling had not come easy after Ianel's death. He knew it would again, but not yet. "I did."

"You?" Lauret frowned. "Did I give birth to a prodigal?"

Ephema tilted her head, "Prodigal? I do not know that word. He unlocked a secret and got what we needed."

"You did?" At Darian's nod, Lauret looked relieved. "Thank heavens for that. It's been a trying time here since you left. Good news is welcome."

"We saw the flags and the smoke." Tabor gestured to the sky, where smoke still trailed off into the clouds. "How many ships were there?"

"Just three. They managed to sink a few merchant ships in the harbor, damage some of the docks, and lob flaming debris into the city before we chased them off. But make no mistake, I expect them to return; they flew the same colors as the ship that attacked us."

"So, they were testing the defenses to see what we might and might not have, and left before too much damage was done to their ships." Darian grimaced. "Did they come from the deep water or the shallows?"

"Deep. They came under the cover of night and storm. They came in with the mainsail hoisted and their topsail furled. The steamers were undergoing repairs, and we never heard them coming. Got their hits in and ran like dogs once we mobilized to return fire, but the damage was done. We lost 15 sailors and one family in town whose house caught fire.

"The Council has been arguing for years about a standing navy, suddenly they're regretting their choices." She shook her head, the thick greying braid of her hair rolling across her shoulders. "And the attackers weren't really serious. They just wanted us to know they're out there and capable of hurting us. They're waiting for an opportunity, and it's not hard to bottle us in here, the bay that protects us also traps us." There was an even calmness to Knight Proctor Lauret's voice that Darian knew quite well. She was beyond angry. People had died.

She'd been unable to protect them, and the persons responsible had gotten away. There would be hell to pay once she caught up with them.

"So, what now? The horses have come a long way. They're going to need to rest up and feed. Ephema's exhausted, Tabor is resolutely Tabor, and I could use a bath and a long nap."

"All of that will have to wait until you've seen the High Priest. Except for the care of the horses, of course."

Darian nodded as they passed deeper into the city, more guard everywhere he looked. "That makes sense. Tonight, we should…" He paused as the sorrow hit him again and cleared his throat. "We should meet with the resident Knights tonight. To honor Ianel."

"Indeed." Tabor muttered.

Behind them the city gates rolled to a close, welcoming them home.

CHAPTER TWENTY-THREE

Ephema sat in a small alcove outside the chamber of the Eternal Flame. After their report to the High Priest, she had slept hard. She remembered dreaming, but she couldn't remember what about, only that this time it wasn't bad. When she woke, she found that Darian had been dragged off by Fressin to work on the scroll. Tabor had left the High Temple, but no one knew where he'd gone.

She'd spent part of the evening in the stables with the horses before finding this quiet spot. She didn't want to talk to the worshippers or the devout. They all had questions in their eyes that she didn't know how to answer. It seemed so unfair that life should go on so normally when it didn't go on for Ianel at all. What was the point of connecting yourself to people when they all went away?

Footsteps from the hallway caught her attention, and she looked up just as Fressin strode by the alcove. He caught her eye and came to a halt, one eyebrow raised in question. "Good evening. You haven't, by chance, seen my brother, have you?"

Ephema shook her head, careful not to knock her head against the stone wall she leaned on. "Not since earlier. I think he was hoping for sleep."

"Drat. He took the necklace with him, and I've had an idea." Fressin leaned up against the wall. "Typical of him, really. No matter, I'll get it from him in the morning." He smiled, the first time Ephema had ever seen him truly smile. "You held your promise. You brought him back. Thank you."

The smile surprised her. Ephema blinked and then nodded, drawing her knees to her chest and resting her arms around them. "You're welcome. I wanted to bring them all back, but there were so many wights."

"Well, not to be a jerk, but I didn't ask you to bring them all back. Just Darian. The rest of them can fend for themselves." He coughed to the side. "Ugh, this cold weather kills me every time it starts to come in, I swear. But, I'm guessing you've never encountered a wight before?"

"I don't think so. I don't have the same names for all of the undead." She peered at him before adding. "You should rest. Your body is tired, even if your mind isn't."

Fressin snorted, then reached for a handkerchief and blotted his nose. "There's the pot calling the kettle black. How many days were you gone? You fought bandits and undead, rode almost the entire time, and have only had half a day's worth of recuperation? Yet here you are." He shook his head and tucked the cloth away. "I'll rest when the job is done. I might not be worth much with a mace or a spear, but I know languages, and with what Darian managed to bring with him I will decipher that scroll. Soon."

He scratched at his side as he continued, "As for the wights, they really should have been expected. Wights are typically found around old religious sites and are thought to be the risen followers of the deities, still bound to the temples. They're stupid strong, easily two or three times as strong as a man. They live in nests and they never age. There's usually no more than ten to a nest, but from what Tabor said that nest had lots more." Fressin's voice dropped as he continued, "Usually, a Knight is considered equal to no more than one or two wights at once. Any more than that and the best option is retreat."

Ephema listened, her mind flashing back to that night, to the creatures crawling out of the wreckage. She wondered if Tabor had expected the wights, but never told her. Finally, she sighed. "How do they do it? Keep fighting when there is so much death? When everything wants to hurt them? When it never stops? This scroll is supposed to tell us where something is, something important. That means going to get it. What if we run into more wights, or something else? Something worse? I brought Darian back this time, but what if it's him next time? I can't stand it!"

"I used to wonder the same thing." Fressin crouched down to be at her level. "My Father used to tell me something about the Knights when Mother would go for weeks on end. I never understood it then, but I do now. When I'd ask him why she had to leave, he'd look at me and say, 'Because if they don't, no one else will. They risk everything so we can be safe.' And he's right. They keep fighting, much as I hate to say it, because they know if they don't, no one else will step up to take their place.

"This world is down to just one defender and his servants against the undead and the Lich. Without the Knights, towns would gradually be overrun, slowly but inexorably, until none were left. So, we're glad to have them. Though," he paused, flicking a finger at the globe she wore. "maybe it's more than just one defender. You've shown the Goddess is still out there, fighting through her insanity, doing everything She is able to do. And, Darian spoke to another God thought dead for a century. So maybe more than one."

Ephema fell silent for a long moment before she met Fressin's gaze. She didn't understand everything he had said, his accent and word choice still sometimes beyond her, but she understood what he meant. "You will be honest with me, yes? Is it worth the risk of going out again?"

"Before you left, I'd have said no. No way in all the hells." Fressin stroked his chin, contemplating the question. "Now, there's new information I didn't have access to. I don't have an answer to your question just yet; much will depend on what the scroll actually says. But," he stood back up and stretched. "If what Whilpow told my brother is even remotely true, then without a doubt it is worth going out again. It would even be worth me risking my life if it would actually bring an end to this madness.

"I, however, would be slaughtered within a few days out there. The Knights will fare much better. So, I daresay, would you. So, my answer to your question is a very solid, 'maybe.'"

Ephema considered his answer, finding herself somewhat comforted by it. He was an odd man still, but she was beginning to understand him. She even thought she might like him. "Then I will try to do what must be done. And pray for no more losses."

"You serve a Goddess of Life. They serve a God of Death." Fressin tapped on his temple. "There will forever be one massive difference between you and them. They literally do not fear death, because they know what's waiting for them in the afterlife. It's unnatural. But against the horror of the undead, no better weapon exists." He placed a hand on her shoulder, squeezing gently. "You've proven yourself, at least to me. My door is always open, if you need it. Even if you want out of this. I'll help you. And, I think you're right. Since Darian squirreled off somewhere with my new toy, I might as well get some sleep."

"It is good advice. I am to join Darian and Tabor later to honor Ianel's passing. Darian says it's like a funeral, but not. I do not understand what he means."

Fressin rubbed the back of his neck. "It's a rite they perform when a Knight dies. I've never seen it. Usually, the only ones allowed to join are Knights, and the rare priest. I suppose they are doing you an honor by letting you come. Good luck." He pushed away from the wall and walked down the corridor, disappearing around a corner.

Ephema watched him go, then leaned her head against the wall, closing her eyes. She would rest here for just a minute and then return to her room. Her breathing deepened and sleep claimed her. This time she did not dream.

DARIAN TILTED HIS HEAD, listening as the tower bell rang the midnight hour. To him, the bells were comforting, reassuring that all was well. He knew some people who disliked the bell's chiming, though the farther you were from the center of town the quieter they were. He'd become accustomed to the sound as a child and now the sound brought comfort and a sense of home.

He looked up as soft steps approached, watching Ephema

make her way down the hallway. She stopped a few feet away from him, a questioning look in his gaze. "Am I late?"

"No. The other Knights only just went inside."

She nodded, toying with a lock of her hair. "What is going to happen?"

Darian smiled and raised his hand to push the door open. "I don't entirely know. I've heard of the Rite of Passage but it's restricted by rank, so I've never participated until now. I don't think you'll need to do anything. Just take the chance to remember Ianel and wish him well as his soul enters the Halls of Osephetin's faithful."

"All right."

He opened the door just enough for them both to pass, his armor and weaponry requiring more space than Ephema's slender form. Before them the Eternal Flame of the temple burned merrily, though the chapel pews were empty. Only a half a dozen armored Knights and the Knight Proctor were present in the room. They stood in a rough circle before the flame, obviously waiting.

Lauret looked up, waving toward the seats nearest the back of the chamber. "Ephema, choose a seat. This can be loud, but I assure you there's no danger. Darian to me. It's time to begin." Her tone brokered neither argument nor explanation, and they hurried to obey, Ephema slid onto one of the benches as Darian hurried down the aisle.

He stepped into the empty place in the circle, his gaze coming to rest on a small table where a few of Ianel's things rested. He knew that the ritual was usually conducted over a Knight's body, but in this case, there was no body, armor, or weapon to consecrate. The thought brought a new pain to Darian's heart.

Lauret thumped the end of her staff on the floor, the

sound stark, cutting through the whisper of the Eternal Flame. A second thump and each Knight drew their soul weapon, holding them across their bodies in a guarded stance. Darian followed suit, a tingle running along the bottoms of his feet and rising through his body. A third thump, and the Knights spoke, for an instant Darian was lost, but the words quickly resolved to the familiar.

"Osephetin. Guide me."

The weapons came to life, shining with blue eldritch energy that swirled about hammer, flail, mace, staff, and mauls, the weapons designed to destroy the undead. Tonight, the Goddess-blessed runes on Darian's mace remained quiet, filling with shadow where they usually blazed with golden light, blue flames dancing about the skull that topped the weapon.

Lauret stepped forward, touching the tip of her staff to the table. The Knight beside her followed suit, the movement continuing around the circle until all eight weapons rested on the wood. Blue flame poured onto the table consuming Ianel's items without leaving so much as a scorch mark where they passed. A silent wind swirled in the center of the circle, carrying the ashes into a slowly twisting cloud that settled into the Eternal Flame. Like small stars each piece of ash burst and glittered as it fell, utterly consumed.

"Ianel, Ianel, Ianel, Ianel…" The men and women of Osephetin chanted the name of their fallen comrade, pounding their weapons on the floor or against their shields. The noise grew until it filled Darian's ears, the scent of ash and fire hot in his nostrils. He didn't know when he'd gone from a chant to a scream, though his throat burned with the effort. A strike of blue lightning lashed from the center of the Eternal Flame, slamming into the wooden table and destroying it with one strike, knocking the Knights from their feet and scattering them.

Darian lay on the floor, his breath coming in gasps, his ears ringing. A voice he remembered from his Knight's Challenge echoed through his mind.

"He has been found…worthy."

EPILOGUE

Adaman blinked as he sat up and swung his legs over the side of the bed. He was wrapped in an overall feeling of calm, and knew immediately he was having a vision, and he was asleep. He cast his gaze about, nodding in appreciation of his surroundings. He stood in a forested glen, surrounded by trees decorated in early spring blooms. Thin grasses tickled his feet as he stood, and a warm breeze chased the chill from his bones.

He held out his hand to pick out a flower, but the flower disappeared, replaced by the globe amulet Ephema wore. He took a step back, letting his hand drop as the amulet began to spin.

A flash of light sparked from the amulet, and time froze around him. The trees and grasses stopped moving in the wind and all sound ceased. The amulet still hovered in the air, though it was now motionless. Then a new sound rose and caught his attention.

Laughter.

Deep, cruel, foreboding laughter. The laughter of misery.

He took a sharp breath when first one, then many, skeletons appeared at the edge of the forest. These skeletons were old, older than any he'd ever seen. Many were missing limbs and the bone that remained was twisted into shapes that were no longer human. For a heartbeat, the skeletons and he matched empty gazes; then they advanced, one step at a time. The ground shuddered with each footfall.

Adaman found he could not move as the skeletons came ever closer, until they were no more than a body's length away. He tried to scream as the first reached him, but his voice failed him.

"That is quite enough of that." A man's voice came from behind him, calm and reserved, breaking the spell. A rather short, chubby, balding man walked in front of him and touched Adaman on the center of his forehead. "This vision will only do you harm. The Lich is on the move and the time of his rising is now. You must tell your people to guard their dreams, and your Knights must act now. This is the last time. Their last chance with the last Daughter. They have the keys to the information they need, and they must not fail. Now wake up, Priest of Osephetin and get to work." He snapped his fingers in front of Adaman's face, breaking the vision.

Gasping in fear, Adaman jolted awake from his bed, covered in sweat. He wasn't sure who had saved him, but he recognized a directive from on high when he heard one. At least this time the interpretation was clear. The danger of the Lich was growing, but they had a real chance to stop him.

A chance was all they'd ever asked for.

And by the Dark One, they were going to take it.

. . .

BRINGING the Scroll of Lianna home was just the beginning. The followers of the Lich attack from the land and the sea, and personal politics threaten the Order from within. A dying High Priest sends Darian and Ephema beyond the borders of the realm with one last hope to put an end to the Great Lich forever...

Continue the adventure in *Life's Daughter,* Book 2 of the War of the Lich. books2read.com/u/47Yp5N

ABOUT THE AUTHORS

Matthew T. Summers

In the quiet Virginia mountains, Matt Summers whiles away the day with his wife and two kids and whatever menagerie of pets have made their way to his door. He has written in multiple genres for more years than he cares to admit, and will soundly deny rumors that he initially started writing to impress a girl.

Jena Rey

Writer of the weird and the wonderful, Jena Rey has long been a fan of science fiction and fantasy. She finds inspiration in the Utah landscape where she lives with the best kids, husband, and furry sidekicks.

ACKNOWLEDGMENTS

Thank you to: Melissa McShane, Patrick Roddy, A. Nixon, Bryan Brown, Veronica Mulik, and Anna the one and only for your reading and encouragement.

Love this book? Drop a review on GoodReads or your favorite e-book distributor.

Made in the USA
Las Vegas, NV
14 February 2023